Praise for Morris's Earlier Works

Morris...has a dreamlike obsession with the past and with the politics of family life.

—Los Angeles Times

Morris excels in providing new dimensions to conventional narrative.

—Dallas Morning News

Morris's gift for exact detail is fine-honed. She also gives us fully developed characters and her use of suspense is skillful.

—Houston Chronicle

Suzanne Morris writes with all the bark off. She has a capacious imagination for characterization and psychological dilemmas.

—Columbus (Ohio) Dispatch

AFTERMATH

a novel of the New London school tragedy

March 18th, 1937

Continued Praise for *AFTERMATH*

From the ashes and rubble of one of America's worst tragedies, Suzanne Morris has created a story of survival, remorse, pain and love in the only way it could be fully expressed–through a novel–one that will break and warm the hearts of readers. As in all her work, she expertly captures the era with its clothing, events, dialogue, and societal norms I still long for. And she does it without intruding on our reading pleasure.

—Jim H. Ainsworth, author of thirteen books, including seven novels.

In Delys Lithingate, a survivor of the 1937 New London school disaster that shocked Texas and the nation, Suzanne Morris has created a memorable character. The continuing and deepening impact that the loss has throughout Delys' life helps us feel again the ongoing reality of that disaster. *AFTERMATH* is a well told tale of continuing significance in Texas.

—Milton Jordan, Past President, East Texas Historical Association

For more information:
Stephen F. Austin State University Press
P.O. Box 13007 SFA Station
Nacogdoches, Texas 75962
sfapress@sfasu.edu
www.sfasu.edu/sfapress

Book design: Tinesha Mix
Cover design: Tinesha Mix
Cover photo: Lori Janick
Distributed by Texas A&M Consortium
www.tamupress.com

LIBRARY OF CONGRESS CATALOGING-IN-PUBLICATION DATA
Morris, Suzanne
Aftermath / Suzanne Morris

ISBN: 978-1-62288-116-1

AFTERMATH

a novel of the New London school tragedy

March 18th, 1937

by Suzanne Morris

Also by Suzanne Morris

Novels

Galveston
Keeping Secrets
Skychild
Wives and Mistresses
The Clearharbour Trilogy

History

The Browns of Ashton Villa—a Family History

Contents

In memory of

Fred Tarpley

who encouraged me in the writing of this novel
but did not live to read it.

ACKNOWLEDGMENTS

I extend my heartfelt thanks to those who assisted me in the research and writing of AFTERMATH.

For aid in New London and Overton research: Bobby Johnson, Robert Jordan, Marvin Dees; John Davidson and the volunteer staff of the London Museum and Tea Room; staff members of the Houston Metropolitan Research Center, Houston Public Library, and the East Texas Research Center, Stephen F. Austin University Library;

For sharing their personal memories of the Scottish Brigade of Austin High School, Houston, Texas, and for dusting off my own: Dorothy Niland, Jennifer Pichinson, Nancy Grissom, and all the former brigadiers who contributed essays to A SCOTTISH BRIGADE ANTHOLOGY;

For early readings and helpful critiques of the manuscript: Anne and Milton Jordan, Karen and C. R. Javellana, John Davidson, and Nancy Grissom;

Likewise, with regard to the New London poems: Fran Levy and Lori Janick;

For hospitality when I returned to soak up the atmosphere of Idylwood–little changed since I grew up there–Karen and Barney Giesen;

Through forty years and eight novels: for editorial guidance, encouragement, and moral support, Susan Schwartz; and for steadfast friendship and expert proofreading, Karen Giesen.

Though, sadly, it is too late to express my gratitude to Fred Tarpley for being a source of inspiration, not only in this latest endeavor but throughout my career as a novelist, I wish to note here that it was he who urged me to write A NEW LONDON ANTHOLOGY when, for a ime, the novel seemed to elude me. I hope he would be pleased with both outcomes.

Valedictory

To the Victims of the New London Tragedy,
March 18th, 1937

I don't dwell on it much anymore,
having lived far longer since
than I had lived
before it happened.
Only now and then,
my mind circling back to what might have been.

Bruce and I would be married, of course.
And Edna would write for some
paper up East,
exposing true stories of honor breached,
saving lives.

(Did you see Mr. Berger's fine piece
in the New York Times? No, of course not.
But, years later, I did.
Fading words on a yellowed page
attempt to bring order to jumble
by lining up one after another.)

And Bucky? A shingle would hang there in Overton.
Dr. Peter Buckstrum, Sr., and Son
would treat sickly children
of oil field hands,
set bones, and cure grown-up diseases.
House Calls Available.

As for Lanelle—the distinguished woman of letters
would travel the world, ambassadors meeting her plane.
On what subject she'd lecture,
who could tell?

Rich now, hours spent on her feet,
she would indulge her taste in fanciful shoes.

And Mama and Daddy would have retired
under the wisteria, on that little porch
facing the poplars,
while Rusty's descendants, with wagging tails,
explored the nearby creek.

I still think of Bruce with a clutch of regret,
boarding a war-time ship and
sailing away from his demons.
How I wish I knew that he made it back.

If only I could see him again,
I'd love all he was as I did in the days when he
saved me a seat on the London School bus—
confused, he even saved me a seat
when the school had collapsed on pier and beam.

But I wouldn't come.
I awoke to see Jesus Praying
in the Garden of Gethsemane,
then Daddy, standing at the door.
"Where is Mama?" I asked.
He studied the floor.

Do you ever think of those who lived,
while riding the clouds
in your heavenly sleigh desks?
Dip pens in ink pots and
write of all, given the chance,
you might have become?

I say to you now:
There is no justice on earth,
no day of accounting for death's random hand.
For you, there is only the silent
waiting for all of time to spend.

And for us? A life of wondering
what you, and we, might have been.

–Delys Lithingate
#106/106
A NEW LONDON ANTHOLOGY

Part One

Chapter 1

Saturday, March 4th, 1978

A letter came today that the Scottish Brigade is being disbanded.

The news struck me like a blow to my sternum. Not that I was surprised; the organization's approaching demise has been all too apparent in the shrinking of the ranks a little more with every year. At its peak, membership numbered two hundred and fifty. One day last year—my final year before retirement from teaching English at Austin High—I looked down from my third floor classroom window as they assembled on the campus for after-school drill, and did a quick, heart-sinking, head count. There were but forty-four young women out there. It pained me to watch them in their white shirts and shorts, practicing so valiantly, keeping those lines straight, determined for all they were worth to uphold a proud tradition that was sagging under the inevitable weight of change. After a few minutes, I had to look away as though I had just witnessed a rare poor performance during half-time at a football game.

It's understandable, of course, young women being so different nowadays. (Trying to sneak a stash of liquor onto the bus for a field trip would have been unthinkable in my day.) Well, to be fair, it isn't strictly young women who have changed, but society in general. Young women just mirror what's going on all around them. Back then—I refer in particular to the late thirties and early forties, when I was in Brigade—it seemed natural for young people to want to pull together and do something that reflected well on all, something that we could be proud of, and celebrate together. You could honestly say—further—that observing these principles, plus having a healthy respect for authority, were fundamental to our winning the war in Europe and the Pacific that we soon found ourselves embroiled in. How proudly I wheeled Aunt Allie's gardening wagon up and down the sloping streets of Idylwood, collecting pots and pans. How diligently I labored in Miss Lytle's First Aid class, the better to be prepared for shortages in medical personnel. Later, in Viet Nam, the erosion of these principles in society, plus a growing suspicion of authority, were major reasons why we lost; I am convinced of this. Our idealism was slain along with our President in 1963. What could we believe in after that? What possessed our government to think that we would buy into that jungle war, just a few years later, with all the romantic fervor that had swept us to victory in World War II?

Ideals. In Brigade back then it was all about upholding the highest ideals. About not compromising just because it would be easier. Not doing something wrong when no one was looking (I had the thin white booklet containing the Honor Code practically memorized). The ideals were what restored my equilibrium after I had been exiled to Houston, and what I clung to desperately after I discovered the winking morals and handshake deals in the dark that wrought the tragedy at my school and cost me everything that I had always counted on. The Scottish Brigade was what saved me from God knows what fate, bitter and angry and rebellious as I was from having been thrust away from my home and the New London community that I knew and loved, pawned off to relatives I hardly knew and my daddy off to the California oil fields, leaving me behind. But those high ideals could be turned into stern rigidity, as I learned too late, and could exact a price so high that ideals were all you were left with. By themselves, they make for cold companions. I sit out here on my porch and look up at the stars, and remember some things and imagine the rest....

For instance, my mother, on that night, and the following morning, before the tragedy that changed everything; the last time I saw her. Something significant happened between her and Daddy in those few hours. What I have always believed, and what I was told, many years later, by the one person who had the power to manipulate the truth of their relationship to personal advantage, are poles apart. So I imagine the truth was somewhere in between. I know they loved each other; I'll stand by that to my dying breath. But they had come to an impasse somehow. Mama had followed Daddy all over Texas and up into Oklahoma as he pursued his chosen vocation of oil field worker—I use the word chosen with some gravity; Daddy turned down the opportunity to take over his father's long-established business, Houston Specialty Glass, that made beakers and test tubes and such. He had gone away to serve in France during World War I, leaving a diamond engagement ring on my mother's finger. He had come home a changed man. He did not wish to spend long hours, day after day, confined in a tomb-like building, engaged in work that was largely predictable.

As I say, Mama followed him, and this was at the expense of the goodwill of her parents, who felt Daddy had misled her and that she ought to have broken the engagement right on the spot, rather than going through with marrying him. The fancy church wedding they were paying for was canceled. Mama and Daddy eloped to Galveston. Early in their marriage they spent a long stretch living in a tent camp at Sour Lake, hauling their water from a communal well; other times they lived in oil field housing which, given the absence of indoor plumbing or electricity, was not much better. By the time they got to East Texas, Daddy had risen through the ranks and become a well-respected oil well driller. Mama believed she had done her duty. Besides, I would soon be the age to enter first grade. It was time to settle down. Daddy built us a house between Overton and New London. Mama bought cemetery lots at Pleasant Hill, and accepted a place on the faculty of the London School in 1932, the year the new facility opened.

Just two words, "I'm going," in my father's voice, is all I can remember. I heard these words from Mama and Daddy's room that night after Daddy lit the gas heaters and we all went to bed. And this memory didn't come back to me for years and years. What didn't get blown out of my memory for good the next afternoon often didn't come back in the right order. My memory was a whole library exploding, and the books tumbling from the shelves that were not destroyed were all jumbled up and out of order, their pages flung open and their backs broken.

The home Daddy built for us in East Texas was a farmhouse-looking affair, raised up on brick pedestals that were higher in back than in front, owing to the gentle slope of the land as it stretched down toward the creek. It had a covered front porch overlooking the broad expanse of poplars and oaks that stood between the house and the road. Altogether it was a substantial structure, well-crafted. But the wall between the two bedrooms was thin enough that on some nights I would overhear rapidly creaking bed springs, and giggles, maybe; a breath catching, then swooning sounds. Happy noises, even to my uninitiated ears. But then that night: "I'm going." Such weighty words. I see my parents even now, lying in bed, facing each other and exchanging sharp whispers. Daddy is slender and long-legged with fine, straight, smoky blond hair and light blue eyes. I believe it is when Daddy turns away from Mama toward the wall separating our bedrooms, one broad shoulder stubbornly thrust up, that I hear him, because his voice is very clear, as though he has only just begun to speak. I pick up on the mutiny in his tone and it stops my heart cold.

I listen for him to speak my name and assign me some place in these deliberations. I am named Delys for my paternal grandmother. The name is pronounced Delees, with the stress on the second syllable. But Daddy has always called me Dee, his special name for me.

I do not hear him say my name. I do not hear anything more at all except the low rumble of the blue gas tongues, licking up the grate in the corner of my room.

I knew Daddy's voice and its many intonations better than any voice on earth, having spent most evenings of my life sitting out on the back porch, under the stars, talking with him. So if I was inclined to believe there was mutiny in his voice as he turned away from my mother, then I was probably right. But that is not to say he didn't love her anymore, or that he really would have left us behind, for all my worries that he may one day do so. I was so in tune with Daddy's thinking that I knew even when he wished silently for something on a star, and I knew, without ever being told, that very often his wish was to be somewhere else. At least in his heart, he was what my Aunt Allie would one day call him to my face: a wanderlust.

I see myself the next morning, sitting sleepily before a bowl of hot Cream of Wheat and a piece of cinnamon toast. I am dressed for school in a white blouse, blue cardigan sweater, and blue and maroon plaid skirt. Saddle shoes and blue socks. Mama still has to brush my hair and put the bow in, a ritual carried out with me on her dresser bench every school morning, which winds up with a hug and a kiss.

I see Mama in profile, standing at the sink on tiptoes, watering her African violets that grow on the windowsill above. She is not very tall— I take my height and long limbs from Daddy. Her hair is chestnut-colored and slightly wavy, as is mine. Her skin is fair. She plucks her eyebrows up high and she has a perfectly shaped cupid's bow mouth.

"Where's Daddy going?" I ask, because I have been sleepless with worry all night. No sooner are the words spoken than I realize with a tight squeeze of my diaphragm that I have given away my eavesdropping to Mama.

Mama turns abruptly, her eyes wide, and her deep red-painted lips slightly parted, as though I have slapped her face. "What do you mean? Nowhere. He has gone to work."

I shrug, not sure what to say, still afraid I may be in trouble for eavesdropping. "I thought I heard him say he was going somewhere. Maybe I was dreaming."

"Must have been."

I am aware, even then, that Mama is letting me off the hook, but more important, she is reassuring herself. We are reassuring each other.

Mama pours herself a cup of coffee from the pot on the stove, and comes to sit across from me. "Feeling okay this morning?" She takes a sip of coffee, her eyelids fluttering above the steam coming from the cup.

"Yes, ma'am."

"No headache?"

I shake my head and dip my spoon into the Cream of Wheat. Though my head does not ache this morning, I did have a headache yesterday. I have been troubled by headaches for a couple of weeks at school, and since I am not having trouble seeing the black board, which would suggest eye strain, Mama believes the headaches are caused by my focusing too hard on the spelling words for tomorrow's competition. *Serendipity. Permutation.* I go around spelling the words in my head all the time. *Loquacious* (I tend to forget the "u" after "q" because it sounds like it's already there). *Idiosyncrasy* (I mistake the second "s" for a "c"). Our team won a trophy last year. I will die if we don't win another one, and especially if it's my fault. Last year we got the winning point when I took a lucky guess and correctly spelled the word *strait.*

A few minutes later, just before I go out through the back door to fill Rusty's water bowl and wait for the bus, Mama comes into the kitchen. "Is my slip showing, hon?" she asks, her back turned toward me, looking over her padded shoulder.

I glance at the hem of the deep red, slightly flared skirt of her dress and down her shapely calves along the straight seam of her stockings, all of which I quite admire; then back up again. There is just the merest hint of black lace peeking out. I say, "No, Mama," because it is hardly detectable, and if I tell her the truth, she will want me to wait while she goes in the bedroom to adjust her slip straps, then check again. Mama has certain aversions: to people tracking red dirt in the house, to swallows building red mud nests in the porch eaves, and to her slip showing. If I tell her the truth I might miss my bus, and have to ride to school with her and Queen Price. I do not, above all things, want to miss the bus because I have a boyfriend named Bruce Buckstrum who saves me a seat every morning and afternoon. I savor the recent memory of the two of us, arm in arm, skating round and round the Overton Skating rink. I am wearing a white felt skating skirt with red heart appliqués, which Mama made for me. Bruce is wearing a red shirt. The clunky rollers under our rented skates have become sleek, sharp blades, and we are gliding on ice. When we stop, Bruce presses a small red, heart-shaped card into my hand that says, "LOVE" in the center, and at the bottom of which he has scrawled in pencil, "Be my valentine. Bruce." His big sister Edna, with sexy eyes, a small waist and glamourous long legs, sinks down on one knee and snaps our picture. And from that day, I know that Bruce will be my valentine for the rest of my life.

Mama turns, smiling. "Thanks, hon, have a good day. See you this afternoon. Love you."

I avert my eyes. "You too, Mama," I tell her, guilt muting my voice so I can barely be heard. Then I dash out. The lie I have told Mama is already so indelibly marked on my soul that even the force of the day's event will not dislodge it from memory.

Chapter 2

There is a picture of my mother as an angel—well, it isn't really my mother, but in my mind's eye, I've superimposed Mama's face on the angel for so many years, it seems that it is. She wears a voluminous gown, and has great sheltering wings. Her face sweet and benign, she hovers protectively behind the shoulder of a small girl who is crossing a narrow footbridge into the darkness. The highly sentimental pastel illustration fills a whole page at the front of the *Book of Memories* that was published in lieu of the *Londana*—our school annual—in 1937, because annuals are celebrations of life, with snapshots chronicling a snowball fight on campus, and kids in saddle shoes and letter sweaters posing on the running board of a convertible, and the football pass that won the game. A space must be cleared in between two *Londanas* where major epochs can be separated into Before and After, a volume devoted entirely to memorializing the dead, their pictures lined up and bleeding the margins of page after page, with cloying poetry interspersed, and with an angel to guide them safely through the darkness of death, to the Other Side. Bruce mailed a copy of the *Book of Memories* to me in Houston. Stranded as I was, with no information available except what Bruce provided, he hoped the book would satisfy my fervent desire to fill in the blanks of who had died at 3:17 p.m. on Thursday, March 18th of 1937. Bruce was my lifeline to New London, and the only link to my past there.

While I was nowhere near my mother when disaster struck—the junior high classrooms were in the opposite wing of the building, separated by the huge, balconied auditorium—I listened to my daddy recount details he learned during the rescue effort that got underway even before the dust had begun to settle, and eventually I read the story of Mama's heroism in *The Henderson Daily News*, a story that included testimonials from several of her sixth-period students. I know the family concerns that haunted Mama all through that day, and that doubtless had already kept her awake all night. On many previous afternoons I had sat quietly waiting at the back of her classroom as she concluded her workday, so I am familiar with its arrangement. So vividly can I see Mama as those final minutes of her life ticked away, I feel as if I am witnessing everything from the back of that room.

Mrs. Vinia Lithingate's classroom is at the rear of the second floor in the handsome, five-year-old brick school building, with red tile roof, that oil money built. Behind her desk stands a wooden case where leather-bound *World Book Encyclopedia* volumes are cradled, and high above is the small speaker through which the Pledge of Allegiance and announcements stream from the Principal's office. At the edge of her glass-topped desk is a large globe with green land masses clustered in oceans of blue, poised to spin in a brass frame.

One wall of the room has a row of those sash windows so familiar in classrooms— reaching so high that the top portions are opened and closed with a hook on the end of a long pole. Along this wall, beneath the windows, a gas radiator stretches out accordion-like, with a control valve that students are strictly forbidden to touch. All day long Vinia has been administering tests, pacing up and down the hardwood floors between the rows of sleigh desks with their black iron filigree pedestals. Usually Friday, not Thursday, is test day, but tomorrow is the county meet in Henderson, and the superintendent has declared a school holiday, encouraging all students and the faculty to attend.

By the time sixth period arrives, the air in Vinia's classroom is soured with a day's worth of teenagers' sweaty hands and feet, spilled ink, graphite and chalk dust. The floor is scuffed-up and gritty. She passes out exams to seniors who have been studying the Treaty of Versailles and the deep and severe ramifications of its passage for the future of Germany, a study which has ultimately led to free-ranging discussions on the likelihood of yet another war in Europe, and how it might inevitably involve the United States. Ordinarily Vinia glories in class discussions that spring up spontaneously as this one has, in which the material she is teaching takes on a life of its own. But it is clear her senior boys are already preoccupied by the possibility that they could be called up to the armed forces. Senior girls are worried about their boyfriends; some already wear engagement rings. Vinia does not like to think that this generation of young people will have to go through the same ordeal as her generation, and that some of the young men she has taught could lose their lives. Such good children, and many of them quite promising—well, it's too depressing to think about, and besides, she has enough on her mind already.

This period passes by in much the same way as earlier periods today. Vinia sits down behind her desk, waiting out the time allotted for the exams to be completed. From the carryall at her feet, she withdraws a sheaf of papers curled at the edges, engraved with the concentrated points of ink pens, and secured with a rubber band, then tries to concentrate on grading them, to save time over the weekend. But she is preoccupied by Dan's threat to go away to California, and so she often pauses to sit quietly, staring through the window into the depths of the blue sky, furled with white clouds. Her thoughts vacillate between hoping with all her heart that Dan will not destroy their lives by leaving, and preparing herself for all it will mean, if he does. Practical things like the need to buy a car spring to mind, and the question of how much financial help Dan might provide for the wife and daughter he is leaving behind. She and Delys will not starve, she consoles herself. The London School hires only the most qualified teachers, and the pay scale is among the highest in the nation. Still, there will be less than half the amount of income they are used to, and scarcely any left over to stash into savings or to keep up the regular contributions into Delys' college fund.

Up to now, they have been living very well, she thinks; and a feeling of resentment swells up and stops her short: Why is it she has always been expected to accommodate Dan's wishes, and never the other way around? She loves this job more than any other she has had, and Delys! Her little spelling champion who works so hard at everything and earns all A's and B's, and who makes friends with everybody. How much has Delys figured out from what she obviously overheard last night, as opposed to what little she admitted to her mother this morning, then quickly retreated from, sitting before her breakfast, her hair tossed and tangled from sleep? How much will it affect her ability to concentrate tomorrow? Perhaps a great deal, depending upon what happens tonight. And what will happen tonight? She imagines Dan walking through the door with a stormy face. Heading for the bedroom and packing his bags. Imagines her daughter's terror. It makes her sick inside. This is the first time in her marriage that she has not been able to count on her husband's steadfast goodwill; the first time she has felt stranded. It is like walking through a maze in the dark.

It isn't fair for Dan to expect them to uproot their lives just because he is bored with the East Texas oil field and eager for the challenges of drilling in an unfamiliar geological formation, hundreds of miles away. For that matter, how long will Dan stay in California, and will he come back to them when he again becomes bored? But what if he falls in love with another woman in the meantime, and decides to divorce her, Vinia, and remarry? What if Delys blames her mother for breaking up their family? She has always been crazy about her father, and if forced to take sides—

Vinia's mind spins and spins, with questions buffeting her from every side, yet she reaches no solution except to wish all this would just go away.

At around ten minutes past three, she asks for a show of hands if anyone needs more time to complete the test. Apparently not, so she walks up and down the aisles, collecting the tests, avoiding collision with the impossibly large and cumbersome feet of senior boys. She is thankful the day is coming to a close, and already envisions herself at home, dispensing with stockings and garters, changing into a comfortable house dress and low-heeled shoes, and having a nice cup of hot tea out on the front porch swing, glancing through today's *Houston Chronicle* and waiting for Delys' bus to arrive. *Let Dan do as he pleases. Think how much you love that swing, and cherish the sense of tranquility that fills your soul whenever you sit out there.* Yet...maybe tonight when Dan comes home and Delys flies into his arms, he will suddenly know that he cannot live without that awkward twelve-year-old girl, all arms and legs, flinging herself on him every single night when he comes through the door. Maybe she'll fry chicken for supper: Dan's perennial favorite. Put on a loving face as if nothing had happened. Woo him. *Oh, how can he think of leaving us? But regardless, I'm not going. I'm just not....*

Standing behind her desk, she stretches a rubber band around the stack of exams she has just collected, heaves the leather carryall from under the desk—with sixty some odd tests already inside, it weighs almost as much as she does—and plops it on top to finish loading up. She lets out a breath.

When Vinia glances up at the round clock on the wall opposite her desk, the hands are pointing at twelve after three. Shortly, a long arm shoots up from the middle of the room, fingers outstretched. It is Peter "Bucky" Buckstrum. Vinia has both the older Buckstrum kids this semester—Edna the sister, a junior, is in her first period class. The Buckstrum kids are both straight-A students; they are good-looking, and popular. Bucky is the Captain of the marching band, and has already been accepted at Rice Institute in the fall. A Rice graduate herself, class of 1919, Vinia wrote him a letter of recommendation in fact. Peter Buckstrum, Sr., is her family's doctor in Overton, and Bucky hopes to join his practice one day. Edna intends to study journalism. She writes for the school paper. Her prose is crisp and concise. They will both make their goals, no doubt about it. Now the younger boy, Bruce, is another matter. From what she has heard, Bruce has a real struggle in school. It is mildly troubling that he and Delys are sweet on each other— in fact she was remarking on this to her sister, Allie, the weekend before last when she and Delys went down to Allie's for a visit. True, they are young yet. Still, Delys can be stubborn when she makes her mind up to something. Besides, her body is beginning to show signs that she is blossoming into a young woman, and soon—

"Yes, Peter?" Vinia always calls her pupils by their given names at school. In her opinion, the use of nicknames would undermine the dignity of the classroom.

Bucky has blond hair, large eyes set in a round face, and dimples—a real charmer and full of fun; all the girls adore him. He is wearing a royal blue letter sweater that accentuates the deep blue of his eyes. "Miz Lithingate," he addresses her politely, and asks permission to head out a little early to the band room. The band is leaving on the bus at five o'clock for Lon Morris College in Jacksonville, where they will perform in a concert tonight.

Vinia fills in Bucky's name on a hall pass, signs it, and wishes him good luck on the concert. He thanks her. In a flash, he is out the door.

"Now, who wants to erase the blackboard?"

Vinia nods at Geraldine Murphy on the front row, the first to raise her hand. Then she glances at the clock again. The long hand ticks over to 3:16. *Just fourteen minutes to go*, she thinks gratefully. It seems this day has lasted an eternity, and she was exhausted to begin with. Oh, for things to just go back to normal tonight, everyone cosy in their bed, sleeping soundly....

Watching Geraldine stretch her arm up and begin to erase the board, Vinia remembers that she needs to walk over and close the window before leaving. Her room has been so stuffy these past few days, and her pupils have complained. Regardless of the chill outside, she has been leaving a window cracked during the day. A small gas leak, maybe? Probably not, but just in case, she resolves to hunt down the janitor before she leaves today.

When she is a few steps from the window, the room abruptly goes so quiet it is as if the earth has stopped spinning. She pauses in her steps, reflecting. Not that the students have stopped their whispering that always commences when they are idle just before the bell, the minutes ticking by until the sound pulsates through the building. They are still whispering. It is just a missing background noise, that's what it is, a noise that you are never much aware of until—

As if the power plant has suddenly gone dead, she realizes. But why—? She glances at the clock face: 3:17. Reflexively, she glances up at the speaker for an explanation from the Principal. Then some primal instinct sends a chill down her spine. She wheels around. "Children—under your desks!"

Amazed at her own outcry, she watches them dive, Geraldine dashing by from the blackboard, her eyes wide and her arms flung out. Her calves and shoe soles are just disappearing when the walls thunder. Then the plaster is ripping into jagged chunks and crashing down, spewing clouds of white dust. Oh my God, we're at war; but why bomb a school? The oil field, of course. They are targeting the biggest oil field in the country. Thank God, the children are safe!

My mother cannot see, through the blinding dust, her own desk, just a few feet away. She ducks her head, reaches out a hand and gropes her way forward. She has never seemed more slight in figure or more vulnerable to me than when I think of her in her deep red dress, with a tiny fringe of black lace peeping out, undertaking that short journey into blindness.

Whenever I see Mama's face on the angel, I think of her taking all those children under the shelter of her wings. Her sharp instinct and quick thinking saved the life of every pupil in the room that day. Granted, I can only imagine her last movements. Still the fact remains that in the very same room, inches from the cover of her own desk or some other vacant one, she lost her life. Such was the random nature of the tragedy. Now, tell me you believe in God's grace.

Chapter 3

Mind you, I mean no disrespect. Only that if you were to say, "There, but for the grace of God, go I," you would be saying that God looks with favor on some of us, and not the rest, that God picks and chooses whom to save from harm for some unfathomable reason that we are not meant to know or understand unless it is that God has a special purpose in mind for some lives to continue—hardly a source of comfort for those of us who buried a loved one, if not two or three, up at Pleasant Hill Cemetery or elsewhere. I would rather believe that God's grace had nothing to do with those choices, but that who stayed home from school that day with a case of sniffles, or who played hookey without being caught and hauled by the ear to the schoolhouse before the day was over; who switched desks with somebody else, or walked through one of the doors marked, EXIT, just in time; or simply wound up in a place from which escape from death was possible—as I did—was all a matter of chance because, to believe that what happened was an act of God, as a judge would later assert in tossing out the lawsuits brought by the victims' families, would be to believe in a God more cruel and indifferent than any mortal enemy.

I would rather believe God set the world spinning, then left us to our own devices, than to believe God was that fickle toward people who believed so hard and never missed a Sunday of church or a Wednesday night either, and whose children came to Jesus.

I would not know for some time after the catastrophe how it was that I came to lie twisted in an unconscious heap out on the campus, in the moments following 3:17 in the afternoon.

No sooner had I gotten to school that morning than my head had begun to ache. And all through the day, it ached without relenting. Whenever I remembered that bowl of cream of wheat with a dollop of butter melting in the center, I became half nauseous, and at lunch time I could only pick at the roast beef sandwich with pickle and mayonnaise that Mama had packed in my dinner pail. All this was punishment for lying to Mama, I scolded myself, plus all the worrying about Daddy last night which had robbed me of sleep.

To live with a father who worked in the oil fields was to live with the ever-present danger that he could be seriously injured or killed one day on the job. When I was around four years old there was a blowout on the drilling rig where Daddy was employed. Having heard the report from a neighbor, Mama and I sat up through the night by a kerosene lamp in the kitchen. The windows of our little oil camp house rattled like castanets. I was so terrified I sat trembling on Mama's lap and would not get down. She hugged me to her and smoothed my hair, tapped her foot on the floor and watched the door. "Where's Daddy?" I kept demanding. "He'll be here soon, Delys, it will be alright." Finally, sometime after midnight, there was a knock on the door. With a quick intake of breath, Mama shoved me off her knees and ran to open it. Daddy was soon carted feet first through the door on a makeshift stretcher. The two crew members who were carrying him said he had been safe until he broke cover and tried to make his way through the flying pipe joints and wildly sinuous cables raining down, to pull the derrick man to safety. The derrick man had fallen eighty feet to the ground, and lay there, out in the open, defenseless. (He would later die from his injuries, leaving a wife and four children behind.) The men had finally gotten Daddy to a doctor, who sewed up a gash on the back of his head, declared he had suffered a mild concussion, and gave him some strong pain medicine. Seeing his body lying horizontally, with his eyes closed and his face pale and lifeless, I started screaming because I thought he was dead.

Daddy was off work for two weeks, and I begged him not to go back. Mama was traumatized, too, and took the opportunity to beg Daddy to forget oil field work and take his rightful position at the glass company; but he wouldn't listen. He loved his work, and was proud whenever his crew brought in a well. There was a picture in my scrapbook of a bunch of haggard-looking workmen posing in front of a drilling rig in tall boots and grimy overalls and hats, and me in my ruffled bonnet and Sunday dress and high-topped shoes, perched like a sunbeam on Daddy's shoulder. A line of men, cleanly-shaven and dressed in suits, stretched out on each side: the newly prospered well owners. Everyone was smiling.

But because Daddy had no further interest in being around a well once it was producing at its optimum, bringing in a well often meant it was time to move on to some other location. By the time Daddy finally wound up at the vast East Texas Field, which stretched across the whole northeastern corner of Texas, and spread into seven different counties, we had moved from Odessa and Burkburnett out in West Texas, up into Oklahoma—we lived for a few months in Tulsa, then headed to Lawton for a while—then moved back down to Texas, to live in Corpus Christi. Even though all through my childhood, until Mama's death, I often heard her and Daddy talk about their many moves from one oil field to another, I believe my first real memory of being surrounded by boxes as Mama scurried around packing up was when we relocated from Tulsa to Lawton, a few months after Daddy was injured in that blowout; and I might say here that there is nothing like living in fear on a daily basis for making a child keenly vigilant, even more so because that fear is rarely articulated. Perhaps this is why I was acutely sensitive to the moods of my parents from a very early age, particularly of Daddy whom— ironically—we always assumed to be the only one of us in real danger. When the well he was drilling was about to hit pay sands, his workdays would lengthen, and when he came home at night he would be taciturn. Out on the porch before bedtime, I would be hard put to keep his attention long enough to identify the Big and Little Dipper for him before he fell silent and barely answered my questions. He would mostly just sit smoking his cigarette. Scooted up next to him in my thin nightgown, I would feel the tension in his arm and thigh muscles. After Mama called me inside to bed, he would continue sitting out there for a long time. I would know, because I could not go to sleep until I heard the kitchen door open and shut and knew he had come in.

Then one day he'd come home smiling. And if the well that had come in was the last one on the lease, often we would have to move. Sometimes Mama would become tense, and withdraw from me, and I would worry that I had done something to displease her. Only when I was older did I come to understand that as time went on she grew more and more weary of moving, desperate to put down roots. I distinctly remember she did not want to leave Corpus Christi because I had started kindergarten, and she had accepted a teaching job at my school. She was also tutoring two high school students that year. I overheard her arguing with Daddy one late night, and I was afraid Daddy would go off and leave us. Eventually I would overhear him say to Mama, "Now see, Vinia? I was right all along. Just look at the great job you got here, pays a lot more than the one in Corpus."

The job he referred to, of course, was teaching at the London School.

So on the night before Mama was killed, when I heard Daddy say, "I'm going," I was worried that the time had finally come when we would have to leave East Texas, or Mama and I would be left behind. Further complicating matters, while I couldn't imagine living without Daddy, I could hardly bear the thought of being uprooted from the life that I loved, and my school, in order go with him.

Of course, my nausea of that morning was no doubt due, at least in part, to nervousness over tomorrow's spelling contest. Lanelle Oberlin, one of my two partners, had such a severe case of nerves that, right in the middle of lunch, her stomach groaned loudly. Her face blanched, she clutched her abdomen and fled the table for the restroom. Lanelle lived in the Tidewater Oil Camp, nearby the school, and was very poor. She wore dresses made of feed sacks and hand-me-down coats and shoes from her several older siblings, clothing to be passed along to her younger siblings as well. She had dingy blond hair that she wore in a braid down her back, and freckles. Sometimes she didn't smell very good, which I would complain about to Mama. And Mama would shush me and say Lanelle couldn't help it, and not to say anything about the subject to anyone at school, and that was final.

Lanelle was the smartest person in sixth grade. Somehow, in the crowded, confused conditions in which she lived, she managed to focus obsessively on her studies. She was my best friend, along with my other spelling partner Eva Ruth Halsey. I was never envious of Eva Ruth, in spite of her long, silky dark hair, her deep green eyes and china doll complexion, because spelling was her best subject; in others she was only average. Besides, Bruce had stopped liking Eva Ruth for me. But I was envious of Lanelle every time she made a higher grade on a test than I did. And I was mortified whenever I got a B on my report card, because Lanelle never, ever did.

My head throbbed and throbbed. After lunch I considered asking to go to the nurse's office, but if I did she might make me lie down, and send for Mama. Mama might think I was coming down with something and insist that I ride home with her and Queen Price instead of taking the bus, and I didn't want to do that because Bruce had told me that morning that he had something to ask me on the way home in the afternoon. On most mornings, Bruce was the first person to board the bus and I was the second. We had five minutes or so to talk before anyone else got on, and we'd sit far enough back so that the driver couldn't see us holding hands, or listen in on our conversation, though as loud and clattering as the school bus was, bumping along the country byways, I have often wondered why we were so concerned. In the afternoon we had another five minutes of privacy before I got off the bus, my dog, Rusty, circling and barking in joyful greeting.

It seems odd now to look back on an age in life when you were always subject to the will of the adults in charge, and how you relied on your wits to exercise some control over your life. And as guilty as this always made me feel, if Bruce had something to ask me, nothing could stop me from being available to give him my answer. And anyway, I thought I knew what it was, given the fact that we had been valentines for over a month, and by the way his dark eyes shifted off to the side, and his voice grew soft and secretive under those straight brown brows, when he alerted me.

And so the hours passed, and during last period, English, we took a test on *Silas Marner*, including a reading comprehension question which I found easy in spite of my throbbing head, English being my best subject, and *Silas Marner* being a story I loved so much that by then I had read it several times. And when everyone was done, Miss Tadlock took up the papers. It was just after three o'clock then, and Bruce's eyes suddenly met mine from across the room—neither of us planned it, I don't think—widening and holding my gaze in a way I thought was meaningful. But my head hurt so bad that I dreaded the jostling on the bus ride home, and almost wished I had gone to the nurse's office after all. Miss Tadlock said, "Now, Eva Ruth, Lanelle and Delys—"

And that's the last thing I would remember for a very long time.

Chapter 4

I am lying on my back with my eyes closed. From somewhere far away I can hear the wailing sound of sirens, a great many of them, eclipsing one another as though there is some kind of traffic jam. Heels clatter loudly along the floor. I am bumped and jostled. Pushed at. "'Scuse me." Pain clenches my head like a vise, and radiates from my right shoulder down the whole length of my arm; my fingernails feel on fire. I do not know where I am but the surface underneath me is as cold and hard as a marble slab. I want Daddy to move me up on the couch but I cannot speak with my mouth full. I need a bath before the spelling contest. My whole body feels caked with dust, as though dust had been hurled at me with such force that it penetrated all my pores. Was there a dust storm? Are we in Odessa? I try to open my eyes, but when I do the lids feel heavy like water balloons, and they scratch against my pupils as if they were made of sandpaper. There are noises all around me, a cacophony of talking, moaning, pitiful whimpering, and desperate sobs that sound as if they are coming at me through a long tunnel. And all the while, from far off, the wailing sirens. There is no such place as where I am. I am trapped in a Halloween nightmare; locked inside the haunted house. Just need to wake up and— The air smells of blood and ammonia and rancidness, like dirty sheets. And dust. It's lodged far up in my nose and crammed up under my eyes. My face throbs with it. My cover is gently lifted. "It ain't him, Louise. Sorry, miss." My cover drifts back down like a cloud.

Then I hear a somber male voice as though from high above, and approaching steps. "There is nothing I can do for your daughter; I'm sorry." From far away there are high-pitched, ragged voices, arguing: a man and a woman. A brief scuffle seems to erupt, with grunts and shuffling. "Now, Henry—" says the woman. "You didn't half look at her," comes the man's sharp, threatening rebuke. "I have to move on," apologizes the somber voice, sounding weary. "I'm so sorry. But you can see all the others that are here. And still coming. I have to try and see them before...." The voice trails off. So then I know I am dying, and Mama and Daddy are upset. But it's alright. Tell them I'm not afraid. My head aches so hard I want to tear out my hair and run as fast as I can. I did not know that headaches could kill people.

And then I feel a sudden chill, the cover being rudely thrown off, exposing me. "A female," says the somber voice, and then a cold hard thumb is pressed against my chest, first one location then another. After a few beats, the voice reports, "Heartbeat's strong." Next my eyes are forced open, one then the other, and held open while the light from a train shines in. I feel a heavy breath close by and something large and warm and fleshy, pressing against my side. My eyes sting like fire. I paw the air with one hand, to force the intruder away. "I'm Doctor Buckstrum. How are you? Can you talk to me? Tell me your name."

I wonder if I have heard him right. I can hardly believe my own doctor, whom everyone calls Doc, and who is Bruce's father, doesn't even recognize me. Not that I am sick that often. Still. I would recognize him. He is a large man, barrel-chested, with thick graying hair and sad-looking, hooded eyes. Doc is a sad person; widowed when Bruce was five. "Duh-hhhh—" I try hard for him, but no sound comes, just air. The sound is caught behind the grit crammed in my throat and caked on my tongue and my teeth. Now his large hands are groping over my body, my abdomen, legs, feet; brief but painful pressing, pressing. "Contusions. Let's see if we can turn her," says Doc. But when he touches my right shoulder a shaft of pain strikes at me like lightning shooting through it, and I groan in terror. Releasing my shoulder, Doc utters a string of doctor words. A female voice answers, "Yes, I've got it."

"Send her on."

I sense the doctor drawing away. *My head hurts*, I try to say before he goes. I feel a sharp jab in my hip then a sensation of melting. Hot wax spreading under my skin, and spreading farther and farther, until it over-takes my whole body.

It is Saturday afternoon when I finally come fully awake and at that time I do not recall anything about the bad dream. The first thing I see is Jesus praying in the Garden of Gethsemane, a Biblical event which I have seen depicted in a colored print on the wall of my Sunday School room. Momentarily dismissing the context of a sea of floral wallpaper, I believe that my head has exploded and I am dead.

Abruptly Daddy's figure nears, blocking out the picture. The sleeves of his khaki shirt are rolled up to the elbows, and his forearms and hands are covered in red scabs and purple bruises, the real significance of which will not register in my mind for years. At the time I vaguely assume Daddy has hurt himself at work.

When Daddy sees that I am awake, he inquires in a soft, husky voice, "How's my Dee?" Then his face twists up and his eyes gush with tears.

I remember all this, or believe I do, though I had suffered a serious head injury (having nothing, and everything, to do with my day-long headache), and those next few days in the Mother Frances Hospital, in which I spent as much time sleeping as staying awake, have never seemed altogether real. I could not say with any authority whether what I remember actually happened, or was only a dream. There is one conversation with Daddy, that day or the next, that I have always held in my heart as real, and never even had reason to question until many years later, after my father's death, when I was confronted with a new set of facts about his relationship with my mother.

After Daddy delivered the shocking news of a gas explosion at my school, in which Mama died along with many others, we held each other to the extent that we could—my right shoulder, dislocated, had been put back in place, then bandaged—and sobbed until we shook, though of course I had not even begun to absorb the reality that my mother was gone, and scarcely any of the rest of the report either. But then I suddenly remembered my lie to Mama just hours before her death. I was so filled with remorse, I began to sob anew and had to compose myself all over again before I could make a halting confession to Daddy.

As he listened, he smiled tenderly at Mama's well-known fetish about her slip showing. Afterward, he took hold of my hands. His hands felt rough and scabby. His face grim, he said, "Oh, Dee, I wish I could take back something I did, too." He paused. Swallowed hard. "Your mother and I had a disagreement the night before, and in the morning when I left she was standing in the kitchen in her robe. She said to me, 'Dan, I am sorry you are unhappy.' I did not say a word, but picked up the dinner pail she had filled for me, and walked out. I got in my truck and drove to work."

Daddy gripped my hands harder then, and went on, "All day long it kept crossing my mind, I was going to make it up to her that night. Try to put everything to rights. Then—it was too late."

I have always felt my father gave me a generous gift in that confession. For one thing, he convinced me that I was not a bad person, as only a loving father could do for a young daughter who idolized him. This assurance lasted until I grew old enough to know I would have to sort out my guilt for myself. And in truth, as the years have gone by, I have realized the obvious: being a good daughter to Mama overall—which I certainly was—counted far more than one transgression at the end of her life. Yet, the harder truth is that even now I still have the occasional dream in which I see Mama's slip showing and try to tell her; yet I cannot make the words come out, and gradually she recedes then vanishes.

The other thing Daddy did was to confirm that he and Mama were truly in love when she was killed and, had she survived the blast, would have made up as they always did after a quarrel, their devotion to each other continuing as ever.

Of course, as I say, what was claimed to me years later does not support the reality of this conversation, and many times since hearing the opposing view I have found myself suddenly becoming prone, as though under attack, and forced to question whether Daddy really made any such admission to me, or I dreamed it up because every word is exactly what I want to believe.

By the time I was released from the hospital, six days after the explosion, Mama had been buried at Pleasant Hill Cemetery. Not in the plot she had purchased several years earlier, and where she anticipated one distant day being laid to rest beside her husband, but in a special new section near the road, surrounded by pupils she had taught. "I believe it's what she would have wanted," Daddy said. At the time I thought he had reached a very strange conclusion, but that was because I knew so little about the nature or the scope of the tragedy, how it could never be looked at as a number of separate individuals dying, but rather, one whole community, with everyone interconnected. One could imagine—and I have, many times—a whole host of spirits rising all at once above that rolling countryside, holding hands and reassuring one another. Yes, the bodies of some victims were taken far away, to other cities, to be buried, and some were taken to other cemeteries close by, in Overton, for instance. But it doesn't really matter. It was still a collective disaster, one whole group of people who knew one another and saw one another every day, destroyed together, in a single stroke. Daddy must have felt deeply that sense of their being connected, and wanted to honor it.

Or, was he already thinking that he wasn't about to stay around East Texas any longer than necessary, so there was no use in Mama's remains lying there in the Pleasant Hill Cemetery, waiting for his to be buried beside them someday? My daddy was a complex person, with finely-tuned sensitivities on the one hand, which made him an insightful listener and conversationalist, and a streak of cold logic on the other, which made him good at his job. So I believe it is possible that he was answering to more than one set of dictates at the same time.

And maybe, in fact, he was struggling between them, moment by moment. One thing I know is that, shocked and confused as Daddy must have been—and far more than I could have possibly fathomed at that early point in my life—he was understandably vulnerable to the counsel of Aunt Allie, who arrived with her husband on the very night of the tragedy, the tires of Uncle Logan's big sedan making ruts in the red clay around our house. Which—now that I think of it—was another of Mama's fetishes.

Anyway, driving me home from the Tyler hospital, Daddy was quiet for a good while. I sat beside him wearing a new robe and pair of slippers that Allie had bought for me in Henderson, dreading the thought of walking inside our house, knowing Mama would not be there waiting, cooking supper maybe, or hanging clothes out on the line. To think: I would never again hug her hello and burrow my face in the sweet-fragranced, sun-warmed bib of her apron. I tried to brace myself for the days ahead, thinking how I would take care of her garden beds, in which daffodils were already starting to bloom. How I would learn to cook Daddy's supper.

Then all at once Daddy was clearing his throat loudly enough that it stirred me from my ruminations. I turned toward him. Squaring his shoulders, he announced his decision to move to California, and leave me to the good offices of my mother's only sibling, whom Mama had adored and trusted in every way. "There is no doubt in my mind this is what Vinia would have me do," he said firmly. I can't give you the kind of life she wanted for you, but your Aunt Allie can, and she is eager to step in. Especially as she has never had any children of her own."

Before I had time to absorb the shocking news that even the last remnant of the life I had known was about to be ripped away, he hastened to add a few words of caution that have stayed with me to this day, along with the vehemence with which he uttered them. Many times I have turned over in my mind how much they revealed about how proud my father was, and how sensitive to being looked down on by my mother's family for the way he had chosen to earn his living—feelings which I never heard him openly admit. In a strident voice, he said, "I don't mean to say that I'll be relying on the Fletchers' *charity*. I will continue providing for you just as though your mother were alive. I made that clear to Allie; and it's important for you to understand, too, and not be asking her and Logan for things instead of looking to me."

He glanced my way, his eyes blazing. "Is that clear?"

"Yessir," I murmured, my heart hammering against my chest.

He nodded and let out a breath, then reached over to pat my knee tenderly as though to soften the blow, either of his decision to leave me behind, or the brusque way he issued his words of warning. I've never known. Perhaps it was both.

Of course, none of this was really clear to me at all. My father's unexpected determination to cast me aside was almost as disorienting as waking up in the hospital after the explosion. After a few minutes, I managed to ask, "What will become of our house?" To me, our house that Daddy built was our holy sanctuary; it had never belonged to anyone else, and I never wanted it to.

Daddy stared dully at the road ahead, his knuckles whitening as he tightened his grip on the steering wheel. "I'm going to put it up for sale," he said with a sigh of resignation. "Your aunt and your grandmother are helping me get it packed up now. Your grandfather is going through Mama's papers."

Mama's parents, the Maddens—Roy and Sarah—had arrived the day after the explosion. In fact, it was in the Maddens' nice big automobile that we were riding now, owing to the fact that Daddy's oil field truck was too bumpy a ride for someone recovering from head and shoulder injuries. I didn't particularly like my grandparents because they had always been cold to Daddy and not especially friendly toward me. When Mama and I would go down to Houston, to visit Aunt Allie, we would stop by for only a brief visit with the Maddens. And Mama always seemed relieved when we departed. I didn't like to think of my grandfather opening Mama's cardboard boxes where she kept her papers so meticulously, and looking inside. It didn't seem to be any of his business going in there. He may as well have gone in her underwear drawer. The thought of which made me consider drawers and closets and kitchen cabinets being thrown open and emptied of Mama's things, when she had taken such pride in keeping our house in order. "We don't have a great big house, but as long as we keep the clutter picked up, and everything in its place, we'll have plenty of room," she would say.

I felt sick inside. To live with my aunt and uncle was the last thing I wanted. Though Allie was always kind, sending me presents through the mail and remembering my birthday every year, I felt I hardly knew her at all. And her husband, even less so, because he never came with Aunt Allie when she visited us, and never paid me any attention when Mama and I visited in his home. Uncle Logan had a quiet demeanor and a nasal voice, and was hard of hearing in one ear. I had never once seen him without a suit and a tie. His car was always immaculate, and never had red mud on the fenders as Daddy's truck did.

If we stayed, even if our house would be unbearably sad without Mama, at least Daddy and I would still have each other, to love and care for, and I would still have all my friends. In the hospital, as I recovered day by day, when I had not been grieving over the loss of Mama, I had been fearing that some of my friends had been hurt, or killed, as well. It didn't seem likely, because the junior high wing was so far away from the senior high wing. Still, I could hardly wait to go back to school and find out for sure. I could hardly wait to see the bus coming in the morning, and Bruce inside, saving me a seat, waving his hand at me through the window. Surely he would be there.

Which did not answer the question of how I got hurled out on the campus by the explosion. While I was in the hospital, Daddy had asked me where I was when the explosion occurred, and I didn't know. I didn't remember anything at all. He said, "It's alright. Don't worry about it," and patted my hand. He hadn't gone into any detail about the explosion. It never occurred to me that he was trying to protect me from the shock of the truth. I just assumed he didn't know anything more.

Now, panicked, I argued, "But why do we have to leave? We've got our house, and all our friends here. And I need to go back to school, Daddy! It's the middle of the semester. I can't just go off now!"

Daddy sighed. Then he glanced my way sadly. "There is no school, Dee. What little was left—they've about knocked it all down. Safety reasons."

For a few moments I stared at Daddy blankly, trying to conceive of what he had said. When construction of the school began years earlier, Mama and I walked down the road some afternoons, to stand watching on the sidelines as the building gradually rose up from the bald prairie. The London School was the most formidable building around. It stood out singularly, in proud relief against the broad blue sky. And now, suddenly, it wasn't there at all.

And if this were true, my thoughts raced on, then was the junior high wing affected too? Or was it just part of the building taken down afterward for safety reasons? "Daddy, what about my classroom? What about my—my friends?" I implored.

"Your classroom was destroyed. But that doesn't mean all your friends were killed necessarily. I just don't know. All I know is, my little girl escaped, and I don't know how, but I thank God for that." He bit his lip.

Again I tried to think back to where I was when it happened. But

Miss Tadlock calling out my name and Eva Ruth and Lanelle was all I could remember. What did she want with us? Did we go up to the front of the room so she could call out words to us? Somehow, it didn't seem quite right, though I couldn't say why. But if she did, then Eva Ruth and Lanelle, and Miss Tadlock must have wound up out on the campus where I did. But what about the rest of the class? What about Bruce? Oh my, what about Bruce?

Bruce is dead, I despaired.

Chapter 5

I make no apologies for my feelings for Bruce Buckstrum, or that he has been—in spite of everything—the love of my life. From the beginning I was drawn to qualities in him that others failed to discern, busy as they were weighing his promise against the many accomplishments of his older sister and brother, and concluding his prospects fell short. My mother made this error. Not that she said a word to me, but it was obvious that she took far more interest in Edna that night the two of them accepted an invitation to stay for supper at our house, following the Valentine's skating party. "What are you writing this week for the paper, Edna? I thought your piece on Mr. Maxwell's plans for campus beautification was quite well done, and so did Miss Price...." While Bruce politely listened, I waited in vain for Mama to engage him in conversation too.

Then, after Mama's death, Aunt Allie spurned Bruce as well. Eventually I would come to realize that Mama had colored Allie's opinion of Bruce so that he was all but doomed to fulfil her low expectations. Everything Allie did on my behalf sprang from her sense of loyalty to her late sister, and inherent in this were her relentless efforts to discern my mother's wishes and carry them out. Of course, even aside from this, Bruce was a part of the tragedy that Allie abhorred, and was urging me daily to move on and forget. But I would have given all those dates in high school that Allie would one day insist I accept, for one illicit phone call from Bruce. Or—I should say—to Bruce, for after my aunt forbade us to be in contact, he and I would work out a new system of communication. And I make no apologies for that deception either, nor did I feel the least regret during the time it was going on. Well, not for a long time, anyway.

From the night I arrived home from the hospital and Bruce stopped by, concerned about me despite being shaken by the horrors he had experienced among his own family, we pledged ourselves to each other. And I will be quick to say that, in my opinion, the first romance of any girl's life carves the most indelible impression in the walls of her heart, no matter how many romances follow.

But I'm racing ahead. First, my homecoming from the hospital, around nightfall. That would have been Wednesday the 24th of March. What an empty celebration. I remember approaching our house, which retreated far back from the highway so that only if all the house lights were thrown on (they seldom were, when Mama was alive) would it be clearly visible through the trees. And indeed that night every front window was flooded with light. I hated the garish sight as we turned off the road, and was as embarrassed for Mama as if she had been surprised by an unwitting intruder while stepping out of the bathtub and reaching for a towel. I could see even as we pulled to a halt that the walls were bare of Mama's framed prints of bucolic landscapes and still lifes.

Rusty, the stray I had adopted and named for the color of his fur, who had one ear that stood up and one that drooped, yelped excitedly and sought my hands for licking as we made our way across the yard. "Confound it, watch out!" Daddy scolded, fearing Rusty would trip my feet no doubt. But I leaned down a little so he could lick my face, and told him I was glad to see him, too. What will become of Rusty? I suddenly wondered with dread. Rusty was my faithful companion, making up for the fact that I had no brothers or sisters. And this fact gave me one more reason to set myself against my aunt and uncle, for I doubted they would allow my dog to come to live with me in Houston. I had never seen a pet at their house, and I once heard my uncle complain of a neighbor's dog barking in the night and keeping him awake. When I stood straight again, my head felt like a boulder that had been knocked lopsided. I wobbled a little. For the moment I forgot my worries about Rusty.

Daddy was guiding my elbow toward the back porch when the screen door swung open and Aunt Allie stepped out to greet us. She was taller than Mama, her narrow torso and long limbs taken from their father's side of the family. Whereas Mama's steps were quick and lively, as if to make up for her shortness, Allie's steps were slower and more measured. And she spoke more slowly, too. She styled her honey blond hair in tight finger waves around her oval face, the back rolled into a crescent that stretched from ear to ear. Allie's eyes were long and tapered, set above high cheekbones. Her skin was smooth, and darker in tone than Mama's. According to Mama, Allie had always been considered the beauty of the family.

Now she was wearing Mama's favorite apron, trimmed in yellow rick rack, I observed, and I resented her removing it from the hook where it belonged, slipping her long arms through the sleeves and tying the sash behind her waist. *"Take it off! It's too little for you!"* I wanted to lash out.

"Welcome home, darling," she said warmly. But when my figure came within the glow of light stretching out beyond the porch, my shoulder bandaged and my eyes still black and purple, Allie took a look at me and brought a hand to her chest. "Child!" she gasped, her eyes wide and glassy. She stood aside and let Daddy and me pass through the door. I heard her murmur uncertainly from behind, "I've got chicken and dumplings on the table. We—we weren't sure when to expect you."

The thought of sitting down with my visiting relatives to a plate of chicken and dumplings, without Mama at the table, nearly brought me to my knees with nausea. And now there they were, Uncle Logan behind Mama's copy of *The Houston Chronicle*—Mama liked to keep up with her hometown news—and my grandparents, two round figures, one of them bald and the other with a fading red topknot, looking anxiously toward the door. Along one wall, empty cardboard grocery boxes lay in wait for filling. Mama was hardly cold in her grave, and already—

"I've got to go lie down," I said, overcome. "I feel dizzy." Daddy steered me to my room, and I lay down on the bed, dots appearing before my eyes.

"Well, they told us to expect this, didn't they?" said Daddy. He tucked the quilt around my shoulders, then switched on the dim bedside lamp. "I'll bring the kaopectate and some water."

Kaopectate was vile. "I'll be alright. I just need to be quiet for a little while," I said.

What I really needed was for the last six days never to have happened, I lamented as Daddy walked out. How could he go off to California, and leave me behind? Didn't he have the same feelings I did as we walked through the kitchen just now? Didn't he know how wrong all this was, that we were about to abandon the home that Mama loved, and separate from each other? She would never have wanted that, surely. I started to cry, and to strongly consider calling Bruce on the telephone. I could never lightly call up any boy on the telephone. As a rule, nice girls did not do so. Yet surely Bruce would understand my breach of etiquette after all that had happened. And now that I thought about it, he may be worried about me. If only I could know that he was safe and well, and longing to know that I was safe and well, too, everything would be better, I thought. Then I remembered I was about to be forced away from Bruce too, assuming he was alive. *Oh please, let him be alive!* My valentine. We must never, ever lose each other, no matter what.

Abruptly I remembered Bruce wanted to ask me something. Something significant, I thought. The memory of his saying so dropped into place as though it had fallen right into my lap. Suddenly I felt aglow inside, that I could remember something—anything—concrete from that day. I strained to see if I could remember anything else while I was at it. But I could not. And I might say right here that through all the years of my life since the explosion, whenever a memory of the time shortly preceding it strikes me hard, and of a piece, as this one did, I am inclined to believe in its accuracy even if it is never proved. Otherwise I am often skeptical. The slipperiness of memory has made me yearn for certainty in my life. Perhaps more than I should, more than is healthy.

In a few minutes Aunt Allie came into the room and stood beside the bed. She had removed Mama's apron. She wore a greenish-brown gabardine dress with a shirt collar, self-belted waist, and large buttons down the front. "Better?" she asked kindly.

"Some."

"Mind if I sit on the bed with you, so we can talk a little?"

"No, ma'am. I don't mind," I said. Yet in fact I was nervous about talking to this aunt who had suddenly taken over my life. Already I had a suspicion she would ask things of me that I would not want to give.

Cautiously, she lowered herself onto the end of the bed and turned toward me. She seemed a little lost. "I can only imagine how you must be grieving for your mother right now," she said. Then she added, haltingly, "And—you know, Vinia–she meant the world to me, too. Why, we shared everything our whole lives! Who will I...?" Her voice drifted off. Her eyes searching mine, she waited for an assurance that I was incapable of providing.

Momentarily her lips curled into a wistful smile as she recalled, "When I couldn't have a little girl of my own, Vinia told me she wanted me always to think of you as belonging partly to me. And I've always held that wish of hers sacred." Her voice caught on the last word. Her eyes sparkled; tears dribbled out. Pursing her lips, she withdrew the handkerchief from her skirt pocket and wiped her eyes, then composed her face. It seemed to me that my aunt was very conscious of how she appeared, even when she became upset. When Mama cried— which was not very often—she let all her sadness out before she stopped herself. Her eyes grew pinched and her face grew blotchy. Somehow Mama's crying seemed more authentic.

Poor Allie. How lonely she must have been; how high her hopes that I could fill the empty places in her life. Yet to this baring of her heart, which would be the first of many times my aunt reached out in vain to establish some form of intimacy with me, I could say nothing. I wished Mama had never given Allie to believe she had some claim on me. If Mama had known she would not live to see me grown up, surely she would not have done so. And Daddy and I would be staying together now, right here—

"So it isn't like your uncle and I are just trying to be nice," Allie continued. "We really do want you to live with us, and I know, in my heart of hearts, *that* is what your mother would have wanted. We can give you *such* a good home. I promise you."

I could not help interjecting, "I'd rather live with my daddy, though."

Allie gazed at me for a long moment, as though trying to assess the difficulty ahead. "Oh, I know that, honey, I really do," she said then. "But Dan's going to be moving around now. All over the place. If you went with him, you would have to live in one oil camp after another." She shrugged. "It wouldn't be any life for you, and what would become of your education?"

I resented her slur against oil camps. Mama and Daddy and I had lived in oil camps when I was little, and we were happy. What really counted was that we were together. It occurred to me then that Allie had used this line of argument to Daddy, and made him feel he would be selfish if he failed to do as she advised.

"My friend Lanelle lives in the Tidewater oil camp, and she is the smartest person in sixth grade," I said defensively, feeling a little guilty for the times I had felt jealous because she made a higher grade than I did.

"Still, I'm sure your friend's parents would provide better for her if they could," Aunt Allie pointed out.

I could not argue with that.

Allie reached for my hands and gave them a gentle squeeze. She looked earnestly into my eyes. "So. This is going to be real hard for a while. But the two of us will help each other, huh? Take one day at a time? And we'll get through it. I know we will," she said bracingly. Yet again, I resisted her attempt to draw me close. My grief was my own, and had nothing to do with hers.

However, it dawned on me this was the perfect time to ask Aunt Allie if I could bring Rusty to live with me. In that moment I was sure I could convince her of how much it would help.

Before I could speak, there came a light tap on the door and Uncle Logan looked in. "Delys has a visitor, a young man. I told him I would check, that he might have to come back some other time."

My heart leapt. "Bruce Buckstrum?" I cried.

"Bruce something. I didn't quite catch the last name."

It seems to me as I reflect on this moment that a kind of recognition passed between my aunt and uncle, followed by a slight lift of Allie's brow as though she had been placed on alert. But perhaps I'm only filling in the picture a bit, inserting a fact to coincide with what I now know was my aunt's obsession with getting rid of Bruce.

I threw off the quilt and brought my feet to the floor so fast that dizziness overtook me again. I braced myself with both hands on the edge of the bed, and hung my head, my breath heaving. Aunt Allie gripped my arm. "Are you alright?" "Yes, ma'am." She rose and smoothed down her skirt front. With a touch of uneasiness in her voice, she said, "Better you stay there. I don't see why your friend can't visit you in your room. But not too long. We'll leave the door ajar."

As my aunt and uncle walked out, I was all too aware of my puffy, discolored eyes and swollen face. Reflexively, I ran my fingers through my hair. I should at least take a minute or two, to run a brush through—

But then it was too late. Bruce had come into my bedroom and I was inviting him to sit down on my dresser bench. Bruce looked as if he were dressed up for school picture day. As if coming to visit me were a special occasion. His brown hair appeared to be freshly washed, its side part a straight line from front to back. He wore a plaid shirt with long sleeves and the collar opened and smoothed down. His slacks were neatly creased and his belt buckle shined. But his shoes bore a thin layer of telltale red dust. Realizing he had walked all the way from home—a good three miles from here—I had that heady sensation of knowing my affections for Bruce were returned in full, a feeling I had when I boarded the bus every day and made my way toward the seat he was saving for me. I do not believe that grown-up love can ever be quite that intoxicating, maybe because only the young have yet to experience the kind of disillusionment that will one day make them more cautious about trusting those feelings.

"Hey," he said, lowering himself onto the bench. Now, with his dark eyes under those straight brows narrowed on my face as though he were slightly unnerved by my appearance, I felt frightened that he would stop liking me. Should I tell him that the doctor at Mother Frances assured me I would look normal in a few weeks? Yet, what good would it do? I was going away. What if Bruce always remembered me as I looked tonight?

"Gee, it's good to see you," I told him. "I was worried about you."

Bruce only nodded, continuing to study my face as if he could not take his eyes off me. "Guess I look pretty bad, huh?" I remarked uneasily.

"Aw, you can't help that," he said quietly. His eyes dropped as though he suddenly realized he had been staring. He sighed, and gazed off into the distance. *You are sorry you came*, I thought with dread.

Abruptly he looked back at me. "I've come by every night since it happened. Your aunt said you still weren't home."

So Bruce had been concerned about me, I thought with relish. It saddened me, though, to think of him getting dressed up and walking all the way here, only to find his efforts were in vain.

Why hadn't Daddy told me about this? I wondered. Then I realized he was probably sitting out on the back porch when Bruce arrived, and didn't know. He was probably out there right now.

"I heard Miz Lithingate was killed. I'm real sorry," Bruce said, his brows hitched together, his eyes crinkled, searching my face. Empathy was one of those qualities that I sensed and admired in Bruce, even before I knew there was a term for being able to enter into another's feelings as if they were your own.

I nodded. "It is said that she saved every person in her room," I told him proudly, and my voice broke.

A pained expression crossed his face. He clenched his jaw. Then he asked, "Is someone moving in with you now? I saw all the boxes."

I shook my head, wishing that were true. I told him Daddy and I were moving away.

Bruce screwed up his face. "But why? You don't have to go. We're still going to have school. And they're going to build us a new building, just as good as the one we had."

His words made my heart ache more. To think: all my friends were staying behind together, while I was forced to go away. I felt nothing could be more unjust, and to this day I feel the same. As a teacher I watched many a teenage heart broken by a family move. Adults often pay little notice to the worlds their children have carefully constructed for themselves, fragile as a spider web in a door frame.

I told Bruce there was nothing I'd rather do than stay here and go to the new school, but it had already been decided that I would move to Houston with my aunt and uncle. I thought of Eva Ruth, of how Bruce might decide to like her again, when I was gone, and I felt so jealous my eyes blurred. But then it struck me that Eva Ruth may not have survived. I was seized with guilt and worry. Still, not quite wanting to mention Eva Ruth's name because it might prompt Bruce to start thinking about how pretty she was, I asked about our class, if everyone was alright.

Bruce shook his head. "Our grade was hit hardest of all, they said. Most everyone in our class was killed, including Miss Tadlock."

He may as well have socked me in the chin. I shrank back on the pillows. I thought of Miss Tadlock, a kind spinster who lived with Miss Higgins, a fellow teacher, behind the school. "But how did you— How did I—?"

Again, Bruce screwed up his face. "You don't remember leaving the room?"

No, I don't remember that at all."

"Miss Tadlock sent you and Lanelle and Eva Ruth somewhere to practice spelling words. I didn't hear what she said about where. Then a couple of minutes later, she sent me to the elementary school building with a note for Mr. Fielding. He was at the P.T.A. meeting.

"I had just given him the note, and I was walking out the door, on my way back, when I heard a huge rumble, and the ground rocked. It threw me off balance, and my rib cage knocked the doorjamb," he said, wincing, easing one hand around his ribs. He went on in a trembling voice, "People were running out the doors, screaming. Nobody seemed to notice me. I couldn't see anything from there except a lot of smoke. I couldn't see any flames. I knew something terrible had happened, but I didn't know what." He paused and swallowed before continuing.

"From where I was, I—I could see the buses parked, you know, where they always are. It looked like it was safe there. I thought the driver might be inside, and he would know what happened. So I went on to our bus and got in. But no one was there except me. So I decided to wait and see if anyone else would come. I waited a good while." Again he paused, and our eyes met.

"I saved you a seat," he said tenderly.

I loved Bruce mightily then. We went on looking at each other for a long moment. Then I nodded, and lay there thinking. It was too much to take in. A memory was teasing at the edges of my mind, of standing in a brightly lit place, maybe by a window? And a sense that I was not alone. But it wasn't much to go on, and I could not say that's where I was when the school blew up. I shook my head, then I realized something. "I guess Eva Ruth and Lanelle must be okay, too, huh?"

"Eva Ruth moved away," he said. "A lot of people up and left as quick as they could. Like they were afraid it might happen again. But Lanelle—" he thought a moment. "I don't know about Lanelle. I haven't heard."

I could not help but take a moment to rejoice in the fact that Eva Ruth had moved away.

Bruce told me of the fates of his brother and sister then. Someone had seen Bucky just a few steps from the back door leading out to the band room, right before the explosion, he said. "But that's wrong. Bucky was in Mama's sixth period," I corrected him.

He squared his shoulders and took in a breath. "Yeah, but I guess she let him go early. He didn't make it."

I let out a mournful sigh. I was coming to realize that whether you lived or died was just a matter of chance. Mama would have saved Bucky along with the others. He was going to be a doctor. He had been accepted at Rice—

"Edna was taken, too," Bruce was saying, his voice barely above a whisper. "They were both laid out in the Overton skating rink."

My hands flew to my cheeks and I stared at him. I could see Edna going down on one knee, taking our picture together on Valentine's Day, the flash bulb exploding as others skated round and round behind us and the music played on the nickelodeon. "Where—?" was all I could choke out in disbelief.

"The Overton rink was one of the buildings they turned into a morgue."

Now I was thoroughly unnerved. The image of many, many dead bodies covered with sheets, rows and rows of them, came to mind. I believe it was in this moment the true scope of the disaster finally began to sink in.

Bruce took in a quick breath, and latched his hands together tightly, as though bracing himself. Shifting his eyes from mine and staring out into space, he went on in a soft voice, his eyes glassy, "It took me a while to find them. There was a lot of confusion."

My eyes widened in fright. Did he mean that he identified the dead bodies of his own sister and brother? At that time I had no idea of the brutal nature of injuries to those killed in a gas explosion, and all I could imagine was Bucky and Edna laid out under sheets as though peacefully sleeping, their bodies intact. But even so, identifying bodies was something a grown-up did; no one could have forced me to be that brave.

"But why didn't Doc—?"

"He was busy, helping Doctor Potts up there at the hospital. They were receiving patients to evaluate. Patients were lined up all over the floor when I went there. You had to step over one to get to the next," he said. "And they were still bringing them in."

Overton's hospital was in a small, two-story frame building up on Brandon Hill. I had never been in there, but I had seen it from the outside. Doctor Potts ran the hospital with the help of one Registered Nurse. I was trying to imagine the scene Bruce was describing, when suddenly I realized that what I had thought to be a nightmare was real, after all. "Bruce, I was there! I was on the floor. Doc—"

At this point the door swung open and Allie looked from one of us to the other. "We don't want Delys to overdo, her first night home," she said with a smile that seemed forced, though perhaps again I am reconciling what I actually observed then, with what I know now. It is tempting to improve on memories over time, making the stories we tell line up as they should.

At least I am sure that I resented Allie's interruption at that moment. What was the hurry? If we could just go on talking for a while, maybe I would remember more. Oh, why could she not leave us alone?

The spell was broken. Bruce looked up at her and blinked, as though his mind had been so far away, he could not quite remember who she was or what she wanted. "Yes, ma'am," he said politely. Allie withdrew, the damage done.

Bruce rose from the bench and came to stand a couple of feet from the bed where I lay. "I guess I have to go."

"When will I see you again, though?" I implored.

He thought about this. "There's going to be a big memorial service on Sunday afternoon. There on the school grounds. Reckon you can come?"

"I'll be there," I promised, thinking how good it would be to see everybody again, until it dawned on me how many people I knew would be part of the reason for the gathering.

"I'll save you a seat next to mine," Bruce promised.

"That will be swell," I said, and attempted to smile through the taut skin of my jaw and the weight of sadness I was feeling. "Oh, and Bruce, what was it you were going to ask me? Remember, you were going to ask me something on the bus?"

Bruce nodded. "I remember. I was going to ask you to be my steady girl friend," he said. Then he shrugged and looked at me miserably. "Guess you don't want to be that now, if you're moving away."

"I don't care. I still want to be. If you want me to," I said.

He smiled then. "I do," he said. He stood there for a long moment, looking indecisive. Abruptly he glanced at the half-closed door, then moved right up to the side of the bed, leaned near and boldly kissed my mouth.

I was much too surprised to say anything. Bruce's eyes avoided mine. He tucked his head down and started for the door.

"See you on Sunday," I called out anxiously, but I could not be sure he had heard me.

Chapter 6

On Friday Daddy came home from work early and suggested we take a drive over to see Mama's grave. "We can take your grandfather's car," he said.

I hesitated. Secretly I had felt relieved that I was not sufficiently recovered to attend Mama's funeral, and grateful that the grown-ups did not talk about it in front of me afterward. I felt Daddy should have discerned this and left me to my memories of when Mama was alive. Yet, seeing the hopeful look in his eyes I felt guilty and selfish for wanting to be spared. Mama would be ashamed of me. "Yes, alright," I said uneasily.

"We'll have to hurry, while there's daylight," said Daddy. "Take a sweater. The wind is chilly up there." As we walked out of the house, he draped my sweater around my shoulders.

The fact that we would be driving past the school—there was no other route to the Pleasant Hill Cemetery unless you went miles out of the way—added to my trepidation. As we crested the gentle hill that had always been the overture to seeing the red tile roof of the school just ahead, and for me was, and ever shall be, associated with riding the school bus with Bruce at my side, my stomach cringed and my heart picked up speed. *I don't have to look.*

Daddy didn't say anything. I sensed he wanted to leave it to me, whether or not to slow down and take a good long look, even talk about it, maybe.

With my right arm in its sling wrapped around my waist, fingers pinching the skin tightly, I held out until we reached the place where the road forked around an esplanade, directly across from the long walkway leading to the main entrance of the school; and then I could not help myself. I turned my head to the left, only to find what used to be our handsome, sprawling campus was only mud now, churned up like the sea during a violent storm. Sprouting from this was a rude structure resembling a slender, grayish plaster box, several stories high and stripped of all adornment, with squarish, gaping holes here and there over its surface; and a squattier box that thrust out to the side like an arm, with elongated holes, regularly spaced, up and down its length. None of this bore any resemblance to my school building, or to anything else I had ever seen. I faced ahead again.

Gradually I let out my breath, feeling somewhat gratified that I had conquered my fears and looked. Somehow the whole affair of the explosion seemed less real than ever, though. What I had seen might have been just some abandoned dump along the highway. I glanced at Daddy. His profile was stern, his jaw clenched tight. He had not even slowed down.

A mile or so more and we reached the point where this road intersected with the cemetery road, and we turned left and soon started winding a distance of about four miles, give or take, to our destination. Just a pretty, peaceful-looking stretch of rolling rural highway, overhung with trees and scattered with modest dwellings, which I realized suddenly I was going to miss. I thought despairingly of Houston, with its sharp corners and big buildings and traffic lights.

I suppose I must have assumed that, having gotten this far, I would go all the way to Mama's grave. Yet, when I came within sight of the scores of fresh red dirt mounds at the front of the cemetery, bedecked with garden flowers, I could hear the anguished sounds of moaning and sobbing, and Doc Buckstrum's solemn voice: "There is nothing I can do...." *They were laughing and gay and now their flesh is dissolving on their bones. Oh my soul! Why was I spared this? Why are they there, and I am here?*

Daddy gently steered the big sedan to the shoulder of the road and brought it to a stop, then turned to look at me. "Are you alright?" he asked.

"In a minute," I told him. I felt I was strangling for air. I wanted to crawl out of my skin. Surely if I sat still for a little while, I would be able to compose myself and go up there. *"Yes, I drove by the site of the school before I moved away, and to the cemetery where Mama is buried,"* I might say to someone bravely.

But then I looked up at the tall stairs leading to the entrance, with the iron arch overhead, and my mind returned to the days when I was small, and would come here with Mama for the annual cemetery clean-up day, and picnic. I could feel the smooth warmth of her hand clasping mine, see her red cupid's bow mouth parted, her eyes and forehead lost in the shadow of her sun hat as she warned me from above, "Slowly now, Delys. Mind, you don't want to fall on these stairs and skin your knees." I could feel the sun on my back and shoulders, and smell the grassy scent of the broad-brimmed straw hat on my head; feel the press of the knot in the ribbon under my chin. I could hear the friendly banter and frequent ripples of laughter of women who had arrived ahead of us.

I shook my head and clutched my arms around me. I couldn't go up there now. "I am sorry."

After a pause, Daddy said in a nasal voice, "I understand. Maybe we can try again before you leave; that is, if you want to." He sniffed. "Course, you don't have to. There will be other times. I'll come down to Houston."

"Yes, let's be sure and come back together. Some other time. When I feel stronger," I said, my sense of relief mixed with regret that I had failed Mama, and the others, too.

When we arrived at home I learned that I would be moving on Saturday. My uncle was scheduled to usher for the Easter service— my aunt had forgotten Sunday was Easter until Logan reminded her—and he had no way of finding a substitute while up here. Besides, my grandparents wanted to get back because Roy had been off work for a week—he was the chief accountant for a Houston entrepreneur—and needed to catch up at his desk before Monday morning. Allie assessed there was just enough time to finish packing and leave around noon on Saturday.

I felt panicked. I wasn't ready. The memorial service— "But there's a memorial service on Sunday. I was going to attend."

Allie gave me a look of sad forbearance. "All it would do is upset you. And besides, there's nothing your uncle can do about it. He has a commitment."

But I have, too, I wanted to shout.

Boldly I placed a call to Bruce's house, to inform him of the plans. But no one answered. When I put down the receiver I thought of Rusty.

Afraid of being denied, I had been putting off making my plea to bring Rusty to Houston. Well, there would be no more putting off my request.

When I walked into the kitchen to make my case, Aunt Allie and my grandmother were preparing supper. Allie was standing at the sink, and Grandmother was sitting at the table, peeling potatoes. After hearing me out, Allie stared at me blankly, as if she had been taken completely by surprise. What did she think we would do with Rusty? Abandon him? Finally she shook her head. "I'm afraid that would be impossible, Delys. We are not set up to take care of a pet. Your father mentioned he was going to find him a home up here," she said.

I was flabbergasted, not to mention, hurt. Daddy had said nothing about this to me.

"For heaven's sake, Allie, the child has lost everything," Sarah snapped up from the table. "She ought to be able to take her dog. You've got a fenced-in yard, Allie. For heaven's sake." She made a clicking sound with her tongue; then, without so much as a glance in my direction, she went back to peeling potatoes.

It was the first, and would be the only, time in my life Sarah ever troubled herself to look out for my interests; and as I remember this little scene I suspect she did so, at least in part, because she took satisfaction in dominating Allie. *"Stop letting Mama boss you around,"* I once overheard my mother say to Allie. Mama had always been something of a rebel in her family. Proof positive: she married my father over all objections. Allie was the opposite of Mama, always trying to please her parents.

Regardless of the reason, I would always be grateful to Sarah for taking my side that night, and would try to keep this in mind on the occasions when she made thinly-veiled, slighting remarks about my father, which she was wont to do more and more as time went by.

Allie reddened. "But how are we going to get the dog down to Houston? He certainly cannot ride in the car with us."

I thought fast. Daddy would be driving the truck down on Sunday, carrying my things in boxes in the back. "Rusty can ride in the back of the truck. He has done that before. He cut his paw real bad once, on a piece of glass, when we were down at the creek, and Daddy took him to have it stitched up," I assured the two women. Already I was imagining Rusty waiting for me when I came home from school, as he had always done. I would take him for a walk every day. I'd have to get him a leash, though. He had never been on a leash. But oh, just the thought that I would not have to leave him behind made me feel happy as I had not felt since Bruce came to visit on the night I came home from the hospital.

Logan walked through the back door then. He had been leaving the house every morning in his suit and tie, carrying his briefcase, and staying out all day. I had no interest in my uncle at all, and did not ask what he was doing all those hours he spent away.

He removed his hat. "What's this about the dog?" he asked, turning his good ear to Allie while cutting his eyes at me. I braced myself. Everything was about to come unraveled.

"We're taking it with us," Allie told him icily, half closing her eyes and lifting a hand to her brow.

Rusty was not an *it*, I wanted to correct her. Logan looked slightly vexed, but he did not respond.

There was a lot revealed in that brief exchange about the nature of my aunt and uncle's relationship, although I was much too absorbed in my own concerns to notice it except to feel slightly discomfited that I had already caused a strain between them. Was my uncle perhaps not as keen on me coming to live with them as was my aunt? I wondered uneasily.

Much relieved about my dog in any case, I lumbered into the living room— this was the slow, labored way I was getting around, with my head subject to aching at the slightest jerk, and my shoulder still exceedingly painful. Daddy was sitting alone there, reading the *Chronicle*. Since coming home I had noticed how he kept to himself, and avoided getting into long conversations with the relatives. At the supper table, he hardly said a word. After supper was over, he would spend the rest of the evening out on the back porch. Unfortunately, I had already found I could not sit out there comfortably with him.

I told Daddy my aunt and uncle had agreed to let Rusty come and live in Houston. To my consternation, he put down his paper and gave me an irritated look. "That's a very bad idea, Dee. I wish you had asked me first. Not that I mind carrying Rusty down there, but he won't like living there. He is a country dog, used to being free to run around. He'll be miserable and bored cooped up behind a fence.

"I was going to find him a home up here."

I didn't say that I already knew that. Daddy was making a good point, and I knew he had given the matter considerable thought. But the fact that, as sensitive as he was, he had failed to foresee my heartache if I were to be separated from my dog, and that he didn't discuss the subject with me, bore out what I had always known: to Daddy, there was nothing special about Rusty. He was just a dumb animal. How could I trust Daddy to find a family who would treat Rusty as I treated him, especially when he was in a hurry to get off to California? "Rusty's my dog. He belongs with me," I argued, my voice trembling.

"Have it your way," Daddy said contrarily, and returned to his newspaper.

Again, I felt relieved. Yet, inevitably, I began to fear that I was making a terrible mistake. What if Rusty escaped from the back yard in Houston, and ran off? He wasn't used to city streets. What if he got run over by a car, and killed? I would know that I had been responsible for his death, that if not for me he might have been living with some new boy or girl here, who loved him as much as I did. Still, Rusty would not understand me just driving away and never coming back. He would think I didn't love him any more. I could not bear that.

I struggled and struggled, but I always came back to the same conclusion: I could not abandon Rusty.

Before we left town on Saturday I telephoned Bruce again, and this time he answered. Hearing his voice flooded me with awareness that my life was about to change completely. It almost brought me to tears. I bit down on my lip. I told Bruce I could not come to the memorial service after all, and that we were getting ready to leave in a little while. He only sighed as though in resignation.

I found myself saying, "Would you do me a big, big favor? Would you let Rusty come live with you?"

There was a long pause. Then Bruce said, "Hold on. I'll have to ask my dad." He put the receiver down with a thud.

I could hardly believe what I had just done. Having Rusty go and live with Bruce would be the only way I could leave him behind. Rusty liked Bruce. He wagged his tail when Bruce came around, and Bruce would always give him a nice pat behind his ears, and speak kindly to him. And now Bruce didn't have a brother and sister anymore. Maybe this was meant to be. I felt almost elated. But if Doc said no, then I could still—

"He said okay. I reckon I can walk on over. That way it will be easier when you leave."

He did not say for whom it would be easier, but it did not matter. It is one more reason that I have always loved Bruce Buckstrum.

I can still see him there in the yard, as Logan wheels his big automobile around so that it points toward the road. He is crouching next to an anxious Rusty, an arm around the animal's furry chest. He is patting him gently there and speaking to the dog as if to comfort him. When we drive away, Rusty lunges forward but Bruce lowers his head and holds him fast, cuddling him as though he were a child whose heartache mirrors his own. I dig my fingers into the upholstery, and will myself not to cry in front of the aunt and uncle I hardly know and whom I will never trust with my feelings.

Part Two

Chapter 7

Long ago I made my peace with Aunt Allie. This is a considerable statement given that our life together started out at cross purposes, and only grew more so as time went by. My aunt died in 1964, having survived my uncle by six years. Through a series of conversations near the end of her life, progressing over several months as she lay in her sickbed in the house on Park Lane, we finally became reconciled; at least to the extent possible. Which is to say, we agreed that we had both done our best in a long and difficult period of our lives. Ours could never be the kind of reconciliation that brings both parties a sense of reward and joy, eliciting a warm and tearful embrace. There had been too much pain on both sides. For Allie, the pain of my rejection, which—I'll admit—was not always warranted. For my part, too much wondering what my life might have been like if not for Allie's steering me on the course she was certain Mama would have chosen for me. What she could never understand was that meddling in my life could not bring Mama back. And maybe Mama would have approved of the counsel Allie dispensed to me in the beginning, encouraging me to move on from New London, not only in body but in spirit, too. Even—I'll grant this much—encouraging me to be open to the attentions of boys I met in Houston. But surely by the time I had entered high school, Mama would have noticed that Bruce and I were deeply in love, as she and Daddy had been. She would have remembered the grief her parents caused her, stopped interfering with Bruce and me, and let us take what enjoyment we could. The time for prom gowns and corsages, and believing all good things are waiting just around the corner, is all too fleeting, and was especially so for our generation with most young men marching off to war. For heaven's sake, I was grown up and teaching school before Allie ceased her meddling—

Well no, wait. I cannot claim with certitude that Allie interfered with Bruce and me any time after our nation went to war in 1941, although she certainly wound up giving me reason to speculate: under the influence of a number of strong medications during those months when we talked, my aunt sometimes contradicted herself. Misremembered things. I can't begrudge her this. I remember her fretfulness at being confused, the long lacy sleeve of her nightdress sliding down on her thin arm as she pressed a hand to her furrowed brow. There had been a letter for me from Bruce, after the war, she said once, with no preamble whatsoever, as if the fact had simply tumbled into her memory. She had been rambling a bit beforehand and I, half-listening. "When? How long after?" I asked, now fully alert. She did not know. Abruptly she dozed off, leaving me stranded, daring to hope we might pick up again on the subject, and tortured in the meantime.

When next we talked, there had been no letter; I was mistaken, she said ....

My Aunt Allie was a patient person. She waited a long while before pressing her case about Bruce, to give me what she thought would be ample time to become invested in a new life in Houston.

She must have realized pretty quickly that she would have a long wait. I made no secret of the fact that I was miserable. Granted, part of this stemmed from my physical health—I had not yet fully recovered from my injuries. I suffered from terrible headaches and bouts of nausea. Often I had nightmares. Not that I relived the explosion, the details of which continued to elude my memory. I dreamed that the school was being invaded by hordes of people, of all ages. There were so many people crowded into the building that I could not move, and could scarcely even breathe. They were yelling at me, their words incomprehensible. They hung from the windows, arms and legs flailing. They spilled out the doorways and onto the sidewalks, tumbling over one another. The details varied—sometimes I was outside the building and the campus was overrun by vehicles, hundreds of them, honking their horns, their head lamps blinding me, their front bumpers forcing me back until I was pressed flat against the building wall and could not escape. But this theme of being invaded and overrun recurred again and again. The dreams were so immediate and real, I would wake up terrified and lie awake for the remainder of the night. The fact that the dreams are yet so vivid, all these years later, leads me to believe that they were a bizarre twist on the explosion after all, and that I witnessed a lot more of the event than I thought I did, or could ever consciously remember.

On weekdays there was the prison-like atmosphere of Jackson Junior High, so different from that of my school in New London. Intuiting this on the day I enrolled, I had been filled with dread. Leaving the school office afterward, all my old report cards having been scrutinized—skeptically, I thought—then returned to the envelope Mama had kept them in, I refused to go with my aunt for ice cream, or to let her clasp my hand. Even if I had wanted to, I could not. I was nauseated, and becoming more so by the moment. At home I fled to the bathroom, locked the door and vomited violently into the toilet. Allie stood outside in the hall, desperately knocking, begging me to let her in, to let her help. "Go away. I don't want your help," I gasped. Did I have any sense that I was driving a knife through her heart, as she would claim years later from her sickbed? No, I don't believe I did. Young people assume that adults are impervious to wounded feelings.

The Principal at Jackson walked around with a scowl on his face, as if he hated and mistrusted the pupils. And this attitude seemed to infiltrate the student body. (I say this, having spent many years of my life in a school where the Principal loved the teachers and the students, and this great goodwill was felt throughout–Austin was so like London in this regard.) Allie would not let me tell anyone where I was from or what happened there. Her eyes blazing, she warned, "If you do, it is all they will ever want to know about you. They will question you relentlessly about the sordid details, then gossip behind your back. Just say you are from up near Tyler, that your mother died and your father travels in his work so you came to live with your aunt and uncle."

Sordid details. Though I did not see it then, I eventually came to realize that part of Aunt Allie's motivation was to invent a background for me that she felt was more desirable than my own: how she would have liked for me to have lived in the city, my father wearing a suit to work and driving a shiny auto, while Mama, dressed in muslim and lace, hosted afternoon teas to benefit charity. In any case, I resented Allie so much at that point, I would do anything to defy her. If anyone asked me where I was from and how I happened to show up at Jackson six weeks before the end of the spring semester, I would tell them I was from East Texas. Thus I was pegged as a hick, who came from a one-room country school house. It did not help that I had a flat East Texas drawl, which I had never realized until I got to Jackson, my mother having been strict about the correct use of English. It did not help, either, when I was heard to refer to my lunch kit as a dinner pail. However, the insulting remarks only made me more determined to show everyone how smart I was. In spite of the weeks of classes that I had missed, I excelled in every subject—Jackson was less challenging than my former school. I managed to flash around my high test grades so people who sat near me would be sure to see them.

At Jackson a girl who was taller and larger than I was had been assigned the locker below mine. Her name was Nancy Jo. One day when I was standing there, turning the dial on my combination lock, she came up and pushed me so hard that I lost my balance and nearly fell down. She had nudged me before, whenever we would arrive at our lockers at the same time, testing me no doubt, to see how much I would let her get away with. Until that day I had ignored her. I had no experience with bullies, and I lacked the courage to stand up for myself. But inside I was seething with anger. "Get out of my way," she threatened now, leering at me.

I moved away as I always did, but just then something in me snapped. Nancy Jo probably would have been alarmed at the murderous thoughts going through my head. While she busied herself digging through her locker, I went down the hall and waited behind a door that was open. When Nancy Jo had closed her locker and started down the hall, I lunged at her, and kicked her shin so hard that she cried out and grabbed her leg, her books spilling to the floor. I kicked her in the other shin, harder this time. Had not a male teacher grabbed my arm from behind, I do not know when I would have stopped kicking Nancy Jo. I wanted to go on striking her until she shattered into pieces. I wanted to bash her head against the lockers until her teeth rained out. Given the right circumstances, I believe I would have been capable of killing her.

I was sent to the office along with Nancy Jo, and her mother and my aunt were called and told that if this ever happened again, we would be expelled.

My aunt was beside herself. "Why didn't you report what the girl did to you, instead of taking matters into your own hands?"

I didn't want to. I wanted to show her.

That evening, after my uncle came home from work and we sat down to supper, Aunt Allie told Logan of the incident. His face went scarlet. He looked at me. "It's no wonder. You've been mad at the world since you got here," he swore.

I was a bit surprised Logan had noticed how I was feeling. He largely ignored me, rarely turning his good ear my way. Not that he paid all that much attention to his wife. Whereas my parents used to talk to each other about the day's events while at the supper table, sometimes lingering a while even after everyone had finished eating, and I had been dismissed to get my lessons, my aunt and uncle were more subdued. Usually Logan talked and Allie listened. And sometimes I suspected she wasn't really listening at all. "If this happens again—" Logan continued, and I braced myself for a threat.

"I am sure it won't happen again, dear," Allie cut in, with a glance at me. "Delys is very conscientious about school."

Logan glared at her for a long moment, then shrugged. He picked up his fork.

I relaxed my breath. I had the distinct impression that Allie and Logan had settled on the fact that she alone was in charge when it came to matters concerning me. Did this cause bad feelings between them? Regardless, I wondered why she had even brought the matter up to my uncle. I think now that she was probably reluctant to leave the impression that she kept secrets from her husband, the head of the household. Allie hewed to tradition and was very conscious of appearances.

I remember wondering if she would notify Daddy of what I had done. If so, I reasoned, maybe he would come and get me, and take me to live with him as he should have done in the first place. But probably not. Earlier, when I complained in a letter that Allie had made me lie about where I came from, he wrote back in clear language that he would not interfere with Aunt Allie, that I was to follow her rules for as long as I lived under her roof.

Later that night in my room, brushing my hair before bed, I mulled over the events of the day. Amazed, and frankly even exhilarated, at how fearless and bloodthirsty I could be when provoked, I put down the brush, stared into my luminous eyes reflected in the mirror, crossed my arms before me and said defiantly to the world: "Don't mess with me."

My bravado lasted no more than a few seconds. As I turned out the light and slipped under the covers, I knew in my heart that the angry, hateful person I was becoming was not who I wanted to be; and certainly not the person Mama would want me to be. Tears came to my eyes. Maybe I would quit school one day and be done with it. I hated my life. I wished I had been killed in the explosion.

All through those early months in Houston, both during school and in the long dreary days of summer, the only thing I had to live for was Bruce's frequent letters. As the days went by his swift kiss upon my lips seemed ever sweeter, and I vowed that no other boy would ever be allowed to brush that kiss away with another. The fact that I could see no possible way we would actually see each other again only made me long for him more, only made his every good quality stand out in greater relief from most of the boys I knew at Jackson, who traded dirty jokes and ogled girls' developing breasts.

I remember my aunt would raise an eyebrow whenever she saw me affixing a letter addressed to Bruce on the mailbox, with the clothespin we kept there. And once she warned, "Don't expect that boy to stay interested for long, Delys. Males are fickle by nature. He may string you along for a while, but believe me, one day he'll find a new sweetheart, close by. You would be smart to stop writing him before that happens."

I always felt a little smug when still another letter arrived from Bruce, proving my aunt was wrong about him. I had no idea she was already laying the ground work to put an end to our relationship, yet hoping that by sowing the seeds of distrust in me early, she might be spared a confrontation later. I believe now that, deep down, Allie was a little afraid of me; or at least, fearful her efforts to guide me could backfire. She was conflicted by wanting me to love her, and yet wanting to be faithful to Mama. Unfortunately, she lacked the imagination to see that one need not preclude the other.

Bruce kept me informed whenever he discovered some news about one of our friends—the first and most devastating item being that Lanelle Oberlin had lost her life in the explosion. How could this be? I wondered in agony, when she and Eva Ruth and I were in the same room? It defied logic. I strained hard to remember details of those last few minutes we were together practicing, but none would come. I felt guilty about all the times I had been jealous of Lanelle. She had so few nice things during her brief life, while I possessed so many, and she had very little freedom because she was expected to look after her younger siblings a lot of the time. School chums would sometimes talk about what they wanted to be when they grew up. I wanted to be a teacher, like Mama. But Lanelle had higher aspirations. She told me once with a resolute look in her eyes, "I don't know what I'm going to be, but it will be something important, and I'll make a lot of money. I'm going to see the world someday, too."

At the end of May, Bruce sent me the *Book of Memories* devoted to photos of students and faculty who had lost their lives in the explosion, a volume I feverishly perused because it told me so much more. For instance, that fourteen teachers—half the London faculty—had been killed, including Mama's friend and fellow gardener, Queen Price, with whom she rode to school. After noting the sad outcome of Miss Price, I found myself looking away from the book, trying to imagine her and my mother together that last morning of their lives. What had they talked about on the way to school? Did either have an intuition that they would not live to board the car and ride home at the end of the day? The possibility nearly made me swoon, and I shut it out at once. Oh, to have been riding in the back seat, listening to their usual light chitchat. It would have given me one more happy memory of Mama, to be treasured always. Instead I had told a lie that assured I would not be in that car, a lie that I could never forget.

Naturally, that Bruce was so good to my beloved Rusty endeared him to me all the more, and provided me yet another lifeline.

For weeks after I moved away, Bruce wrote, Rusty would trot to our old house—still on the market— every day, and wait for me out front. This broke my heart. I could only imagine the loneliness and disorientation the dog must have felt as he stood sentinel outside our sad, abandoned home. To my great relief, Bruce would go down and walk Rusty back to his new home, a round trip of six miles. "I reckon he'll get used to things eventually," he remarked. Bruce would toss Rusty a ball in the afternoons, when he could have ignored my dog and joined pals in a game of tin can shinny in the empty lot near where the school used to be, and where I had often watched the boys at play.

One day in the summer, Bruce discovered Rusty missing as usual, and walked to my old house to lead him back home. At first he could not find him. Walking around to the back of the house, he heard a whimpering sound. He found Rusty underneath the house near the back door, inside the dark enclave created by the tall brick piers. This was where Rusty would always go to get out of the summer heat or the winter cold, or to take shelter during a storm. His old blanket was still there.

"At first he growled at me and bared his teeth. But I figured he was hurt, so I just slid him out on his blanket, and had a look. Someone had shot him," Bruce wrote. Reading this, my heart froze. "Luckily he was just clipped on his right hip. I wrapped the blanket around him and carried him to my dad's office. Doc removed the bullet and sewed him up. Looks like he'll be okay."

After reading the letter, I cried and cried. It was all my fault for leaving my dog behind. How was it we had not even thought to send Rusty's blanket with him to his new home? He might have been able to accept living there more easily. No doubt he routinely trespassed on someone's property as he made his way to our house. It was only a matter of time until someone picked up a gun and aimed at him.

As I began writing a letter to Bruce, to thank him and Doc for saving Rusty, I missed my dog more than ever. I would have given anything to be able to put my arms around Rusty's neck, and tell him I loved him. And this led me to wish I at least had a picture of him to prop upon my dresser. I wrote to Bruce, "Would you please take a picture of Rusty when he's well again, and send it to me? All that time when he was living with us, it never occurred to me one day we would be separated, or I would have asked Mama to take our picture together. I would be deeply appreciative if you could do this for me, Bruce. You do so much, and I am more grateful than you could ever know. You are MY HERO."

In practically every letter Bruce and I exchanged, we renewed our pledge of fidelity to each other. I was sure we would marry one day, as soon as we were old enough. And I envisioned living in a house like Daddy built, maybe even the same one, and Rusty with us, too.

For Allie the Scottish Brigade must have seemed an answer to a prayer.

One day in the fall of 1937 I waited in the car while my aunt picked up my uncle's starched white shirts at the laundry, a few blocks away from where the new Stephen F. Austin Senior High School had been constructed. Allie dropped off and picked up Logan's shirts every Thursday, after picking me up from school. From there we drove to Henke and Pillot's grocery store on Cullen Boulevard. Allie always had a long list to fill because on Friday nights the Maddens came to supper and the whole day would be devoted to preparing a meal that would, hopefully, earn Sarah's approval.

The Scottish Brigade drill team was so new, they had not even begun raising funds to acquire the highly expensive bagpipes and chanters that would one day mark them as unique from every other high school drill team for many miles around. While waiting in Allie's car, the windows rolled down to catch the September breeze, I was ruminating on the apparent fact that I had developed a reputation at Jackson since the incident with Nancy Jo last semester. No one taunted me anymore. Instead, people largely ignored me. Good, I told myself. Just let someone try pushing me around again, and—

My thoughts were arrested by a blare of bugles, then a sudden and dramatic thunder of drums. I sat straight for the next few minutes, listening closely. This music was different from the marching music of the London High School band, though I could not put my finger on exactly how except it seemed to be comprised of drums and bugles only. No flutes or clarinets or trombones could I hear. And the tune they played was more bold and commanding, too, which I found especially appealing in my current state of mind.

At my insistence, when Allie returned to the car, she drove me to the school so that I could see where the music was coming from. There were, I estimated, a hundred or so high school girls—many carrying drums or bugles, others not— marching out there on the broad green campus of this handsome and formidable three story brick school, wearing white shorts and shirts, lace-up shoes and white socks, their columns taut and straight. I was immediately drawn to the group. I would have given anything to leap out of Allie's sedan and lose myself among them. I kept my aunt there for a long time, parked in front of the little church across the street, my fingers gripping the car door frame, my gaze fixed on the scene.

Walking to and fro before the columns of girls, her hands locked behind her, was a severe looking woman whom I assumed to be the teacher in charge. Clad in a loose shirt that buttoned down the front, a dark skirt, and low-heeled shoes and stockings, she wore her short, dark hair in a diagonal part that made me think of a lightning strike. All at once, crossing her forearms, the woman sliced the air violently, two, three times. A tall, dark-haired girl standing nearby raised her whistle and blew it once, sharply. I gathered she must be the first in charge, after the woman. All motion and sound halted at the shrill report of her whistle, as though abruptly switched off. Everyone stood stock still as the woman barked out several apparent criticisms. I found my heart was pounding as if I, too, were being dressed down. I checked myself. I would not be afraid of this woman.

The girl with the whistle spoke up and dismissed everyone for a ten-minute break. Then she drew close to the woman and they began conferring, the woman gesturing extravagantly with her arms, the girl nodding, interjecting a remark now and then. Watching them, I felt attracted in a way that I could not have identified except that it seemed obvious the girl with the whistle was not afraid of the woman.

The others seemed to relax now, laughing and chattering companionably. They were glad to be there, comfortable with one another. I found myself nearly in tears with longing. The spirit of kinship that I strongly sensed among these girls was exactly what I had experienced at the London School, where I knew who I was and had a sense of belonging.

I heard Allie say she had read about the new drill team in the newspaper.

"I am going to be one of them," I said, feeling my chest swell with the gravity of the words, knowing what I was really saying was that I was going to start over, to be as fresh and clean in my spirit as those white shorts and shirts; and my instinct was strong that in this convivial group I would have that chance. "I'll learn to play the snare drum." To me, the deep pounding of the bass and tenor drums, together with the crisp cadence of the snare drums, was a powerhouse. I knew I could never carry the heavy weight of a bass drum. But I had already taken note that the strap of the lighter drums was worn over the left shoulder, rather than the right. It seemed a good omen. And I was particularly attracted to the complex rhythms and rat-a-tat-tat of the snare drums. I was already counting up the days I must endure Jackson School before I would, presumably, be eligible. I had all of this school year and the next at Jackson. It seemed an eternity.

Allie did not comment either way on my wish to join the Scottish Brigade. She only said, doubtfully, "The thing is—I don't know if we'll be living in the Austin district by then. We haven't decided where to build yet."

Currently my aunt and uncle and I resided in a small, wood frame rent house on Collier Street, a block or so from Logan's office up on Lawndale Avenue. For several years he and Allie had been saving up to build a custom brick home in a nicer neighborhood, one that reflected well on my uncle's prospering law practice.

So now, instead of looking forward to joining the Scottish Brigade, I would have to worry that I may not have a chance, I thought bitterly.

Not until one of those conversations many years later would my aunt admit to having set out on that very day to persuade her husband to build their dream home within the Austin School boundaries. Hearing this, I wondered if her determination to stay in the area was driven by her desire to divert me from my relationship with Bruce, or her wish for me, otherwise, to have what I most wanted. I suspect now that it was both. The young women's organization was quickly growing in prestige, and certainly fit in with Allie's idea of the right kind of extracurricular activity to advance a proper young woman in her life.

I do not believe my aunt ever had what she truly desired in her own life, apart from a lovely home in a mildly upscale neighborhood that she would one day leave to me, her only surviving relative. I have come to feel a sadness about the limited options that were available to Allie, especially nowadays when young women are seeing so many doors opening to them, if only they will get an education. As a young girl, Allie must have seen little advantage in acquiring more than a certificate from an office skills course, taken right out of high school. In those days, marrying well was a young woman's ticket to a comfortable living, and would remain so for years to come. Yet, I might add that my astute mother, coming along five years after Allie, and perhaps sensing—if not knowing for certain—that Logan fell far short of Allie's expectations except as a provider, chose to get an education before she married my father.

In April of 1939, the Fletchers purchased a lot in the then new subdivision called Idylwood, on a street that curved gently down toward the banks of Bray's Bayou, at a point where the bayou took a deep bend. Across the street was a pleasant neighborhood park shaded by tall pine trees. House plans were drawn up and construction soon began. At the end of May, I signed up for the Scottish Brigade. Summer drill began in mid-June and continued, Tuesdays through Thursdays, all summer. I was so eager that I could hardly sleep nights. Yet to my consternation, a letter soon arrived from Daddy that he had been able to get time off the first two weeks in July. "I'll be there to pick you up around the Fourth."

Though I knew of Daddy's plans to take me on a vacation this summer, his choice of words struck a disagreeable chord. Last August had been the first time since Daddy moved to California that he was able to get enough days off from work to come and see me. We spent eight days touring San Antonio, Austin, and New Braunfels. While I was glad to see my father arrive, and hugged his neck, I felt strangely detached from him. Over the course of the holiday I kept thinking I would feel differently; and there were times when some expression on his face, or something he said, took me back to the days we used to sit out on the porch together, and reminded me how much I loved him. But the sentiment never lasted long. His attempts to bridge the gap and draw me close again seemed obvious, and frankly rather pitiful.

Before we parted, he promised we would take a trip every summer. "It'll be something you can count on, Dee," he said earnestly. "We both can."

"That will be nice," I told him indifferently. Admittedly, I took some satisfaction in the crestfallen look on his face.

And now he presumed that I would drop everything and be waiting for him with my suitcase packed. "Won't we go down to New Orleans, and over into Mississippi, and up the coast?" he wrote. "We can do that easily in eight days."

I had no intention of missing a single day of summer drill. It seemed too mean just to tell him I would not be available, however. I wrote him and explained that I would be tied up on Tuesdays through Thursdays. "Summer drill is very important, and I can't miss," I told him. In truth, vacation days were excused. But not for me.

Shortly before summer drill began, Daddy wrote that he understood, and we would work around my schedule. Then of course I felt guilty. I know from my years of teaching high school students that it is difficult to make a transition from spending the most important occasions in life with your parents, to developing a life of your own, without feeling disloyal. And that is without all the complications I was forced to deal with, being torn between anger at my father for abandoning me, and loving him deeply, regardless.

Even though I was accepted into the drill team on a probationary basis, I knew more than most of the other new girls because after that first encounter, I had begun spending an hour or so nearly every Thursday afternoon, watching drill practice from the porch steps of the church across from the school, while Allie continued on to Henke & Pillot's store. I can see myself as though it were yesterday, hopes puffed up like the clouds in the bright blue sky above: sitting straight, my circular skirt neatly spread out around me. Feet together, I had beat out the marching rhythm with the toes of my Oxford shoes, my fingertips tapping out the snare drum strikes on the pavement.

Being issued a pair of snare drum sticks, at last, was like receiving a long-awaited, highly coveted award. I wanted to kiss them. And when no one was looking, I did. I pounded those sticks on the sidewalk at home, and on the concrete tops of the picnic tables in the park across the street, and on the stone coping around the big Austin windows during summer drill, until I had worn the rounded tips of one pair into sharp points, then another, and another.

I believe most girls took the high standards and the numerous regulations of Brigade with seriousness, and tried hard to live up to them. But I went further. I read the slim booklet outlining the conduct code in the deeply earnest manner that some read the Holy Bible. I regarded those regulations almost as a religious creed, something to hang my life on. This was my chance, finally to be someone again. I don't mean by that someone of important rank— though I would aspire to that as time went by— I mean, to be someone in whom I could recognize myself, in relation to those around me. I had to do everything exactly right. I hoped no one in the Scottish Brigade would ever find out that I once beat up a girl at Jackson. I would be mortified if they did.

I poured out my heart in a letter to Bruce about all this drill team meant to me, and how determined I was to succeed in it. "How I wish you had something like this in your life," I added, with feeling. Bruce now had serious problems at home and a terrible secret to keep. He had never said much to me about how he dealt with the loss of his sister and brother, and I did not feel I should press him to say more because I figured it was none of my business unless he wanted to tell me. But now he was being forced more and more to deal with Doc's heartache, not only from the loss of his children, but from his inability to save so many others who were injured in the explosion. As I read in Bruce's letters about what he was going through with Doc, I could see in my mind's eye the midnight kitchen with shadowy corners, the table covered with an oil cloth and a bowl of ripening fruit, the dim light overhead. The tortured voice: "Every time I lifted a sheet and found a child beyond saving, I wondered what I would do if I were to lift up a sheet and find myself looking down at you, or Bucky or Edna, in that same state. Could I walk away?" And through Bruce's description I could see myself, one of the many injured children lining the hallways of the receiving hospital on that misbegotten night, waiting obliviously for my turn to be assessed.

In November a place came open in the Brigade regular Drum Corps when some unfortunate girl's family moved away. Among all the drummers on probation, I was chosen to replace her. Never in my life have I felt so excited, or so proud. I was issued a snare drum, painted dark green with white trim, and a dress uniform with so many rules applying as to how it was to be arranged for wearing, it took an hour to get dressed in it:

A tartan woolen kilt—green and black plaid on a red ground—hitting just below the knee, and matching scarf that crossed the breast diagonally in front and fell exactly even with the hemline in back; a tailored green gabardine jacket with high collar and wide white belt; a sleek black glengarry-style hat with plaid ribbon trim and green feather; black lace-up shoes, snowy white spats and plaid leggings.

I will never forget the first time, with Allie's help, I put on the uniform for a football performance. After we finished checking to be sure all the regulations had been obeyed— the conduct code booklet lying open on Allie and Logan's nearby bed, the measuring tape dangling from my aunt's neck—I stood ready before the full-length mirror, my long, thick wavy hair standing out like a halo above the high jacket collar, and my pale skin and the slight blush on my cheeks making me look and feel the part of the Scottish lass. I knew I did the uniform proud. I knew the effect was dazzling.

I turned from the mirror and lifted my hands. "What do you think?"

Allie's eyes filled; she put her trembling fingers over her mouth for a moment, as if to compose herself, then flapped her hand. "Oh honey, it's what I've always wanted for you!"

What went through my mind at that moment—and this I now admit with a cringe at how uncharitable I felt toward Allie—was that it would have been more appropriate for her to say, "Your mama would be so proud if she could see you now!"

I managed to fulfil my small role that night without a mistake. I came home dizzy with relief and happily exhausted, and soon climbed into bed. I fell asleep composing a letter in my thoughts: *"Oh Bruce, I was so nervous out there at the edge of the football field waiting to start, those klieg lights shining down. And when I heard the Major's whistle, then the bugles blared, I was so thrilled my eyes filled up. The Drum Captain's hand went down. Boom! The drums came in with a mighty roar and we stepped off. I felt like my fingers were dancing! The audience went wild. Oh Bruce, it was so powerful. I wish you could have seen us....*"

I awoke late on Saturday morning. When I went into the kitchen for breakfast, my heart was light as a butterfly. Then my Aunt Allie said gravely, "Delys, I need to have a word with you about Bruce."

Chapter 8

She has found out. A sense of alarm overtaking me, I sank down in a kitchen chair. Had Allie stolen into the shoe box hidden at the very back of the top shelf of my closet, and helped herself to Bruce's letters? Or, had she been opening my letters to him before the mailman arrived to pick them up? If either were the case, and she took it upon herself to write a letter notifying some authority—the county medical board, maybe, or even the State?— *"I could not in good conscience allow this to go unexposed when Doctor Buckstrum's patients may be at risk"*—it could prove disastrous for Doc, and ruin Bruce's life in the bargain. Bruce would never speak to me again. What if she had already written a letter?

I stared down at the pancakes and sausage links on my plate—a Saturday favorite for which I had suddenly lost all appetite. "What about Bruce?" I asked with feigned innocence, reaching for my napkin and clutching it between my hands in my lap. I could feel the pulse pounding in my ears.

Almost as if she were delaying the inevitable while she found a delicate way to state her case, Allie lifted the sweaty pitcher of orange juice from the table and slowly filled my glass. I sat twisting the napkin in my fingers.

Finally she sat down across from me. In a forbearing tone, she said, "I have nothing against Bruce personally, mind you; I'm sure he is a good young man..."

Nothing against Bruce.... And so she had found out. A "good young man" would stand by his father and protect him. He would not run away from home as some boys would, leaving Doc to fend for himself in a small community where it was so easy to learn someone else's business. At the risk of being late for school, he would go to the office and open up for Doc on his bad mornings, ushering in patients who waited outside, assuring them the doctor would soon arrive, that he had gone to look in on a patient admitted to the hospital last night.

"...but you can't have a well-rounded life here as long as you continue to be attached to Bruce."

My fingers relaxed their hold on the napkin in my lap. My head felt all fizzy, like a sparkler on the Fourth of July. There was no crisis at hand, after all. The secret was safe. Yet—why, then, did Aunt Allie object to my attachment to Bruce? That she wanted me to be "well-rounded" was obviously an excuse. My life was as well-rounded as anyone else's. If she had nothing against Bruce, as she claimed, was it her concern that my relationship with him was the last remnant of the past she so deeply regretted and wanted me to put aside? Surely not, or she would not have waited so long to bring up the matter.

Her next words at least shed some light on her delay. "Certainly I understood it for a while, when you were adjusting to a whole new life here. Logan said, 'Don't worry. They'll both lose interest in time.' And I thought so too, particularly since you never see each other.

"But lately I notice that you and Bruce are writing each other more often, rather than less. You both need to be looking to the future, rather than tying each other down," she said, then waited.

I could think of nothing to say. How could she be so sure that Bruce and I had no future together, unless she intended to stand in the way of it? Or maybe she meant that there could be no future in letter-writing without some promise that eventually we would again see each other on a regular basis. But first of all, just now, when Bruce's life was in such turmoil, he needed more than ever to be assured that I cared for him, and would be there for him no matter what.

Apart from this, in the very near future we would—to my great joy—be seeing each other again. Bruce had learned to drive a car, and Doc had enlisted his services to drive him to a statewide medical seminar that was held at the Rice Hotel in the spring, summer, and fall of every year–winter meetings were out of the question because of the influenza season. Doc had stopped attending these seminars after the school explosion, but lately he had decided to resume. He had sent in his registration for the next meeting, in April. Bruce thought it was an encouraging sign that his dad might be getting better. To me it was also a sign of Doc's keen sense of personal responsibility that he would appoint Bruce to do his driving for him, just in case. I could hardly wait for April to arrive.

I weighed the possibility of telling Allie that soon Bruce would be coming to see me on a regular basis. Maybe it would put her mind to rest. Yet, on the other hand, I could not risk revealing our plans now, when I was uncertain of the reason for her concern about Bruce.

I searched my mind for a way to persuade her to leave things as they were. If need be, I supposed I could offer to write him less often, though for Bruce's sake, I dreaded doing so. I needed to choose my words carefully.

"Bruce and I are close friends," I said at last, which was true enough. "As you say, he's a good person, and my grades haven't suffered from writing him, you know." I paused, then to drive home my point, I added, "Nor would I ever let Bruce, or—or any other boy—interfere with studying. My education is too important." Perhaps this declaration was somewhat beside the point, but everyone knew that school grades were of primary concern for any responsible adult who was raising a teenager. And the fact that I had kept my end of the bargain would surely weigh in my favor now.

Allie sighed. "Yes, Delys, and I'm proud of you for all that. I really am. But that isn't the point. I want you to be well-rounded and...and happy, my dear."

Again, there was that term, 'well-rounded.' "But look at the Scottish Brigade. It certainly makes my life well-rounded—why, I hardly have time for anything else. And it makes me so happy, too," I pleaded.

Allie smiled tenderly. "I know that, and nobody could have been more proud of you than I was last night," she said. Bringing a hand to her chest, she enthused, "My, my, I could barely see the performance through the blur of tears in my eyes! But Brigade isn't enough, Delys. Most girls your age invite boys over to their house now and then, or arrange to meet for a bowl of ice cream or see a movie. But you never do. And if a boy calls you up on the telephone, why, you act like you're too busy to talk to him." She sat back. "It has crossed my mind that maybe you think boys are drawn to girls who treat them with indifference; but they're not," she counseled, with a lift of her brow. "I know what I'm talking about."

I remembered Mama saying that as a pretty young girl, Allie was popular with boys, and had "a long string of beaux." Which established in my mind an image of Allie as fun-loving and vivacious. I suddenly wondered why she had been attracted to a man like Logan Fletcher, who did not seem to fit into this picture at all, with his cautious, boring personality.

"I haven't been playing games," I assured her. "I cannot pretend I'm interested in someone when I'm not."

"There! That's exactly what I was afraid of," she said triumphantly. She leaned near. Her face alight with conviction, she declared, "Delys, you are such a pretty girl, and you have so much to offer." She crinkled her brow in supplication. "You could have any boy you wanted, don't you see?"

So this was what being 'well-rounded' meant to Allie, I reasoned: being popular with boys, just as she had been. Inexperienced as I was, I did not see that Allie believed my attributes would ultimately make me valuable on the marriage market. Nor did I guess that, through me, she saw an opportunity to reconcile the major mistake of her life, and my mother's as well. I must find true love that never disappoints, as Allie had not. I must find a prosperous, stable partner, as my mother had not. And of course, not for years after we sat talking that morning, my breakfast growing cold before me, did realization dawn: based on slighting remarks Mama made about Bruce, Allie had already disqualified him. At the time I could only wonder naively why she seemed to think I could find a better boyfriend than Bruce, when she didn't even know him.

"So you see, it's necessary that you stop being involved with Bruce," she counseled. "Then at least boys here will have a fighting chance."

Now I was on the verge of panic. "But we can just cut back some, on writing; oh please, Aunt Allie, don't ask me to break up with Bruce, please!"

A look of recognition crossed her face. With a chill in my heart I realized I should never have become so passionate, for now I had confirmed her worst suspicions and increased her sense of urgency. She persisted, "It won't work, Delys. Believe me, breaking it off completely is the only way. I know you think I'm mean, but one day you will thank me. You have nothing whatever in common with that boy except the past that's over and done with."

I felt I had been ambushed, and I hated her for it. I found myself arguing hotly, "Why do you want me to pretend my life in East Texas never happened, Aunt Allie? It's as if you think those people up there aren't as good as you are. Well, they were good enough for Mama."

Almost before the words were out, I realized I had gone too far. Especially that last sentence. I would give anything to retrieve it. Aunt Allie's jaw had stiffened; there were red streaks on her forehead. She rose from her chair and looked at me fiercely. "Yes, and look what it got her!

"No more letters to Bruce. Understood? Break it off, or I'll do it for you."

I did not say a word. In that moment I could see my grandmother Sarah voicing the same heedless words to Mama when she had decided to accept Daddy as he was. But Mama defied Sarah and went off with Daddy. I wouldn't break up with Bruce either, and if that meant running off with him someday, well then I would do it.

By morning I was figuring the best possible way of getting the message to Bruce that I intended to defy my aunt's wish. No matter how I went about this, there would be some risk, I finally concluded. But then I asked myself: What was there to lose? So I wrote to Bruce and told him briefly of the situation. "Write me back and tell me what you think we ought to do. I'll tell my aunt that I am asking you to reply, so I will know you've received my farewell letter. I cannot be sure, but I think she will accept this. Anyhow, it seems the only way."

I don't suppose I ever felt completely right about sneaking around with Bruce. I never regretted the deception itself because my aunt had forced me into it. Yet I knew that part of my life was out of joint, and did not fit with the rest of it. One of the main Articles of the Scottish Brigade honor code stated that members were selected "...on the basis of scholarship (you had to maintain a C average), conduct (you had to maintain an E), and character." No measure was given for character, but its many implications were obvious. I could not count the number of times during drill practice when a voice inside me cried out that a person of good character did not sneak around with the boy she was forbidden to contact. Though I always quickly argued back that I was in the right, I found it nerve-racking to worry all the time about being caught, especially when, in Brigade, you were expected to report the infraction of any regulation, and go before the Officer's Court. Sometimes I would have a foolish dream that I was standing in the middle of the circle of top officers, confessing what I did with Bruce, taking the dreaded demerit that would go against my record.

What I did with Bruce. Well, with letter-writing forbidden and obviously telephone calls as well, we worked out a plan in which I could call him collect whenever the chance arose. It was his idea. His dad didn't mind, he assured me. So, whenever Allie left to go shopping or on some other errand, or she and Logan went out for an evening, I would pick up the telephone and dial the Operator. Should the back door open while I was talking, I would simply hang up in Bruce's ear and hasten into my room located just off the hall where the telephone bench sat. If I wasn't quick enough, and Allie asked who was on the phone, I would say it was someone calling a wrong number. Or, I was suddenly talking to a Drum Corps friend about car pooling to the next slumber party—Friday night slumber parties were a standard part of Brigade life, and were held year-round. Bruce knew the signals.

I always felt unladylike calling up Bruce on the telephone, no matter the arrangements we had made. But after the first few times, at least I stopped being nervous that I might get caught. Occasionally, Doc would answer the telephone. Regardless of the fact that Bruce said he would not mind my calling, I would be so overcome with nervousness, I could hardly find my voice and my knees would shake. Once, I remember, it was on a

Saturday night, Doc's voice seemed slow and thick when he said, "Hello, Doc Buckstrum here." I imagined the half-empty bottle of whisky waiting at the kitchen table for his return. I panicked. "Excuse me, wrong number," I said to the Operator, and hung up. Later I decided I must have imagined Doc's drunken state. Surely patients called his home occasionally in the evenings. If Doc had been drinking, he would doubtless have had Bruce pick up the phone.

I had never been around anyone who drank too much. I had always thought that fathers who drank were cruel and abusive to their families. Bruce said that Doc never was. He told me once, "If my dad ever looks like he's going to take a swing at me, or threatens me in any way, I'll walk right out the door and never come back."

I prayed with all my heart that Bruce would not be forced to run away. I envisioned him hopping railroad cars, or stowing away on a foreign ship, never to be seen or heard from again.

Bruce said that Doc needed someone to listen as he poured out his heart. He could not sleep unless he passed out because he was afraid of his dreams. At the kitchen table, if he was not reliving the school explosion and the horrors he dealt with afterward, he would reminisce about Bucky and Edna as little kids, before Bruce was born. Sometimes he cried because he had not been as good a father to Bruce as he had been to Bucky and Edna. He would apologize for sending him out to locate his brother and sister after the explosion. "A boy your age should not have had to do that. But you acted like a man, son, and I appreciate that more than you will ever know," he said. Bruce seemed to forgive his father, in spite of the fact that he had plenty of his own nightmares, of the scene that met him in the charnel house that the Overton skating rink had become.

Doc often kept Bruce up talking until well past midnight, and then he would either fall asleep at the kitchen table, or Bruce would finally coax him away, and help him up to bed.

"It isn't right!" I cried one night as we talked. Bruce had failed an exam. Not only was school hard. No one—not even the best of students—could perform well without sufficient rest, and a mind free of worries. I began helping Bruce. We were taking mostly the same courses. Sometimes our whole conversation would amount to me helping him with an algebra problem or a chemistry formula.

Sometimes I could forgive Doc; other times I found myself despising him for what he was doing to Bruce. I was inclined to believe—and I still am—that Bruce was ten times as strong a person as Doc was. But then I didn't witness what Doc did; I did not have to decide whether to try and save some poor victim, or not. I did not have to look all those parents in the eye and say, "There is nothing I can do." Then walk away. In some ways I felt I was surely fortunate not to remember any details of that afternoon and night, and Bruce certainly believed that I was. Still, there were so many questions that I longed to have answered; in particular, why had Lanelle been the single unlucky one of the three spelling team members? And then, of course, why was I spared instead of her? I often wondered what became of Eva Ruth. What was she thinking? How did she feel about what happened? What did she remember? But I would never know. She might as well have vanished into thin air.

The seminars Doc attended in Houston brought Bruce and me as close to dating each other as we ever came. And I hold dear the memory of our sweet and sacred, but dangerous, encounters. The meetings began on Friday evening and concluded on Sunday afternoon. Initially I had happily envisioned my many Friday and Saturday dates with Bruce. I figured he would be in town for one football game per season. I would be able to show off the Scottish Brigade to him, and show him off to all my Brigade friends. He might be around for the Bronco Whirl— the most important school dance of the year. And otherwise, we could meet other couples for a movie at the Loew's, or the Metropolitan or Majestic on some nights, and maybe organize a picnic in Galveston, in July.

Unfortunately, now that Aunt Allie had stepped in, none of this could ever be. Dates would be with boys I did not care to be with, accepted in order to keep Allie from being suspicious.

All Bruce and I would get were a couple of hours on Sunday mornings while Allie and Logan were in church. I would feign a stomach ache or sore throat so that I could stay home.

"Where can we meet?" Bruce asked on the phone before that first seminar in April.

"There's the cemetery," I replied, for I had been thinking long and hard on this matter.

"You're kidding," he said darkly.

"No, I'm not," I said. "Forest Park is huge—acres and acres. We'll have privacy there. It is just across the bayou from here—you'll need to pick me up or I'll have to swim," I told him, with an attempt at levity that, given his silence, must have fallen flat. Then I explained he was to turn off Lawndale onto North Macgregor Way, which snaked along between the bayou and one edge of the park. He would pull over and stop even with the back of the park, where the tall stairs led up to a gazebo made of rough timber. It was somewhat secluded there, because behind the gazebo the land tilted steeply down to a tree-shrouded gully. Before getting into Bruce's car, I would check to see that no one was around. I had to be careful I wasn't recognized. I did not know of any other Brigadiers living in Idylwood at the time, or any of my other classmates either, though eventually this would change. But upon moving there, Allie had bought a pair of sturdy walking shoes, and she paced up and down the streets on nice mornings, often getting to know neighbors along the way. Sometimes they would come to our house, to join my aunt in a cup of coffee, and she would introduce me.

Returning when our time was up, Bruce would leave me there. If Allie and Logan had gotten home earlier than expected for some reason, I could simply stroll back to Park Lane and up the block to our house, then explain I had been feeling a little better and had gone out for a walk in the fresh air.

"Alright," Bruce said breathlessly. I believe he was in awe of the thoroughness of my plotting.

Oh my, the quiet meandering lanes of Forest Park Cemetery, overarched with high, moss-hung trees. You could so easily get lost there, and we did. Parked in the shadows of the tiny gothic stone chapel that was quietly nestled near the center, we sat in the car, and we kissed and we kissed and we kissed. With only Bruce's earlier shy peck on my mouth while I was convalescing from my injuries, to measure by, I could hardly have imagined the effect on me now of this handsome, deep-voiced male, how the touch of his tender hands on my face and body brought my every nerve alive. Bruce's warm hand pressed across my abdomen made my eyes glassy. And I gloried in seeing his face and ears grow warm and pink with intensity, his straight dark brows knit together, and the swelling all too evident below his waist. What madness. It was pure midnight-on-Lover's Lane heavy petting in broad daylight. The kind that would later send me home imagining what lay beyond the precipice we had reached. On Sunday afternoon after such a tryst my head would be sunk into my school books across my bed, the better not to reveal myself to my aunt and uncle.

What saved us? Sometimes it was me, realizing we were getting in too deep, my arms stiffening and pushing Bruce's chest. But more often it was the banal sound of another car passing, or even stopping nearby—doors banging shut; someone bringing flowers to a grave. A heart-stopping moment, then we would emerge from our fevered absorption, catching our breaths, and realize our time had already passed. I had to get home. Or, if there was time, we would step out of the car and walk among the granite tombstones, our arms entwined up to our elbows; and sometimes, if no one was about, sit down on a bench beside the duck pond for a while, watching the fat ducks glide serenely up and down, and the trees' shimmering reflection on the water. We wouldn't talk much there. We were too overwhelmed by the recklessness of our encounter just minutes before and the feeling of sweet, unsated desire we were left with, to savor until next time.

I have often thought how different things might have turned out if only we had been left alone to have our dates like other young people. Dances and movies and football games. Just three weekends a year, but otherwise perfectly within the normal bounds of the teenagers' social universe. Instead, our sense of desperation, plus Bruce's loneliness and sense of isolation at home—which so obviously haunted him that even I could feel it in my very bones—added a dark deliciousness to our time together, provoked us to risks that, given enough repeats, certainly would have doomed us to go too far to turn back. But it didn't happen that way.

Chapter 9

In the days of those clandestine meetings with Bruce—so eagerly scheduled then anticipated—and our less predictably timed telephone calls in between, I had more or less accepted that I knew everything I was ever going to know about the tragedy three years earlier that had inevitably led to this arrangement between us. The effects of my head and shoulder injuries had subsided, although I might note here that many years later I would suffer chronic shoulder pain—arthritis burrowing down in a vulnerable zone. This pain would, in fact, make raising my right arm to write on the black board difficult, and would play a part in my decision to retire, and devote full time to building my New London poetry anthology—

But there I go again, rushing ahead to another part of the story—

In those days I still often ached for the presence of my mother. Every school morning when I brushed my hair I remembered sitting on the bench before Mama's dresser mirror as she brushed my long springy hair, placed a pretty bow on the side, just so; then caught me in a hug and kissed my cheek. If I closed my eyes I could feel her arms encircling me. I still had full-blown bouts of homesickness occasionally; sometimes I would imagine myself back in our little country house, Mama's white lace curtain on the back door; see the curtain shudder when the door flew open at night and Daddy walked in, in his stockinged feet, having left his work boots out on the porch stoop. And naturally I still resented my aunt for breaking up my beloved home, and Daddy, too, for permitting her to do it so that he could go off and leave me behind.

Though I continued to be frustrated that I could not remember the circumstances which, apparently, had saved my life and Eva Ruth's but not Lanelle's, at least I had at my fingertips a reference detailing who had not survived. Now and then I would find myself thinking of some schoolmate or teacher I had failed to ask Bruce about. Gingerly I would open the *Book of Memories*, bracing myself lest I find a photograph of that person. Sadly, more often than not I did, and it would throw me into another tailspin of grief.

Other than the fact that I could not quite orient my mind to the way one explosion had affected two separate wings of such a large building, I believed my picture of the tragedy was reasonably complete. As far as I knew, the catastrophe could neither have been anticipated nor prevented.

Then, in that summer of 1940, there was another accident, and everything changed.

Daddy wrote that he had been injured at work when a length of cable on the rig broke loose and whipped around, whacking him across the back and knocking him sideways across a rack where some pipe joints were stored. He suffered several broken ribs and an injured back. He would be living in a convalescent home for the next two months, and it would be still longer before he could return to work. "I'm lucky I wasn't hurt any worse, I guess. The biggest disappointment right now is that I won't be able to come see you this summer...."

In truth I had been torn as this summer approached. Last year Daddy had accommodated my summer drill schedule without complaint. But what if our brief holiday this year coincided with my one opportunity to see Bruce? Now I could not help feeling relieved that Daddy was not coming; at the same time, I felt guilty that my own father was sinking yet another notch on my list of priorities.

While recovering, Daddy would live off some compensation from his employer, and otherwise draw on his savings. He assured me that he would be able to honor his commitment to pay the Fletchers the amount set for my room and board every month. However, there would be nothing left over to cover my routine expenses. "The best solution is for you to find a summer job," he suggested, "and put some money by for the fall, when your expenses always go up."

Find a job. For a long moment I stared at the words on the page, seeing the dire consequences implicit in them. I was about to be cheated out of attending summer drill altogether, and this would hurt my future in Brigade, maybe even ruin it. Though participation in summer drill was not compulsory, a service point was earned for every day attended, and any girl who hoped to attain a high office one day needed a near perfect score. From the beginning, Brigade had grown at such a rapid pace that soon there were routinely more girls running for office than there were places to be filled. This despite the fact that the ranks of officers had now been expanded overall—the top office of Major had been overtaken by that of Colonel—and new office ranks had been added all the way down the line. Missing summer drill, or even part of it, would put me behind the many other contenders.

It seemed to me the obvious solution was to ask my aunt and uncle to help by paying my expenses until Daddy was well again. Yet I was afraid to approach Daddy with the idea because he had been adamant about his intention to provide my living. He didn't want the Fletchers' charity, as he had put it.

Maybe I could find a job that left my afternoons free; but what if I could not? I was sorry Daddy had gotten hurt, truly I was, and thankful his injuries were no worse than they were. And if we would have gone on living in East Texas, I would have been right there to care for him every single day. But it seemed to me that after he had stolen that life from me, at least I ought to be free to make the most of the new life I had so carefully constructed for myself.

As it happened, in spite of spending the whole of the next day after his letter arrived—a Saturday—looking for a job in downtown Houston, I found the summer jobs were already filled by applicants who had applied before school let out. A lady in one personnel department said with a sniff, "You should have thought ahead, and applied earlier."

I returned home on the bus, staring out the window and lamenting the injustice of it all.

That night at supper Uncle Logan abruptly said to his wife, "Delys can work for me. Mrs. Jolly can use the help. We're busy right now, and she's getting behind." Having spoken as if I were not there, he now shifted his gaze and inclined his good ear to me.

"But I don't know anything about working in a law office," I protested. I had already spent an hour lying down in the hall, cooling off under the attic fan and reasoning how I would just do without, until Daddy returned to work. At least I would still be able to go to summer drill, and that was more important than anything I could buy with the money he usually spent on me. Now my new plans were being threatened like the ones they had replaced.

Uncle Logan fixed me with his cool gray eyes. "You took typing, didn't you? And you can file—all you have to know is how to put folders in alphabetical order. Mrs. Jolly can show you the ropes. Let's say, twenty-five cents an hour."

In spite of my misgivings, and my resentment that Logan had taken charge of my problem without even consulting me, his setting of a pay rate did give me pause. Quickly I calculated how much I would make in an eight-hour day, times five. Admittedly, I had never paid attention to how much I spent. Allie kept the receipts and mailed them to Daddy for reimbursement. Still, ten dollars a week seemed a lot, surely ample to meet my needs. I would be a fool to pass it up.

It took all the courage I had to pose the one burning question in my mind, and when I did, my heart was pounding. "Would I be free to leave in time for summer drill?" I asked, then hastened to add so that there would be no room for confusion, "On Tuesdays, Wednesdays, and Thursdays. It starts at four."

Logan thought about this. "I don't see why not. We'll dock you an hour's pay, of course, but as long as you get your work done, and without errors–" He gave me a pointed look. "–we don't tolerate errors in a law office."

That last statement chilled my blood, and would continue to do so for many days to come.

My uncle was not particularly talented, I don't believe, nor was he overly ambitious. He did not aspire to represent the big oil companies, more and more of which were establishing headquarters in the vaulting buildings of downtown Houston. From what I understood, fresh from law school he had started out at one venerable law firm that did so, and soon became swallowed up in the hierarchy. Thus he began making plans to establish his own practice one day.

For his office, Logan had purchased and converted a brick residential cottage harking back to the days before Lawndale began to turn commercial. The entrance door was formidable, made of wide wooden planks painted cordovan red, with a small glass window a few inches above eye level. There was a tiny front porch with a pointed roof that barely sheltered visitors on rainy days–I discovered this my first morning on the job, as rain was pouring when I reported at eight o'clock, and I stood out on that porch struggling to close my umbrella without getting drenched before walking inside.

The interior of the office was no more welcoming, with moss-green walls and dark stained woodwork, and sepia-toned drawings of medieval streets and seascapes, enclosed in black frames upon the walls.

To my relief, Mrs. Jolly was a kindly, mild woman. She wore rimless eyeglasses, perched far down on her turned-up nose; and her graying hair, which looked as soft as a powdered wig, was parted up the center and worked into a frilly knot at the back of her head. Her facial features were narrowly set and seemed bunched together in the center; her cheeks were plump and rosy. She was a member of East End Methodist Church, where the Fletchers worshiped, and where I went along dutifully and sat daydreaming in the pew. I vaguely recognized Mrs. Jolly as a member of the small Sunday choir, wearing a royal blue robe with a white cape collar.

Naturally I took her to be old. But as I look back, I doubt she was as old as forty, if that. She would work for my uncle until he died of pancreatic cancer in 1958. Then she would serve as the church secretary at East End Methodist for at least six years—she was there to greet me after my aunt died, like a long-lost friend rather than the lapsed Christian I had become by then, and to lovingly help me plan Allie's funeral. And while on the subject, I might add that there were many showy flower arrangements for my aunt's funeral, and friends filling the pews. I imagined her smiling down from the heavens, pleased that it was all for her—she had deeply resented the communal nature of Mama's funeral, in which there were four caskets lined up at the front of the sanctuary. Afterward Allie was buried next to Logan in Forest Park Cemetery. I could not escape the irony in that, and during the burials of first my uncle, then my aunt, I fancied Bruce and me hidden nearby in the shadows of the trees, like two ghosts.

My first day on the job, Mrs. Jolly explained that my uncle represented small industrial firms—for instance, the manufacturing shops and supply houses that sold necessities like pipe fittings, valves and gauges to the big oil exploration companies and the refineries along the nearby Houston Ship Channel. "Then of course there's our 'bread and butter'—drawing up lease agreements and wills, and bills of divorce and so forth," she added, as though my uncle's practice belonged partly to her. None of it sounded interesting to me, but I tried not to show this. Just three months and it would be over....

Now she directed my attention to the front office desk on which a black Remington typewriter sat like a hulking rock, with a rather daunting stack of legal-sized documents alongside. "Original and two carbon copies of everything, unless otherwise specified. And by the way, we do try and use carbon paper as many times as we can before discarding it."

I would be answering the telephone, she informed me finally. "That way, I can get something done for a change." I was to answer with the mouthful that I can recite to this day: "Law office of E. Logan Fletcher, Miss Lithingate speaking, may I help you?" I was sure that callers would grow impatient before I finished my spiel. My uncle expected detailed messages, legibly written on the small pad provided. "And don't ever get a telephone number wrong; have the caller repeat it, if you need to. Nothing annoys Mr. Fletcher worse than a wrong telephone number." She looked around with knitted brow, thinking. Then her countenance brightened as if she were about to burst into the singing of a joyous Easter hymn. "I believe that's it. For now, anyway."

Mrs. Jolly turned to the pile of documents. "Now, get started retyping all these drafts. They have already been revised once. If you have trouble with your uncle's handwriting, let me know. I can decipher it, usually.

"Oh yes, and positively no typographical errors allowed. You make one, you start all over at the top of the page."

Mrs. Jolly disappeared through the door leading into the hall, and I picked up the first document, THE LAST WILL AND TESTAMENT OF.... I thumbed through it. Sixteen pages, bleeding with red ink. I felt sick at heart. I could not manage all that was expected of me. I would not last out the week. The only saving grace was that the man behind all these demands spent most of his days out visiting clients, or in court. At least my uncle would not be breathing down my neck, making things worse.

Somehow I got through the day, albeit with aching neck and shoulders plus a heap of discarded pages with typographical errors. Then the next, and the next after that. In a couple of weeks I felt I knew pretty much what was expected of me, and was able at least to breathe a little more deeply and stop being startled every time the phone rang.

Pleasing Uncle Logan was a different matter. He generally read over documents early in the morning, before I got to work. If he wanted any changes made in what I had typewritten, he would bring them to my attention in a note scrawled across the top margin. "Retype with revisions." I proofed everything very carefully in order to avoid mistakes, but inevitably I made a few. Once he wrote, "The word *fiduciary* is misspelled twice. I suggest you learn to make use of the dictionary on the shelf behind your desk." I could feel the blood coming up in my face as I read the snide memorandum. I had thought the word was *fudiciary*.

Another time, "Retype. There is a transposition in Mr. Leland's house number. You need to be more careful of this. We can't have confidential documents winding up in the wrong hands!" I checked. Mr. Leland was the very last of four names with addresses listed beside the designation, "cc:". I had been very concerned to center the short letter on the page—my uncle was particular about this—and had started over three times to get it right. Besides, I could not get an original and five carbon copies in the machine at once, so I had to type two originals and discard one, just to get enough copies out of the deal. Or at least that was the method I used, and had felt pretty smart for devising it. Until now. I felt like a prisoner in this job. As it happened, this was on the Monday morning following my one summertime visit with Bruce, and I was missing him so much that every time I thought about him, I nearly wept. *"Baby, please don't make me wait."*

"Oh Bruce, I don't want to...I wish...oh...!" I wished I could have driven away with Bruce yesterday, and never had to come here again.

Surely my uncle knew how hard I was trying every day. Yet he never said anything when we were home at night. Of course, he did not say that he was unhappy either. He treated me as indifferently as he always had, and let me wonder what he might be thinking. I was not about to humble myself by asking if he was pleased with my work.

Mrs. Jolly was nicer. One day when she paid my work a compliment, I said, "I don't think my uncle realizes how hard I try." Of course, it was a shameless hint that she pass along the message to my uncle, and I am sure she realized it. With a knowing glance, she said, "I've been working in offices since I was seventeen years old, and I've learned that the longer you are around, and the more you learn, the more valuable you become."

I bristled, assuming she was trying to put me in my place. I had no intention of spending my life working in an office. If there had ever been any doubt that Mama was right when she told me I must get a college education, it had been dispelled behind that typewriter.

I remember years later as a teacher, I used to sometimes tell the story of working in my uncle's law firm by way of urging a bright young girl pupil against marrying her heart-throb right out of high school, instead going to college first. Often signs of special aptitude were embedded in essays for extra credit—my satchel was heavy; my grading hours, long. An astute insight into ANNA KARENINA, perhaps, or MY ANTONIA, or another of my extensive list of approved books, would make me want to stand up and cheer. Then one day the promising pupil would walk into class wearing a radiant smile and an Austin boy's green letter sweater, the sleeves sagging over her wrists, and I would think: Oh, no! My advice to the girl—quickly to follow—was usually met with the derisive look accorded to a jealous old maid who does not know what it is to be in love. When eventually I stopped giving such advice, it was as much because I disliked the assumption that I didn't know what it was to be in love, as that I disliked wasting my breath.

As the summer stretched ahead, my only consolation was summer drill on Tuesdays through Thursdays and the paycheck that appeared on my desk on Fridays. And I must say that I felt quite proud one day when, having accidentally split a drum head, I was able to pay for a replacement with my earnings. In fact, remembering now the feeling of awe that washed over me as I opened my handbag and withdrew the money, it occurs to me that in that very moment my fierce determination to be in control of my life came into focus and took hold, after having been only an abstract notion before then.

Came Monday morning of the last week of summer drill, the one week that included Monday practice, and which was compulsory if we were to participate in the Opening Day performance on the campus in front of the school.

While we were at breakfast, Allie and I in our house robes and Logan in his suit—ready to put on his hat and walk out the door—the telephone rang. Logan went into the hall just outside the kitchen door, to answer. Mrs. Jolly had developed a sore throat. She was not coming to work; she had made an appointment with her doctor.

By listening to my uncle's responses, I was able to get the gist of Mrs. Jolly's story. By the time he had wished the woman well, hung up the telephone, and returned to the kitchen to explain the predicament we were left in, my stomach had begun to churn.

I would have to fill in for Mrs. Jolly until she returned. This meant I would be reporting directly to my uncle. Worse still, it also meant longer hours— "As long as I can get off in time for summer drill," I reminded him. "It's compulsory this week," I added.

"I know all that," Logan said wearily. "I'll be in and out, as usual, but I'll take care of going to the post office, and I'll try and be back in the afternoons before Allie picks you up."

Meekly, I thanked him. Disagreeable as my uncle was, I had to admit he was fair, more or less, most of the time. Somehow I seemed to remember Daddy remarking on this once—if begrudgingly—though I could not remember the context of the statement.

I hoped Mrs. Jolly would be back in the office within a day or two. Alas, she called on Monday afternoon to say she had been diagnosed with a severe throat infection and would be out all week, doctor's orders. Oh well, at least it was my last week to endure this job. School started next Tuesday, the day after Labor Day. My goals had been accomplished: I had been able to attend summer drill, and even the several Friday night slumber parties that were always so much fun. And I had saved a little over thirty dollars.

The week sped by quickly as I juggled the two jobs. To my amazement, Logan made an effort to be a little less harsh when I made mistakes. One day he surprised me by expressing his thanks after I completed one of the numerous tasks that usually came within the purview of Mrs. Jolly. In that moment the woman's sage advice finally hit home: Of course Logan was being nicer to me. I was more valuable now. He would be in a real bind if I got mad and quit.

By Thursday morning I was counting the hours until my last summer drill practice, and looking forward to Opening Day performance and the beginning of my junior year in high school. This was the academic year when I would run for office in Brigade–the process would dominate the entire spring semester, in fact. As of now I had every reason to feel confident that I would be among the strongest candidates.

Then I made a shocking discovery.

Up to that time, I had dealt only with the current files of Logan's practice, stored in two cabinets in the corner of the front office. But on Thursday morning my uncle called in from a client's office, and asked me to find a telephone number jotted down inside one of the "inactive" files. These were kept in a cabinet in what was originally the breakfast room of the house, and where Mrs. Jolly and I usually ate our lunch at a small table. I removed the key ring from Mrs. Jolly's desk, found the key designated "Inactive," and hurried to unlock the cabinet. My uncle was waiting on the line.

The name of the file I was looking for was Kubick Manufacturing versus Statewide Insurance. There were no alphabetical dividers as there were in current files— probably one of my uncle's many ways of economizing– therefore, I had to take a lucky guess.

I plunged in among the tightly-packed folders with dog-eared tabs, finding myself in the early M's. Oh well. Impatient—Logan was probably already fuming—I walked my fingers backwards through these and then into the back of the L's— LU...LO.... I started to skip ahead then, but KU would be at the very back of the K's, so I just kept going one or two at a time until— Then: LI—

I was astonished to find myself staring at my own last name. I read across: LITHINGATE, DANIEL v. LONDON SCHOOL BOARD - 1937.

Chapter 10

If the New London tragedy robbed me of the life I had loved, discovering the truth behind the tragedy robbed me of something quite precious that I had continued holding onto. I suppose you might call it the bittersweet comfort of nostalgia, of being convinced as I looked back with yearning on my years in that rural community, that life was as innocent as I had perceived it to be. Truth to tell, unfortunate as the timing seemed—within days of Opening Day performance—at least by then I had in Brigade a reliable compass to guide me forward. Had I learned what really lay behind the tragedy earlier, when the effects of it were fresh, my physical wounds yet unhealed, I believe at the least I would have been unable to trust in the goodness of anyone, ever again; at worst, I might have come unhinged, and remained that way.

As it happened–if memory serves me well–I had a sense of foreboding that made me hesitant to open the file when the opportunity came during my lunch hour, secretly tucked away at the little table in the file room; a feeling of dread that had nothing to do with my fear of being caught–I knew full well I had no business helping myself to a file from my uncle's archives, without his permission, even if my father's name was on the label.

I had always assumed the men who sat on the London school board were above reproach, that for them nothing was more important than looking out for the interests of the student body and faculty. I was wrong. I suspect you would not find their scheming much of a shock nowadays. I certainly would not, given the corruption by public officials frequently exposed in the newspapers and on the television screen. But that day in 1940, after several hours spent with my eyes wide and fixed on the documents at hand, I was shaken to my very roots.

The report of an official inquiry—not a legal brief, as I had expected to find—plus a large envelope stuffed with newspaper clippings, commanded my attention far longer than I anticipated. All the while I was apprehensive of being discovered by my uncle. But, by God, my mother's body had to be clawed out of that rubble, and I had some right to know the— *Sordid details*. Oh yes—it came clear suddenly—these were the details my aunt was thinking of when she applied that disparaging phrase to the New London disaster, insulting me.

And here is what strikes me as bizarre even yet: the paltry motive involved in an act that would lead to monumental consequences. The school board took satisfaction in what my father would have called *chiseling*, and the prospect of saving a few dollars—with no one the wiser as to how they went about it—blinded them to the risks. My parents, and no doubt scores of others, would gladly have paid the niggling amount saved, many times over, to assure the safety of the school building. *"Make your pledge here, and the board will renew our contract with the bona fide natural gas provider, guaranteeing a trained and licensed engineer to monitor said service, and full accountability for the quality of that service. The difference to be made up is two dollars per year, per child."*

Two dollars. The meager amount for which our safety was sacrificed, leapt off the page in front of me. But of course neither the parents of the children nor the faculty members were given the opportunity to make a choice. And all the while, our school district was one of the wealthiest rural districts in the nation. What were they thinking, for heaven's sake? I wondered, my eyes blurring with fury.

Say what you will—that natural gas had no detectable odor in those days, that state regulations were inadequate for the pipelines carrying it. Regardless, as I came to know from the record unfolding before me, the tragedy that occurred at 3:17 on the afternoon of March 18th, 1937, was entirely preventable. My mother should be alive right now, growing old in contentment with my father at our house in East Texas—oh yes, if not for her death, Daddy would have lived many more years than he did; I fully believe that. Bucky should be thriving in his medical practice. Edna should be a respected journalist. Lanelle should be traveling the world; and Bruce and I should be married. All the victims buried in that mountain of steel and glass and concrete should have had the chance to live out their natural destinies. You will pardon my vehemence, but even all these years later, if I think about it long enough, hot tears of anger pierce my eyes like swords and I could shake my fist at the very stars I am gazing at because now, as ever, I am powerless to reverse what should never have happened—

Exhibit A: REPORT OF THE MILITARY BOARD OF INQUIRY. The title in bold letters centered on the front page; very professional looking, with a convincing number of pages following. Here was serious business. Nine gentlemen, with venerable titles attached to their names, swooped down on our tiny hamlet intent on getting at the truth and seeing that justice was served. Or so I thought for the first few pages. I remembered my uncle going out from our little farmhouse every morning in his suit and tie, carrying his briefcase, as though he were off to put in a day's work. So this was where he had gone.

Instead, I soon found a stream of expert witnesses disagreeing with one another about what caused the explosion; school officials, if sincerely apologetic and obviously shaken, ducking responsibility and making excuses. And I remember even a chilling huffiness on the part of one board member, insulted at having his judgment questioned. *"People around here tap into field gas for their homes, and nothing ever happens,"* he informed the assembly.

I remember searching the report in vain for one simple and, to me, obvious question to be resolved: If there was nothing wrong with switching the school to field gas, why did the school board do so in secret, and with nothing in writing, not even so much as a notation in the minutes?

The hearing was all a show, of course, for simple country folk who would not realize they were being patronized. So that they would go off and lick their wounds then return to their jobs in the oil field, making the rich men richer. I know, it sounds cynical; and it was.

Oh, for timid Cora Prince to have been called on as she desperately raised her hand from the back of the room: *"Excuse me, Sir, but the witness is lying. Parade Gasoline did so agree to sell the school field gas! I heard the transaction myself."* It might have changed everything. Or, maybe not. Who knows?

But wait, before I explain about Cora Prince, there is Exhibit B: the newspaper clippings. Or I should say, pictures. For now, I would ignore the stories accompanying the pictures. I was beset with an almost morbid desire to view what the heedless school board had wrought, and besides, I had a long-held wish to make sense visually of what had taken place:

I see myself now, leaning intently over those smudgy broadsheets, my knees clutched tightly together. With the first ragged picture coming into view I feel the sudden and mysterious onset of a dull throbbing behind my eyes and forehead; my stomach is a pot slowly coming to a boil. As though it were happening all around me again; closing in, cutting off the air, my body recalling vividly what is too deeply embedded in memory for my mind to reach.

On page one of the *Henderson Daily News*, a large, poorly reproduced photograph of part of the school building that lay in ruins, bleeding the margin in the top right hand corner; and a jumble of people and motor vehicles dominating the entire lower portion of the picture. I recognize familiar arched windows along one side of a central wall left intact, but a huge section of roof lay in a heap, with one end twisted against the wall, as if it were propped there; and even that part of the structure left standing is lopsided. I blink, and stare harder. The section of roof on top is badly damaged, and does not fit straight anymore. There is a dark shadow all around the eaves, like a space has opened up. I look away, reflecting. While visiting me in the hospital, Daddy had said, "It appears the school blew up then collapsed on itself." Such a clear, compact description, I recall thinking. It had evoked in my mind an image of an overly inflated balloon popping. So...the roof had flown straight up into the sky, and then smacked down on the building again? Yes, of course that's what Daddy was trying to tell me. The ruin I had glimpsed as Daddy and I cruised by, along the way of that aborted trip to Mama's grave, bore little resemblance to what I see before me now. Of course, our excursion had followed at least a partial clearing of the site. This newspaper picture was taken within hours—maybe even within minutes—after the explosion. I am mesmerized by the picture. *My school.* Tenderly I think of the handsome structure that Mama and I once anticipated so eagerly, we would walk down the road on many an afternoon to stand across from the site and watch the building rise up on the gentle slope, brick by brick. What would it have felt like to stand there watching, minutes after the explosion, stupefied by the immensity of horror and confusion on view, yet knowing one thing for certain: the world had just been knocked off its axis?

From the photo, hordes of people had done just that. In fact I cannot even tell what angle the photo was taken from, because I cannot see the campus for all the cars and the people engulfing the scene. Hopefully other photographs will be more explanatory, I reason.

Yet, the next few pictures are no less confusing versions of the first, and I am conscious of running out of time though not so much that I can force my eyes away from what amounts to a kind of bizarre scrapbook. The pain in my forehead is increasing. Angry this physical onslaught should get in my way, I clench my forehead with one hand as if I might strangle the pain, turning pages with the other. Eventually I come across a photo designated, "The rear of the school." Now I am able to get my mind oriented. Practically the whole left side of the building—no, if you were facing the front, it would be the right side—has been blown apart. The junior high wing. Where my classroom was. So that means the part collapsed and hanging down so grotesquely, in the first photo, is the balconied auditorium, which had run from front to back down the center of the school, like the spine. I return to page one for another look, to be sure. Now I notice the arched shape of the roof. Yes, this had been the auditorium where we so often assembled to say the Pledge of Allegiance and watch a program on the stage.

On the other side of that would be the senior high wing, then, which was not as badly damaged as my wing, or so I have been told. Not that it helped Mama, whose room was at the rear on the second floor. And now I find still another picture that includes the senior high wing, and see where the back section of the roof has collapsed, right above Mama's room. My hands fly to my mouth. How complete the destruction looks...yet Mama managed to save all those children before meeting her death.

Tears spring to my eyes. Mama: the angel with great, sheltering wings.... Until this moment I have never fully appreciated how truly heroic she was.

Other photos feature the rescue effort: a desperate plunge into the tower of debris. Throngs of rescuers, many in work clothes and overalls, others in suits and hats— whatever they were wearing when news of the explosion reached them—are picking over the leavings, looking for survivors, with the shattered remains of the building looming behind them. Some are carrying victims from the wreckage on makeshift stretchers. Some are hauling debris away in large baskets. Some stand staring bemused at the mess of mythic proportion, hands on hips, as if trying to decide where to dig in next.

One of those many rescuers—maybe somewhere in one of these very pictures—would have been Daddy, I realize, in his khaki shirt and pants, looking for Mama. Looking for me. How shocked and desperate he must have felt. And a caption states that until acetylene torches had been brought to the scene, the rescuers clawed through the rubble with their bare hands. All at once I remember the cuts and scrapes covering Daddy's hands and arms, when he visited me in the hospital.

I cannot bear to look anymore. In fact, I almost wish I had never opened the file in the first place because I know now that all I have found will prey on my mind for a long time to come. And there is nothing I can do to change what happened. Nothing. By now my head is a torture chamber and my stomach is roiling. I lay my head down on the table and close my eyes, trying to take deep breaths. I have to get out of here or I am going to be so sick, I—

"What do you think you are doing, young lady?" My uncle's angry voice crashes through the silence from the doorway, bringing me straight up from the chair.

Chapter 11

I do not know what prevented me from losing the contents of my stomach in that moment, dispatching them all over Logan's starched white shirt front. Perhaps shock, or fear of reprisal, stunted my impulses momentarily. Nonetheless, my heart was hammering wildly. Feeling that the room around me was tilting forward, and outward, at the same time, I sank down in the chair again, gripping the arms. "I'm going to be sick. My head—do we have any aspirin? I need one, please. Two!"

Logan's eyes widened in alarm. "I think so. In the kitchen." He turned and hastened toward the small kitchen nook, on the other side of the wall. "This is why your aunt didn't want you going in there," he scolded through the wall. "I've been calling since I left the Rotary Club meeting at one."

I had not the breath to explain myself. Lowering my head to the table again, I clutched it on either side as if to keep it from flying apart, my eyes shut tightly.

I heard the cupboard door close with a bang, then the sound of water running in the kitchen faucet. It seemed very far away. Yet Logan was back almost at once. "Well you know what they say about curiosity killing the cat." He handed me the pills and a glass of water. I glanced at him, expecting to find a smirk on his face. Instead he wore a frown of concern; his mouth was drawn down.

Murmuring my thanks, I swallowed the aspirin then pushed the file contents out of the way and laid my head on the bare wood of the table top. The surface felt cool to my cheek. That was better. Oh, for an ice pack right now—

"Shall I call Allie to come get you?" my uncle asked.

With longing I imagined lying in my bed, the wished-for ice pack propped upon my forehead. Yet I had an instinct that if I went home, Logan would consider me weak. What satisfaction that would give him. *Young lady*, he had disparaged, robbing me of the status I felt I had gained over the past week. No. I would finish what was left of this work day, if it killed me. "I'll be alright in a minute."

He hesitated momentarily, then said in a quiet voice, "I'll be in my office."

He shuffled away. Pretty soon I heard him talking on the phone. I remained very still for the next few minutes. I began feeling a little better, the nausea subsiding as the pain in my head lessened. Logan had said that Allie did not want me to see the file. If she feared the contents would upset me, she had certainly guessed right. I would never open the file again.

Or, so I was convinced at the time.

When I felt up to it, I rose ever so carefully, then stepped slowly out of the room and up the hall, to stand at Logan's open office door. By then I had begun to doubt my findings, to wonder if I had misunderstood what I read in the report, or overlooked something important that exonerated the school board. That those men— some of whom lost their own relatives in the explosion—could have behaved so recklessly seemed unreal now that I had gained a little distance. And the fact remained: there was no legal brief in the file. Which seemed to bear out the probability that no wrongdoing was involved; that what happened was a terrible accident, as I had always believed. I wanted very much to have this confirmed.

Logan was down to his shirt sleeves, sitting behind his desk and studying some document that he had aligned perfectly below his marble pen and ink stand. Logan's desk was always immaculately arranged. Like the rest of his life, I thought suddenly. *Nothing bad has ever happened to you*, I thought with contempt. I asked him why Daddy's lawsuit had apparently been dropped.

Logan looked up in surprise, then studied my face. "Sit down," he said.

Inclined to behave as though my head were made of fine porcelain, I cautiously lowered myself into the straight back chair where Mrs. Jolly always sat when my uncle dictated letters, her stenographer's pad prone. I let out a breath.

Logan leaned back in his chair. "Unfortunately, not a shred of evidence had emerged that would stand up in court," he said, "just one person's word against another's. Your daddy was in bad temper with me at first, and I didn't blame him. But he came around to my reasoning."

So the school board was in the wrong, after all? I gathered with sinking heart.

"I was soon proved right," Logan pointed out, with satisfaction. "Some seventy lawsuits were filed. Judge threw them all out. Said what happened was 'an act of God.'"

Before I could even begin to assimilate the fact that a judge had invoked God's name to indemnify the slaughter of nearly four hundred people—indeed, to this day I am still trying to do so—Logan added, "Besides, I had bigger fish to fry."

So then I leapt to the conclusion that he had other, unrelated, cases to work on, and did not want to bother representing Daddy any longer. Which proved once again how little respect he had for my father. Perhaps if he had taken time to dig deeper into the facts. Yet, he was probably afraid Daddy would not be able to pay him what he felt he deserved. But I knew better—

"A young woman came to me at the end of the hearing. She worked for Parade as a stenographer, or had at the time they started peddling their field gas to the school on the sly. She was later let go."

He uttered a rueful laugh and shook his head. "Cora Prince was the most important witness of all, but she was not summoned to testify...."

My uncle commenced to tell me the young woman's story. Yet he did not get very far before I began imagining what happened through her eyes: as a recently hired, single female in the Parade office, Cora Prince was treated with disdain by the mostly male staff, and in particular her boss, the operations manager. "Where'd you dig up that thing, anyway?" he would demand when she showed him the company policy prohibiting the sale of field gas. "H. L. Hunt don't take orders from Legal, and neither do I."

How frustrating to be ignored, then, when Cora gathered the courage to raise her hand in protest during the hearing. However, as my uncle pointed out, who would have believed her? A disgruntled former employee does not make a convincing witness. My uncle believed her; that's what counted. Just as important, apparently Parade eventually took her seriously, too.

But I'm getting ahead of myself—

"She seemed kind of hysterical at first," Logan remarked, as if to say: *Just like a woman.* And I believe that was the moment when I tuned out the drone of my uncle's voice and began to see the story through Cora's eyes. I featured her being a small woman, about Mama's size. I envisioned her seated far back in the Wildcat band room, where the hearing convened even before the victims of the explosion had been buried. And where—ironically—Bucky had been headed when he was killed. The room had been emptied of instruments and music stands, so more chairs could be brought in. The place had quickly become packed with people—friends and relatives of the dead; reporters; lawyers; and no doubt a few morbidly curious onlookers who had no real connection to the proceedings. I could imagine the confusion of many loud voices engaged in conversations before the gavel sounded. The brash sound of chairs scraping the floor as people continued spilling in. And once all the chairs were filled, people lining up around the walls. It was hot in there from the heat of so many bodies, and oppressive, too, the rancid cloud of cigar and cigarette smoke fouling the air. And no doubt there was a certain amount of stinkiness, too, fathers having come directly from an all night tour at the oil field, wanting to know answers, wanting to know who did this to their babies.

As the final day of the hearing brought the conclusion that no one was to blame, all Cora's hopes that justice might be done collapsed. She had seen my uncle writing notes on a pad, and took him to be a reporter. She introduced herself. "Parade was lying and no one cared!" she cried. Tears flooded her eyes. Logan hastened her away so that they could speak in private. He said that she had told him a good bit before she paused to take a breath, and ask him which newspaper he worked for.

"All she told me squared with what I had observed from the hearing, and from talking to people around the community," he said. "As soon as the news broke about the explosion, she had started putting two and two together...."

You can imagine how easily I related to Cora's feelings as she tried hard to make a go of her new job at Parade. Her boss had hired and fired a number of stenographers before her, she told Logan. And no wonder. The man was disagreeable, impatient. His instructions were vague and confusing. But she needed the job desperately, and was determined to get along with him. In three months she would be up for a small raise and a promotion to secretary—the job she was already doing, but not being paid for.

Cora was assigned the task of cleaning out files. Obviously the job had been neglected in the past, and she suspected this was because her predecessors feared tossing out a document by mistake, and being fired as a consequence. One day she discovered the policy on field, or waste gas, in an unmarked manila folder. The policy addressed the serious issue of liability should there be an accident. This was obviously important, she reasoned. Surely, the document belonged with copies of other company policies. Wherever they were. She put the paper aside for the moment, and continued sorting.

Several days later as she returned from lunch, her boss's office door was ajar, and she overheard a conversation inside. A big man, tall and long-limbed, the boss was leaning way back in his chair, his hands locked behind his head, his feet planted upon the edge of his desk. She could just glimpse the soles of his boots there. She felt he was being disrespectful to the guest sitting across from his desk, conveying the message that he was superior.

She did not get a look at the visitor, a fact which she would later regret. She noted that he had a kind of mild, deferential way of speaking.

"...feel like they're taking us for a cleaning, you know...."

"Yeah, I know what you mean. Those big outfits are like that, ain't they?"

"And so we just wondered about—with your line coming within 200 feet of the school and all, and apparently it's no big problem to tap into a line if you have the right fittings."

"Naw it's no problem, really. Anyone with good sense can do it."

"Only—uh—I gather it's alright from your end?"

"Sure. Good way for us to bring in a little extra, when the gas would just go to waste anyway."

It was here that Cora realized what they were talking about. Why was her boss implying it was acceptable to sell waste gas? The policy was clear—

"And I've always been given to understand it's not that much more volatile than any other gas. Why, we use it at my house, and others on the board—"

"Most people do around here, and when did you ever hear of an accident? You just need to have the right kind of regulator. We can give you a hand with that."

"Well, that's good then. Now, I'm not speaking for the whole board, of course. I was just asked to inquire, you know, when I was in the neighborhood. A final decision will be made. Then, someone will get back with you."

"Up to you. Let me know and I'll send the word down."

The big man's chair wheezed as he sat straight again, maybe reached across to shake the visitor's hand. The telephone rang, and Cora answered, grabbing her note pad and pencil. As the visitor walked out, Cora was nervously taking down information the boss had told her to get for him earlier in the day. Fearful she would make an error, she could not so much as raise her head, to get a look at the man from the school board.

At least no deal had been made, as far as she could tell. She would have to figure out a way to show the policy statement to her boss, without offending him. Maybe he was unaware of it. Would he be grateful when she brought it to his attention, so he could inform the school board and make his apologies? Somehow she feared he would not. In a way, she wished she had not overheard this conversation. Then she would not have to worry about making the boss mad.

Working up her courage finally, she went into his office—

Logan was saying, "After she presented him with the document, he reminded her that it was his job to be sure the company made a profit in the East Texas field. It was her job to keep her mouth shut and stay out of his business.

"From thence he kept his office door closed."

"And shortly after, she was let go?"

"That's right. With no reason given."

"So you felt Daddy had a stronger case against Parade?" I suggested, feeling guilty for mistaking his intentions earlier.

Logan was nodding. "H. L. Hunt—the owner—along with Parade. With Cora Prince as a witness, I figured we had a fighting chance. If you had looked one folder up from where you stopped in that file drawer, you would have found it."

As if I should have known to look. And so the notoriously rich oilman was involved. It struck me as interesting that he was not called to testify. "Did you win?" I asked, hoping that at least a modicum of justice was done, that some guilty party was forced to pay.

"We settled out of court," Logan said.

I felt so gratified in that moment, it was almost as if I were the one who had brought the powerful H. L. Hunt to heel. I could imagine Logan collecting a huge amount of money, an amount that would set the wealthy oilman back for years. And yet, obviously my father had not become rich or I would not be working in Logan's office right now.

As though he could tell what was going through my mind, he said, "What we got was pocket change, for Hunt. He just wanted to save himself a public relations nightmare. I would have held out for a lot more. But your dad didn't want to. He was eager to get on with his life out there in California. And I believe he had some unlooked for expenses connected with the move. Replacing a worn-out truck, for one thing. Then, it took him a while to find the right job."

Pocket change. I could imagine Mr. Hunt—a belligerent man by reputation—responding to advice from his attorneys, *"Alright. Give that goddamned rube something to shut him up. With his fancy Houston lawyer—who is he anyway? Nobody? If he's smart, he won't push me very far. Not a goddamned thing in writing. I shouldn't be doing this."*

I wondered then why others didn't sue Mr. Hunt as well, but then if

Cora Prince was the only witness— "What became of Cora Prince?"

"She moved away, leaving no forwarding address. I can only speculate, but I think the Hunt interests paid her something, to keep her quiet. Hunt was nervous. He had come around right after the explosion, visiting his employees who lost children. Oozing sympathy. Peeling off bills from fat rolls of cash."

The telephone was ringing. Logan answered. Shortly he was reaching for his pen, jotting down a note. "I'll find out, and call you right back," he said to the party at the other end of the line. With a glance at me, as if to weigh the possibility of sending me on the errand at hand, he changed his mind, excused himself and walked out.

I went on sitting there, imagining the rich wildcatter, a cigar in his mouth, peeling off bills with his pudgy hand. And then he could breathe a little easier, and go back to conducting important business. Pocket change. It made me sick inside. And for some reason my mind returned to that photo in my scrapbook, depicting a moment of celebration on the drilling rig when Daddy's well had come in. The investors, in their pristine suits, posed with roughnecks in grimy overalls. And there was Daddy, the proud driller, holding me high on his shoulder. I had always taken for granted that my father was the smartest man in that picture. But I was wrong. Men like H. L. Hunt, who showed up for the photos, who reaped all the rewards without ever dirtying their hands, much less, risking life and limb, were the smart ones.

Logan poked his head in the door. "Your aunt just drove up. But maybe you ought to go on home, skip summer drill."

I would not have missed summer drill for anything, if I could help it. And especially now, when I had been exposed to a part of life that was downright seedy...unclean. And—this hurt most of all—in the community that had always seemed so wholesome, where I had trusted everyone completely. Oh, how I longed to be with my fellow Brigadiers, right out in the open, the bright sunlight beating down and nothing for anyone to be ashamed of.

I vaguely realized Logan was trying to be kind, and I would have been smart to acknowledge this by saying thank you. Yet I was too eager to show him that he was not as smart as he thought, if he did not even understand the importance of Brigade in my life. "No, I can't do that. It's the last practice before Opening Day," I reminded him.

"Suit yourself," Logan said. The phone rang again.

Feeling a weight bearing down on my spirits, I doubled back to the file room, reassembled the file and returned it to the drawer. I locked the cabinet and returned the key ring to Mrs. Jolly's desk drawer. Then I hurried to the restroom, to change into my shorts and shirt and loafers.

Chapter 12

I would have given anything to be able to pick up the telephone and call Bruce. Was he aware of all that I had only just now learned? He never mentioned it. But then, after his first few letters following my move to Houston, he had written that in New London no one talked about the explosion anymore. "It's the only way we can keep putting one foot in front of the other," he said, "and besides, people here feel like it's disrespectful to the dead, to keep bringing it up all the time. Like we are invading their privacy or something." I had understood the sub-text to his remark: he was begging me to lay off the subject, too. Which made me feel stranded. How would I know if someone lived, or died, or went away, or stayed around, unless I could ask? But then shortly he sent me the *Book of Memories*, no doubt hoping this would resolve all further need to talk about what happened. And I respected that. Of course, I had not realized then that there was anything further to talk about. Yet now—

Surely sometime over the next few days an opportunity would come for me to talk to Bruce. I was reluctant to feign sickness and stay home to call him on Sunday morning. He would be here to visit in a little over a month, after all, and I would have to pretend to be sick when he came. Best not to risk that any more often than necessary.

When Aunt Allie pulled to a stop at the curb in front of the school and I saw my fellow Brigadiers arriving in their crisp white shorts and shirts—some crisscrossing the lawn, others making their way up the broad front walk—tears sprang to my eyes. I felt as if I had returned home safely after a long and treacherous journey. I wanted to be enveloped in the safe bosom of my—my family. Brigade was my family now, I thought, and felt a glow deep in my heart.

All through practice I found myself struggling to concentrate on the commands that I was supposed to be following. I was not sure why; yet I had a strong, reflexive will to keep the revelations of the past few hours from intruding on my sanctuary here. Perhaps this shut down my thought processes altogether. Miss Beatrice Lytle, our Sponsor, did not appear at summer drill on a regular basis. But today she was pacing up and down the sidewalk, in her straight skirt, low-heeled shoes, and stockings, an inimitable sight which naturally elevated the stress I was already under, and reminded me of the first time I ever saw Brigade practicing. I had told myself then that I would not be afraid of this woman. But in spite of that flash of bravado, I was now as terrified of Miss Lytle as every other Brigadier seemed to be.

I must admit it gives me pause to think how superficial was my view of Miss Lytle then. As though there was no other side to her personality except what was apparent when she was strutting up and down during practice, barking out orders, terrifying her Brigadiers. Later, when I was a teacher, some of my pupils viewed me in much the same way, I fear. Of course, I had not Miss Lytle's sharp, authoritative demeanor, and especially as a young teacher I appeared...well...soft and easy to circumvent. But as soon as I informed my seniors that a comma splice on any paper turned in to me earned an automatic zero, word spread that I was mean and rigid, and heartless. This perception did not hurt my pupils one iota. My job was to prepare them for the demands awaiting them out in the world. The same was true of Miss Lytle.

Only the Colonel appeared to be at ease around our Sponsor, I observed that day in the sunshine, as so often I had. I would be eligible to run for office next spring—the last semester before my senior year. With my high grade average and outstanding record, I could easily envision being awarded Captain of Drums, or even Drum and Bugle Major. Either office would be in keeping with my love for the music that always stirred me so. Yet, secretly I was ever attracted by the camaraderie I sensed between Miss Lytle and the Colonel as they stood with their heads together, obviously discussing important Brigade matters not meant for the rest of us to hear. What would it be like, I wondered, to be the Brigadier whom Miss Lytle relied on and trusted most of all? And too, the girl who led the Scottish Brigade onto the football field, whose name was announced over the loudspeaker, was in all ways the most visible person in the organization. Her picture would appear in the newspaper—for instance, when she accepted an award from the Lion's Club or the Rotary, for her drill team's excellent standing in the community. How would it feel to be a celebrity?

Yet, I realized suddenly, if Brigade failed to perform with the excellence for which it was renowned, who but the Colonel would be held responsible? The very thought of having all Miss Lytle's displeasure centered on me gave me a shudder. Yes, I would be much better off occupying a lower office—. I blinked. What was that command just now? I wondered in alarm. I simply had to start concentrating, or I would look scatterbrained, then all my hard work since the beginning would have gone for naught—

By the time I heard the Colonel's whistle dismissing us, my head had begun to throb again. Thank goodness I had the whole weekend ahead, plus Labor Day, before anything further was expected of me. I must get hold of myself by Tuesday morning when we reported for our performance. After all, we were all dependent on one another; I could not risk letting everyone down

I was so drained by the time I got home that I skipped supper and went straight to bed, falling into a deep and dreamless slumber from which I awoke Friday morning as though drugged, dreading to face my last day at Logan's office. Somehow I managed to get through that day, my uncle occasionally throwing me a doubtful glance. Thankfully, he did not bring up the subject of the explosion.

Over the long weekend I came to see New London through a different perspective. All those memories, once held dear, were tarnished now. Gone was the pleasure in reliving the bus rides to school, sitting next to Bruce. Every time I thought about it, all I could see was these men we assumed could be trusted, hiding from their deeds while sitting at the head tables at banquets and on the stage of the auditorium during assemblies as innocently as though nothing mattered but our well being. Did they ever look out over the sea of our young faces and wonder, just for a moment, if they had made a deadly mistake? How did they sleep at night, knowing they alone would be held accountable if anything went wrong? But of course, they were not held accountable because there was no proof. They had covered their tracks. Again and again I asked myself: *How could they, when we trusted them?*

I had no appetite whatsoever, but sat listless in my room all day long, at times lost in thought, at other times weeping without restraint at some innocent memory that crossed my mind: Edna Buckstrum going down on one shapely knee, and snapping my picture with Bruce at the Overton skating rink on Valentine's Day; Bruce, after the explosion, gazing out the bus window in confusion, but waiting for me, regardless, to come and take my place beside him; my poor dog, Rusty, pacing back to the home that used to be his, wondering why I never was there to greet him. Mama checking to be sure her slip wasn't showing that last morning of her life, and me reassuring her it was not. Mama the angel with great sheltering wings, the pupils fleeing to her bosom, for safety. Bucky just reaching the back door of the school, on his way to the band room, when—

And in that same band room, days later, any hope of justice for the loss of his life and all the others would be betrayed, the parties responsible slithering away like snakes.

My thoughts swirled and swirled, often driving me to the edge of nausea. Aunt Allie was so worried that there was no way she would leave so that I could call Bruce. Just the thought of hearing his voice returned the tears to my eyes. On Saturday evening Allie called Daddy to tell him of my upset. He was worried, and wanted to come see me. I told him no. It was Bruce I needed, not Daddy.

Everything had changed. Nothing seemed real anymore. Even the three years since the explosion, in which I had simply walked around bewildered, did not seem real anymore. Yesterday morning did not seem real anymore. *Who am I?* I despaired. *Who have I ever been?*

Again and again I thought of the *Book of Memories*. How could I have once looked at those photographs without my emotions coming unleashed? I would never open that volume again. Nor would I look at the *Londanas* ever again. Bruce had told me that on the morning of the first day back at school, they woke up to a ground white with snow. All the classes were held in the various outbuildings around the campus, wherever space could be made. Everyone had to wait in line outside before being assigned. Parents built fires outdoors to keep their children warm. Inside the buildings, the rooms were frigid because the school officials were afraid to turn on the gas. Hearing the story, I had felt cheated because I was not there with them. Thinking of their innocence now made me weep.

I cried more tears in those days of the long holiday weekend than ever I cried in the aftermath of the tragedy—

Aftermath. Now there is an interesting word. By definition it refers to the period closely following a terrible, life-changing event. But for me the aftermath of the New London tragedy has never ended. It cannot be usurped by some newer event of equal proportion because there can never be a loss that compares to the one which occurred when the earth rocked beneath my beloved school. Every day brings some fresh and painful sting of sorrow, if not some shocking revelation as in the case of the discovered file. Aftermath is the rest of my life, beginning at 3:17 p.m. on March 18th, 1937.

But back to where I was—

On that Sunday morning I was counting on an opportunity to call Bruce— obviously, I was in no shape to go to church. Yet, to my chagrin, Allie sent Logan off alone while she stayed with me, trying to coax me to eat, trying to help me feel better by saying she was so sorry I had found that file; it was the last thing she would have wanted, but now I must be strong and *will* my thoughts away from the past. I must now concentrate on making the most of every single day, and preparing for the future.

I wanted to cover my ears and scream, *"Be quiet and leave me alone!"* I felt imprisoned in her house as the hours passed and I could not telephone Bruce. And yet I hardly had the energy to move. I must pull myself together. Opening Day was less than forty-eight hours from now. How far away it had seemed on Thursday afternoon. I could not imagine where the time had gone.

On Monday night I had a terrifying nightmare that I had lost my drum key. Hard as I looked, I could not find it anywhere. Then, in the dream, on the morning of the performance the sky clouded over. The snare head sagged in the middle like an under-baked cake and I marched across the field, everyone else in a blur, beating my drum with my sticks and making no sound at all.

By Tuesday morning I barely had the heart or the energy to drag myself out of bed. When I did rise, my head began to pound so hard that I grabbed it on both sides and sank down on the edge of the bed, reeling. When finally I rose to my feet again, I tried to mentally rehearse my part in the performance, as I always did beforehand. My mind drew a blank. What were we playing today? I wondered in panic, the many familiar marching songs scrambled in my brain. Oh yes, "Here They Come," for the entrance, and, and— "Thunder," yes, at the close. I caught my breath in relief. Yet...what if I forgot what I was doing during the performance? One drummer could strike a false beat, and it would reverberate across the campus, breaking the spell. One false step would mar the perfection of a performance. You were on your honor to report any mistake you made, whether or not it was detected, and appear before Officer's Court where, unless you had accidentally stepped into an ant bed or suffered some other mishap that could not have been prevented, you would receive a demerit. I could not afford even one demerit. I—

I am going to be Colonel, I thought suddenly. My heart stood still as the certainty took hold then expanded further: either I would be Colonel, or I would not hold any office at all. From Colonel, all the way down the ranks through corporal, there was nothing in between for me. From the beginning, this had been my destiny. I was like a filly, bred for the racecourse. If I failed— I stopped myself, terrified. What crazy thoughts. I did not want them to be true. What was happening to me? All I should be concerned with right now was how to get through today's performance.

After brushing my teeth and washing my face, I walked bleary-eyed into the kitchen in my robe and slippers. My body was trembling. All I wanted was two aspirin and a cup of cool water, but at Aunt Allie's behest, I accepted a glass of orange juice to chase the aspirin down.

Allie's eyes were shadowed underneath. She looked as if she had not slept all night. She stood by worriedly as I swallowed the aspirin with the juice. Orange juice had never felt so acidic going down; it was like setting fire to my stomach.

"You're in no shape to participate this morning," Allie fretted. "I want you to stay home. I'll call the school. Say you've come down with something."

I clapped down the glass tumbler on the counter, the contents sloshing inside. "But that's a lie! I won't tell a lie."

Allie's eyes widened in surprise. "Then I'll try and reach Miss Lytle at home—hopefully, she is in the phone book—I'll explain what has upset you so. She'll understand, I'm sure."

"So, now you want to tell my secrets?" I cried. "Don't you dare tell Miss Lytle! She's the last person in the world I want to know. She'll think I'm crazy!"

"But, dear—" Allie pleaded, by now on the verge of tears herself.

"It's late. I've got to put my uniform on," I said, and staggered out, dots before my eyes.

The weather was hot and humid that morning, the sun pressing down like a hot iron, with barely a hint of a breeze. As the Brigade filed out the side door to take its place, the campus was teeming with students, gathering in groups, schoolmates talking and joking with one another. Boys and girls were flirting. Everyone was happy. A feeling of high anticipation was in the air. A new beginning. How beautiful it was, I thought, how shiny and golden the day. It broke my heart. My eyes filled. I sniffed back the tears.

My woolen kilt and scarf and heavy jacket made me feel that I was shut up inside an oven; my drum was like a heavy boulder weighing on my hip. My headache had not completely subsided, though, thanks to the aspirin, it was a little less severe. The Brigade stood lined up at attention as the Austin band played "Semper Fidelis," then the cheerleaders, in their white sweater vests with big green "A's" on the front, and lace-up shoes, led the onlookers in an Austin High yell and did a series of acrobatic stunts that brought a cheer from the crowd. The cheerleaders, too, had been practicing hard over the summer. School spirit reigned. The sun in my eyes made them watery. I kept squinting, tears making tiny rivulets out toward my temples.

Then it was time. The crowd grew hushed. The Colonel's sharp whistle pierced the silence. Altogether, in a single instant, the bugles rose in a pitch-perfect clarion. A breathless pause, then the sound of the drums split the air. It sent a thrill up my spine and choked me with emotion. I was hardly aware of my hands holding the sticks and beating out the rhythm. The sticks might have been performing without me.

With her spine perfectly straight, her steps precisely measured, and a kind of shimmering aura surrounding her body, the Colonel led the staff officers onto the performance field, followed by the Flag Corps, then the small band of Bagpipers. The Captain of Drums lifted her hand in a signal, and the Drum Corps stepped off.

When all the corps had entered the field and come to a halt, the bagpipes tuned up with their weird cacophony, quickly resolving into a haunting Scottish melody on a brogue-ish wail; members of the Drill Corps crossed their swords on the ground and executed the Sword Dance around them. The other corps were formed up behind them in twin sets of perfectly straight diagonal lines.

My position was on the very end, closest to the school. The sun beamed on uniform backs. It seemed to inflame my headache again, like waking up a sleeping lion. Then: eyes right, all the way down the line. Now I was suddenly facing the sun's glare, and my tender eyes were boiling; my gaze drooping downward. All I could see were the tips of shiny black lace-up shoes, and snowy white spats above them, lined up perfectly, one pair after another, white on black, angling toward the center—

I am staring at a pair of small, two-toned lace-up shoes, the sun beaming down on them through the tall window. How unusual they are, these shoes; could have clad the feet of Robinhood or Peter Pan: made of dark green suede, with light tan trim and pointy toes, and the tongue of the shoes comes up high, and is flared and scalloped at the top. Scalloped at the top! Imagine! I have never seen such a pair of shoes. And how is it that Lanelle Oberlin has come by them, when Lanelle wears dresses made of feed sacks and never has anything new and fancy like I have? I can hardly concentrate on the spelling words because I am so taken with the shoes, and I am struggling between my wish that they belonged to me and yet knowing that it isn't right to envy Lanelle when the girl never has anything nice to wear. Still, wouldn't those shoes go perfectly with my brown skirt and bolero that Mama made—

"I've got to go to the bathroom. Quick!" cries Lanelle, and the shoes pivot and fly away, because we have all been a little nervous these last few days, and especially today

with the competition coming up tomorrow that we must win again or the whole world will come crashing down around our shoulders; it is enough to give you a headache or...or keep your stomach upset—

I blinked my eyes hard, realizing: Lanelle had fled to the bathroom; that's why she was not in the room where everything was safe. That was what had cost my friend her life.

I was gasping for breath now. The black shoes and white spats had become a long, undulating line. My heart was pounding as if it would burst through my chest. I had to get away from there, or I would collapse on the ground and disrupt the whole performance, and maybe crash into the line of girls in front of me with my heavy drum, send Brigadiers toppling like dominoes. How lucky I was to be on the end. I would pivot around to the left, standing very straight, looking purposeful, the bagpipes playing on and the Drill Corps deftly executing the Sword Dance. And with no one the wiser, I would retreat inside the cool first-floor hallway. Would this mean a demerit? I wondered, my heart seizing up. No, I was only doing what I had to do, to save the performance, the best thing for everyone....

So that was what I did, walking as straight as I could, vaguely sensing the puzzlement of the girl standing next to me, who was forbidden by regulations to turn her head and stare. I clamped my drum sticks tightly against the snare drum head, my heart seeming to beat higher and higher in my throat, choking off the air, and all the while the sun was beating down defiantly, as if determined to follow me, to dare me to escape its vengeance. But if I could just get through the side door and into the cool hall in time, I would be alright—

Reaching the edge of the concrete walk that approached the door, I felt all at once a sensation I have never felt in my life, before or since, of utterly dissolving inside my skin. My head rolled forward like a wheel going down a hill. My chest and shoulders landed on top of the snare drum to which I was tethered, my chin striking the rim as the drum itself struck the edge of the concrete with a loud metallic clap. The last thing I remembered was my hands flying out and my drum sticks clack-clack-clacking, over the concrete, and my certainty that I had failed everyone depending upon me, and ruined the performance we had all strived so hard to make perfect.

Whole generations, or mere moments, might have passed before I became aware of the acrid smell of ammonia flooding my nostrils. And I realized as Miss Lytle, with frowning hawk face and piercing dark eyes, came into view, that all my hopes for high office in the organization that I loved so well, would have given my very *life* for, had come crashing down along with me.

Then I remembered my prescient feeling as I rose from the bed this morning.

Chapter 13

As I stammered my apologies, I became aware that my drum strap had been unhooked from my waist and I was lying on my back in the grass, my uniform jacket unbuttoned part of the way, and something tucked up to make a pillow under my head. "Is my drum okay?" I inquired, raising my head, still dazed.

"I doubt it, but never mind that for now," Miss Lytle answered in a mild, reassuring tone that surprised me.

Regardless, I could easily imagine the cool observation going through her mind: that Delys Lithingate was subject to giving way under pressure. Point well taken as she began considering officer candidates for next year.

"We're going to get you inside now," I heard Miss Lytle say, and I hated all the fuss I had caused, which I knew she must deplore. Two male teachers, Mr. Jacobs and Mr. Clemenger, positioned themselves on either side, and helped me to my feet. "Steady now...." My body came straight up from the grass as though I had been resurrected from the grave. As I paused to get my bearings, the men still holding my arms above the elbows, I noticed Miss Lytle shaking out her suit jacket, and was mortified to realize my head had been lying on it.

Through all this I could hear the final notes of "Thunder" in the background as Brigade exited the field without me; then the loud cheers that broke out. I was only so thankful that apparently I had not disrupted the performance.

With assurances to Mr. Clemenger that he could handle things from here, Mr. Jacobs walked me to the school nurse's office where I was to spend home room and part of first period—Brigade period for the Drum and Bugle Corps— lying down with an ice pack on my battered chin. As I look back on that day, it hardly seems possible that some six years hence, I would be attending faculty meetings alongside these two gentlemen; that I would watch them grow old, their hairlines receding, and eventually reach retirement. And so it seems a good time to remark that Austin teachers tended to stay put, which was a strong testimony to the quality of life in that school, at that time. Is it as good these days? No. But if you look, you can still find glimmers of hope for a renaissance someday. My, what an inspiring cloud of witnesses—students, faculty, administrators, all—make silent footfalls up and down those aging corridors now.

The school nurse called Aunt Allie to explain what happened. "She struck her chin pretty hard, though she doesn't appear to have any loose teeth. Um-hum...yes, the heat, probably, plus maybe a case of opening day jitters. You know how it is." *But not with me!* I wanted to shout. I could overhear my aunt's frazzled reaction through the receiver. Presently the nurse turned to me. "Mrs. Fletcher is worried your right shoulder may have come out—"

I had been warned initially that my shoulder could become dislocated again, perhaps many times. "No, no, I didn't hit my shoulder. It's fine."

"She's coming to get you," said the nurse.

Panicked, I rose up from the waist and grabbed the tumbling ice pack. Our first football game of the season was less than two weeks from today. "No, tell her I don't want to go home. I need to get to Brigade period. I'm alright."

The nurse said to my aunt, "She thinks she will be fine, and her vital signs are normal. I'll give her a pass to come back and see me if she needs to. Um-hum. Alright. Yes, ma'am, you're welcome."

No one at school was told anything about my fainting spell except what the nurse reported to Allie. As the days went by I was thankful at least to have finally remembered the circumstances that led to Lanelle Oberlin's death, though I despised myself for having envied the unusual pair of shoes she was wearing, during the last few minutes we were together, the last few minutes of her life. I felt almost as if I had some part in causing her death. I was struck anew by how cruelly capricious the disaster was. An upset stomach meant the difference between life and death. If I had suffered that affliction, rather than Lanelle, then she might be alive today, and I might be dead. Sometimes I felt that would have been more fair. I would hasten to shake off the feeling, for I knew it was ridiculous. All the same, I was possessed of a notion that I must try somehow to make up for the loss of this girl who could have accomplished so much in her life, given the chance. Lanelle Oberlin was smarter than I was. Oh, how generously I could bestow that recognition upon her now, after having withheld it for all the time I had known her; and I deeply regretted that I could give her nothing more. If shoes were worn in heaven, I wished for my friend Lanelle multitudes of the most fanciful ones, to give wings to her feet.

A couple of weeks after school started, I finally had an opportunity to telephone Bruce. Every time I called him, I half-expected my aunt or uncle to return home before we got very far into our conversation. So I started right in with my tale of finding the file, anticipating I might be cut off before I finished. Noting my every pause was met with silence, I began to suspect Bruce was as shocked as I had been. At the end, I paused yet again before adding, "I wondered if you knew about it—you never said. Oh Bruce, I was so upset by Opening Day that I—"

"Of course I knew! Everybody did. But I've told you before, Delys, I'm through talking about all that," he snapped. "I wish you'd—" he added, but then his voice dropped off. I could hear his frazzled breathing into the receiver.

I was too stunned to respond. Not so much because Bruce was obviously aware that what happened to us was no accident; more, because of his rudeness in saying so, his acting as if I had no right to be upset. I didn't like this side of him, which I had never known existed. It frightened me.

"Why don't you just come on up here? You and Doc can talk about it all night, and maybe I can get some sleep," he went on, in a nasty voice.

Now I sat back. I was still thrown off by Bruce's rudeness; but at least now it made more sense. Apparently I had reached him following a bad night with Doc, or maybe a string of bad nights. Poor Bruce. I found myself offering at least a qualified apology. "I'm—I'm sorry. But I had no idea you were having a rough day." Should I add that I was sure he must have many rough days? It was not as if I didn't know what he was living through with Doc. And yet, until today he had always seemed to keep his perspective.

It was so long before Bruce spoke again, I began to fear he had hung up in my ear. Then he said, miserably, "I'm sorry. It isn't your fault. But I can't take much more of this, I swear, I can't."

"I understand," I said with feeling. Yet, I was alarmed. What did he mean? What was going to happen now? Was he leaving?

"I've gotta go study. We had a pop quiz in chemistry today, and *guess what?*"

So failing the quiz had sent his nerves over the edge. At least he wasn't giving up I realized, encouraged. "Can I help? I'd be glad to–" I began, yet wondering suddenly if I had picked up the sound of a car cruising up the driveway.

"No. Not now. I gotta go. I'll see you in October."

"Yes, of course! I can't wait. Bye, Bruce. I love you."

"You too," he said, his voice so constricted that I thought he was going to cry.

When I hung up the receiver, my hand was trembling.

From that day I feared that Bruce would greet me in October with the announcement: *"I'm leaving. I came to say goodbye." "Where will you go? When will I see you?" "I don't know. I don't know. Just kiss me...."*

While agonizing over the thought of losing Bruce, I realized that if he left home, my dog would be stranded. I thought of poor Rusty, faithfully guarding the Buckstrum house and property, trusting Bruce as he once trusted me. If Bruce left, I could not expect Doc to care for him. Yet, nor could I beg my aunt and uncle to provide Rusty a home, because doing so would tip them off that I was still in touch with Bruce. On the other hand, what reprisal could they devise that would make any difference to me, if I lost Bruce? They could refuse to give my dog a home, that was what. Could they be that cruel? I wondered with a chill. *Oh, please don't go off, Bruce!* I pleaded in silence. My life had become a house of cards.

In the long weeks that ensued, Bruce and I talked but once, and briefly. I could not get an idea of his mood. No sooner had he confirmed our meeting coming up in a few days than I heard the back door open and had to hang up.

I remember he was nervous when he picked me up that Sunday; I could sense this from the moment he opened the door of the car and I slid in beside him. Though it was not a warm day—in fact, I was wearing a sweater set and wishing I had brought a jacket along—I noticed a telltale wet spot on the under side of his shirt sleeve as he reached out his arm to greet me. He said nothing, but smiled—a melancholy smile? I wondered—and squeezed my hand. I noticed his hand was moist. *I'm leaving....*

No sooner were we tucked away on a shady lane in Forest Park Cemetery than Bruce grabbed me close and kissed me as though he had waited forever to do so. Which left me breathless and filled with sweet longing, but did little to allay my fears. Then he pulled back, let out his breath and looked at me, his face earnest. "How'd you like to be a doctor's wife one day?"

It was the last thing I expected. This was the closest Bruce had ever come to proposing marriage, in so many words. Busy as I was, trying to separate what I had expected to hear from what I actually heard, all I could say was, "Why Bruce, what girl wouldn't want to be a doctor's wife?" I smiled tentatively. Was he serious?

"Good, because I've made up my mind to go to medical school one day," he said firmly. His eyes searched my face as if for some sign I believed he could succeed.

Now the far more concrete term, *medical school*, raised a red flag in my mind. Everyone knew that only the brightest pupils, those who excelled at the most difficult subjects, dreamed of going to medical school. Abruptly I remembered this had been Bucky's aim. So Bruce intended to devote his life to fulfilling his brother's promise? How noble of him, and yet surely he was incapable— I stopped myself. Now, who was selling Bruce short? He could do it. Of course he could. "Oh, Bruce, I'm so proud of you!" I cried. I took his hands in mine and kissed his fingers.

He glanced down shyly, then looked into my face again. "Doc's going to help me. I'm already going in with him on Saturdays," he said. He added with gravity, "Last week I sutured up a busted knee. Did alright, too.

"Doc says it seems like people feel easy around me when I'm in there with him, and he says that's as important as all the book learning in medical school, when you want to help someone get well."

Doc had made a very good point, it seemed to me, and it warmed my heart that he had bolstered Bruce in this way. I hastened to say, "I'm sure that's true, Bruce. Why, when anything happens to upset me, I always know that as soon as I can talk to you about it, and hear your voice, I'll feel better." Case in point: my discovery of the ominous file. I still felt stranded by his refusal to help me sort things out. I had needed that, and there was no one else I could turn to. As though reading my mind, Bruce's eyes dropped. I thought for a moment he might relent and open the subject. But no. When he looked up again, he said, "You know, I think my decision has made Doc happier, given him something to look forward to. He seems better lately."

Did he mean that Doc had cut back on his drinking? Even stopped? I hoped so, but again I felt alarmed. Bruce was at the breaking point a few weeks ago. How long had he been racking his brain to figure out how to help his father to get well, so that he would not be driven to leave home? He had not mentioned it to me, but then, he did not dwell on Doc's drinking problem very much when we were together. No doubt he did not wish to waste his only hours of escape dredging it up. Had he seized on the idea of medical school in one last desperate hope it might work? And what if he failed to get into medical school? What would become of Doc then? No, I was not going to think that Bruce might fail.

Perhaps sensing my reluctance now, he went on uncertainly, "Only, I just hope I can get through the courses, that's all."

"Keep reminding yourself of what Doc said, that you have a natural ability to help people feel better. Then nothing can stop you," I told him bracingly.

Bruce's eyes grew lustrous. "I reckon as long as I have you, why, I could do just about anything I put my mind to," he swore, his dark brows hitched together.

I wish I had been discerning enough in that moment to appreciate what was at stake when he said those words. I would see, by and by, but unfortunately not soon enough.

Gradually Bruce's countenance brightened. He began talking about his hopes and dreams. At one point he told me he had started reading Doc's medical books. "Most of it is way over my head, though now and then a light comes on," he said, "and I sit there and think about that a little."

I nodded my head earnestly, knowing exactly what he meant; and somehow Bruce seemed older to me then, wiser. Maybe, from now on, he would do better and better in school. It seemed anything was possible.

As I reflect back on that conversation from the distance of many years, I believe Bruce came as close then as ever he would come to fully believing in himself. After all, he knew his father believed in him; and he knew I believed in him. We were the two people dearest to his heart, the two he most respected.

To this day I am haunted by a question: if not for the blunder I would commit a few months later, would Bruce have been able to scale the heights of medical school and fulfil the dream that burned in him? I see him on the day he receives his diploma, flush with pride, having fought long and hard, and succeeded. I am his wife, standing at his side and knowing I helped him reach this day when he will finally pack the books away and put his good instincts to work, helping people get well.

Thinking of the innate kindness and empathy that I remember so well in Bruce, it is easy to imagine him entering an examining room in his crisp white coat and sitting down with a patient, his very presence reassuring: the first step toward healing....

I was never anyone's wife and helpmate, of course, but having taught school for many years and having seen the tender shoots of ambition in a fair number of pupils, I have often found myself hoping I did manage, perhaps in small ways, to encourage them and thereby redeem the way I let Bruce down.

Oh precious children, who made your wobbly way across my path long after, I hope I helped you stand a little taller. With love, your teacher, Miss Lithingate.

It was a day in early January, under low shelves of gray clouds. Snow was predicted before the night was over. My English Literature teacher, Mrs. Hathaway, opened the class by telling us to pull out a blank sheet of paper. We were about to start a unit on the famous American poets. Like Aunt Allie, Mrs. Hathaway was tall and slender. But she had an athletic build, with muscular calves and forearms, and she told us once that she had been a champion swimmer in college. Her hair was very light, almost platinum, and she had twinkling blue eyes and girlish freckles. Brightly she said, "I want everyone to write a poem for me. Just a few lines. I want you to see how it feels."

Inevitably, hands were soon going up: What did she want us to write about?

"The first thing that comes to your mind, of course," she said. "We'll take, say, fifteen minutes. If you don't finish, it's alright. I'm not grading these, though I'll have a look at them, so put your name at the top."

Mrs. Hathaway had taught me English the previous semester, too. I was grateful to have her again, because I liked her. She was an engaging teacher, as Mama had been, and I think if Mama had not already inspired me to pursue that vocation one day, Mrs. Hathaway would have done so.

I don't know what made me think of the lines I soon found myself writing down, though most likely I was responding to the weather. New London was never far from my thoughts, of course. And since the radiator in our third floor classroom was crackling with steam heat, and if we were very lucky—we seldom were in Houston—there would be snow on the ground tomorrow, the first thing that crossed my mind was how Bruce had described that first day back at school after the explosion:

> *His words painted a picture for me:*
> *The campus of snow white;*
> *Snow studding the gaping wound where*
> *the school once stood;*
> *Flickers of orange and yellow light,*
> *Children huddling by the fires.*
> *I wanted to be there with them then.*
> *But now I don't know.*
> *We were all such fools.*

I was doubling back to the third line, wondering if there might be a better word than *gaping*, when Mrs. Hathaway called time and started taking up the papers. I would leave it, I decided. I jotted a title across the top of the page, "The First Day Back," then quickly read through all I had written. A feeling rose in me. There was significance in those few lines. I had gone inside myself and drawn out something I had not known was there.

Late that night I lay awake in bed, staring into the darkness and marveling at the process—so new to me—of writing verse. In the fleeting time when I was immersed in my poem, only the ideas flowing from my mind and being shaped into words existed; all else fell away, even my anger and sense of powerlessness about the tragedy that had inspired them.

Chapter 14

Remembering my conflicted feelings as the days lengthened and grew warmer in early spring of that year, and the long-awaited time approached when I would become an officer candidate, I find myself wondering: Since my days in the Scottish Brigade, has any part of my life or experience ever been as intense as those? Have I ever again felt as if my very life depended upon a set of outcomes, one after another? Has anything ever mattered quite that much to me? I don't believe it has; nor was I unique in feeling as I did. Perhaps that was what made Brigade so magical, so that even now as I look back, my memory has an otherworldly quality about it, the band of young women in plaid kilts and green jackets and feathered hats floating above an emerald field with our very breaths in perfect unison. We could not have been that good, and yet we were; and it was our intensity that made us that way.

Even after all this time, it pains me to recall how lost and dejected I felt, when surely by all rights I should have been confident about my prospects. After all, from the time I enrolled in the Scottish Brigade—indeed, even before I enrolled—I had set my goals, then achieved them one by one. Yet now, every morning during Brigade period, and during practice in the afternoons, I had an uneasy sense that I did not belong there, that I had lost my bearings in the organization. Even as I prepared for the tests that would be a part of running for office, my courage was flagging. I could not shake off the notion that there was only one office with my name on it, and that office had been lost to me on Opening Day: one more casualty of the debacle in New London. Worse, increasingly I felt that my fate was obvious to my fellow Brigadiers. I was embarrassed to think I had once felt so sure of myself, and I feared I may have flaunted this. Everyone now hated me and could hardly wait for me to receive my comeuppance at Installation. Should I boldly ask to speak to Miss Lytle, and explain the state I was in on Opening Day? But no. It was too late. She would see through my ploy and lose respect for me in yet another way. I could not bear to think of the look of derision on her face, the knowing eyes above the tight mouth.

Then one day I thought: *I don't have to put myself through this; I don't have to run for office.* In that moment I felt as though a heavy weight were lifting from my shoulders. Even so, perhaps I should not be too hasty, an inner voice warned; there was plenty of time. I told no one what was on my mind, in case I changed it. Yet, over the days that followed, the conviction grew. Not to run for office would be the only way to take charge of a situation that had gone beyond my control. I would not be forced to sit through the ceremony with my heart sinking more and more until it was all over. I would know from the start that I would leave with the same rank as when I entered the auditorium.

On the morning of the official starting day, I awoke feeling strong in my resolve: I would not participate. Resigned to the decision, I felt nonetheless that some part of me had died.

Later in Brigade period, I watched inert as girls all around me bent over sheets of notebook paper, bravely listing three offices they most desired to hold, in order of the first to the last. I knew the dearest wishes of their hearts were engraved on those three lines. But I could relax, I told myself; for me it was over before it had begun, and I was free. Then as I saw the first papers turned in, and watched the girls return to their chairs, the heightened glow on their faces saying, *"Maybe, just maybe...,"* I became terrified that I might be cheating myself, might always regret not having at least tried. For the next few minutes I suffered such an agony of confusion, I could scarcely take a breath.

I don't remember consciously changing my mind. Rather, quite impulsively, my throat dry with anxiety, I pulled out a sheet of paper, wrote my name at the top, then listed: 1. Colonel; 2. Drum and Bugle Major; 3. Captain of Drums. Bracing myself, I quickly turned in my choices. I was the last one to return to my chair. I felt all eyes were upon me.

A few days later the testing began out on the campus behind the gym, Miss Lytle enthroned on a wooden student desk, employing writing pen and pad while the March wind riffled her short hair and the corners of the pages before her. In the next few weeks, every time I stood before our Sponsor—say, soloing on my snare drum, or showing that I could issue a Brigade command with that special way of throwing the voice that made each syllable carry clearly and distinctly—or any of the other tests, I did my best. But it seemed to me that the other candidates were better prepared, and whenever my eyes met Miss Lytle's, I sensed the harsh judgment behind her inscrutable look. She did not like me, for I was weak. And maybe she was right. Maybe anyone with real fortitude would be able to hold herself together for the few minutes of a performance, no matter what was going on in her personal life. And so, maybe this was turning out for the best after all; maybe I was not as capable as I thought and would wind up letting everyone down if I were made Colonel—my thoughts skidded to a halt. *Or any other office,* I corrected myself. Why could I not let go of that feeling it would be all or nothing for me? I did not even want to be Colonel anymore, I realized. The idea had soured for me. Now I wished I had stuck to my decision not to run for office. Why could I never do anything right? I hated myself.

At nights I would close my eyes, counting like sheep the days remaining until Installation Day, May 15th. Then—thankfully—it would be over with and I would be getting past the hurt. I would go back to playing my drum which was what— *Remember this, Delys!*—I had wanted from the start, to be the heartbeat of the Scottish Brigade. And it would be fine, like brand new...

...only it would not be brand new because there would no longer be any new accomplishment to strive for....

The final test was an essay, to be written at home. The topic was, "Discuss the Scottish Brigade honor code." I began to jot down ideas as they came to me: that the honor code forced each member to take responsibility for herself, and therefore strengthened the organization throughout. Which ultimately would make us better citizens, I added. I wrote several more sentences. I read through them. They seemed more a definition than an essay. And yet, as far as I could tell, what I had written was accurate.

Still, I yearned to write something original.

I thought and thought. Then I found myself writing, "The honor code is a mirror. It shows us who we are."

I sat back, feeling as I had felt when I penned those lines of verse for Mrs. Hathaway: that they had come from deep within me. I believed there was more to be revealed if I just kept writing in this vein. And I remember now that inevitably the Article about membership being based, in part, on character, ballooned in my mind like a genie escaping a bottle. I remember how quickly I forced it back inside.

Of course, I reasoned, Miss Lytle didn't seem like a person who would appreciate having her honor code turned into a metaphor; so perhaps my first try was better. I returned to it and read it through. This time I felt an acute sense of distaste. Anyone could have written those words. They lay inanimate on the page.

Oh, what difference did it make when my chances were doomed anyway? I may as well write what I wanted to write....

To my great surprise, around the first of May I received a call from Daddy. He was coming to Houston "for your big day."

I had not seen my father since before his accident, but we exchanged letters occasionally, and he called me long distance around once a month. His voice always sounded tired and raspy on the telephone, and tonight was no exception. I knew that even though Daddy had returned to work at the end of the summer last year, he still suffered back pain on many days. Surely the long motor trip to Texas would be miserable. I felt a little sorry for him. "Daddy, I'm not going to get an office," I said. "You'll just be disappointed, after coming all this way."

There was a pause. Then, his voice thick, he said, "I could never be disappointed in you, Dee." More cheerfully, he added, "Besides, it's high time we had a nice visit, whatever comes."

Hearing that last qualifying phrase, I suspected Daddy feared the worst.

He said that he would probably arrive on the afternoon of the ceremony. "Tell me where we can meet, and we'll sit together," he suggested.

I sensed he wanted to be nearby, to comfort me. "No. I have to sit with Brigade," I told him. "I can't even speak to you until it's over." Again, I felt a little sorry for Daddy. "You can sit with Aunt Allie, though. I'll see you afterward."

As we hung up, I felt guilty. Just three days earlier, Bruce had come to visit. For all my attempts to remain dispassionate, I was a bundle of nerves by then, and there were no more tests to serve as an outlet for my energy. I felt more eager than ever for Bruce's mouth on mine, for the warmth of his body pressed against me and the sound of his heartbeat as I lay my head on his chest. It had been harder than ever for me to stop things from going too far. Ever since we parted, I had been missing my sweetheart and wishing he could attend Installation, and be waiting for me when the ceremony was over. Whatever came...as Daddy put it. I resented being cheated out of sharing with Bruce every significant event in my life, or even being free to acknowledge him to my friends. Several times over the past year, I had imagined myself reminding Allie of the many dates I had accepted with Austin boys, then saying, quite innocently, "I still like Bruce, though. Can't I be in touch with him again, as long as I continue dating other boys?"

And it seemed that my aunt would surely relent, and give her blessing. But then, having sneaked around with Bruce behind her back, I feared that my voice would begin to shake as I spoke, or my face would turn scarlet with guilt. Or, if we talked very long, I might let some piece of information slip out that would reveal I had been seeing him. For instance: what would impress my status-conscious aunt more than to know that Bruce was going to be a doctor? And yet I could not tell her this, for obvious reasons.

How many facts about Bruce's life had I come to know since Allie forced us apart? Just one slip, and the scheme would backfire.

When I think now of my aunt's prejudice against Bruce—which, by the way, would not dissipate over time—I almost believe that she was a little crazy. That what happened to my mother made her that way. Then too, her frame of reference may have come from her own life. On her sickbed she startled me with the disclosure that she had come close to backing out of marrying Logan "after the gifts began arriving," because she no longer felt he was right for her. She did not say why, though by then I had my own ideas. But her mother Sarah forced her to go through with the wedding, bluntly pointing out that Logan would provide her the same status in life that she had grown up with, and this was what counted in the end. "'You've just got a case of the jitters; that's all that's wrong with you,' Allie parroted her mother. "I knew better, but I did as she said. And eventually I came to see that she had been right," she told me.

Allie was certain that Bruce was wrong for me. Perhaps she assumed when she forced us apart that I would obey her as dutifully as she had obeyed Sarah, though she may never have been completely certain. For a long time she managed to retrieve each day's mail delivery before I did. A coincidence? And later, during the period I speak of now, when I was stealing away to the cemetery with Bruce, there were times when, for a day or so afterward, she seemed to be especially attentive to me for no apparent reason, as though perhaps trying to see some sign of treachery in my face. Of course, all this may have been imaginary, stemming from my fear of being discovered.

In any case, every time I felt tempted to try and persuade Allie to let me resume contact with Bruce, I wound up checking myself for fear it would make matters worse. And admittedly, I had come to regard those hours Bruce and I were together as all the more sacred because they were stolen, and to feel twice the excitement because of the risk they carried. It was as if Forest Park Cemetery was our own secret universe, always waiting to enfold us.

As I look back on that sunny afternoon of May 15th, 1941, I can still see the packed school auditorium, and smell the fragrance of ligustrum wafting through the high sash windows. I can only imagine that what Daddy was going through was far more complicated than what I was experiencing: a simple, full-blown case of nerves that no amount of trying to be prepared for the worst could alleviate.

I see Daddy sitting alone among strangers, having avoided a rendezvous with my aunt and uncle on pain of encountering my grandparents. *"I'm sure that, in your own way, you are a good man, Dan Lithingate*, said Sarah Madden, her eyes red-rimmed, on the day Mama was buried, *"But I curse the day my daughter met you."* And now Daddy is somewhat relieved to be on his own because he has seen how dressed up people are—men in suits, women in Sunday dresses and hats and gloves. And here he sits, dressed in a fresh pair of starched khaki trousers and shirt, which he changed into after he showered and shaved at the tourist court. Had he only known.... The last suit he owned was the one he got married in. What had become of it? Discarded, along the way of his and Vinia's many moves, no doubt, just like anything else that had worn out its usefulness. Suits went along with that whole way of life he wanted no part of. But he could have worn one today, for Dee's sake. He hopes his Dee will not be ashamed when she sees him.

It was Allie who urged him to come. She wrote of Dee's fears—and she admitted to sharing them—that the mishap during that performance last September had ruined her chances. "If Delys attains an office, nothing will thrill her more than that you are on hand for her big day. If she is met with disappointment, however, you are the one person capable of consoling her."

Reading those words, Dan immediately bristled with insult that whoever made these decisions might overlook his daughter. It was easy enough to tell from Dee's letters that she put her whole heart into this drill team. She seldom wrote of anything else. But he was cut to the quick to realize when he called from California to say he was coming today, Dee had kept from him the reason she feared being left out when the offices were awarded. The truth was, Dee didn't share her feelings with him as she used to do. Well, whose fault was that?

He is bone weary now, and this auditorium seat is not the most comfortable in the world. He shifts around a bit as people continue pouring in to be seated. He glances up and behind him. Even the balcony is starting to fill. He wishes they would just get on with the show, get it over with. His little girl is not going away with a broken heart today, not if he can help it. Ever since his accident, he has been turning over in his mind the idea of making a change. Nothing like being laid up for months, to give a man a new perspective on life. The truth is, he is getting too old to work in the oil fields. He is tired of being dirty all the time, too, tired of being so worn out at the end of the day that he barely has the energy to wash off the grime before dropping into bed. Returning to work after all those weeks of being off was among the most disagreeable things he had ever done. But oil field work was the only thing he had ever known, and to have gotten as far as he had, earning well above what most workers would ever take home, well, how could he walk away?

Then, right on the heels of it, he learned that Dee had something of a crisis in her life, brought on by finding that file about the school explosion inquiry in her uncle's office.

It broke his heart when Allie called him over Labor Day weekend to say Dee was in the throes of despair. His first thought was that he must go to her and console her. He had hardly gotten his bearings back, at work, but he was determined to take time off regardless.

"I don't need you," she said bluntly. "I'll be alright."

Her words brought a chill to his heart.

That night he woke up in a cold sweat. *I wasn't there for Dee when she lost her mother and needed me more than ever. I let her down. I let Vinia down, too. I was wrong. And now Dee doesn't want me anymore.*

He had never told Dee how hard it was the day she left him and moved to Houston, to watch Logan's big sedan drive away toward the highway, that little hand fluttering goodbye to him through the back window. He went out on the back porch that night, looked up at the stars, and cried so hard his body was quaking. He cried for Vinia. He cried for Delys. He cried for their shattered lives. He pounded his fist in his hand. He had intended to stay until the house sold, but he knew that night he could not stomach being around for that long. He hated the very thought of East Texas.

At first he got letters from Dee, saying how unhappy she was, begging him to come get her: the simplest and dearest request from a little girl to her daddy, whom she had always adored. She never knew how much he wanted to, how those letters grieved him, kept him awake nights. But he felt sure she was better off down in Houston. He didn't have anything to offer her. He buried himself in work to hold his sadness at bay.

He has been doing it ever since.

Lately he has been considering his options, though; in fact he spent a good part of the trip to Texas thinking long and hard. With Europe embroiled in another war, business was booming at the U.S. refineries. He could never go back to live in Houston; there are too many bad associations there. But he has heard that Standard Oil is hiring up at their plant in Cleveland, Ohio. He wouldn't mind living up East. His sisters Florence and Hannah, and their families, live practically next door, in Indiana. A few years ago, Pop sold the glass business and moved up there, too.

He thinks he sees everything clearly now. Dee has one more year in high school. If she gets an office today, he won't say anything to rock the boat, but will hold off telling her his thoughts. After all, he may get cold feet before it's all over with, or jobs up in Cleveland may not pay enough to suit him. Best not to get Dee's hopes up too soon. But if he does go to work at a refinery in Cleveland, then he'll contact Dee about going to college nearby.

On the other hand, if she doesn't get an office, and her whole world is shattered, maybe he'll throw caution to the winds, take her in his arms and say, "How about coming to live with Daddy, Dee?" That will turn her sadness into joy. And somehow, regardless of the job situation, he will find a way to make everything come out right for them.

By now, Dan is so eager to begin making up for lost time with his daughter, he is half wishing she will not get an office. What is it, anyway? A little high school drill team. They probably have something similar there in Cleveland....

The stage is set up with a wooden lectern, front and center, and a semicircle of folding chairs behind it. A large arrangement of fresh flowers sits at the base of the lectern, and a tall stack of white envelopes waits on top. The sight of those envelopes makes Dan's heart turn over.

Three people are seated up there, two men and one woman. The woman wears a dark tailored dress with a belted waist and crisp white collar. She has a flinty smile on her face as she chats with the rakish-looking man with dark hair and moustache, seated next to her. Dan takes the woman to be the Sponsor—he can't recall her name for now; starts with an L, he thinks. "A formidable spinster, whom no girl in her right mind would cross," Allie described the woman in her letter. "Brigade is apparently her whole life," she said. In truth she puts him in mind of his drill sergeant at Camp Polk, strutting around, dressing down recruits until they felt so reduced their trousers might slide off. And all the while they were being trained on toy wooden rifles—there being a shortage of munitions at the moment—to face an enemy who had real and lethal guns. It was how the war was fought. One day at a time, improvising as they went along. Putting aside all the horrors that were best forgotten, this part of being an Army soldier—the unpredictability of the proposition—had a certain appeal for Dan, and taught him a little about himself and what he wanted out of life. He had come home determined that he was not going to bury himself in that tomb on Congress Avenue that had consumed Pop's whole life. Vinia would just have to—

Realizing his mind had wandered off, now he shifts again, clenches his jaw, wishing for an aspirin or two. But he'll never get through all these people and out of here, to find a drinking fountain, then get back in time—

A whistle blows crisply. Conversations in the audience die down as a small corps of bagpipe players rise and tune up to play. Girls in their Scottish uniforms, hands at their sides, begin filing down both aisles, two by two, spacing their steps, then taking their places in rows that are roped off in front. After about the first couple of dozen, Dee appears alongside a partner in the doorway to his right, her head held high, her eyes facing straight ahead, her shoulders squared. Dan all but swoons at the sight of her. She looks so much like her mother it is as if Vinia had just walked through the door of the auditorium and stood there. *Oh Vinia, if you could only see our little girl at this moment!* Until now Dan has only seen a photograph of Dee in her uniform, her snare drum belted on her waist. He has nearly worn out the picture, showing it to his buddies at work. But today there is a radiance about Dee that no photograph could capture: her eyes luminous, cheeks rosy; her shiny brown waves framing her face underneath that slanted, feathered hat. And there is something more, he thinks, searching for the way to describe it. Proud. Yes, that is how she looks. As if wearing that uniform makes her more proud than anything in the world. She never said, *Daddy, I feel proud of being in the Scottish Brigade.* But he can sure see that now. Suddenly he wonders how he could have ever wished she would not get an office today, regardless of the reason.

With her mouth turned up ever so slightly at the edges, Dee seems the soul of composure, ready for whatever comes. But he knows, if he could see up close, her mouth is trembling. He knows that inside she is a jumble of fears and expectations— *Please, God, she has lost so much in her life, there must be a card with her name on it somewhere in that stack of envelopes!*

Now, at the proper interval Dee and her partner step off and start down the aisle. Dan soon loses his daughter in the sea of red and green plaid. The sight of all these young girls assembling in their colorful kilts and scarves, and cloud-white spats, increasing in number until they seem like a whole battalion, makes his throat swell with pride. Not a one looks any more capable than his Dee, though, he thinks stubbornly. Not a one is more composed. Suddenly he dreads what is to come, and wishes it would never have to happen. God almighty, how is he going to make it through this thing?

A few minutes later, the retiring officers, all wearing party dresses and high heeled shoes, have been seated. Six of them, with bouquets of roses draped over their arms, are up on the stage in the semi-circle of chairs, each leaving an empty seat beside her. Will Dee get to go up and sit in one of those? Well, even if not, there are lots more offices to be given out. The stack of envelopes is high. Dee will do herself proud, no matter what office she gets. And even if it's a low one, he'll make over her as if he thinks it's the greatest thing in the world. *My Dee....*

Of course, if she doesn't get an office at all—he thinks, hope rising again as he remembers the surprise he has waiting just in case. But no—

Now the Sponsor is standing at the lectern, speaking in a brisk tone, setting out the goals of the organization. He pays little attention to her words, but he sees what Allie was talking about. Without a doubt she is rigid and exacting; she would not brook any weakness...such as a girl fainting during a performance. Dan's heart sags. He imagines the stack of envelopes going down, and down, without Dee's name ever being called.

The Sponsor takes her seat. The young girl to her immediate left in the circle of chairs rises to her feet, the skirt of her pretty dress puffing like a cloud around her. She is small-boned, with a head of full blond hair, and straight posture. She has a pleasant expression on her face. She is undoubtedly the top officer. A pregnant hush comes over the audience. The sense of anticipation is palpable. Dan can hardly get his breath. His knees are banging against each other, and his fingers have a death grip on the brim of the hat resting on his lap. *Calm down. This is just the first one. There are many more to go, he tells himself. All those envelopes....*

The girl steps up to the lectern and flashes an all-American smile at the audience, then picks up the envelope at the top of the stack. She lifts the envelope flap, then gazes out at the audience. "The new Colonel is...." she begins with a firm but feminine voice. She reaches for the card inside. It is a tight fit. As she works the card all the way out, it is all Dan can do not to leap up on the stage and help her. Finally she pulls it free. She unfolds the card and silently reads the name on it. Her face lights up in a broad smile. She looks out at the audience. Head held high, she calls the name clearly.

The audience goes wild. The pulse is throbbing so hard behind Dan's temples, he is not sure he heard the name right. Maybe— *And he is waiting and waiting, watching the stack of envelopes dwindle....*

Then, amidst all the shrieks and applause, he sees his daughter bolt up from her chair and make her way toward the aisle, the girls she passes grabbing her hands all along the way. *Look at all those girls who love my daughter, and are happy for her!* In a flash she is in the aisle and bounding up the stairs to the stage, her kilt and scarf flying, her hands pressed to her cheeks. Dee and the retiring Colonel hold out their arms and reach for each other, and then they are locked in an embrace, dancing around. The audience continues cheering. Dan cannot tell if Dee is crying or laughing. Probably a little of both. His heart swells. *Colonel. Colonel of the Scottish Brigade. My Dee...of course I knew all along....* Tears are running down his face. The girls retreat to their chairs, and as the new Colonel is fitted with all her regalia, the next retiring officer steps up to the lectern. Dee is hidden from her father's view.

Dan expels a soughing breath, and comes down to earth. He feels a stab of loneliness deeper than any he has experienced since he lost Vinia. For now, Dee will not be coming to live with him; and somehow, he has an instinct that he has waited too long to make right his mistake of leaving her behind. With that trip down the aisle and up those stairs to the stage, Dee has gone beyond his reach forever.

Chapter 15

Oh my. Colonel of the Scottish Brigade. Colonel *Delys Lithingate*, of the Scottish Brigade, of Stephen F. Austin High School, of Houston, Texas. I did feel, even before stepping down from the stage after all the envelopes had been opened and all the names called, and the ceremony was finally over, that I had ceased to breathe the same air as before. I felt as if I had been transformed into some high, ethereal being, so fragile that if I took a false step the spell would be broken and I would shatter into pieces like glass.

I had not ruined my chances after all. It seemed a miracle. Taking my hand, and with a stiff, off-center smile, Miss Lytle had said bracingly, "Congratulations, Delys. Let's make it a great year!" I wanted to bow down before her in gratitude. I would go to the ends of the earth to deliver on the promise she had seen in me.

When I got home that evening I went into my room and closed the door. I stood before my dresser mirror and gazed at my uniformed figure. On my shoulders were white fringed epaulets, with a looped braid draping down over the left upper arm of my jacket. On each side of my high stand-up collar sprouted brass eagles with spreading wings: the Colonel's traditional insignia, enameled in white. Below my waist hung a curled horsehair sporran, with a small purse of good luck trinkets from previous colonels concealed on the back side. Around my neck hung a silver whistle on a long white braided lanyard.

I took my whistle in my left hand. I snapped up my right arm, at an exact right angle, as though in readiness to give a command. I had given my first official command— to dismiss the new Brigade— at the end of Installation. I could not see myself then. Now. This was what it looked like to be Colonel Delys Lithingate....

What it looked like. I sank down on the dresser bench, fingering the shiny surface of the whistle, thinking. A colonel of Brigade was colonel all the time, and not just when she was wearing this uniform. Scholarship. Conduct. Character.... If high standards of behavior were expected of every member of the drill team, yet more was expected of the girl who led them.

A colonel did not stay home on a Sunday morning, feigning illness, and sneak out with her boyfriend. How close Bruce and I had come to crossing the age-old line from safety into hazard the last time we sat in his car together, under the shade of the newly-budding branches of Forest Park trees. His warm fingers had stolen under my skirt hem and traced halfway up my thigh before I—. Or—was it possible? Had we *done it* after all? I wondered, seized with fright, my face and neck burning. Of course not, how ridiculous! Yet...how easily it could happen before we even realized. And then one day, to the Sponsor who exemplified fine character, "*Miss Lytle, I'm pregnant.*" It would be a heavy stone cast into the pond, the ultimate descent, unforgivable shame brought down on the whole organization. And Miss Lytle would rue the day she took a chance and awarded me, out of all the many qualified candidates, the highest office. If she knew what I had been doing with Bruce in the Forest Park Cemetery, or even the way I sneaked telephone calls to him when Allie was unaware, she would regret her choice.

I had to break up with Bruce. I must not ever see him again.

Feeling shaken but nonetheless resolute, as one would feel when realizing some deeply ingrained, hazardous addiction must be broken or death was certain, I rose from the bench and opened the top drawer of my chest of drawers. I gathered up the socks and stockings and scarves I usually kept there, and heaped them all on the bed. I would reserve this drawer for my new regalia. As I began removing each article from my uniform and laying it reverently inside, I felt that somehow I had already besmirched my office. But no. I was Colonel starting today. My year as Colonel must and would be unimpeachable.

The problem was, when and how to go about breaking up with Bruce. Write him a letter? That would be the least painful for me, but it seemed wrong when he was powerless to write back in response. Should I telephone him? Yet I featured him innocently picking up the phone, anxious to hear whether or not I had gotten an office—he had taken such an interest over the months, always reassuring me as only Bruce could do—and all the while I— No. The best and fairest way would be to tell him in person. Yet, he would not be back in Houston until August. If I waited that long, it would mean dragging this burden around for practically the whole length of summer drill. And then, Bruce would have come all this way thinking we would be together like two lovers, only to be told that everything had changed, and it was all over. Oh, it did seem to me then that everything had changed; even my feelings toward him. *I don't love Bruce anymore*, I told myself, and was terrified at how quickly I could fall out of love with a person who had meant so much to me, for so long. A person who had never failed to honor me and respect my feelings, and love me in return. *He is taking care of my dog*, I recalled with a start. Would he abandon Rusty out of spite? Surely not. Bruce wasn't the kind of person who would do harm to a helpless animal. I thought of Rusty, waiting for Bruce to come home from school in the afternoons, as he used to wait for me. It made me sick at heart.

Eventually I concluded that I would have to break up with Bruce over the telephone, and the sooner the better. But how I dreaded it. I reasoned that it might well be days and days before I had an opportunity, in which time I could work up my courage, think how best to put my decision into words that he would understand and that would persuade him to forgive me. For I did want Bruce's forgiveness. I could not bear the thought that he might spend the rest of his life hating me.

After supper Daddy came over, and we sat out on the Fletcher porch together until well after dark. Daddy had to head back to California first thing in the morning, and report for work on Tuesday—such a short stay, between two legs of a long and exhausting journey, and all for me. And of course I had to go to school in the morning; tomorrow was Friday.

The porch occupied one whole corner of the Fletcher house front, under the tall sloping roof, and was framed in iron filigree railing. Sitting out there on the top step, our thighs touching, with a bright moon and a scattering of stars gradually lighting up the sky, I felt a strong sense of kinship with Daddy that I had not felt since before Mama died.

Daddy revealed to me many of the thoughts and feelings he had experienced as he waited out the opening of the envelopes that afternoon. He told me he was struck to see how much I looked like Mama. "The sight of you almost took my breath away, Dee," he said, his eyes glassy. He grabbed my hand in his and gave it a tight squeeze.

We talked about visiting the Pleasant Hill Cemetery next time Daddy came to Houston, a promise we had made to each other right after Mama died but had postponed repeatedly. Except for a moment of dread when I considered how close that excursion would take me to where Bruce was, I found myself eager to visit Mama's grave, and imagined conveying to her from my heart the news of the day. How proud she would be! After that we swapped a few stories about life with Mama, even laughing sometimes as we recalled funny moments; whereas before, we had always found it too painful to talk about the happy days when Mama was alive.

Daddy was unaware that I had continued to be in contact with Bruce after Allie ordered me to stop, let alone that for a year I had been sneaking off to be with him. He felt so strongly that I should abide by my aunt's wishes as long as I lived in her home, he would most certainly have taken her side. Now that I was feeling so close to Daddy, though, I was tempted to make a full confession to him. He would certainly approve of my decision to bring the relationship with Bruce to a close, I reasoned. But then I decided it would be best to keep the whole matter to myself. Why should I risk Daddy being disappointed in me on this night of all nights, when he was obviously as proud of his daughter as ever a father could be? Besides, I felt confident that we would never again retreat from each other, but only grow closer. So it was easy to imagine the day would come when I would make that confession freely. And Daddy would understand, I just knew he would.

Around nine o'clock we hugged and kissed and said goodbye, both of us teary-eyed. Daddy drove off, the moonlight catching his salute to me from his truck window. I watched as the head lamps of the truck made elongated beams all the way down to where the street curved at the end of the block, then he made his turn onto North Macgregor Way and disappeared from view. I did not want him to go away. I had not felt like this since the night he left me for the first time, my belongings having been unloaded from his truck and deposited in my new room at the Fletchers'. Of course, then I was heartbroken because he refused to take me away with him. Now, I would not have given up my life in Houston for anything in the world. Colonel of the Scottish Brigade. *What if this is only a dream, and I wake up in the morning to remember instead how that stack of envelopes vanished without my name ever having been called?*

Still, it saddened me that Daddy was going off alone to spend the night at a tourist court. He had barely even stepped inside the Fletcher house when he arrived tonight, just long enough to say hello and ask Allie to tell me he was here.

First period on Friday was sheer euphoria, with Brigadiers hugging one another and chattering happily, and not much else. I still felt as though I were floating on air. However, I could not help noticing the stoic looks on the faces of the girls whose names were not called out from the stage. *That could easily have been me*, I thought soberly. I did not know if I should go over and hug those unlucky girls, many of whom I knew personally. Would they appreciate the gesture? Or would they feel I was patronizing them? I asked myself how I would feel in their shoes, and decided I'd probably rather be left alone, at least at this early point. So I kept my distance, and resolved to find a way to make some kind gesture toward each one during the coming year.

Did I carry through? I wonder now. I think possibly I did with a few, but certainly not with every girl. Which does not mean that eventually I became indifferent. Quite the contrary. I was present at most Installations over the years that I taught, and those girls who were passed over for an office never failed to evoke my sympathy. I always made a point of offering a word of encouragement whenever the opportunity arose. After all, each girl was still a very important part of the organization. Eventually there would come a brief period when it was my duty to help select new officers. No one ever knew how I agonized, often losing sleep, or how hard it was to look certain Brigadiers in the eye when the final decisions had been made before Installation Day, and know they would be disappointed.

Soon first period was over, and all the rest of the day my stomach churned as I thought of having to call Bruce. I must have changed my mind twenty times. I didn't have to break up with him, did I? We could be careful, somehow.... But I always came back to the same conclusion. Any way I looked at it, sneaking around was wrong, and particularly unbecoming to one who held my office. I could not help but feel thankful it would probably be a while before I could make the call.

Friday night there were slumber parties for every corps, and the new Lt. Colonel of Records—the only one of the top officers who had use of a car—took several of us from house to house, visiting, before we finally wound up in her living room and fell into a dead sleep on blankets and pillows spread out on the floor. I never gave Bruce a thought.

But then, returning home on Saturday morning I found a note on the kitchen table from Allie, addressed, "To the new Colonel—". I remembered her standing outside the auditorium after Installation, with Logan and my grandparents. Allie was beside herself with joy. She hugged me tightly and pressed her wet cheek to mine. All around, Brigadiers were gratefully embracing their "Brigade moms," as the mothers were affectionately known. Like those women, Allie had sacrificed her time and energy, transporting Brigadiers by the carload to all the places we needed to be; making sure my uniform was picked up from the dry cleaners; that my spats were bleached snow white, and loose buttons were sewn fast. The list went on, and I was grateful. Yet I would never accept Allie even as my surrogate mother, no matter what she had done for me. Besides, my gratitude was tempered in that moment by my sharp awareness that Allie had robbed me of Bruce's presence on what had turned out to be the most important day of my life.

As I struggled to find the proper words to thank her while remaining aloof as I always did, I noticed Daddy waiting alone several yards away, his hat held politely in his hands. He looked a little awkward as he—all too obviously— avoided an encounter with Mama's relatives. And it brought home how they had snubbed him all these years. I turned away from my aunt and hurried to where he was.

Not until those conversations with Allie during her long illness, years later, would I express my gratitude for her support while I was in Brigade. Far too late, of course, and it probably seemed a little staged. As if I were checking off my list of obligations before she passed from this world into the next. Which, of course, I was, though not without feeling. She responded in a dry tone with one word: "Well." Then she followed up with an ironic smile. As I have implied, such was the nature of our exchanges. I remember her clouded eyes above the smile had grown large in proportion to her face, the disease having emaciated her flesh. The private duty nurse appeared at the door then, in her starched white cap and Sani-White shoes, the rubber soles as silent as cat paws. It was time for Allie's medicine. This was near the end.

The note from Allie that Saturday morning after Installation conveyed that she and my uncle had gone for a drive to Kerrville, to visit friends there. "We'll probably be late getting back this evening— nine o'clock or so. Be sure to turn on the porch light for us."

I'm not ready, I thought, feeling I had suddenly been given a shove toward the telephone. On the other hand, I had all day and most of the evening to call Bruce. First I needed to get busy on homework assignments that were due on Monday. I lay down across my bed and opened my U.S. History book. Yet I could only stare blankly at the page, the words running together as I thought of reciting Bruce's number to the long distance operator, trying to marshal my courage and arrange in my mind the words that I must say to him.

At three o'clock, feeling all but overcome with anxiety, I picked up the receiver, realizing as soon as I did so that calling Bruce collect in order to break up with him would obviously add insult to injury. I returned the receiver to the cradle and buried my face in my hands. What to do? I probably had enough money in my purse to talk for a few minutes on a public telephone. The nearest one was within walking distance—at the gas station and ice house up at the corner of Lawndale and Wayside, at the edge of the neighborhood. But what if I ran out of money when we were halfway through the conversation? Or, what if someone approached to make a call, and stood there waiting impatiently for me to finish?

How ironic, I thought. This was the first occasion when I had plenty of time to sit at home and talk to Bruce, without fear of being interrupted. Yet I would have given anything to avoid it.

I picked up the telephone. I dialed the long distance operator. Within less than a minute Bruce picked up and accepted the charges. My heart seemed to contract into a knot, and my knees quivered violently.

"Delys? Hey, well what happened? How'd you come out?"

The sound of his voice, carrying all the anxiousness I knew he had felt for me, nearly brought me to tears. After a prolonged pause, I said, "I've been made Colonel, Bruce. It's the highest honor I've ever–"

"Wow, that's great! Hey, Dad, Delys got Colonel of her drill team. It's the top office." A pause. Doc's deep voice booming in the background. He was happy for me, too. "Dad says, congratulations. Oh Delys, I just knew you'd get something real high—"

I struggled to squeeze out the words. "Bruce, I—I have to talk to you. Can you—I mean—is Doc right there?"

"Naw, he went on upstairs. We just got in from the office," he said. Did I only imagine the new ring of confidence in Bruce's voice? He was engaged in something important, too, by golly. "What is it, hon?" he asked sweetly.

Whether it was the endearment he used—sometimes in the car, he would call me hon, or babe, and it would send a thrill up and down my body—or just the fact that the full weight of what I was about to do was finally registering emotionally, I started to cry. Haltingly, I tried as best I could to explain to Bruce the position I found myself in. "It isn't what I want, you understand?" I hastened to add. Suddenly I was no longer sure I did not love Bruce anymore, was not even sure what I was doing was right. But then again I thought of all that could happen if I did not break up with Bruce.

His voice hollow with astonishment, the note of confidence abruptly gone, Bruce said, "But it's not like we get to see each other all that often—"

"I know. It's what we do when we are together. And the fact that—"

"But we'll be careful—"

"I don't trust us, Bruce. Besides, it's the fact that—"

"Well we can at least talk on the phone, anyway," he said. Then as I could not quite get my voice past the lump in my throat, he added plaintively, "Can't we?"

Feeling like the lowest kind of heel, I let out a breath. "I wish we could, I really do. But you see, we can't talk without me sneaking around, and that's what I can't do any more, Bruce. Sneak around. It isn't right. Please try to understand. Being Colonel changes everything."

For a few moments he was silent, as if he were letting this sink in. "But what about your helping me, sometimes, Delys? When I have trouble getting something right? You know how much it means," he said finally, and the strain of alarm in his voice made me feel lower than ever.

"I—I know, Bruce. Maybe you can find someone up there to help you," I suggested. After all, I could not have been that much help to Bruce, not when our phone conversations were so erratic. We were very lucky if we talked once a week. Usually it was every other week or so. Bruce needed to believe in himself more, that was all.

Again, he did not answer right away. Then, his voice so low and tight that I could literally feel the gulf now spreading between us, he said, "I don't need any help. Never mind."

Only then did I recognize my cruelty. Not only was I leaving Bruce stranded, which was bad enough; worse, I was humiliating him by proposing he find help in that small community, where the tutor would surely be thinking—and maybe even remarking to others—Isn't it a shame, Bruce's sister and brother were so much smarter than he is. And if that person came to Bruce's house–as Mama often went to the home of a student she was tutoring, when Daddy was working nights and he slept during the day—she might figure out Doc was drinking, and spread the word. Bruce had never told me Doc had stopped drinking altogether. I had only hoped this was the case, now that Bruce was going to be a doctor.

If you were to ask me what is the worst thing I have done in my life, the answer would not be that I broke off my relationship with Bruce. The worst thing I have done is abandon Bruce in his struggle to make his greatest dream come true. That is nothing short of a crime because I destroyed a part of him, and I will never forgive myself. *"...find someone up there to help you,"* I suggested at the tail end of that misbegotten phone call. Bruce must have wondered if he had ever really known me at all.

"Bruce, I'm so sorry. Please forgive me, and try to understand. I can't do anything about this. I really can't," I said, then I found myself heading for the coward's exit. I told him that my aunt had just driven up in the driveway. "I will always treasure what we–" I quickly began to assure him.

But then the operator came back on the line. Bruce had hung up.

Chapter 16

I never felt right about what I did to Bruce. Whenever I reflected on our telephone conversation, which I was condemned to do, time and again, I could see his troubled eyes staring through me as if we had been standing in the same room together, face to face. Lying in bed at night, unable to sleep, I would stare at the ceiling, his words of an earlier time haunting me: "*...as long as I have you...I could do just about anything.*" My callous suggestion that he go elsewhere for help most likely ensured that he would never forgive me.

The spring semester drew to a close. Summer drill began. Whenever I stood in the midst of Brigadiers arriving on the campus, and gave the command to assemble, or issued the command of dismissal at the end, Bruce would cross my mind. And in between, his face would loom in my peripheral vision as if he were standing at the curb, watching.

I missed him. Missed knowing he loved me and was always there for me. The source of reassurance and comfort that I had taken away from him, I had also robbed of myself. My fellow officers all had steady boyfriends. At slumber parties when we sat around talking about the vicissitudes of being in love, I had nothing to contribute to the conversation. There was nothing new about this, of course, but now I could not even savor the secret happy knowledge that I cared for someone more sensitive and loving than any of the boys being talked about, and he cared for me; that this someone would be on the other end of the telephone line in a day or two, and would come for me at the back of the park on certain Sundays, and we'd speed away in his car. Well, I deserved it, I told myself. Then my mind would go back to the cogent reasons I had broken up with Bruce, and temporarily I would feel justified. But it was never long before my sense of guilt returned.

After a few weeks it occurred to me that I might have asked Bruce if we could stop being in contact only until I had fulfilled the obligation of my new office, rather than breaking up altogether. How unfortunate this possibility had not crossed my mind either before or during our conversation. When I picked up the phone to call Bruce, I still thought I had fallen out of love with him. Yet, hearing his voice, I found myself less sure. What a perfect juncture to get my bearings and turn in a different direction.

Of course, I consoled myself, Bruce might have suggested a temporary parting, yet he had not.

Thinking of this now, I cannot help but observe that the length of a year stretching out before a teenager is like an eternity; it is only as we grow older that the span appears to shorten. I wonder if this youthful perception inhibited my ability at the outset to conceive of a more sensible solution than severing my relationship to Bruce. I honestly do not know. I only know the sense of urgency I felt at the time, to live up to the honor that had been bestowed upon me.

As the first of August rolled around, I regretted as never before that we would not be seeing each other when Bruce drove his father down for the summer conference. Now that I had broken up with him, I could not quite believe that we had behaved so dangerously after all, when we were together; and anyway, it was only for two hours. Two hours, three times a year was all we ever had together. Why was it so wrong? No, it wasn't wrong, I thought mutinously. It was Allie who had been wrong, in coming between us.

The conferences were customarily held the third weekend of the month. As the days on the August calendar melted away one by one, I felt more and more inclined to take advantage of the opportunity to rectify my mistake. I would simply telephone the Rice Hotel and ask to be rung through to Doc's room. I would tell Bruce how much I missed him, and regretted what I had done. I would ask if he could forgive me, then wait to resume seeing me after my year as Colonel. Oh yes, that was the thing to do. Already I felt better.

Yet...what if Doc answered? He surely resented me. He might remember with insult how I had telephoned collect to break up with Bruce. I would brace myself and ask for Bruce. And if Doc recognized my voice and hung up in my ear...well...I would have to figure out my next step from there. For I was now determined to get Bruce back and never let him go again. Stupid me! That's what I would say: *"Bruce, I've been stupid. Forgive me, please!"* And he would, I knew that he would.

I had no choice but to make the call while my aunt and uncle were away from the house so, unfortunately, even that would be sneaking around. Well, I would have to live with that. After all, it was only to suggest to Bruce the logical arrangement that I surely would have suggested before, if only I had not felt panic-stricken. Bruce and Doc usually arrived late on Friday evening, so Saturday morning would be a good time to call. Logan worked on most Saturday mornings, so it was unlikely I would have to worry about him. I had to hope that Allie would leave for a while.

I slept poorly that Friday night, and when I woke up on Saturday Allie was not in the house. I dressed quickly and walked out on the back porch. From there I could see if her car was in the detached garage. Spotting it there, I concluded she had gone for her morning walk. But I had no idea how long she had been gone. I hurried back inside, and sat down on the telephone bench. I looked up the Rice Hotel number in the directory, then picked up the telephone and dialed. I was so nervous that my tongue felt lashed to the bottom of my mouth.

"Dr. Peter Buckstrum, please. I don't know his room number," I said.

"One moment, please," said the hotel operator. And the next thing I knew, the phone was ringing. *"Bruce, forgive me, I've changed my mind...."* Abruptly I remembered how I had felt when I decided to break up with Bruce, how I thought I did not love him anymore. What if my reawakened affections did not last out the year? Would it be fair to tie up Bruce for all that time, only to disappoint him at the end? I asked myself. Then, in the next breath I realized that what I was about to do was cheap and disrespectful. I should have asked him to wait in the first place. And there was another question teasing at the edge of my mind that I would rather have ignored, because I did not want to know the answer: Could I truly respect Bruce if he was willing to take me back now?

On the second ring, Doc answered. My heart froze. I hung up.

With the Opening Day performance approaching—how hard it was to believe a whole year had passed since the crisis that marked the last one—Miss Lytle came to oversee the last few sessions of summer drill. Over the summer I had gradually developed confidence in my ability to lead. But now that she was present I felt ill-at-ease. When Miss Lytle and I stood off to the side conferring, I would remember how I used to dream of one day being drawn into her privileged orbit. Yet I was so frightened of misinterpreting her instructions, or making some unintelligent remark, that I could only be thankful when we parted.

Nonetheless, Opening Day went as smoothly as I could have hoped, bringing a nod of approval from our Sponsor. And the first few football performances were stellar: the lines blade straight, the formations without fault, the music and dancing as crisp and precise as ever. I was deeply proud, and it seemed a miracle every time I heard my name over the loudspeaker as we entered the broad green field, shimmering under the bright klieg lights, the crowds cheering: *"...under the leadership of Colonel Delys*

Lithingate...."

Then, near the end of October, came the fall seminar that would once again bring Bruce and his father to Houston. Its approach preoccupied me for days as I talked myself in and out of making the call I had failed to complete in August. On that Friday night we had a home game; I have long since forgotten the team we played or even if we won. I remember our treading in single file down from the stands as half-time approached, pausing on the ground to cross arms, lock hands, and recite the traditional good luck chant, *sotto voce*; then lining up in companies under the stadium on the north end of the field. There we waited in the semi-darkness, and I watched until Miss Lytle signaled from her position out along the track that it was time to move onto the field. I remember our eyes meeting, then the discreet wave of her hand. My left hand closed around my whistle below my waist. My right arm went up to signal Brigade, first to mark time, then to march. I remember our emerging silently from under the stadium into the shock of the bright lights, then coming to a halt just behind the goal post, where we waited to be announced. I remember my awareness—always stirring—that we moved as one.

Standing there in the interim, I heard a deep voice call from somewhere off to the side and above, "Delys!" A chill went down my spine. Bruce. I knew it was him and with all my heart I wanted to turn and look. Yet the rule prohibiting a Brigadier from averting her gaze on the performance field was so thoroughly drilled into me that my eyes remained locked ahead. I was immediately distracted, nevertheless, as doubt followed certainty and I argued back and forth in my head about whether it was actually my name I had heard. Had I only imagined Bruce calling out to me because he had been so much on my mind? Or—

Abruptly I heard Miss Lytle bark loudly: "GO!"

My eyes widened in alarm. I had not even been conscious of the announcement over the loudspeaker, or the cheers that had invariably broken out. My right arm snapped up and I raised the whistle to my mouth: one long tweet; one short, my arm swinging down on the second tweet. The bugles blared. The drums thundered. Soon I was stepping off. Somehow my feet moved forward to the beat although they did not feel as if they were coming into contact with the ground beneath me. I could hardly think what to do from one step to the next. My body seemed to move on its own volition, like a wind-up toy. I remember how high was the wind that night, how it tossed our hat ribbons and whipped up our long scarf tails as the bagpipe music flared and the dancing commenced; I remember the sound of the flags snapping behind me as they were buffeted like the masts of sailing ships.

Then, suddenly it was all over and we were exiting the field. Performances always seemed breathtakingly short.

Afterward, when we had filed back into the stands, it was all I could do to keep from looking this way and that, in hopes I might spot Bruce. But such overt conduct would have been unbecoming to a colonel even if I had not already raised the ire of Miss Lytle; and besides, even if I spotted Bruce, I could not acknowledge him until Brigade was dismissed at the end of the game.

We took our seats on the bleachers. While Brigadiers all around eagerly unscrewed the lids on thermos bottles of steaming cocoa brought from home—our traditional after-performance treat—I could only sit with my hands in my lap, still agonizing over whether it actually had been Bruce calling to me, or rather my wish that he would be here playing a trick. Could it have been some other boy calling out another name, distorted as it was carried on the chill October breeze sweeping across the field? But no, I did not think so, and whenever I turned over in my mind the sound of Bruce's voice, I believed there may have been desperation in it. Had I turned to acknowledge him, would he have said more? *"Delys! I need to talk to you, please! It's important."*

All weekend I anguished. By Sunday morning I could take it no longer. I stayed home from church to boldly call Bruce at the Rice Hotel, only to be told there was no Doctor Peter Buckstrum registered. I was so taken by surprise that I could see dots before my eyes. Certain there must be some mistake, I asked the operator to check again, that Doctor Buckstrum was attending a conference there. And so she did, but to no avail. "Some of the doctors have already checked out," she said. "Sorry." She hung up. And indeed, some emergency may have cropped up at home in Overton, I realized.

Just in case, I waited until the usual time of my meetings with Bruce, then stood cautiously at the back of Idylwood park, watching for his car. If Bruce came I would not go off to the cemetery with him, or so I told myself, but just lean near his open car window and ask if everything was alright. But Bruce did not come. What had possessed me to believe he might discern that I would be waiting for him? So then I was left feeling both concern for Bruce and let down that I had not been able to respond to him, plus a sense of guilt for having sneaked around yet again. I felt my life was going around in circles. I must get hold of myself.

On Monday morning, Miss Lytle met with the Majors and me at her desk as usual, to discuss the performance just passed, and lay out plans for the next one. She made no comment about my distraction of Friday night, but I knew it was coming—another preoccupation of the tortured weekend. Although she had been able to get my attention and—thank goodness—avert disaster, she was going to demand an explanation as to why she had been forced to act.

Since school started I had met with Miss Lytle in her office on a number of occasions—including one in which I explained in great detail what had really caused my fainting spell that time. Though she was not generous in conversation and I never felt quite sure where I stood with her, at least I had begun to feel a little easier around her. Until today.

When the meeting was over, and the Majors went out to join their corps and begin teaching their part of the next performance, she looked at me solemnly. "Sit down," she said.

My stomach roiling, I took a chair in front of her desk. My glance took in the wall behind, filled with framed pictures of Brigade arranged in various formations over the five years since Miss Lytle had started it: a gallery of her pride and joy. There were individual studio portraits of each of the four top officers preceding me, lined up in a row. How poised and dignified they all appeared, how confident. As though they never experienced the struggles in life that I did, never wondered what was right, or made significant blunders. As close as I had come to wreaking disaster on Friday night, would Miss Lytle be proud to add my picture to these four one day?

She folded her hands on her desk and leaned near. "Well? What happened out there?" she asked, her brow lifted imperiously.

My eyes cast down in shame, my palms turned up, I said in a trembling voice, "I heard my name called. It was—I think—a boy I knew in New London." I looked up at her. "I liked him. A lot," I said, tears forming behind my eyes.

She thought about this. "He came down to see you perform?"

"I—I guess so. But his father is a doctor. Bruce comes into Houston with him three times a year, for a conference," I told her. "He wants to be a doctor too, you see," I added after a pause, though that was entirely beside the point. I just liked giving Bruce credit for his aspirations.

Miss Lytle frowned. "He didn't wait to say hello, after the game?"

I shook my head. I had a date, which complicated matters once the boy had joined me to walk to the parking lot. It was hard to search for Bruce in the crowd without being obvious. "No. You see, I broke up with him." I took in a breath. "Months ago."

I wished I had said more vaguely, "Long ago." I was sure it was obvious that I cared for Bruce a great deal. I could only imagine the calculations Miss Lytle must be making behind her laser-like gaze.

After a long moment she said, as though in dismissal, "Well then." She picked up a paper from her desk and started to read. I rose from my chair, feeling at loose ends. I should have said more, and might have done so if she had only shown any interest, or empathy. As I started out the door, she added without looking up, "Be sure your next boyfriend knows better than to call out to you when you're on the field."

I nearly broke down then. I wanted to defend Bruce and say that he would not have come to the stadium and called out to me unless he had good reason, especially since I had broken up with him; and that I had a strong instinct that my failure to turn to him might have left him stranded in some way that I may never become aware of.

"Yes, ma'am," I said tightly. And I concluded—oh, how naively!—*"You have never been in love."*

I won't ever have a "next" boyfriend, I thought, and in this regard I was wise beyond my years.

Chapter 17

I have come to be wary of second chances in life. Often enough, one will seem to emerge, perhaps at what appears a more opportune moment than the first time. Yet complications inevitably arise that were nonexistent before, because life never stands still. I am thinking now how much better the outcome would have been if Daddy had realized after Mama's death that nothing was more important than our staying together. I was already twelve years old, for heaven's sake. We could have had...maybe...five or so years together. How unfortunate that Daddy didn't stop to reason, *My Dee will be in college in a few years; how can I let her go now?* Well, I have no business pointing my finger. How much better the outcome would have been for Bruce and me if I had only asked him to wait in the wings while I completed my term as Colonel, rather than breaking up with him?

But to Daddy—. When he called to say he was moving to Cleveland, Ohio, and wanted me to come and live with him after graduation, my mind was still in turmoil over what happened at the football game. All I could think was that it seemed inconceivable for me to move even farther away from Bruce than where I lived already.

Only the day before, I had mailed Bruce a letter asking if he had tried to reach me at the game, as I believed, and telling him that if this were so, I was anxious to know why. I told him that I would call in a few days. Frankly, I was pretty sure that unless I wrote to him first, Bruce would not accept my telephone call. He may not even yet. What a blow that would be, yet who could blame him?

The letter required many rewrites, as I had to choose my words carefully. At first I included several paragraphs about my anguished weekend following the game, and my attempts to reach him in Houston. Then I removed them lest I leave the impression that I'd had a change of heart and wanted our relationship to return to the way it used to be. In fact, if I had been mistaken about Bruce coming to the game, he would think my letter was a cheap ploy to that end. He would believe I had been lying in the first place about my reason for breaking up with him. Perhaps he would think so anyway, I realized, but I felt I must take the risk. I could not bear to continue wondering if some crisis had befallen him. And of course, whenever the word crisis went through my mind, it was quickly followed by thoughts of Doc's drinking problem, which led me to imagine the worst.

Had Doc caused Bruce's life to come tumbling down around him for the second time? How I hoped not. Yet if so, it seemed likely that there was no one else in the world he could turn to except for me.

Having mailed my letter, I felt a little unsettled, as though I had started sneaking around again. Yet I was not asking Bruce to take me back. I was only checking on a dear friend who may be in need. As soon as I found out he was fine, I would...well...I did not know what I would do. But I had to know that he was fine.

As I hesitated on the phone perhaps longer than Daddy had hoped, he said in an injured voice, "Guess you are not interested, then."

"I— it's all so sudden—"

Hoarsely he pleaded, "It's our last chance, Dee. You're nearly grown up. You have your own life ahead. This would give us three or four years together."

"But Daddy, why do you have to go so far? We have a bunch of refineries in Houston. You could come here, and I could move in with you." In fact I had assumed I would attend college at Mama's alma mater, and the Fletchers had already invited me to live with them until I finished my degree. Daddy knew all this. If he would only move here—and the sooner, the better—it would be like a dream come true. Gone would be the need to apologize to Bruce. *Everything has changed! Daddy is moving to Houston and I'm going to live with him. Daddy would not object to our seeing each other*, I would tell him. With half the school year left, we could go out on dates like other kids. And Bruce could be in the audience when I gave away my Brigade office next spring. Admittedly, it crossed my mind that if need be, I could make Bruce's reentry into my life a condition of living with Daddy. But then I felt mean. Daddy would never stand in our way.

Yet Daddy was saying with forced patience, "I don't want to live in Houston, Dee. It's the last place on earth I want to be. Except for East Texas."

I sensed he was disappointed for needing to explain something that I would have intuited once upon a time when we used to be close. It made me feel guilty, and to miss him suddenly, achingly, and long to recapture that time. I remembered how close we had drawn to each other on just that one night, of Installation, and how I regretted saying goodbye at the end.

He went on, "Besides, my family is all up in that area now—Cleveland is no farther from Fort Wayne than Houston is from San Antonio, you know. We could spend holidays with them; wouldn't that be nice?"

I allowed that it would. Poor Daddy. His holidays had been lonely since Mama died. He often volunteered for tours at work so that others could stay home with their families.

"It would give you a chance to really get to know Pop. He won't live forever," Daddy pointed out.

And Pop was such a nice man, too, I thought warmly, so different from my grandparents the Maddens. I remembered riding around the glass factory on his shoulder, past enormous brick ovens that scared me and made me cling to his neck; remembered him saying proudly along the way, to workmen holding long iron rods with amazing bubbles of glass on the end, "This is my granddaughter, Delys." Still, I felt too conflicted to give Daddy an answer now. Nor could I speak freely of my concern about Bruce. My aunt was around the corner in the kitchen.

Yet, now that I thought about it...I had no idea where Bruce would attend college. Assuming there had been no life-changing crisis, surely he could go wherever he desired. Even Ohio. And suppose we did not get back together? I might forfeit my chance to live with Daddy, for nothing. Suddenly life seemed simple. Bruce and I had only to want to be together. Everything else would fall into place. How fortunate that I had written him. Now all I had to do was call. "Well then alright," I heard myself telling Daddy, somewhat in wonder.

After the few beats it must have taken Daddy to absorb my consent, he cheered, "Good girl! Oh, Dee, it's going to be so fine! Now I'm going on up there; I start to work week after next. I'll rent a room somewhere until you come. There is no sense wasting money on a larger place until then. Besides, you can help me decide where to move to. We might even get a house, I don't know.

"But meantime, I'll be looking into the colleges. I understand there are several up there in the Cleveland vicinity."

"Yes, fine," I said, feeling lighthearted. The whole idea was beginning to sound very exciting indeed.

Before we hung up Daddy said in a gravelly voice, "Dee, you never knew how much I've missed you. If I could have seen any way"— he hesitated for a beat or two, cleared his throat, "—why, I would have had you with me from the start. Now we've got so much to make up for; and we will, I promise."

The sincerity in his voice, and his almost palpable sense of lingering regret, flooded me with love for him. "Oh Daddy, we'll sit out on the porch together, just like we used to," I said with a catch in my voice, tears forming in my eyes.

Oh my, what a bittersweet memory that conversation is for me now, and in spite of everything that happened, I am grateful beyond words that I talked myself into saying yes to moving up north with Daddy.

Granted, I was not as thrilled as I would have been had he asked me much earlier, when he was still like a god to me, the center of my universe. Yet I would grow more and more excited as the weeks passed and the prospect became increasingly real; and we inevitably grew closer. I remember how often we would chat on the phone about our future. And how often we wrote letters, too. They all concluded, "Love you," a sentiment that seemed to mean more than ever it had since Mama died, and to reinforce the bond between us.

As I said, in spite of everything—. I have come to believe that anticipation itself is one of life's sweet blessings, and that is what Daddy and I shared. It was somewhat like the way I would later anticipate going overseas in the summers—the months beforehand of reading travel books, ordering tickets, reserving a room in some charming little inn, located in a remote village of Tuscany or Cornwall, maybe. Putting money by, a little at a time, to pay for it. Yet our anticipation was so much more special because it was ours together, the last thing Daddy and I would ever have. The memory of that golden time is an antidote to the anger that still bubbles up occasionally toward the woman who wound up destroying our plans, reminding me that although she robbed Daddy and me of so much, she could not take everything.

"Oh, Dee, it's going to be so fine!" Daddy had predicted of our new life together. And though it may sound strange, I would add that as our new life was never tested by reality, I can always believe it would have been as good as I can imagine.

I remember I could hardly wait for the upcoming long Thanksgiving weekend to arrive, when I was sure to have a chance to call Bruce. Yet, as it happened, though I tried two times, I failed to reach him. Somehow I doubted he and Doc were spending the holiday out of town. I knew they sometimes accepted an invitation for Thanksgiving dinner with the family of one of Doc's patients. Unfortunately, last year Bruce confided to me afterward that they had backed out at the last minute because Doc "wasn't up to it." Which could mean only one thing, adding to my worry now that something was seriously wrong, and ongoing.

The first of December Daddy wrote that he thought I would like Oberlin College. "I've enclosed some information that will give you an idea," he said. I put his letter aside and looked over the one-page flyer. Oberlin included a distinguished school of arts and sciences, plus a world-renowned conservatory of music—I had heard of this conservatory. Oberlin was a co-ed university, admitting students regardless of race, creed, or color, and was the first college in the United States to offer degrees to women, in 1841.

Yes, I thought with an unexpected thrill, Daddy was right. And it struck me that the name of the school was a positive omen. Going there would be a way of paying homage to my slain friend Lanelle Oberlin, who would no doubt be entering some prestigious university on full scholarship next fall, had she lived. My heart was thumping as I studied the photograph on the flyer: a stately library built of stone, with steep gables and big windows and climbing chimneys, offset by vaulting trees. I imagined myself in that picture, strolling along a shady lane with my books in my arms....

"But Dee, it's expensive," Daddy's letter continued. "And unfortunately, being off my feet for all those months last year, I got behind putting money away for your college fund. I'd like you to apply for scholarships to help us out. With your grades, surely you ought to get something."

As a matter of fact, when classes resumed after the Christmas holidays, seniors at Austin would begin meeting with the guidance counselor about filling out college enrollment applications, and applying for scholarships. Logan had already mentioned there were scholarships available from the Houston Chamber of Commerce, of which he had long been a member. "You know, with Dan being an oil field worker, subject to getting injured and being without a paycheck for long stretches, you'd be smart to get as much help as you could," he had said. It was certainly practical advice, but I had sensed Logan was leveling an insult against my father along with it so I had shrugged off the idea. Besides, tuition was free at Rice, so I would not need much money.

That night I asked my uncle to bring a scholarship application for me next time he stopped by the Chamber headquarters. By the next evening I was looking it over. According to the instruction sheet, the deadline was Monday, January 5th. Unfortunately, that was the day we returned to school after the Christmas holidays, and started finals. Well, I could manage, I supposed. I read on.... Several letters of recommendation were required; categories were listed. No problem there. And a transcript, of course, with final approval of applications pending grade averages received after the deadline.

The last requirement was to "write an essay of at least 1,000 words discussing the person, or persons, who have had the strongest influence on your life, and in what way (i.e., a parent or other relative, family friend, neighbor, teacher, employer, clergyman, etc.).

"Note: Essays submitted by the top three scholarship winners each year are published in the Chamber's *Houston* magazine, which is circulated to Chamber of Commerce offices all over Texas and beyond."

The top scholarship was for $250 per year, for four years. Otherwise, there were two scholarships awarded for $100 per year, and four, for $50 per year.

Surely two hundred and fifty dollars per year would go a long way in paying for college, no matter where I was enrolled.

Finally, stated the instructions, the decision on awarding of scholarships each year was made by an independent panel of judges composed of "five distinguished educators from Texas institutes of higher learning," and was "exclusive of any member of the Houston Chamber of Commerce or any other Chamber of Commerce chapter."

Well, this certainly seemed fair, although I could not help imagining five men in academic robes sitting high above in some hallowed academic chamber, frowning down skeptically at my essay.

The following Saturday I went to work on the project. First I had to decide whom to write about. Miss Lytle seemed a good choice, especially when I considered the fine example she set with her Scottish Brigade; yet Miss Lytle was larger than life. I did not feel I knew her well enough personally to write a thousand-word essay.

Now...on the other hand...Mrs. Hathaway had guided me in a very personal way since I wrote my first few lines of poetry. After class the next day, she had called me up to her desk and handed me my poem, "The First Day Back." The words, "Very good—Evocative," were scrawled across the top and underlined. So my instincts had been right, even though I had never written a poem before. I could hardly believe my eyes.

"I see real promise here, Delys," she said earnestly. She spoke of the vivid language, of the picture the poem evoked in her mind as she read, of the overtones of tragedy and loss that pervaded it. "Speaking of the site of the destroyed school as a 'wound'—it just went right to my heart," she said with shining eyes, pressing her fingers against her chest. Noticing she did not say "*gaping* wound," I wondered again if I might have found a better adjective.

"By the way, what happened to the school, and why did you feel someone had made fools of you?" she asked with a sympathetic frown.

Luckily, English class was right before my lunch period, which gave me time to answer her question fully that day, and later, would offer many opportunities for her to guide me further as to how to shape my life experience into poems. Pretty soon I thought of my future not only as one of teaching, but also of writing poetry. Granted, all my attempts since the first had proven discouraging. It seemed to me that a good poem should always flow out as readily as that one. I found it hard to accept the principle espoused by Mrs. Hathaway that most poems must be worked on long and hard, just like any other work of literary art. That sometimes they needed to be put away and forgotten for a long period of time, then returned to. "Now and then you get lucky— as you did on the first try—" she allowed, "but most of the time you have to rewrite and rewrite before a poem even comes close to feeling right." Mrs. Hathaway loaned me her three personal volumes of the poetry of Emily Dickinson, to study and dream on. In reading her notations scrawled in the margins as I went along, and pausing to consider lines of verse she had been moved to underscore, I felt my teacher had shared something intimate with me. And this encouraged me not to give up my own efforts.

Truth to tell, I had quickly become drawn to Mrs. Hathaway as though she were a kind of second mother. At that point I had never even heard of the word *mentor*, which I would eventually come to see as a more appropriate description. But then, deep inside I longed for someone to take the place of my mother, to be that pillar of strength and wisdom that Mama had been for me. I had never been able to find it in my heart to accept Allie to fill that role, probably because I felt she had forced herself on me. Mrs. Hathaway, on the other hand, had nurtured my innermost being.

I considered writing about both my mother and Mrs. Hathaway, tying these two strong women together in one essay.

Yet...I thought ahead. If I won a top scholarship and my essay was published in the Chamber magazine, I would be inferring that the aunt who had taken me under her roof when my mother died was less special to me than Mrs. Hathaway. Allie would most certainly wind up reading the essay, and would feel deeply insulted. No. Whatever my feelings for Allie, or lack of them, she was Mama's beloved sister. I could not do anything so injurious to her.

Feeling disappointed, nonetheless I began to formulate my thoughts on writing about my mother alone. Certainly there was a great deal I could say about Mama; how, for instance, I used to sit at the back of her classroom and observe her at work teaching, and how that inspired me to want to emulate her. I could write, too, about observing her with the children she tutored at our kitchen table, how she showed patience and sympathy, even while demanding they do the hard work of learning. I wound up jotting down more notes about Mama than I had expected. But then...the ending. I considered this carefully. I would write of her heroism that day of the explosion. I would write about how it had felt to lose her.

Yet, I dreaded writing this. And somehow I did not like the idea of some businessman strolling into a Chamber office to wait for an appointment, opening the magazine to my essay, reading a few paragraphs, then—*'Mr. so and so will see you now—'*' And the inevitable casting aside of my mother's tender story. Of course, I may not win. Still....

On Sunday afternoon I was closeted in my room, still considering my options, when Allie opened my door, her face white. "The Japanese attacked Pearl Harbor this morning," she said in a quavering voice. "It was just on the radio. Our ships have been sunk in the harbor. Many people have been killed. President Roosevelt has asked the Congress to declare war."

I could not take in the news. I had always believed our country was utterly safe from enemy invasion. How dare the Japanese attack us, and in broad daylight? And now war would be declared, for how could the Congress refuse the President's request? I struggled to grasp all this would mean, but I could not.

The doorbell rang. Aunt Allie and I waited in silence, staring at each other as if we expected someone to be waiting outside to explain the unfathomable.

Presently Uncle Logan came up behind Allie. His eyes looked vacant, as if he were in a state of shock. He touched Allie's shoulder, then gave it a gentle pat. Even in my state of distraction I could not help taking note of this. Given the fact that Logan was never in the least demonstrative toward Allie or anyone else, the ordinary gesture seemed almost intimate. Was it meant to reassure her? Of course it was. As she turned to him, I felt scared.

In a hollow voice he said, "There's to be a meeting at the Spurlocks'. Five o'clock." He looked at his watch. "It's four-thirty now. I said we'd come."

"Yes, I'll get ready," said Allie, in a breathless voice.

When I heard the back door close, I rushed to the phone bench to call Bruce—now there was still one more topic of urgency to talk over with him.

To my shock, no sooner had I placed the call than I found myself staring at my uncle's belt buckle. I had not heard Logan come through the door. How much had he overheard? My mind began to backstroke through every incriminating word of my instructions to the operator, including Bruce's number, "Overton 379." *"I'll take that, young lady!" and I am handing him the receiver.* I raised my head to face him, eyes wide with fright.

"For me?" he asked.

"N—n—no," I stammered.

"Forgot my wallet," he said, shaking his head to himself as though astounded by his forgetfulness, even with Pearl Harbor going up in flames. He turned and walked down the hall to his and Allie's room. My heart was beating like an angry fist against my chest. The operator was speaking to me now, but I could not make out what she said for the pounding in my ears. Abruptly the line went dead. I sat holding the receiver to my ear as though it were glued there, looking numbly down at my lap, until I heard the back door open then close.

I let out a breath, waited a few seconds to be sure Logan did not come back yet again, hoping he was not at that very moment reporting my strange behavior to Aunt Allie. Then I re-dialed long distance. Not surprisingly, the lines were jammed with callers.

It took me more than an hour to get the call through. And then I worried that my aunt and uncle would come through the door in the moment Bruce answered. Oh, how I hated this! No matter the consequences, I would not hang up until I had a chance to talk to Bruce. *Oh Bruce, please, please be there!*

But when the call finally went through the operator reported, "No one answers. Try again later."

Chapter 18

War was declared three days later. Everyone was immediately caught up in it. Logan volunteered to head up a campaign to sell war bonds. Allie and several neighbors drew up plans for a victory garden on the vacant corner lot next to our house. Gravely, Miss Lytle and the top officers began to devise ways for Brigade to participate in the war effort. Our uniforms would soon be six years old, and the plaid was showing wear. We had hoped to launch a fund-raising campaign in January, to order new plaid from Scotland—a major expenditure. I had enjoyed knowing that such a milestone would be part of my year as Colonel. Now the idea would have to be shelved. Brigade would make do until the war was over.

I could not help comparing the attack on Pearl Harbor to the London School explosion. The total unexpectedness. The complete devastation of property. The suddenness of lives lost; the way the lives of those who survived were altered forever. Daddy and I often talked about this in the ensuing weeks. I would have given anything to talk to Bruce, and find out if he was having similar thoughts. More and more I regretted breaking up with him, especially as every attempt to rectify that mistake failed more miserably than the one before. Often I thought of that morning in August when I could have reached Bruce if only I had not lost courage at the sound of Doc's voice on the telephone. That was as close as ever I had come to putting things right. Then the October night on the football field when I believed—and still believe—that he called to me from the sidelines. Why had I not broken a rule for once, and acknowledged him? Surely the price would have been no higher than the price I paid for my distraction. And now I had an uneasy feeling that Bruce was retreating farther and farther from me.

As the days passed and the essay deadline grew nearer, I decided the most sensible choice was to write about Mama's positive influence on my life. Somehow I would have to steel myself and get through the painful ending.

As I sat reading through my notes, trying to formulate a strong opening sentence, I was gradually overtaken by a feeling so powerful that my eyes were swimming: I had been wrong; the story behind Mama's death—the shady dealings, the failure of justice to be done—was crying out for me to write it. I felt as if Mama were standing over my shoulder willing me to recognize this opportunity and seize it.

I sat back, thinking. Had the instructions specified that the influence of the person...or, persons...on my life be a positive one? I looked back at the instruction sheet, my fingers trembling as I clutched it. No. The word *positive* did not appear. Admittedly, it was probably implied. Still.... Now I picked up on the paragraph stating that essays of the top three winners would be published in *Houston* magazine, circulated all over Texas and beyond. I thought some more. I remembered my surprise when Miss Lytle told me that she had closely followed the newspaper accounts after the explosion, and had assumed it was a terrible accident with no one to blame. Indeed, why would she—or anyone else—conclude otherwise, given the outcome of the one hearing that took place? I reasoned. And though it did not occur to me then, I cannot help thinking now how relieved people must have felt to be left with the impression that the tragedy could not have been prevented. Who would have rather believed the harder truth, that the men charged with making decisions about the school were reckless scoundrels?

The changes in the laws that resulted were a sedative.

All I knew then was that I had at my disposal incriminating evidence that so far had not been revealed. More meaningful still: I spoke as one of the many victims whose lives had been wrecked.

Was Mama urging me to set the record straight?

I began immediately. I wrote passionately, crossing out words, crossing out paragraphs, tearing up the page, starting again. After several attempts, I decided to open with a description of the beautiful school, and tell of our deep sense of pride as we watched it rise up on the side of a hill, brick by brick. Then, I began filling in the story of deception that was unfolding behind the scenes even as we watched; the seeds of destruction being sown....

The first Friday night of Christmas break I worked until two in the morning; then I rose on Saturday and continued. I finished a draft. I decided rather than to double back and begin revising, I would put the essay aside until Christmas Day, using the week in between to get some distance from it, and to study for finals.

Alas, when I picked up the essay again, all I could see was angry ranting, riddled with exclamation points. This would not do. Over the next few days I rewrote the piece entirely, tightening the sentences, trying to seem more evenhanded. I completed another draft There, that was better. The information was the same, but now it seemed more convincing. In a way this draft had been easier than the first, for this time I had something to work against. I thought of Edna Buckstrum and her aspirations. *I could be a journalist*, I thought with a start, amazed as the door to a whole new career seemed to open before me. Then, in a moment of inspiration, I decided to strike the final paragraph and write a new one, to end the essay on that note, of how I was doing what Edna Buckstrum would have done, had she survived.

I finished at last, entitling the essay, *A Miscarriage of Justice*. I felt completely drained. I knew deep in my heart that I had written something truly powerful. I imagined my story spreading with lightning force from *Houston* magazine to major newspapers and periodicals all over the country....

I longed to show the essay to Mrs. Hathaway, to see what she would think. Unfortunately there would be no opportunity. I thought of Bruce. How he would love the fact that his sister was honored in this essay that people far and wide might one day read, and be brought to feel the great loss of Edna and a score of other talented individuals. Perhaps it would even allay some of the pain that made him so resistant to talking about what happened. Allie's remark of long ago came to mind now. That Bruce and I had nothing left in common except the past could not have been more misguided. Indeed, it was because of our shared history that we would always have something of great importance in common.

Again, I was emboldened to call Bruce. Again, there was no answer. Before I tried the next time I asked the long distance operator to see if the number had changed. As she did so, I began to wonder, could it be that Bruce changed his number in order to avoid me? Surely not, and yet—

No, the number had not changed. I was baffled; and unreasonable as it was, I could not help but feel somehow Bruce really was trying to avoid me. I had been right to sense his retreat. How he must hate me. It was just as I had feared.

Then I hit on the idea of writing Bruce again, referring to my previous letter and saying I had been trying to reach him. "I have important news that has developed in the interim. It changes everything for us. I will keep trying to call, so please be listening. My love, Delys." Reading the letter through, I wondered if I should have been more specific. Yet I did not have time to even begin to say all that I longed to say to Bruce. I underlined, "My love," then underlined it again, bearing down with the tip of my pen.

On the Saturday morning before the scholarship application deadline, I rode the bus to my uncle's office and typed up the essay there, making an extra carbon copy to save for Bruce, to give him someday when he would be able to appreciate it, and to fill in the application and attach my letters of recommendation from Mrs. Hathaway and Miss Lytle, which I had procured before the holiday. When Logan left at lunchtime he offered me a ride home. But I was still typing, and after that I had to proof everything. Plus, with my uncle none the wiser, I had to walk my letter to Bruce down to the mailbox a block away on Telephone Road.

"I'll write my letter of recommendation early Monday morning, and take everything by the Chamber before the day is out," Logan promised. I thanked him and said I would leave everything in an envelope on his desk. He asked me to lock up before I left. I promised I would.

Earlier Uncle Logan had asked me what I was writing about, and I told him I had decided on Mama. I never had mentioned that I changed my mind. It would be a nice surprise for him, I reasoned, inasmuch as our conversation after I discovered the incriminating file figured strongly in my essay. In a way, I mused, Uncle Logan had been an influence on my life. His perfectionism when it came to office work had made me a more accurate, and speedier, typist than I had been before. And the week I filled in for Mrs. Jolly improved my skills at focusing on several tasks at once, all the while dealing with frequent interruptions.

Finally, at two-thirty, I rose from the desk with a yawn and a stretch, and inserted all the documents inside the large envelope I had brought along. I felt proud of myself, vindicated. Was it the same as the way I felt about my first poem? Not exactly. The essay did not satisfy the creative urge that had awakened in me when I dashed off those few lines and looked at them staring up from the page, and that I always felt, somewhere in the back of my mind, the craving to exercise again. But then, who would ever read my poems? Many people would read my essay...that is, if I placed among the top three winners. Surely all this was meant to be. I blinked, and gazed ahead, revelation sweeping over me: I had survived the explosion in order to tell this story.

I took the envelope and placed it on my uncle's desk, retaining my copy of the essay and the one for Bruce. Writing the essay had only strengthened my belief that we would always be inextricably bound to each other. I imagined Bruce sitting in the empty school bus, wondering what catastrophe had befallen the school and peering anxiously through the window in hopes I would appear and come to take the seat he was saving for me. I would never love any boy but Bruce.

Before dropping my letter to him into the hopper, I pressed it to my lips.

On Monday during finals, I would often find myself distracted, wondering if Uncle Logan had been to the Chamber yet, and dropped off my essay. How soon would the judges begin reading the material? What would they think of mine? Out of the tall stack of paeans to upright teachers, relatives, and members of the clergy, would be one essay that took a brave stand against a small group of individuals who participated in a terrible act of deceit.

It pains me now to think what a great deal I had to learn about life then, and how soon I was to receive a brutal lesson. But to be honest, in spite of it all, I never outgrew my yearning for justice. I mean by this that a certain chain of actions should produce a corresponding result. I am still always shocked, and then disappointed, when life shows me otherwise. It is my nature, I guess.

On Monday night I helped Aunt Allie prepare supper, layering potato slices, onion and cheddar cheese in a baking dish for scalloped potatoes. All the while I kept glancing toward the back door glass, anxious to see my uncle approach.

Yet, when he walked in, I was astonished to see my envelope in the crook of his arm. Today was the deadline. I stared at him, speechless.

Uncle Logan removed his hat and placed it on the edge of the counter. Looking at me, his face pinched, he handed me the envelope. "I couldn't submit this," he said bluntly, as if I should have realized. Allie and I looked at each other, bewildered. I clutched the envelope to my waist.

"What's the matter with it?" I asked, breathless, thinking idiotically that he had discovered a typographical error.

"If this wins—and it's damn well written, and probably will—I could be sued. I could also lose important clients—not to mention, potential ones."

I had no idea what he was talking about. All I could see was my hopes dashed for getting the truth out, not to mention my hopes of winning a scholarship. I screwed up my face in disbelief. "Sued? What—for a paper I wrote?"

"For violating the settlement of the suit we filed against H. L. Hunt and Parade. The terms were never to be disclosed. It's what we agreed to, in writing."

"But you did not tell me that," I argued, my voice quavering.

He shrugged. "It never came up in our conversation. How was I to know you were going to blab about it one day? I thought you had written an essay about your mother, for Pete's sake."

"I was going to, then—"

Allie cut in, her voice low and measured, "But you did not tell her about those terms, Logan, so you can't blame her now for not knowing. *Can you?*"

Logan wagged his head. "That isn't what I'm blaming her for. She should have given some thought of how her—her *diatribe*—against one of the most powerful men in the oil and gas industry could hurt me," he fired back, his face florid. Then he looked at me again. "You worked in my office all one summer, Delys. Didn't you notice the majority of my clients supply the big oil interests?"

"Oh Logan, surely—" Allie began.

Logan cut his eyes at her. "Word gets around, Allie, and Hunt's people know who I am."

I was shaking my head, my thoughts in disarray. "But I don't understand. You weren't afraid of Mr. Hunt when you encouraged Daddy to sue him."

"That was before my practice revolved around oil and gas—just as most businesses in this town eventually do, by the way, or they won't stay afloat."

"You mean, you would keep the truth from coming out, because it might hurt your business?" I asked, appalled.

Logan looked a little nonplused. Then his shoulders dropped and he sighed. "You're damned right I would. Look here. Don't try and make out that I did something wrong now. Christ! Why–"

"*Logan...!*" Allie began threateningly.

"Why didn't you ask me before you did this?" he whined.

"I—I didn't know. I—I thought you'd be proud of me," I said. By now I was nearly in tears. "I—I'm sorry!" I cried helplessly, and rushed out of the kitchen and into my room, slamming my door. I threw the envelope on the floor, fell across my bed and wept.

It was not long before Aunt Allie tapped on my door. I ignored her. She came in anyway, and sat on the edge of the bed. She patted my back and squeezed my hand. I pulled my hand away. I felt embarrassed.

"Delys, dear, I'm sorry," she said gently. "Logan didn't mean—he just, well, you know, he does have a lot at stake here. But all the same, I'm really sorry it turned out this way. I know it hurts."

"It doesn't matter, leave me alone, please," I said, my voice flat.

She rose from the bed. "Logan has already said that you can apply for another scholarship, still use those letters from your teachers. And he'll still write a letter for you, too, of course, as your employer."

I did not answer. Allie left the room.

Much later that night, after my aunt and uncle had gone to bed, I rose and changed into my pajamas. My whole face felt blistered, as if I had received a powerful slap. I had never felt like such a fool. For thinking I had the power to do anything meaningful. For thinking there had been a purpose in my life being spared. I had believed I could expose those people who had caused the explosion for what they were. And yet, all my efforts would do nothing more than hurt others who were innocent of any wrongdoing. For the first time in my life, I understood the staggering power of great wealth. Without so much as lifting a finger or even knowing there might be a reason to, H. L. Hunt had dictated the outcome of this situation. Had silenced me. Who was I to think I could buck H. L. Hunt? I wanted to crawl in a hole and never come out again.

I had to go to the bathroom suddenly. I opened the door of my room. All the lights were out, but the bathroom door was open and the moonlight poured through the window, lighting the hallway. I walked to the bathroom and closed the door. On the other side of the wall was my aunt and uncle's bedroom. No sooner had I sat down on the toilet than I heard my aunt's voice.

"—she has feelings?" Allie said, her voice an angry snarl. "How could you lash out at her like that? How *could* you?"

My uncle responded in a mumble; I could not hear what he said.

"You know her whole life was shattered by what happened. Has it never occurred to you how—how *powerless* she has felt?"

He said something else, but all I could make out was the phrase, "food on this table." I wrapped my arms around my abdomen, my bladder frozen up.

"Oh, we know all about that!" she accused. Then in a queer falsetto voice, as though parroting him, she said, "Didn't you remember to bring a *towel*? I'll have to go back and get one; we can't have blood on the seat."

Blood on the seat. The image made me feel suddenly faint. I brought a hand to my forehead. What were they—

"—already too late, as we found out; and besides, how long did it take, thirty seconds—?" Uncle Logan countered, and somehow I gathered he had made this argument before and was summoning patience to make it again.

"Never mind what I might have been *feeling*," she interrupted. "Just be sure we take care of Logan's business car," Allie went on, her voice pitching higher. "A client might see the stain and realize you were flesh and blood after all. You never wanted our baby! Just say so!"

Baby? What baby? My heart was slamming in my chest.

"–now. You're being unfair," Logan said firmly.

They went on arguing. I had never heard my aunt and uncle fight before, and it was unnerving. It was like listening to my parents quarrel on the night before Mama lost her life, only it was more vicious. No. Only Aunt Allie was more vicious. My uncle was clearly on the defensive. A baby—

And here I was, stuck in the bathroom. I didn't know whether to stay, or go back to my room. I found myself lifting my bare feet off the floor and curling my toes under, for fear I'd make a noise. A few minutes later their bedroom door opened and slammed shut. I heard heavy footfalls down the hall, then the back door open, and slam shut. Who had stomped out? Allie, or Logan? Soon I saw car lights flash by the bathroom window, heard the hum of the motor as the car tilted down the driveway toward the street.

Apparently no one had realized that I was eavesdropping. Well, not really eavesdropping. I could not help what I heard. I waited a few moments. When I failed to hear anything else, I took a chance and raced to my bedroom, taking care to shut the door ever so quietly behind me. Then I stood there with my hands still gripping the door knob, catching my breath, thinking about what I had heard. It was as if Allie hated Logan. And it had all erupted because of me. Allie was mistaken. Only my pride was hurt, not my feelings. Logan was just being Logan. I found out what he was like while working for him.

But as I stood there, the pulse pounding in my ears, I began to think of Allie, how she had tried to comfort me. Well, that wasn't much, after all, I supposed. But later, when she and Logan were alone, she had stood up to her husband on my behalf. That took real courage. And, she understood how powerless I had felt all these years. I never knew that. She was more sensitive than I had thought.

I felt different toward Allie...more appreciative...more forgiving. And she had lost a baby. That Logan had not wanted. Surely Logan could not be that heartless. Or, could he?

I crept to the bed and beneath the covers, shivering. I lay awake for most of the night, fearing I may have been responsible for breaking up my aunt and uncle's marriage. I began reflecting on my observations when they were together. The cold looks they exchanged now and then, and the curt way they talked to each other; their silences at the supper table. How often Allie's mind seemed to be elsewhere when Logan was talking. Finally the image came to mind of Logan patting Allie's shoulder affectionately, that day we learned of the attack on Pearl Harbor. Something had always bothered me about that gesture, though I had never stopped to puzzle it out. Now I knew what it was. Allie had not reached up to touch his hand in return, as Mama would have done with Daddy. *Allie has hated Logan since they lost their child, and what happened tonight was the final insult.* I was amazed at how far-reaching the consequences could be of something I had written in earnest, fully believing in its value to others. At last, in spite of the fact that my bladder was full to aching, I fell asleep.

To this day I do not know who walked out on whom that night, where my aunt or my uncle went, or for how long. When I walked into the kitchen the next morning, no one was there. But I noted two empty plates, juice glasses and coffee cups waiting on the counter to be washed. The household appeared to be back to normal. In a way this was reassuring. And yet, everything seemed different to me. As if I had gone to sleep and awakened in a new world.

Years would pass before I came to recognize that my aunt and uncle's marriage had been in no danger of collapsing the night before that one, and to believe, rather, that the failure for which Allie berated Logan had given their marriage a kind of parity it may have lacked earlier.

On that morning, though, standing in Allie's kitchen, all I could think was that I wanted nothing to do with a career in journalism. Before the day was out I had torn up all three copies of my essay and thrown them away.

Chapter 19

During first period on the Monday morning after I stepped down as Colonel, I stood at the edge of the practice field with Miss Lytle and watched the new Brigade assemble. My eyes were brimming with tears. It seemed but yesterday that I stood out there where my successor now stood, the whistle hanging from the lanyard around my neck—

"Well. It was a good year. No major mishaps!" Miss Lytle said brusquely, facing ahead, her chin thrust out, her hands locked behind her waist.

"*Let's make it a* great *year!*" she had said at the beginning. Was she a little disappointed? I wondered apprehensively. Then I decided I was foolish to make a distinction between the two words. Unless—. I found myself saying, "I apologize for that night when I got distracted. I'll never forgive myself." Well, maybe that sounded a bit melodramatic—

"Bah!" she said dismissively.

How I would have liked to hear her modify that terse response, adding, "No harm done." But she did not. Her satisfaction with the year overall would have to suffice. I would have to work out the rest within myself.

For a long while we stood there side by side, yet alone with our thoughts, watching. At length there came the sound of a lone snare drum roll: the new Captain of Drums testing the tightness of her drum head. She withdrew the drum key from its clasp on the side of the drum and began tightening the spokes— crossing back and forth from one to another, inclining an ear as she tested the tautness in between, until she was satisfied. I could almost feel the smooth metal, the T shape of the drum key, in my fingers. I found myself remembering that day long ago when Aunt Allie drove me over here to follow the captivating sound of the drums and see the Scottish Brigade for the first time. On that day I knew this was where I was supposed to be. But now I had no place here any longer. Would I ever again feel with certainty that I belonged somewhere? At this point, Oberlin College loomed larger than life. I could imagine its huge campus teeming with strangers who rushed past me as I made my confused way along. Just thinking about it made me feel lightheaded with anxiety. Two smaller scholarships had made up for my misfired attempt to win the Chamber of Commerce prize. I had already applied and received my acceptance letter. I was due to move in with Daddy on the first of July.

Abruptly the new Colonel sounded her whistle, and my heart seized up. *"The next Colonel is...Delys Lithingate...."*

As she began making her first announcements to the assembly before her, I found myself asking Miss Lytle boldly, "Why did you choose me to be Colonel?"

Immediately I wished I could withdraw the question because I felt she might consider it fresh, and brush me off. Even after a full year of working closely with Miss Lytle, I still had no clear idea of how—or even whether or not—to approach her.

Yet she inclined her head thoughtfully. After a few moments she said, "I could see from your essay on the honor code that you were a person who takes life seriously. Reflects on what she has observed. All other things being equal, it's what I look for in a colonel."

I considered her words a great compliment, though I was not sure they were intended as such. As I struggled over how to respond, she went on, "Of course, later you told me about what happened in New London. Then it all made sense." She looked at me. "You know, Delys, I rely a lot on instinct when I choose my officers. And one thing I've learned over the years: it isn't only about what the girl will do for the office...but sometimes what the office will do for the girl," she said. Then, her brow knitted, she added gravely in a soft voice, "You'll be able to go on now."

It was the last thing I expected to hear. For a long moment I met her intense gaze with my own; then I had to look ahead again. My eyes were stinging. Beatrice Lytle had a much deeper understanding of what I carried away from New London than ever she revealed, and she also knew me better than I realized. If only we had had this conversation a few months ago, I might have written a fine essay about her for the scholarship contest, and saved myself a lot of grief. All at once I was flooded with love for this starchy woman, and tempted to reach my arms around her neck and hug her. I checked myself. She would not like that.

Before I spoke, I looked up at the sky, then at the bright green field of white-clad girls below, my wet eyes making the scene all shimmery, as though it were part of a dream. As in a way it was, all of it, from start to finish, because the rest of my life could never be equal to it. "Yes," I allowed, "but I will miss all this...having a *place* here!" My guard was down now. My voice cracked on the last phrase.

For a few moments Miss Lytle was silent. Then, her voice husky, she said, "You must come back and see us, when you are in town. Come to a game now and then. Sit with me in the stands." She cleared her throat. With a twinkling glance and a slight nudge at my elbow, she added, "You bring the hot chocolate."

That I would one day not only come back, but also accept an offer to be Miss Lytle's Co-Sponsor, is not a story that needs to be included here. To be interesting, a story must have conflict, and serious obstacles to overcome. There were no such elements in my tenure as Co-Sponsor. Put simply, Miss Lytle needed help at the time—the ranks of Brigade had swelled to 250 girls by then— but she was not quite ready to think ahead to the day she would pass on the reins of the organization to a new Sponsor. For me, the experience as Co-Sponsor was rewarding enough that I might indeed have held on that long. But in just a couple of years I could see what the future held. Not that I could see what Brigade would eventually devolve into. No, not that. More than a decade would pass before society started to change in ways that made such organizations seem quaint and irrelevant. None of my ladies—as I fondly referred to them—would complain that the rules were too strict, or the uniforms old-fashioned. Nor would they pull any shenanigans like a few of the later ones did; but then, to be fair, my ladies lived in a more sheltered world, and this included the neighborhood where they went to school. They had long since moved on, for instance, when a male flasher exposed himself during drill practice one afternoon, sending frightened Brigadiers scurrying inside the building. The man had positioned himself, in fact, on the sidewalk across from the church steps where I had once sat alone observing Brigade with rapt focus, and had no cause to doubt I was safe there.

No. I would wind up stepping aside as Co-Sponsor because I could see how easily I might turn out to be like Miss Lytle if I stayed: tethered to an organization my whole life, and no one to go home to when the performance was over. Of course, the argument could be made that I did wind up being tethered—to a man with whom I was not destined to spend my life, regardless of our love for each other—so I might have done just as well to follow in Miss Lytle's footsteps.

As I stood there with her that Monday morning after having passed from my office, I was already turning over in my mind the possibility of trying to reach Bruce once more. After all, how many times had I tried, really? It seemed like a hundred, but it could not have been more than half a dozen. Bruce was spending his spare time helping Doc, after all. And maybe his apprenticeship was occupying more and more of his time. An encouraging thought. Maybe Bruce would show so much practical knowledge and innate ability by the time he began his formal study of medicine, his professors would be forced to see that he was sorely needed in the field, no matter the struggle he had keeping up his grades in class. I had never tried calling Doc's office. I didn't even know the number. And the last time I telephoned his residence was in early January, the opportunity coming four days after I had put my handwritten note in the mail. Feeling bitter when no one answered, I had vowed never to try again.

But now I was free of the constrictions of being Colonel. I had some idea that if only I could reach Bruce, I could make him see that I had been serious about my reason for breaking up with him, and wasn't making up an excuse. And then I would leave things up to him. Once more. That is all I would try.

The opportunity came two days later, on Wednesday night, when Allie and Logan went to a covered dish supper at the church, to welcome the new Minister who had been assigned there when the previous Minister abruptly volunteered to be an Army chaplain. Allie was proudly taking a pot of fresh string beans and red skin potatoes, from the first fruits of the victory garden to which she was dedicating a good portion of her time these days.

Of the many times I had telephoned Bruce on the sly, seldom had I done so on a week night because usually my aunt and uncle were in the house. Therefore this seemed a particularly auspicious time to find Bruce at home. *This time he will be there*, I told myself, a nervous thrill running through me.

Soon I was awaiting the connection to be made, bracing myself for the sound of the ringing telephone, and ultimately the voice on the other end. At this time of the evening, it was as likely that Doc would answer as it was that Bruce would pick up the receiver. How I hated this. I would absolutely not put myself through this again. If—

Yet after one ring, and that not even a complete one, there was a click and a local operator's voice: "This line has been disconnected." Another click. Then the long distance operator was asking me to verify the number. Which I did, Overton 379. Surely there was some mistake—

"One moment please," she said. I could not bear to stay seated; I stood up to wait, tapping my foot.

When the operator returned to the line, she confirmed that Overton 379 was no longer in service. She had also checked and found there was no new listing under the name of Peter Buckstrum.

Feeling pre-empted and slightly unnerved, I thanked her and hung up. I brought a hand to my forehead, trying to think what to do next. I had an eerie feeling that Bruce and Doc had simply vanished into thin air. Then I thought of one other possibility, and dialed the long distance operator again. Certainly, it did not seem likely that Doc would give up his residential listing unless he had moved away. Yet, why would he move away when— "Would you please check listings for a Doctor Peter Buckstrum, you know, a professional office. A business listing."

"One moment," she said. Shortly she returned to the line to report, "Sorry, no listing under the name Buckstrum at all. Is there anything else I can help you with?"

"No thanks," I said, and hung up the phone in despair.

I lowered myself down to the bench, feeling heavy as a stone. So Doc and Bruce had moved away. Was that what Bruce was trying to tell me last October? Of course it was. And it wasn't all that hard to imagine the reason, really. No doubt Doc had stayed in New London after the debacle because he had a successful practice there, and was reluctant to pull up stakes and start all over somewhere else. But maybe he finally concluded he could not chase away the ghosts of the past while remaining there. Maybe he had resumed heavy drinking. His own survival meant leaving for good. Yes, of course that's what must have happened.

But had they stayed around long enough for Bruce to receive my second note? As in the case of my first note, I had not put a return address on it for fear it might be returned and wind up in Aunt Allie's hands. So, how would I ever know unless Bruce contacted me one day in spite of my aunt?

Inevitably I imagined my poor dog, Rusty, standing guard, once again, in front of an empty house. It broke my heart and frustrated me; and I started to cry and beat my thighs with my fists.

I spent the next hour or so quietly thinking, reality continuing to sink in. Bruce was gone. Gone. He probably had another girl friend by now. And I would be moving away soon, with all kinds of new opportunities for meeting young men and falling in love. Well granted, better once the war was over, which hopefully would be soon. Nowadays young men were succumbing to the military recruiters on the Austin campus and entering the armed forces at an accelerating rate, eager to trade cap and gown for a uniform. In any case, it was obvious that if I didn't let go of Bruce, I was going to ruin my life. And for what? He was never coming back. *He hates me.*

Filled with resolve, I had an urge to do something to mark this decision, in the interest of keeping myself from reverting back to false hopes once the force of my feelings wore off. Before my aunt and uncle returned I had opened the box of Bruce's letters far back on my closet shelf, torn those letters in half, heaped them in a brown grocery bag, and carried them out to the trash.

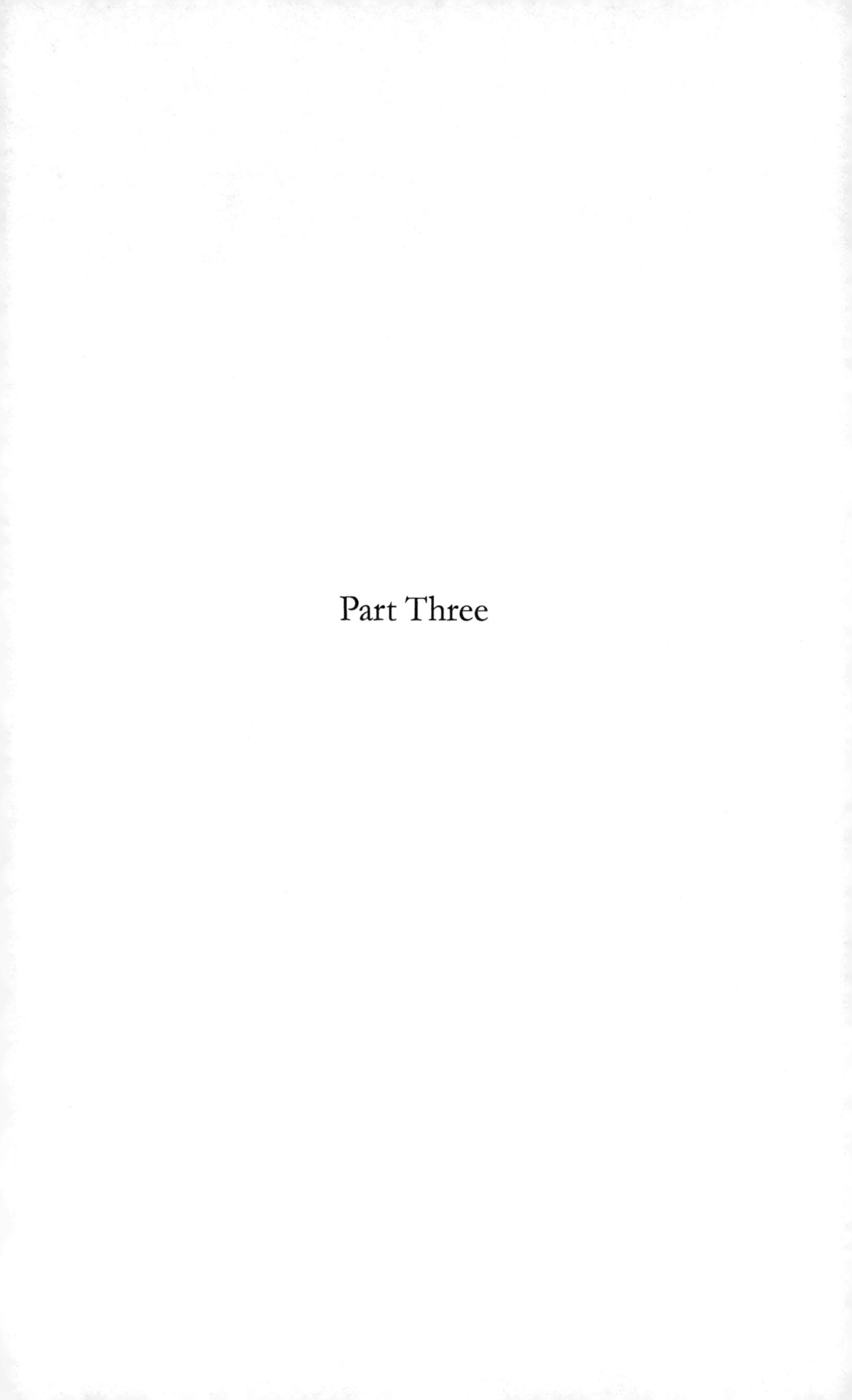

Part Three

Chapter 20

I remember the first time I went back to New London.

The circumstances were far different from those that I had once anticipated —making good at last on a promise my father and I made long ago, to visit my mother's grave together. No. I would not have crossed the street to be with my father then. I made the trip alone. I had just finished my final courses at Rice— due to war-time changes, classes entering in 1941 and 1942 were given three, instead of four, years to complete requirements for a bachelor's degree. By virtue of working a few hours a week in my uncle's law office while pursuing my studies, I had saved enough money in my second year to acquire a used roadster from a history instructor who was going away to the war.

My aunt had taught me how to drive on the slanting streets of Idylwood. With a death grip on the wheel as I strived to coordinate my feet between clutch and accelerator, down to the end of the block we would go. A right turn, then up North Macgregor Way—the street that hugged the grassy promenade fronting Brays Bayou, with Forest Park Cemetery on the opposite banks, and that inevitably brought back the secret memory of emerging on foot from the back of the park to hop in the car with Bruce—we curved around to Sylvan Road which, like all Idylwood streets running parallel, was cut off abruptly at the intersection of Wayside Drive. There a whole new, and far bigger driving challenge, awaited, as I was more apt to encounter other vehicles along the city thoroughfare. A perilous turning around in the last driveway before Wayside—backing up was unnerving for me—then we retraced our route part way before cutting back and forth, up and down Idylwood's cross streets marked by spiky concrete signposts, engraved with black letters.

Even given the privations of wartime, I had found having an auto at my disposal quite liberating, something my aunt understood. During one driving lesson, she told me that early in the days when Logan had established his law practice, a client hard up for cash had paid his fee with an old car. Allie, who was then helping out until Logan could afford to hire an assistant, had quickly appropriated the car for herself. "I have never been without my own means of transportation since, and I never intend to be," she swore.

I have often wondered if the transaction over the client's car came before, or after, Allie's miscarriage. I have a suspicion it was after. On many occasions over the years, I have found myself privately dividing my aunt and uncle's marriage into two separate epochs.

During that period when I was learning to drive, I was already making plans for the trip to visit Mama's grave. So I continued riding the bus back and forth to school and work, in order to have a sufficient number of gas coupons saved up for the nearly 400-mile round trip.

My estrangement from Daddy had made me feel the loss of Mama more acutely than I had for a long while. It also awakened a deep sense of guilt. I should have visited Mama's grave much sooner; should have boarded a bus or a train, rather than put off going until Daddy and I could make the trip together. And in fact I wondered: had Daddy chosen to work somewhere in Texas or even Oklahoma, after Mama's death, so that he could visit her grave periodically and be reminded how much he loved her, would things have turned out differently? Would he have followed through with the two of us living together, as I had agreed to, and had come to count on, rather than letting someone else intrude, driving a wedge between us? Daddy had been widowed and living alone for five years by the time he moved to Ohio, and he knew that within a few short months, I would be at his side.

Here was my plan: to drive first to the Pleasant Hill Cemetery, then from there to the house where Mama and Daddy and I once lived together so happily. No, innocently. That was a more apt description, and the happiness we had shared was part of that innocent belief that the place would always be ours. Who could say whether I might feel a sense of Mama's presence lingering there, more so than at the cemetery? If the garden she had so lovingly tended survived, then surely I would feel her presence there. Or, no, maybe on the porch swing under the wisteria vine, where she used to sit resting her feet and reading the *Houston Chronicle* after a long day of teaching. That is, if the porch swing and prodigious blooming vine had survived. I had no idea who lived in our house now, however; whether it was the family who bought the house and acre of land from Daddy, or a subsequent owner. A lot can change in seven years. Maybe I would find the place looking so changed through remodeling, or—worse—so run down, I would take one look and speed away.

There was one other possible destination at the end of my long road trip, the thought of which had been keeping me awake nights since I made my decision to undertake it: I could drive into Overton and see if anyone knew what had become of Bruce and his father. If I were lucky, some other family doctor may now occupy Doc's old examining rooms, and would fill in the blanks of information for me. Yet, I might be wise to stay away. Since disposing of Bruce's letters two years ago, I had gradually stopped agonizing over the relationship I had failed so miserably. There were even days when Bruce never crossed my mind. I had actually come to enjoy the occasional evening out or study date with young men I met at Rice. So far, nothing had clicked romantically on these dates, but I always accepted an invitation with an open mind, which I never did while in high school. In fact sometimes I cringed when I recalled how close-minded I was then about any boy except Bruce.

Still, from time to time I did find myself wondering what had become of Bruce and his father. If I knew the answer, and had some new context in which I might think of Bruce, most likely with a wife and children, then perhaps I could finally move on for good.

Through all my arguing back and forth about whether I ought to inquire about Bruce and his father, I often found myself fantasizing about going by the Buckstrum house, to check and see if Rusty had been left behind. I envisioned myself offering to buy my dog outright, for a price so high that his current owners could not refuse it, then taking him back to Houston in the passenger seat. This fantasy set me to thinking about how my aunt and uncle might react to seeing me with my ten-year-old dog in tow. Which brought to mind that I was growing tired of having someone else make the rules about how I lived. *"There are only two bedrooms in the house, so we'll just have to make do until I can get around to finishing out the attic,"* said Daddy's letter. He had figured on squeezing himself and his new bride Maxine, along with her son and daughter from a previous marriage, plus yours truly, into the small cottage he was planning to buy in Cleveland. Oh yes, and also the baby now on the way, who was, according to my math, the reason for the abrupt change in Daddy's original plan. It may well have been this one reckless act that I most resented. As a teenager, I had soberly considered the possible consequences of having sex with Bruce, and determined to prevent it from happening, regardless of how much I wanted to continue seeing him and to give in to the longing he aroused in my body whenever we were alone together. Daddy was a grown man in his forties, and yet he had exercised no such restraint, let alone, foresight. He never stopped to think: *I could lose Delys over this woman. Is she worth that much?* Had he impregnated some woman, without benefit of marriage, while I was Colonel of the Scottish Brigade, I would have been mortified to think that Miss Lytle might find out, let alone any of the other girls in the organization that I was leading. Of course, had Daddy taken up with Maxine that early, he would not have proposed that I come to live with him after graduation. My hopes would not have been built up in the first place.

Driving north along the highway on that Saturday morning at the end of April, I felt refreshed and equal to the day ahead. The night before had been my first peaceful night's sleep following a string of nights tossing and turning, my indecision as to inquiring about Bruce bouncing off the walls of my mind. After all, by the time I had gone to bed, the only thing left was to wake up this morning, get dressed, and make the trip. Then, whatever I decided about Bruce, at least by the end of this day, the agonizing would be over and I would be on my way back.

The sun shone benignly through a soft blue sky, and the air was crisp and cool. The rolling fields and pastures along the byways were scattered with a vast array of wildflowers in bloom— morning glories and goldenrod; red buckeye and brown-eyed Susans and wild asters were a few that I could still identify after all these years of living in Houston and rarely seeing any. Most prominent of all was the wild crimson clover that spread prodigiously through East Texas whenever the spring weather conditions were just right. Some years it would turn the entire roadbed in front of our house strawberry red. I wondered why Mama always planted a garden, pulling up and dispensing with any wildflowers that got in her way. Maybe—I thought now—because she had grown up in the city, and could not appreciate the simple gift of flowers that required no work on her part and gave her no feeling of reward. And I found myself smiling because I felt as if I had just gotten to know Mama a little better.

By the time I approached the cemetery a bouquet of pink and white carnations wrapped in wax paper, purchased from a roadside stand just outside Henderson, lay nearby on the passenger seat. I was not sure how Mama felt about carnations, but they were the only variety of flowers that seemed to be on offer.

Soon I was pulling off the gravel road across from the entrance to Pleasant Hill and turning off the car engine. I was struck by how far away I suddenly felt from the rest of civilization. In fact, not for several miles had I passed another vehicle on the road. I had been so preoccupied with the question of looking up Bruce, I had not given as much thought to this moment as I might have. In truth I did not fear this place as I had when Daddy and I first made an attempt to visit, just days after the explosion. After all, I had spent considerable time perusing the pages of the *Book of Memories* and so there would be no surprises awaiting me, I didn't think. And anyhow, it had been seven years, and much had happened in my life to give me some distance. I wasn't sure what I would feel, or even ought to feel, as I walked among those graves. Well, maybe I did feel a little apprehensive now that the prospect was staring me in the face. No need to hurry....

I sat behind the wheel and surveyed the cemetery grounds sloping upward from the road. It seemed to me that when I was a little girl, coming here with Mama for the annual day of cleaning up, there were a lot more trees at the front. Which would make sense because this was where the ground had been cleared for the graves of explosion victims. The early graves of this cemetery were located far back on the tract of land set aside for it, and then gradually built out toward the road. Of course there was nothing gradual about the digging of the London School graves. Once Allie had remarked of the day of Mama's burial, "It had rained hard, and the smell of pine sap from all the trees they had cut down was very strong."

I stepped out of the car with Mama's flowers in the crook of my arm, mounted the front steps and walked beneath the iron archway. It was eerily quiet and still. No sound of leaves rustling or birds looping from tree to tree. I paused to take a long look at the grounds stretching out on all sides. When it came right down to it, Pleasant Hill looked pretty much like any other cemetery I had seen except for the far larger and more voluptuous Forest Park, with its winding lanes and so many trees that it seemed more like the grounds of a landed estate than a cemetery. Here cedars, oaks, magnolias, and pines thickened toward the back, some of them quite old and large. And beyond those trees, small clearings around graves, then more trees; and though I could not see from here I knew that way back in the shadows was the burial plot Mama had purchased for us, the plot that remained empty while her bones resided up here. The Lithingate plot backed up to a fence, I seemed to recall, although I was so young when last I came here, in my sunbonnet and tiny sandals, my hand clutched in Mama's, how could I remember anything for sure?

I had no idea where Mama was buried, only that it was somewhere among those of her pupils who had perished. I began to walk around a bit, the ground soft and spongy under foot as if there had lately been a nice spring rain. I noted many of the graves had flowers tucked beneath the headstones, no doubt by families more attentive than Mama's. Many were offset by low concrete borders, and this was often the only delineation between them. I felt ill-at-ease being forced to walk across one grave to get to the next, but there was no other choice. At first my eyes were drawn to the dates of decease even more so than to the names written above, none of which I recognized. March 18th, 1937. March 18th, 1937. March 18th, 1937. With few exceptions, the date was etched in stone again and again. You would have thought no one died anywhere else in the world on that day except in the London School explosion. And now I recalled overhearing Allie remark once in a voice tinged with bitterness, that the graves of the victims were so close to one another that during Mama's burial she was afraid to back up for fear of slipping down into the next grave over. She had stood clasping Logan's elbow. How counterintuitive that must have seemed to her, and maybe to him as well....

I was soon startled to find a young male victim staring back at me from an oval-shaped tile fixed in a headstone. Though I had not known him, the sight of that smiling, innocent boy's face made my knees quiver. From the date of his birth, I concluded he was a fifth grader. How happy he looked. I had seen many such happy faces in the *Book of Memories*, but that was different somehow, less unsettling...less finger-pointing. I walked on. Here was another oval picture, there still another. The pictures made me think of the delicate paintings on porcelain set in jewelry in antique shops, except these were black and white photos that apparently had been applied to the tile, then weather-proofed with lacquer or varnish. I suddenly felt as if I had been let in on some secret that was kept from me for years. As I encountered more and more of the photos, I could only think: here was a life not lived. Here, another life not lived. What might he have become? What had been in store for her future? I sensed these children, who had not lived long enough to outgrow the clothing they wore in their pictures, were following me with their eyes as I passed on, judging me. *What have you done to justify the fact that you lived?*

As I continued to walk along, I began seeing more faces I recognized, either from my class or from having seen them around the school. How well I remembered Myrtle Hopkins. She often wore flowers in her hair, just as she did in the memorial picture right here. She was very quiet and had problems in reading. Joe Silverman was a practical joker whose teeth stuck out in front. He got in trouble a lot, but everyone liked him. Steve Swann had a speech impediment. Queen Price was helping him to overcome it. John Carver was a senior, on the basketball team. Mama had taught him, and she used to laugh and say, "John is twice as tall as I am, but he knows better than to act like it." In the picture he was wearing his cap and gown. Right on the verge—

Abruptly I stopped and wiped a tear from my eye. I wished I had brought flowers for every one of these children. *Children. I have grown up, but they will always be children, never any older than they were in that moment when our school exploded....*

I stood there considering. Some headstones bore the indentation that apparently meant a picture was intended to be placed there but had been left off. Why? I wondered. Or, had they come unstuck over time, dropped off and been taken away? More surprising, even after seven years, some graves still had temporary markers—puny tin rectangular signs with names and life spans scrolled across them, and a stake for fixing them in the ground. Why would any family neglect to place a permanent marker? Even now I could not always make out the names scrolled on them, the information faded to near invisible. A temporary marker could be destroyed, or in certain types of violent weather, be uprooted and swept away. In such cases, how could anyone ever identify the grave again? I felt defensive. It seemed the family didn't care. Then again, maybe they could not afford a permanent marker. How sad....

Somewhat to my relief, I did not see Lanelle's grave. To have found her staring back at me would have been totally unnerving. But then, maybe I had passed right by my friend's grave. Her family was very poor. Maybe Lanelle's grave was one with a tin marker. This girl should have grown up to become famous, and yet perhaps by now you could not even tell where she was buried, her large family scattered to wherever the winds blew them.

Eventually I did find Bucky and Edna. I was mesmerized by the single headstone and two pictures, the kind of arrangement that in normal times would memorialize a husband and wife: Bucky in his band uniform, with enormous plumaged hat and belts criss-crossing his chest. Edna with her good looks and smile that invited the boys' notice, made them wish she would take that mouth and whisper sweet things in their ears then kiss them. She had attracted me, for that matter. How could any young girl not dream of looking like Edna Buckstrum one day? And not only look like her, but be that smart and sexy too?

At last I found my mother's grave, just two over from Edna's. Somehow this was comforting. Mama thought a lot of Edna. *Lavinia Pearl Madden Lithingate.* There was no picture, just the stone with Mama's name etched on it, and the span of her life beneath, ending with that unequivocal date that was beginning to make me feel as if I had slammed into a brick wall every time I saw it. Then, below this, *In Loving Memory.* At first I felt relieved not to find Mama staring back at me, with that smiling cupid's-bow mouth, and her eyebrows plucked up high, which always seemed to denote her level of expectations for her daughter and everyone else. Yet, soon I felt somehow we, her loved ones, had let her down, the same as we had let her down by not coming here before now and leaving flowers. Why had Daddy not chosen a headstone with a place for her photo? And by the way, had he stayed around long enough to be sure everything was correct on the stone? (It was.) In our few exchanges about coming here together, he never mentioned having come back to check the stone for accuracy.

"Mama." In my mind I forced the word out, like a child first learning to say the most endearing word she will ever know. *"Mama. I am here."* I knelt down on one knee, and as I did so I realized I was still gripping the flowers I had brought her. I laid them gently down and pressed my hand against the thin grass that grew over the warm red dirt. I thought how furiously Mama used to sweep that dirt off the floor of our house, and I smiled and then brushed a tear from my eye. Seven years....

Rising to my feet, I considered Daddy's decision to bury Mama among her pupils. And while I would one day have a compelling reason to doubt his wisdom in so doing and regret his choice, then it seemed clear enough to me. Mama would have been unfairly isolated way back there in our family plot, after having died among her students; indeed, having given her life only after making sure that others were safe. And quite likely she would remain without Daddy's companionship for decades and decades. No. He must have felt it would not seem right to put her back there, casting her out of the community she loved. I found myself thinking how the dead might carry on conversations here, as in the cemetery of Thornton Wilder's *Our Town*. How ridiculous, and yet the thought was comforting to me.

Now I promised Mama that I would be back, that I would never again neglect her grave. I would come back at Christmas, and Easter, I vowed. And on her birthday, for sure. Yet...I thought about this. Mama's birthday was June 17th. Could I save enough gas coupons by then to come back again? Oh, damn the war! Why couldn't they get the thing over with?

As I returned to the car, I felt guilty turning my back on all those graves, felt those who occupied them were staring at my back. *You can turn and walk away, but we can't.* My every step felt heavier than the one before, and the car seemed ten miles away. As soon as I slipped behind the steering wheel, gripped the door handle and heard the heavy door slam shut, I was overwhelmed, my spirits suffocating under a weight as heavy as all those stone markers engraved March 18th, 1937, piled one on top of the other. I rested my head on the wheel and started to sob and to shake. At length I became aware that I had made one hand into a fist and brought it to my mouth. I was biting down so hard that I made teeth marks in the skin, tears showering all the way down my forearm. *Oh my God, they are all gone, consumed in a single stroke as if swiped away by some giant, indifferent hand.* How could this be? I demanded. Of course, I knew the grim answer; still, the magnitude of the loss was incomprehensible.

I found myself wanting Bruce as I had not wanted him in a very long while. Wanting him to hold me close. To feel the strong undercurrent that always ran between our bodies. It seemed amazing that, for all we had both lost on that one day of our lives, there had never been a time when we cried together, and held and consoled each other. It was one more loss, added to the many others. I bitterly resented it.

Once I finally composed myself, I thought how Bruce and the whole community had chosen not to talk about the explosion. From far off it had seemed puzzling. But no longer. I knew that if I drove into town right now and encountered anyone I had known there, I would not be able to force out a single word on the subject. I was not sure I could even open my mouth in greeting.

I continued sitting there for a few minutes, plucking out the sticker burrs that I had picked up on my shoe soles, and thinking of Bruce. All those times I listened to the phone ring and ring, and no answer. And then he was gone. "Where are you?" I cried angrily into the silence. And I knew that if only I could find out today where Bruce had gone, I would go to where he was. I would get him to look at me, to *acknowledge* me. To at least hear me say that I was sorry for what I had done.

I sat catching my breath. The hands on my watch pointed at eleven-forty. I had plenty of time to drive into Overton, to Doc's old office. It would seem wise to go there first; then if need be, I would backtrack to see if I could locate the turn-off for the Buckstrum house, and ask questions there. Wouldn't it be amazing if Rusty appeared in the yard? I thought with a warm feeling in my heart. And now that I considered this possibility, I knew that unless I learned what had become of Rusty while at Doc's old office, I would still try and find Bruce's old house. If Rusty was there and remembered me, by golly, I would not leave him behind again, not for anything. Even if I had to steal him. Finally I would stop at our old house. I wanted to have time to linger there for a while before driving back to Houston. I started the car, feeling a little steadier now.

Soon I was driving along Poplar Row in Overton—the main street, so-named for the row of poplars planted along the esplanade—passing by the small building fronts. Some of them were brick, others had wood siding;

some had awnings, some not. Overton used to seem bigger on the Saturdays when I came into town with Mama in Daddy's truck, and sat reading in the tiny library while Mama ran her errands. Or, on the rare occasions when I got sick and had to come in and see Doc. When the East Texas field came in, Overton had spread out from a tiny hamlet into a fair-sized town, with new streets carved through the red dirt and buildings and houses erected. After having lived in Houston for so long now, it seemed to me small and sleepy and dusty, as if it had shrunk back after all the excitement of the new oil field died down. And indeed there were few cars traveling on the thoroughfare today, and a mere scattering of cars parked along both sides of the street. Of course, there may be more traffic on weekdays.

As I recalled, Doc Buckstrum's old office was located in the middle of the block. It was a flat-faced brick front, two stories high. I cruised down the avenue slowly, not sure I could recognize it by now. Then, abruptly there it was. I probably would not have known it except for the gold leaf lettering on the downstairs window: Sylvan Malone, MD. Open Monday thru Friday 7:30 till 6:00. Saturdays 8:00 till Noon. Closed Sundays. Underneath it all, an emergency phone number. Only the name of the doctor and the phone number had changed. Indeed I could tell that the new gold lettering was fresher and more glossy than the old. The fact that a doctor had apparently taken over in Doc's place made me feel hopeful. I glanced at my watch. Luckily, I had made it with five minutes to spare before closing time.

I hurried up to the door and tried the brass knob. To my relief, the door swung open. Inside the lights were out, though. Three walls were lined with Windsor chairs, enameled black. All empty. A glass window had been cut out of the wall across from the entrance, next to the door leading to the examining rooms. There was a buzzer on the wall next to the window with a small sign above: "Please ring, and be seated." I was sure this window was not there in my childhood days. However, other than Bruce, Doc had no one to assist him in his practice, no one to sit behind the window. I walked up to it. No one was sitting at the desk on the other side. A ruby red cardigan hung like a cape over the back of the office chair. I rang the bell and waited. Presently a man opened the door leading into the hallway, and looked out. He was putting on his suit jacket. One sleeve was on, and one was dangling down his back. He was a short man, tidily built, with straight, light brown hair and glasses. "May I help you?"

"Doctor Malone?"

"Yes." He seemed to be struggling to recognize me.

"I won't take much of your time," I promised. "I'm not sick or anything. My name is Delys Lithingate. I used to live around here. I was just wondering if you have any idea where Doc Buckstrum relocated?"

The doctor seemed surprised. He stood in the doorway putting the other sleeve on before answering me, as if he needed time to compose his reply.

"Perhaps you didn't actually know him. He left sometime in the spring of 1942, or maybe earlier; I'm not sure exactly," I said. "I went to school with his son Bruce, the one who survived the explosion. But we've—" I took in a hasty breath. "—lost contact."

Doctor Malone let the door close behind him then considered me for a moment. "Didn't you know? Doc passed away at the end of 1941," he said.

"No, no. I didn't know, I— was gone by then," I stammered. With all my being I resisted this complicating fact. Why had I never considered the possibility that Doc was dead? My mind felt scrambled now. I had to rethink everything. "I'm so sorry. I had no idea he was ill. The last time I was in touch with Bruce—it was a few months before that—Doc was fine. As far as I knew."

Quietly he said, "Peter died of liver disease. A couple of months after being diagnosed. With the liver, you don't even know you're sick until it's too late to do anything. He died the day Pearl Harbor was attacked." He paused, knitting his brow. "You were in school the day of the explosion?"

"Yes. My mother was a teacher. She was killed."

He pursed his lips, shaking his head. "Such a tragedy," he said.

"I was sent away to live with relatives in Houston. My father was an oilfield worker. He couldn't take care of me," I said. I could hardly believe I had just used the very language Allie once urged me to use when explaining my abrupt appearance in Jackson school, and that had so appalled me because it reflected poorly on my father.

I went on, "I've been to visit my mother's grave today. The first time I've been back. I saw Bucky—Peter, Jr.—and Edna's graves too. They were Doc's children–"

"I know. I had known Peter since we were in medical school in Galveston. Bucky was going to be a doctor. Peter brought him to visit my office in Dallas one day—I was in a practice with two partners then. He was a sharp young man. Too bad."

"Yes, it was. You know, Bruce decided to be a doctor after Bucky died. He used to work with Doc some."

The doctor looked at me vaguely. Apparently no one had told him about Bruce's aspirations. I felt Bruce had been slighted and that I should rise to his defense. But then Doctor Malone said, "I've always thought it was that explosion that really killed Peter. Of course, he had a rough life anyway. Married a nursing student in Galveston. Pretty girl, and smart. But she was poison. Never gave Peter anything but trouble, or so I gathered from what I heard. Peter and I lost contact there for a few years, went our separate ways.

"Of course, I'm speaking out of school I guess."

Indeed he was being more frank than I would have expected. But then, what was the point of being discreet now? Doc was dead. I lived in Houston. And Bruce— "Do you have any idea what became of Bruce?" I asked now.

"He quit school and joined the Navy."

I could only stare in amazement, the news seeming as big as the ocean Bruce had sailed into, and equally perilous. I should have thought of that possibility. It seemed so obvious now. My voice was trembling when I said, "I see. I guess that makes sense. Though I am sorry he didn't get to finish school." How would Bruce become a doctor once the war was over? Assuming—God grant—he survived. It had been more than three years already. *Please God, don't let it be that Bruce lost his life in the war. Or will, yet.*

Doctor Malone was nodding. "The one time I saw him after Peter's death—at the funeral—he seemed in a bad way. Doc was all he had left. I felt terrible for him, I sure did. That's when he said he had joined up."

I felt crushed with guilt. I should have been there for Bruce. He should not have gone through the loss of his father alone. I knew now what he was trying to tell me that night at the football game: *"I need to see you. My father is dying...."* It was worse than anything I had ever imagined him wanting to say. He must have needed me far worse than I had ever imagined, too. "I don't suppose Bruce left any forwarding address with you?" I asked, then felt ridiculous. Forwarding where? To a ship in the Pacific Ocean?

He shook his head. "I'm sorry. You know, Bruce always struck me as pretty much a loner. He used to drive Doc down to meetings there at the Rice Hotel in Houston. And I would see him around and think to myself, he just didn't seem to have much of a life. Except for...well...looking after his dad." Doctor Malone studied me for a moment, as though wondering how much I knew about Doc's personal life.

So he was aware that Doc had a drinking problem, perhaps long before Doc was taken ill. I imagined Doc having to be helped out of the Rice

Hotel bar, Bruce on one side and Doctor Malone on the other.

But Bruce did have a life then, and it was all wrapped up in mine. Had I known then what I knew now, I would never, ever have left him stranded no matter what. I was on the verge of tears. "Yes.... Well, I won't trouble you anymore. Thanks for everything," I said, then hesitated. I wanted with all my soul to beg this man to urge Bruce to contact me at once, should he ever see him again. Maybe even go so far as to say I had wronged Bruce, and wanted more than anything to say I was sorry, and beg his forgiveness. But somehow I could not bring myself to reveal these secrets to a stranger. Besides, what were the chances Bruce would ever come back to Overton?

Doctor Malone shifted his feet. Pulled out his pocket watch to check the time. I was detaining him. I imagined a wife waiting at home, their hot lunch laid out on the table: an everyday scene from a happy, well-balanced life that Doc and Bruce never had. Finally, I said limply, "But—should Bruce ever stop by, after the war is over, would you tell him that Delys asked about him? I'd just like him to know that I hope things turned out well for him."

"I'd be happy to," said the doctor, as anyone would. I only hoped he had discerned the depth of feeling behind my appeal, and would take me seriously. I felt certain that without his help, I would never be able to contact Bruce. Worse still, I may never even know if Bruce came home from the war.

Only as I was walking out did I think of Rusty. I pivoted around. "By the way, Bruce used to have a dog named Rusty. Do you know what became of him?"

Doctor Malone frowned slightly, perhaps put off now by being further detained. "No, I don't," he said.

"I remember he was a sweet animal," I said sadly, and walked out.

I heard the door lock behind me.

Chapter 21

The most thrilling moment of reaching full-fledged adulthood was the first time I slipped the key into the front door of the smaller side of a wood frame duplex at 4011-1/2 Rusk Street in Houston's East End. This was in mid-July of 1945. Graduation from Rice in May certainly had been gratifying, although the occasion was eclipsed by the electrifying news of Victory in Europe, broadcast a few days before. Being hired to replace my beloved English teacher on the Austin faculty— Mrs. Hathaway and her husband had decided to start a family—was probably the second largest thrill. At long last, I would provide my own living and cease depending on the kindness of my aunt and uncle to give me a roof over my head, or on my father to help cover my expenses.

Since Daddy married Maxine, I had felt reluctant to accept his financial help because doing so seemed to compromise my position. I had not been able to bring myself to spell out in so many words why I felt Daddy had let me down. How do you tell your father that he should have kept his pants buttoned up? Instead, I had implied my disillusionment mostly by long silences, and continuing refusal to move up to Cleveland and live with him and his new family. And then of course I had not invited Daddy to my graduation. The problem was that I did not know how to do so without inviting his new family as well. I could imagine him driving up with that wife and all those kids in tow. No, I couldn't. Maybe it was mean, but I did not want them to be a part of my big day. I did not want Daddy saying to people, "This is my wife Maxine, and my son, Daniel, Junior." Daddy had written me when his little boy was born and said they named him Daniel, Junior. "He's a right handsome little thing," he wrote. I think he was hoping that this news, so dear to his heart, would warm mine as well. But instead I felt insulted because it seemed to me that the designation, "junior," ought to have been reserved for the first son by a man's original wife. And it was also unseemly, I thought, that a man old enough to be a grandfather was boasting of having a brand new child.

But on that day when I turned the key and walked into that cozy nook—and nook is what it amounted to—I was overcome with a sense of joy that the place was mine. Of course I was only a renter then, but strictly speaking, I was not concerned about a property deed or a mortgage with my name on it. And by the way, it didn't do me much good that we owned our home in East Texas when Daddy decided to walk away from it. What I was experiencing at 4011-1/2 Rusk Street was the realization that I would never again be forced to move because the person in charge of my life decided it should be so; no one could ever make an abrupt change in plans that would take precedence over mine. No, absent some major reversal in my health which rendered me unable to hold a job or live alone and care for myself, no one could ever again make a decision for me about where or how I would live. I stood in my tiny living room and wheeled around, clapping my hands, and yelping, "Oh my oh my oh my!" Had there been sufficient space I would have kicked up my heels and danced a jig.

Some people could hardly wait until the first shiny new cars rolled off the assembly line so they could trade in their worn-out pre-war vehicles, but I would have driven my roadster until the wheels fell off in order to devote the money at my disposal to fixing up my new home. How like Mama I was turning out to be! Scouring the classifieds for used furniture, I found a serviceable love seat and easy chair, plus a magazine table that looked brand new after I covered the nicks and glass rings with an embroidered table runner. Aunt Allie made me a parting gift of the maple bedroom furniture from my old room. I bought unfinished shelving, bricks and a gallon of white enamel, and fashioned bookcases to climb up both sides of my tiny gas-log fireplace. (The shelves would soon prove insufficient to hold all my books; I have lived my whole adult life with at least three boxes of unshelved books in my home at all times.) I bought ruffled cotton tie-back curtains for the windows, and colorful braided rugs for the hardwood floors. Going from my single room at Aunt Allie's, into quarters that included my own kitchen and bath, seemed like moving into a palace. All this, and I had less than a five-minute drive to work. If not for the hefty satchel of papers I always carried, I could have easily walked.

An add-on to what had originated as a single-family residence, my side of the duplex was set back from the larger portion of the house front, with a small stoop and a tall window next to the front door. Outside, the street was quiet. The noise from bustling McKinney Avenue, two blocks over, plus other nearby thoroughfares feeding traffic into downtown Houston, was muffled by the spreading oak trees on both sides, up and down the block, some of their old, gnarly limbs overlapping to form the occasional archway. Auto tires crunched on acorns fallen to the ground and overlooked by the squirrels. Tangled tree roots rose up in places to buckle the concrete sidewalk. All of which gave me a sense of permanence that I found I craved as much as Mama had.

But what really sold me on the duplex was my side of the fenced back yard, which was overlooked by a large double window in the kitchen. Tall shrubs growing along the fence line gave the yard a measure of privacy. An outsized fig tree grew in the center of the yard, providing a nice leafy view as I sat at the kitchen table with my morning coffee; and later in the day, a shady area outdoors where I could put a lawn chair and settle comfortably to read a book, or grade papers. Or...maybe someday...write poems once again. Sometimes I felt guilty for having abandoned my efforts at writing about New London. Going to college year-round, I seemed always to be overwhelmed with course work. And now—well, teaching kept me busy, and gave me a feeling of satisfaction that made it easy to put off other ambitions. The strong creative urge that had overtaken me upon writing my first lines of verse had gradually receded to a nice warm memory that came to mind now and then, maybe when I read a poem published in a magazine that seemed especially meaningful and...well...was written plain enough to make me feel I could do that too, if I put my mind to it.

I don't know that there has ever been a time when I enjoyed my life more than in that first year or so of teaching and living alone. I did get invited out on dates pretty often. Anthony Delahasse, a divorcé from Louisiana, joined the faculty at the same time I did. We enjoyed a few evenings out and chaperoned a Bronco Whirl together. Then his mother was taken ill in Mandeville, and at the end of the semester he returned to care for her and teach there. Anthony promised to write, but so far he had not. It seemed like someone was always introducing me to a brother or a cousin or a good friend who was single. And let some nice unattached man show up new at East End Methodist, and Allie was planning a dinner at her house where she could introduce us. But again, as in my dating days at Rice, I never felt convinced that I had finally found the right man. I told myself that I had not fallen back into longing for Bruce, not at all; that I only longed for the excitement I used to experience when I was with Bruce, being so drawn to him both physically and emotionally that I dreaded parting from him, even for a little while. And I felt I was being truthful with myself. But then, one comment from a date that struck me as something Bruce would have been too kind, or too respectful, to say, and whatever attraction I might have been feeling would vanish. Can it be that for some of us, there is only one mate born into this world? I don't know. It seems reasonable, given the number of people who never marry. On the other hand, maybe for each of us there are many people out there who might cause the bell to ring, but some of us are not lucky enough to encounter more than one of them.

It wasn't long before I was considering buying the whole duplex where I lived, should the opportunity arise. And I was pretty sure it would. My landlords were a retired couple in their late sixties, Clyde and Ruby Taylor. They occupied the larger side of the duplex. A few chats over the fence dividing our back yards revealed that the Taylors anticipated moving to Arizona. One morning in a bold mood, I spotted Mr. Taylor trimming grass on his side of the fence, and stopped to tell him that when they were ready to sell out, I'd like the opportunity to make an offer.

Mr. Taylor was a tall, rangy man with a long slender face and the hard-baked complexion of one who has spent a good bit of time outdoors. He paused to pull out his handkerchief and mop his perspiring brow. "I don't see why not. Ye'll have to deal with my son, though. We are having one of those—" he paused in thought, frowning to himself— "Oh, heck, what you call those things? I'm always forgetting a word I used just the day before—"

"Power of Attorney?" I suggested.

"That's it!" he said, obviously surprised I knew the term.

"I used to work in my uncle's law office," I explained, hoping Mr. Taylor's son was as easy to get along with as he was.

He made a gesture toward the house. "She's good and sturdy, well-built. When we had that attachment put on, cut out a section in the wall to redo the electrical and run the gas line, and so forth, the workman went through four saw blades." Clearly, this was a point of pride with my landlord. I could not help remembering my feelings upon seeing the house Daddy had built, when I went back to New London that first time. The paint was peeling and the window screens were ragged, but as I observed the straightness of lines and the solid, square look overall, in spite of neglect, it seemed to me the house had a proud look, as if it were waiting patiently for a more responsible party to assume ownership. By then, Daddy had built two attic bedrooms with a bath in between at his house in Cleveland, hoping in vain that I would change my mind and move up there.

"You know, we always liked it here," Mr. Taylor said now, "but Ruby's allergies get worse and worse as time goes on. It's that darned humidity. Whenever we go out to Arizona, to visit, why, she feels like a new person."

"Well, I'm glad to hear that, Mr. Taylor," I said, backing away because I needed to leave for school.

"Next time my son stops by, I'll tell him what you said. Knowing me, I'll forget all about it by the time we get ready to put the house on the market. He'll remember."

"Thank you, Mr. Taylor," I said. I felt a little frightened of the commitment I would be making if all this happened, and through the school day my mind was preoccupied with wondering if I could find a way to start increasing what I saved each month.

From then on, I often found myself dreaming of improvements I might make to the duplex one day, when it was really mine. I would move into the larger side, of course, and rent out the smaller one. The larger side of the back yard was shaded by two tall, shaggy sweet gum trees, and there was room for a nice garden out there. I could see roses climbing up the fence, and maybe a bulb garden with all kinds of colorful blooms in the spring. Once I owned the place, I was determined to have a dog again, too— my lease with the Taylors prohibited pets. Only this time, my dog would have run of the house, sleep on a nice rug at the foot of my bed, and be my companion always. And I would take pictures of my dog, too. As many times as I had reminded Bruce, he never sent me a picture of Rusty. *"Problem is, every time I aim the camera at him, he runs toward me before I can release the shutter, and all I get is a blur. If I wait until Doc comes home, it's dark. Or else I forget. But I'll keep trying."* And then it was too late. I hoped Bruce had been able to find Rusty a good home when he went away to the Navy. I managed to locate the turn-off to the old Buckstrum house that first time I went back up there, but I saw no sign of Rusty or any other dog. The place was currently occupied, and was kept up nicely. I knocked on the door, but no one answered. I drove around the area a little more, to see if I could spot Rusty on someone else's place. But I never found him. On all my trips up there since that first time, I had visited only the cemetery.

Soon after moving in on Rusk, I had sent Daddy my new address and phone number–another thrill, having my own telephone number, WA 4191. Did he feel as if I were turning a knife inside his heart, when he received them? I wondered. In any case, he had written to wish me well. Since then, we had exchanged a few letters, and he would occasionally pick up the telephone and call. But we did not have much to say in our letters, and whenever he called, his voice was a little strained. I sensed he was trying to create a new opening for us to draw close to each other again, but he was at a loss to find the right words.

I think if Daddy had ever admitted to me the astonishing truth about his marriage to Maxine that I would later learn from his sister, my Aunt Florence, I might have been more forgiving. But he never said in so many words that he regretted having let me down. Maybe he was too proud.

He always seemed to hope I would eventually come around to accept his choices, and consider everything the same as it used to be between us.

As the months went by and I grew more and more absorbed in a life that was independent of Daddy's support, I spent less and less time dwelling on my anger at him. Now and then I would tell myself that someday he would see why I was so disillusioned and make amends, and we'd kiss and make up.

But that day never came.

Chapter 22

Around noon on the Sunday before Halloween, I was setting about to carve a small Jack-O-Lantern to put out on the front porch stoop. When the telephone rang my hands were immersed in squishy pumpkin pulp and seeds. I quickly rinsed them off and hurried to answer.

When the long distance operator announced a call for me from Mrs. Dan Lithingate, my mind stumbled in disbelief and confusion as an image appeared of Mama holding the receiver on the other end. No sooner had I shaken this off, realized who was calling me and answered, "Speaking," than I had a chilling intuition that Daddy was dead. I sank down on the bench with my knees clamped together.

Maxine came on the line. She was very sorry to report that my father had passed away. My hand flew to my chest, my mind in a whiplash as I was forced to accept that my intuition had been correct. Daddy was dead. *Passed away*, Maxine had termed it. How oddly the age-old phrase struck my ears. As if Daddy had just dematerialized into thin air one day—. "What...happened?" I murmured, barely able to find my voice.

"It was a heart attack," Maxine replied. "Danny had complained of feeling tired lately, but I thought it was from overwork, you know," she said. Her voice had a kind of nasal quality that was just short of sounding whiny, and she spoke with the elongated "i" vowel sound that I associated with people from up north. Just then my mind snagged on the fact that she had called my father by a name he never used. Danny. No one ever called him that. I was quite sure he would not have liked it. Dan, he was called. *Dan*, I wanted to correct her—

Her voice growing tremulous, she went on to explain that she had found him collapsed at his workbench in the basement.

I sat there mute as I tried to feature my daddy, a slender man of middle age who always took care of his health—well, except that he smoked cigarettes—and rarely suffered so much as a head cold, dying from a heart attack. I despaired at the thought of Daddy grabbing his chest, crying out in agony, then lying hunched over that workbench, all alone, desperately hoping someone would come and help. Surely if he could have gotten to a hospital quickly enough— "Where were you?" I blurted out to Maxine, then realized I must have sounded as if I were accusing her of neglecting him.

"I had taken Daniel and gone to the store," she said stiffly. "I found Danny when we got home. It was the worst—" she began, then the sentence abruptly halted. After a pause, she murmured "It was already too late."

"I see.... When did this—did it happen?" I asked, endeavoring to sound a little more forbearing.

"Yesterday, sometime around noon. I would have called you sooner but the operator said your number is unlisted."

Yes. A result of following the advice of more seasoned teachers who had learned from experience that it was wise to exercise control over such information.

"Your Aunt Florence didn't know what it was. Just now I found the number written down on a slip of paper, folded up in Danny's wallet," she said. Which brought to mind an image of Daddy standing furtively before a pay phone, reading my number off to a long distance operator.

It sounded as if Maxine and Daddy's sister were well acquainted. I had never even met my Aunt Florence, as she had moved to Fort Wayne, Indiana, long before I was born. It sounded odd for her to be referred to as my aunt. I was about to apologize for the trouble Maxine had in reaching me, but she spoke first.

"Florence and I—she's on her way here now—we felt you should be in on the plans for the funeral and all, so please try and get up here right away," she said, on a note of high stress, as if she was barely holding herself together. And no wonder, after the shock she had been through. I knew she deserved my sympathy, but I could feel nothing for her at this moment. I was numb.

Certainly I wanted to help plan the funeral, and I also felt instinctively that I needed to protect Mama and Daddy's interests somehow, though at the moment I could not think what they might be—*Oh God, Daddy is dead!* Tears gushed from my eyes.

"—and he adored his son," Maxine was saying now, but I had not heard the first part of the sentence. Was it, *"Your father adored you...."*? I could not help wanting that to be what I missed hearing, in spite of the fact that Daddy and I had our differences. "I'm having quite a hard time explaining this to a four-year-old who had just seen his father an hour or so before his death," she said, then added thinly, "Danny had sat him on a stool and helped him lace up his shoes before we left for the store."

The remark veered agonizingly close to my own fond memories of Daddy's gentle touch in caring for me. "I'll be on the next train leaving

Houston," I hastened to tell her, not wanting to hear anymore about Daddy caring for his son.

I was already thinking ahead. Before leaving I must be sure to notify Mrs. Sessions from the school, and ask her to find a substitute for me. Fortunately, my lesson plans for next week were on my desk. I had never questioned the importance of obeying this imperative, but nor had I ever imagined it might one day apply to my own circumstances.

"Oh, good!" said Maxine, sounding relieved. "Pastor is leaving town on Thursday, so we need to hold the service on Wednesday. Otherwise he'll have to find a clergy to take his place. And I don't want someone I don't even know standing up there."

Someone I don't even know. Daddy never went to church when Mama was alive, and apparently he had not changed his ways after he married Maxine.

"Darrell and Sheilah will stay with friends," she was saying. "So you and Florence can stay here with me." I sensed that having things to organize was helping to sustain Maxine right now. I presumed Darrell and Sheilah were the children by her previous marriage. Maxine's son and daughter, Daddy always called them. I did not recall him ever mentioning their proper names. Which may have been a measure of his sensitivity to my indifference. Daddy had another sister over in Fort Wayne, named Hannah. I wondered why she was not coming with Florence. I remembered the time when Daddy and I were planning for me to move to Cleveland, how he had looked forward to our spending holidays with these sisters and with Pop. Pop was ancient now, and his health was failing. Daddy visited him as often as he could. He wrote once, "Pop is a little worse off every time I see him." How did Pop feel when he learned his only son had died?

Belatedly, I realized that Maxine was expecting me to be her house guest. That was the last thing I wanted.

"It's alright, I can stay in a hotel," I suggested.

An audible sigh, the kind a mother utters when she is running out of patience with her uncooperative child. "Really, there's so much to do and very little time at this point. It would be easier on everybody if you were here," she insisted. Then, after a few beats, she added in an acidic tone, "Surely it won't hurt you to stay here just a couple of nights."

It occurred to me that Maxine probably resented me as much as I resented her. Reluctantly, I gave in to her wish.

Sitting there trying to collect myself, after we said goodbye, I felt there had been some deeper meaning in Maxine's rebuke. But my thoughts were too scattered to put my finger on what the meaning was. I dreaded the next few days. And yet Daddy's death seemed unreal. If the telephone had rung again in that moment, with his voice on the other end of the line, I would not have found it the least bit strange. How I wished Daddy would call right now, and Maxine's call had been nothing but a bad dream.

I soon learned from checking with the ticket agent at Union Station that I had just missed a twelve-thirty train, and the next available one left at five-thirty. I could easily make that one. Unfortunately I would have no choice but to spend the night on the train. I did not want to call Maxine again. I took the easy way out and called Western Union. "Will arrive in Cleveland 9:30 a.m. Monday, and take a taxi to your house," I advised in the telegram. Then I wondered about the words, "your house." Had this sounded as if I was rubbing in the fact that I had refused to make my home with Daddy and her? Which was true, of course; still there was no reason to seem—Oh well. I called Mrs. Sessions at home, then hurried to get my hair washed so it would have time to dry, to iron a few articles fresh from the laundry, then pack my clothes. I felt oddly removed from my surroundings, as if I had been sucked into a different dimension, and was viewing everything from a distance. After some deliberation while standing in front of my open closet, I decided on my straight black skirt, black crepe blouse and double-breasted herringbone jacket to wear to Daddy's funeral. I had not wanted the black blouse, I recalled now. I had chosen a white one of the same style from the Foley's rack. But the sales clerk insisted black looked much smarter with the herringbone, so I acquiesced. At home from shopping, I had taken the blouse from the bag, and wondered why I had ignored my instinct and given in. Now, unfortunately, the choice seemed prophetic.

Finally, when I was ready to leave, I called Allie to tell her that Daddy had died and that I was leaving for Cleveland. There was a long moment of silence. Daddy's decision to remarry suddenly, after having invited me to share his life in Cleveland, was another black mark against him in Allie's already low estimation. Eventually she said quietly, "Well, what a shock. How old was Dan? I should know, but I—. Wait a minute." She turned from the phone and conveyed to Logan that Dan had died suddenly.

Was Daddy forty-eight, or forty-nine? I had to think. "Nearly forty-nine. His birthday is in January," I reported when Allie came back on the line. Forty-nine seemed too old for Daddy suddenly. Technically this made him past middle-age. Still, he was an active, vigorous man. And that took off the years. Not so long ago he had remodeled his house, doing most of the work himself. You had to be in very good shape to—

"That's awfully young," Allie was saying now, as if she had been privy to my thoughts. "But all that time he worked in the oil fields. That takes a toll on a man, I'm sure," she added. So now I wondered if Allie felt Daddy had gotten what he deserved, for his foolish choice of a vocation had already cost my mother her life.

"Well, I am sorry, I really am. I know you loved your daddy," she said with feeling. Which returned the tears to my eyes. I blinked them back. "Would you like for Logan and me to come for the funeral?" she added on the same note. I had not expected this at all, and for a moment I hesitated. While I appreciated the offer, it seemed their presence at Daddy's funeral would be inappropriate given how they felt about him. Besides, I could imagine the strain between Maxine and Allie.

"Thanks, but I would not want you to go to all that trouble," I told her.

"Very well. Will you phone me the arrangements then? Logan and I will send flowers."

Sensing she was relieved to be off the hook, I promised I would.

"And be sure you take your heavy coat. It will be colder up there."

I walked through the front door at four-thirty to wait for the taxi I had ordered, first stopping at the Taylors' to ask them to collect my mail until I returned. I always collected their mail when they went out of town. Mrs. Taylor came to the screen door. She was a compact woman with tightly curled gray hair and gold-rimmed bifocals that made her eyes look larger than they were. When I imparted the news, she clicked her tongue and said sweetly, "Oh, honey!" Mrs. Taylor didn't know me personally all that well, and yet I felt as though she truly empathized with what I was feeling. Again, tears raced to my eyes. I braced myself to keep from completely breaking down. "Come on in, have a cup of coffee with us, before you go; I just made a fresh pot," she urged. She pushed on the screen door. But I did not have time. Anyway, I would have been a total wreck if I had sat down with her. I declined, but thanked her for her kindness. The taxi appeared at the curb. I waved at the driver, hurried back to my front porch stoop, and picked up my suitcase.

"Did Dan ever make out a new Will, after he remarried?" Logan had asked worriedly, having taken the phone from Allie after she and I finished talking.

"I— I don't know," I stammered.

"Well, if so he should have sent you a copy. Take your copy of the

Will your parents drew up. And if Dan did make out a new one at some point, say you will need a copy for your attorney to review."

"And if he didn't?"

Logan sighed. "Let's just hope he did. Otherwise, this could get messy."

"Well I'm sure he did," I had told Logan, yet more out of an instinct to defend Daddy than out of any sense of real certainty. "He was always very responsible about things like that," I added. And that was the truth. Daddy might have reasoned that to send me a copy of any new Will that provided for his latecomer family would be like throwing salt on an open wound.

As the train lumbered out of the station, the sky was quickly darkening. I switched on the reading light above my seat, withdrew the Will from my handbag, removed it from its envelope and unfolded it. The document was a little over a page long, and was dated just a few months after I was born. We were then living in Wichita Falls, Texas, I was reminded by seeing Mama and Daddy's place of residence typed in. I had no memory of Wichita Falls except I thought I had been told at one time that Daddy was working at the Burkburnett field when I was born, and he rode back and forth every day on the train. Oh yes, and there were so many oil field workers on the train, Daddy often made each leg of the trip standing up in the aisle. Poor Daddy....

I indulged in running my fingers lightly over the familiar signatures now: here a pen held in Mama's and Daddy's grip had made fleeting impressions long ago. Mama's signature was gently slanted and feminine, the Ls of Lavinia and Lithingate extravagantly looped. Daddy's letters were straight up and down jabs at the page, the L of his last name exaggerated, out of proportion to the other letters. I closed my eyes and tried to imagine the two of them sitting on hard wood chairs in a little office, leaning earnestly over the document, poring over every word. Mama wearing her Sunday dress and hat, her small pair of gloves folded neatly over her handbag; Daddy in a fresh set of khakis, creased and starched. The scene as wholesome and American as a Norman Rockwell cover on the *Saturday Evening Post.* Could either of them ever have imagined that their lives would end as they had? Surely not. I would be willing to bet, in fact, that what was going through their minds as they sat there was the very real danger that Daddy could be killed on an oil rig one day and leave Mama and me to fend for ourselves. I paused to count up the years Daddy had outlived Mama: less than ten.

Starting at the beginning, I read through the provisions of the Will.

I was familiar with the ornate language of such documents, and this one was about as simple and straightforward as they came. Though Mama and Daddy did not own much at the time—a savings account, some jewelry, household goods, and a truck—they were obviously looking to the future. The Will provided for any real property, buildings thereon, stocks, and shares in any oil or gas well they might one day acquire. And naturally, as their only survivor, I would be their sole heir.

But that was then.

I sat there thinking. Maxine's seeming resentment of me came to mind. Could it be that Daddy had not made a new Will after all, and she was anticipating a fight with me, and maybe Daddy's sisters, to get what she felt was rightfully hers from his estate? And what would there be? The house they lived in, of course, and a vehicle. A savings account, probably. Some stocks, maybe? Though Daddy wasn't by nature a speculator. And as far as I knew he had never bought shares in any well he helped to drill. I didn't feel I was deserving of any of his estate, though I might feel differently if I were still in college and needed his help. In any case, I hoped that he had set out his wishes on paper. Then there would be no confusion about any matter of importance.

After folding up the Will and returning it to the envelope, I gazed through the window and saw not the darkening landscape but the shadowy features of my own face, reflected there like a ghost. At first I thought with regret of the way things had turned out for Daddy and me. I still did not think I had done anything wrong by refusing to move in with him and his new family. Yet, I did regret not inviting Daddy down for my college graduation. I should have done that no matter how I felt about his new wife and family, instead of thinking how ashamed I would be if they all showed up—. Ashamed. That was the other note I picked up in Maxine's voice over the phone, I realized now, the one I could not identify at the time: *You are ashamed of me and I know it. But that's your problem.*

Well, there was nothing I could do about it, I thought, and wondered why Maxine had been so insistent I stay in her home. It seemed to me she should have been relieved when I offered to rent a hotel room. Surely it would not have been all that inconvenient. Oh well, this would all be over in a couple of days, I told myself. Then it occurred to me that I had no idea where Daddy was to be buried. My heart froze. Why had I not thought about this when I was still in Houston, and could seek Logan's advice?

Maxine would probably want to bury him up in Cleveland, but I did not believe that Daddy would want to be buried in a place where he had only lived a few years, and to which he had no connections except for this latecomer family. Unfortunately he could not be buried beside Mama. But on the other hand...he could be buried not so far away, in our family plot, and I could visit his grave every time I visited Mama's. What would Daddy have wanted? That was the question.

In the end he had married someone else, I reminded myself, and it would be the second wife who buried him, therefore— Still.... Many widowers remarried. Was it a given that Daddy be buried beside Maxine, especially—now that I thought about it—given the circumstances of the marriage? I did not know that Daddy had ever been in love with Maxine. He never said so. But I knew without a doubt that he loved Mama. Surely he would want to be buried nearby the woman he loved.

So the question became: wouldn't Mama want that, too? Didn't she matter in all this?

As promised the first time I knelt before Mama's grave, I had been returning to visit with regularity, and more frequently since the war ended and gas rationing ceased. Granted, my first few returns were almost as painful as the initial visit. But finally I had resolved that Mama would not want me to drive all the way up there and spend my time with her grieving, or even succumb to the undertow of guilt I always felt from the graves around hers. She would expect me to remember the good times. So I had endeavored to fulfil what I believed would be her wish. In so doing I had come to feel, when there, that I was in the presence of the life we had shared, as if it were a cloud surrounding me, lifting me up. In that life, with my father steadfast in watching over us, I saw completeness, a kind of trinity. I often found myself staying longer than I intended because I became lost in thought as one might get lost in conversation with a seldom seen relative at a family reunion.

Yet, every time I turned and walked away, I felt sad that Mama may be the only one of us ever to be buried there, in spite of her efforts to be sure we would always be together, even into eternity, in the place we had finally put down roots. If Daddy could be laid to rest just steps away from Mama, it would at least be better than for him to be stranded hundreds of miles away, I reasoned.

Then the obvious solution dawned on me: to not only bring Daddy's body back from Ohio, but also move Mama to lie next to him at Pleasant Hill. How simple. Would it be wrong to remove her from among her pupils, though? I thought about this. Surely after all this time, Mama's husband should take precedence. Was this in the back of his mind, when he buried her there, that when he died, she should be moved to lie beside him? Oh, it seemed so likely now. This was surely what my parents would both want, and would expect me to arrange. For a fleeting moment I imagined Daddy having stated this preference in his new Will— assuming he had one. Yet truly I could not see him making such a provision, on pain of upsetting his current wife who would be privy to it.

I thought further. Even if I could persuade Maxine to permit me to have Daddy's body moved to Texas— and now I remembered her edginess, like the grittier side of a fingernail file— the whole proposition would be frightfully expensive. I could already see my savings account wiped out, and with it my hopes of making a nice down payment on the duplex one day.

I leaned my head back on the seat and closed my eyes, my mind too fuzzy with exhaustion to figure that one out.

Even though it was early still, I felt I could go to sleep and sleep until morning. I was just dozing off when I remembered something else: I had never properly thanked Daddy for supporting me so generously all those years after Mama died, until I had graduated from college and was able to support myself. Of course I had said thank you many times along the way, for instance, in the numerous cases where I needed extra money because some expense came up that I had not anticipated. *"Hello, Daddy. I fainted during the Opening Day performance and destroyed my drum." "How come you to faint...?"* But I had never sat down and assessed all Daddy had done for me—far more, no doubt, than many absent fathers would have done—and written a long letter, pouring out my heart and expressing the gratitude he deserved. A sharp sense of guilt overtook me and brought me fully awake. From then on I was condemned to sit there remembering what a good father Daddy had always been. How his arms always opened wide to me when I was a child and he walked through the door at night after work. No matter how tired he must often have been, or how difficult the day, I could not remember a single time that he was impatient or short with me. And those nights out on the porch under the stars that I had counted on—. It seemed to me now that Daddy had very little time to himself in those days. Surely there were nights when he would have preferred to be left alone with his thoughts and his cigarette out there, but he never made me feel unwelcome. He seemed to appreciate the fact that the day would come when I would outgrow my desire for his undivided attention and prefer being with someone else. *I never did*, I realized now. What I would give to have just one of those nights back at this moment!

Still, in the end, he put someone else before me. His doing so cost us the opportunity to make up for all the years we had already lost. And now that I thought about it, maybe that error was what had cost him his life. Daddy had no doubt overextended himself, physically, building onto his house. I could see him hauling heavy stuff around, and climbing on the roof, nailing on shingles. Apart from that, imagine having a young child to raise and two others to finish raising, when he was old enough to be a grandfather! I suddenly wondered: finding himself responsible for a wife and three children, plus still having some responsibility for my welfare, did Daddy ever lose sleep worrying about money? If so, he never even hinted as much to me. As proud as he was, he would have kept such burdens to himself. I hoped with all my heart that worrying had not shortened Daddy's life.

Now I remembered the time after the New London tragedy that Daddy visited me in the hospital, and admitted his regrets for not having told Mama he loved her on the last morning of her life because he was still miffed from their argument of the night before. Oh, what I would give if only I had swallowed my pride, called up Daddy one day and said, *"I love you no matter what."* The words he wished he had spoken to Mama. Just so, when his last breath passed from his body, he would know.

Chapter 23

As the taxi drove away I lingered on the sidewalk, hugging my coat about me. Allie was right. The wind was icy and the sky had a marble cast that seemed to threaten worse weather to come. I tugged on the broad brim of my hat to keep it from sailing off my head. Now that I was standing in front of the house Daddy had shared with his new family, I felt as if I were being forced to open my mouth and swallow a bitter dose of medicine that I had been putting off for years. But that was not the only reason I was reluctant to go inside.

It must have been at least three o'clock in the morning before I finally fell into a deep sleep in my seat on the train. Just before waking up I had a pleasant dream of the kind that comes sometimes at the surface of sleep, a time when reality is still barely suspended and a person's force of will can make things as they should be. Daddy was sitting at the end of my bed, and we were talking. About what subject I had no idea, nor had I any idea what age I was in the dream, or whether I was in bed because I was sick, or because it was bedtime. But even when I came fully awake and cognizant, I still had a sense of Daddy's presence, as if he were reaching out to comfort me for a loss only he could understand.

All I wanted was to be left alone now, to savor the feeling of Daddy's presence for as long as I could. And I knew once I knocked on the door of this house, the spell would be broken.

Not having attended Mama's funeral, I could have turned around and taken the next train back home, skipping Daddy's as well. After all, this event was Maxine's affair, not mine, and it wouldn't bring Daddy back to me. I had already made up my mind I would not view Daddy's corpse. I wanted to remember him as he looked the last time I saw him: on the happy night I became Colonel of the Scottish Brigade.

Still, the Lithingate family were my blood kin, so if they were to appear at Daddy's funeral, then so should I.

Daddy's street was located in a neighborhood not far from downtown Cleveland, and was built on a grade, like the street where my aunt and uncle lived. The houses were sturdy-looking and boxy, fortresses against the harsh winters around Lake Erie. Daddy had once mentioned in a letter that the winters up here were hard on him. They made his back act up from that old injury. As the street slanted down, the house lots were gradually built up higher and higher with concrete embankments. Daddy's house was in the middle of the block, a one-story cottage with a pointed gable in front. The wood siding was a light caramel brown color, with dark brown trim. Centered on the house front was a small porch, with four steep stairs leading up to it. Some variety of squatty, evergreen bush grew in unruly thatches on each side. Except for these, plus an old tree— maybe some variety of oak—with a knobby trunk and branches that were dropping their brittle leaves even as I stood looking, the front lawn was bare. Maxine was no gardener, obviously. Altogether, house and yard lacked the charm of our place in East Texas, as though it were chosen with less care and forethought. *"This one will do,"* I could imagine Daddy saying indifferently. Then I noticed the roof line built out on either side of the central gable, and I realized that for the moment I had forgotten the attic suite that Daddy built. With lines clean and sharp, it looked professional, as if it had been part of the original house, rather than something added on later by the homeowner. Just what I would expect of Daddy, I thought, sadness creeping over me. But did he really believe that I would be willing to move into those quarters?

Somewhere along last night's journey, in between my other thoughts and conjectures, I had resolved to give Maxine the benefit of the doubt. To be fair, Daddy was the one who had made a promise to me that marriage to her would threaten. She was no more responsible for his actions than any other woman would be in her relationship with a man she loved. And now she had lost that man suddenly, after only a few years of marriage. So far I had not been able to conjure up any real sympathy for Maxine. But as I had accepted her offer of hospitality during a very difficult time for everyone, it was only right that I repay her by being pleasant and helpful. Besides, I felt the obligation of showing respect to one's elders, which my parents had inculcated in me.

I picked up my suitcase and walked to the porch.

Soon the door was swinging open. The woman standing before me bore a strong resemblance to Daddy, which gave my heart a moment of pause. Aunt Florence. Her hair, pulled straight back into a knot, was the same color as his. The gray strands that softened the blond to a pearly tone were barely distinguishable, and made me wonder suddenly if Daddy had amassed any gray in his hair these past few years. Florence had high cheekbones and hazel eyes, and she was slender and long-limbed like Daddy. People had often said that Daddy looked younger than his age, and so it was with his sister. Florence was ten years older than Daddy, around fifty-nine.

"Delys? Come in, child," she said warmly. "I'm your aunt, Florence Bergen. It's good to meet you at last." I could detect no lingering flavor of Texas in her voice. She might have been born and raised up here. Her eyes were puffy and pinkish around the edges; she'd had her weeping spells as I had.

"Thank you, the same to you." I stepped inside a long rectangular living room and put my suitcase down. Florence helped me off with my hat and coat, and hung them on the hat tree nearby the door. I looked around. The room was modestly appointed but comfortable looking, with area rugs of muted tones over the dark wood floor, and crochet doilies on the arms of the overstuffed furniture. An upright piano stood in the center of one wall, with several small framed pictures lined up across it on an embroidered runner. I recognized my own likeness among these, clad in my Brigade uniform with epaulets and whistle. I found this encouraging somehow.

An insubstantial looking fold-out bridge table sat diagonally in the corner to my left, with three unmatched chairs positioned around it. In the center of the table were a Holy Bible, bound in black, and a smaller volume—a hymnal, perhaps?— with a cover of deep blue. At one place were assorted papers, a lead pencil, a writing pad. And—I noticed now—a legal-sized document. Daddy's new Will? I certainly hoped so.

The other places were bare. Altogether, the sight of the little make-shift conference area was slightly unnerving. Having been the last to arrive, I was at a disadvantage regarding whatever proceedings were already under way there. I thought of my hopes of having Daddy's body removed to Texas. Now that I was here, on Maxine's home turf, the prospect seemed even more daunting.

The two adjacent windows at the corner were covered with thin, lacy panels, and the window sashes were cracked a couple of inches at the bottom. Regardless, the air was musty with accumulated layers of cigarette smoke. So apparently Maxine was a smoker. Daddy never smoked indoors. Or, did he? Prohibiting cigarette smoke in the house had been Mama's rule. I could imagine Daddy and his new wife sitting quietly of an evening in the living room, on either end of the sofa, reading the papers or listening to the large radio-phonograph that stood in one corner, and enjoying their smokes.

Florence and I stood looking at each other, neither of us knowing what to say. Should we hug? I wondered. If so, as the older one, Florence should be the one to initiate it. I hoped she would not. If we came into physical contact, I might lose my composure; and I did not want to, not around someone I had only just met. Momentarily she put her head to one side and observed, "You look just like your picture." She gestured toward the piano. "In the uniform."

I smiled politely, though in truth I felt remiss for never having sent Daddy a more recent photo. Yet, circumstances being what they were—my sense of disillusionment, along with the scarcities war—

"Dan was so proud," Florence was saying, upon which we both got tears in our eyes. She went on, "There was Scottish blood in our family, you know—on Mother's side—somewhere up the line."

"Really? I never knew that," I remarked, thinking surely nothing could be more irrelevant. The Scottish theme was chosen because Stephen F. Austin, our school's namesake, was of Scottish descent. Obviously, Florence was searching for some way to start a conversation.

"Our mother died giving birth to Dan," she said now, as though realizing her earlier attempt had failed.

This came as a surprise. I had always understood that Daddy's mother died when he was very young, but neither of my parents ever spoke of the circumstances. Perhaps they were afraid I would be frightened to hear them. "How sad. I am sorry," I said, for I could think of nothing else to say.

"Our house had one of those wide, rounded stair landings where coffins could be pivoted around and brought down. Hannah and I stood with Pop at the bottom of the stairs, watching as they brought our mother down from the second floor. We could hear our new baby brother crying upstairs." She sniffed. "I hadn't thought of that in many years; it's funny how things will come back to you at a time like this—" Her voice broke off. She searched my face. "Are you alright?"

"Yes, ma'am. I think so. Just a little stunned."

She nodded. "We all are. Well. Maxine's in the kitchen; we've just finished breakfast," she said. "Oh—forgive me, have you had anything to eat this morning?"

I told her of the cinnamon roll and orange juice I had eaten in the dining car, thinking it was a good thing I had done so. My stomach felt a little jittery now. "Will your father and sister be coming?" I asked, then realized I had framed the question awkwardly. But I did not feel right calling them by more familiar names when I hardly knew my grandfather and had never laid eyes on my Aunt Hannah.

"It's Pop and Hannah," she said.

"I—I'm sorry—I'm afraid I don't quite know how to—"

"It's alright," she assured me, and flashed a warm smile of understanding that was so like Daddy, it caught me off guard and brought a sharp pang of longing. Immediately I felt a real sense of kinship with my aunt. I sensed that she and I would stand united against Maxine, if the need arrived. I checked myself. I was not going to think that way. Of course, I would like for Florence to know of my preference for Daddy's burial before I brought it up to Maxine. But I could hardly blurt it out at this early point.

Florence was shaking her head sadly. "Pop is not doing well at all. Hannah felt Dan would want her to stay there and care for him."

"Of course, I understand...."

"My husband, your Uncle Joe, will be here on Wednesday," she went on, "and one of our daughters—Harriet—may be coming in from college; I don't know who else at this point. It was all so sudden! Everyone's scattered—

"First, let's take your things upstairs—we're sharing the attic bedroom, looks out on the back yard."

I could see a small stairway leading up from the hallway beyond the living room. I had been given to believe there were two bedrooms in the attic. I had never shared a bedroom in my life, and now the prospect made me feel hemmed in. Oh well, only for a couple of days....

As I reached for my suitcase, Florence said under her breath, "Maybe we can take a minute up there, and talk—"

But just then Maxine walked in, a small boy shadowing her steps. Like Mama, Maxine was small-boned, and she was about Mama's height. But she was a little more hippy and buxom, which of course sent my thoughts spinning off in a direction they had no business going. She wore a white silky blouse with long sleeves and bulky padded shoulders, a straight skirt of deep green, and a pair of brown pumps. Her legs were rather thin, which made her look a little top heavy. Her eyebrows were plucked up high—like Mama's—and her dark hair was parted down the center and neatly waved, with curly bangs across her forehead.

As she came nearer, I noticed there were wrinkles around her mouth. Impossible, surely, but she looked older than Daddy. Yet, I had not seen Daddy in more than five years, so how would I—

"Delys, welcome," she said, taking my hands in hers, her brow knitted as though in concern. Her hands were as soft and smooth as rose petals; her fingernails were neatly manicured, and enameled red. How, and where, had she and Daddy met? I wondered, not for the first time. I had not wanted to give Daddy the satisfaction of showing any curiosity about Maxine.

"Thank you. It was kind of you to invite me to stay," I told her amicably. I was not sure how to address Maxine. Using her first name did not seem appropriate. Yet, what alternative was there? To address her as Mrs. Lithingate was surely no more so. And I certainly was not about to call her Mother.

She lifted her chin. "There's only one bedroom upstairs now. Eventually, we moved Sheilah into the larger room, and made the other into a little rumpus room," she said. "The boys sleep together downstairs." I was not sure if she was simply stating facts, or reminding me that the larger room had sat empty for some time, being reserved, in vain, for me. Had this caused friction between Daddy and his second wife? I wondered. Now I noted a hard look about Maxine's mouth, that suggested she did not take much off anyone else. Again, I reminded myself to give her the benefit of the doubt. Maybe she was only trying to contain her emotions, and the effort had the effect of coarsening her appearance.

Maxine withdrew her hands from mine and turned to the child clutched up to her skirt. "And this is Daniel, Junior. Say hello to Delys, son."

The little boy wore a pair of brown corduroy overalls and a long-sleeved striped jersey. He had dark curls, deep brown eyes and an olive complexion. He looked like his mother. Of Greek extraction maybe, or Italian? I could not see a single trace of Daddy in his features, a fact that I found darkly gratifying. Peering sideways at me, he murmured a shy hello.

"Pleased to meet you," I said, and thought of the child sitting on the stool, Daddy lacing up his shoes. I could not help feeling a little sorry for him, and guilty for being ungenerous. He would grow up with precious few memories of his father, whereas I would have many to call on, for the rest of my life.

"Are you my dad's sister?" he inquired.

"No, dear, Dad's sister is Aunt Florence," Maxine cut in. "Delys is Dad's daughter. Your stepsister. Remember, I told you." She dandled his hand a little, as if to shake loose his recollection. "Now, go in your room and play until we're ready to go. Mommy has business to do with these ladies."

My heart skipped a beat. The child went off, peering at me over his shoulder with eyes wide, as if I were some kind of exotic curio.

Maxine watched him until he disappeared around the corner, then turned to me, looking bereft. I recalled her saying on the telephone that Daniel, Junior did not understand what had happened to his father. I did not envy her the task of trying to explain. "May I bring you some coffee?" she asked.

"No, thank you."

Maxine led Florence and me to the table, where she assiduously claimed the seat with papers and pen. From her skirt pocket she removed a nearly empty pack of Chesterfield cigarettes and a slim silver lighter. As I watched her placing these articles nearby on the table, I stole a quick glimpse at the heading on the legal document. It was indeed a Will. Thank goodness. Maxine caught me peeking. I smiled uncertainly. Her eyes blazed in triumph. *Just you try something, young lady....*

First she asked me to review the typewritten obituary, to be sure there were no errors or misspelled names. "They helped me with it at the funeral home, and your Aunt Florence has already approved it. But your being an English teacher and all, we thought.... I've got to drop it off at the funeral home before noon, so it will be in time for tomorrow's paper."

I read through it, noting that Maxine had named me as Daddy's daughter "by a previous marriage." It seemed to suggest Mama and Daddy had divorced. It made my blood boil for a moment, but then I told myself surely she had not intended to imply that.

"I would prefer my mother's name be included, and the fact that Daddy was widowed in 1937," I told her.

Looking mildly vexed, she said, "I was trying to abide by the word limit suggested at the funeral home. And the only name I knew for your mother was Vinia. I assume that's a nickname. And Florence didn't—" She shrugged, and checked her watch. "But go ahead and rewrite that part."

"Mama's name was Lavinia Pearl," I told her, drawing out the name as prettily as I could. I quickly made the corrections and returned the sheet to her. Putting it aside, she handed me a typewritten form headed up, "Order of Service for a Funeral." I was beginning to appreciate how many tasks must be fulfilled after the death of a spouse. "At least we've got until tomorrow with this. Florence and I have been working on it together," she said.

I glanced at the single sheet, then looked up. "Had Daddy been going to church?" I asked, curious.

Maxine shook her head, pursing her lips. "After I joined, I was hoping he would too. But the only time he came was when Daniel, Junior was christened. That's when we bought your father's suit."

The suit Daddy would be buried in, I presumed. Had I ever seen Daddy wearing a suit? If so, I had no recollection of it.

The names of hymns, and chapter and verse from Scripture, were jotted down on empty lines on the form. There were several places where selections had been marked through and changed. Following Florence's suggestions, perhaps? The handwriting was erratic, rife with angles and back slashes. As I read through, I sensed something artificial, forced, about these funeral details. What a shame there was not some alternative form of final observance for people who had never stepped inside a church if they could help it, and would not have wanted to exit by way of the church either, and certainly not wearing a suit. I vaguely envisioned a simple service outdoors, with readings from some of the great thinkers whose ideas were shaped by an affinity to nature–Emerson and Thoreau, for instance, and Melville and Whitman. Daddy and I had never talked about books—he wasn't much of a reader—and I did not know how familiar he was with the writings of these literary giants. But he was highly intelligent, and he loved the outdoors, so I was sure that he would have admired them. And maybe I would write an elegy that captured Daddy's essence. *We sat out under the stars at night....* The service would close with my elegy. Oh yes, I thought with a thrill, this was exactly what Daddy would have wanted. Regrettably, though, I had arrived too late to make any major changes in the plans–

That was when I noticed the final typewritten entry: "Following the service, interment will be at," then a long underline, one of the few that had been left blank. I could hardly believe my eyes. Apparently Daddy's widow intended for me to have a say in his place of burial. I saw it all clearly now. Maxine could have her stiff, claustrophobic funeral for Daddy up here, satisfying herself that she had done her Christian duty. Afterward I would have the luxury of time to make plans, do the necessary reading, and put together a service that reflected the person Daddy really was.

Referring the two women to the blank space on the page before me, I ventured boldly, "I would like to arrange to bring Daddy back home to Texas. I am sure it's what he would want." I remember being deliberately vague as to my plans. Maxine may very well be jealous of my mother, I thought; best to keep Mama out of the discussion.

Maxine leaned forward, her eyes wide. "You can't be serious."

Florence uttered a weary sigh and sat back in her chair.

So they had been wrangling over this prior to my arrival. But why? Before I could say anything more, Maxine glanced around at Florence, then turned back to me, her eyes steely. "Why Delys, I'm sure your father would be *deeply* touched—" lifting a hand to her chest— "to see you take such an *interest* in him suddenly, after all these years," she said theatrically.

Though I could not see it then, Maxine's surprise—and insult—were surely understandable. After all, she had no basis for believing that I still cared deeply for my father, in spite of our estrangement.

Then I could only blink and stare back wordlessly, as though she had slapped me across the face. My one coherent thought was that I had guessed correctly about her low opinion of me. I was tempted to inform her that Daddy had let me down by marrying her in the first place, but my relationship with Daddy was none of her business.

Abruptly Maxine rose from her chair, grabbing her cigarettes and lighter as though she were afraid Florence or I might steal them. "I've got to get ready to go," she said huffily. "We'll have to take this up later."

Florence handed her the obituary. "Don't forget this," she cautioned.

When Maxine was out of the room, Florence and I slowly looked at each other. Florence patted my arm sweetly and shook her head, never mind. Again I had a glimpse of her intuitive understanding that was so like Daddy and that had drawn me to her. In a voice that was forced, and a little louder than necessary, she said, "This would be a good time for you to have a look at your father's Will, don't you think?"

I was sure that if Maxine overheard, she was not fooled into thinking that we would table the subject of Daddy's burial until she returned. "Alright," I said nonetheless. I reached for the Will, recalling my initial relief that it existed. It brought little comfort now.

I was three or four paragraphs down when I overheard Maxine say from the hallway, "Yes, you do have to wear your coat. You don't want to catch cold." Moments later the back door slammed shut. Florence gestured toward the Will. "That's your copy to keep. You can read it later. We have to talk, and there isn't much time. The funeral home is only a few blocks from here."

Chapter 24

I placed the Will on the table and looked at Florence. She brought a hand to her brow. "I wish I had known ahead of time what you were going to suggest. Why would you want to bring your father back to Texas? From what I understand, he can't be buried next to your mother."

"We own lots in that same cemetery," I told her. "I'll have Mama's body moved from where it is, and placed next to his. I'm sure Daddy assumed that's what would be done after he died. It was just, the circumstances of her death—she was killed along with so many pupils she had taught—" I shrugged helplessly at the doubtful look on my aunt's face. "It's difficult to explain to someone who did not live in the community. I'm sorry."

"But you don't even live up there anymore, where you can visit their graves," she pointed out.

"It isn't so far away. I visit my mother's grave every few weeks," I said.

Florence lifted her brow. "I see. Well, there is no reason to believe that your father wanted to be buried in Cleveland," she admitted. "Maxine only bought the cemetery lots yesterday, when she was at the funeral home."

I leaned forward earnestly. "Then that bolsters my argument. Maxine ought to have waited until you and I got here, before buying cemetery lots."

Florence studied me momentarily, a hint of irony in her gaze. "There is much you don't know about the ways of Maxine, and we don't have time for me to tell you right now.

"I have the solution," she said. "I want to bury Dan in our cemetery."

I was perplexed. I assumed the Lithingates were buried in Houston, where Daddy's mother was buried. "How often could you visit his grave, in Houston?"

She was shaking her head. "No, we had Mother's remains moved up to the cemetery in Fort Wayne, shortly after Pop came to live with Hannah. It was one of his stipulations. So, virtually the whole family is up there."

Virtually. "Well, that leaves me out of the picture, doesn't it," I said in consternation.

"No, not at all," she said, then her eyes grew tender. "Oh Delys, I've been thinking these past two days of all the time we've wasted, never getting to know you. And after chatting with you this morning, I feel it more strongly. We should have never let ourselves drift apart from my brother and his family."

Though I had never been told, I surmised their drifting apart stemmed from Daddy's refusal to assume his rightful place in Pop's business. If so, then he must have hoped, rather than believed, that we would be one big happy family once he and I moved up here. I was glad at least part of his wish had come true.

"If we buried Dan in Fort Wayne, you could come stay with us, and visit his grave. You could come any time you wanted. In the summer, for instance, when you have all that time off from teaching. And at Christmas, maybe. We nearly always have a white Christmas. It's beautiful. Like a picture on a calendar," she enthused.

Truly, she made the idea sound so appealing, I found myself imagining sleigh rides and sledding parties; and ice skating couples gliding gracefully around the frozen pond, as I used to love to pretend Bruce and I were doing as we rolled around the Overton Skating Rink on our clunky rented roller skates. Oh my....

"We have a big old two-story house with plenty of spare bedrooms," she said, then went on describing the house and grounds, with relish, before concluding her offer, "It would give all of us a chance to get to know each other, finally."

I could see myself knocking on the front door of a big house with a tree lit in the window, my arms filled with Christmas gifts for my family—a loving group, I strongly sensed—who eagerly awaited my arrival. I had never felt lonely; no, I quite liked living alone. But to have this held out to me, when least expected—

Yet, I thought of Mama. If Daddy was buried up in Fort Wayne, then it was only right that Mama's remains would be moved up there too. Then it dawned on me that Mama would not want to be buried hundreds of miles from home, in a place she had never been to in her life. And it was doubtful she had ever met anyone in Daddy's family except for Pop. Suddenly not liking any of this except the part where I visited my newly acquainted relatives, I argued, "No, my parents belong together, back in Texas where they're from. That's where I want—"

We heard a door shut, and voices in the kitchen.

Florence said quietly, "Leave this to me. We'll get it sorted out later. If we don't stand together, neither of us will prevail. I know how Maxine is."

Odd that I had envisioned a united front earlier, though not for what she had in mind.

Maxine came in and sat down. It was evident she had been crying. "They have him ready," she said stoically.

Florence reached across and touched her arm comfortingly, her eyes glassy.

Maxine squared her shoulders, rebuffing the kind gesture as though she now regarded Florence as an enemy in league with me. Her voice trembling, she said, "They've done a good job. He looks very well. You just never know."

Boxed up in a suit, looking like someone he wasn't, I thought grimly.

Maxine turned to me. "You've read the Will now, I hope."

I glanced at Florence. "Not all of it."

"Well, I hope you will do it soon. Obviously, Danny was of sound mind when he drew it up; no one forced anything on him. And bear in mind, I have a mortgage to pay and a child to raise, and no job at this point." Her mouth quivering, she added, "I want everything settled between us, before the funeral."

I fully agreed. I could not imagine anything worse than interrupting an argument to leave for the funeral. Trying to appear generous, I said, "I've read enough to see that Daddy left his estate to you and to his son. That's perfectly fitting as far as I am concerned—in fact, I would have expected nothing less of my father." I studied her face for a sign she felt at least relieved, if not grateful. Maybe now she would be inclined to cooperate with me about Daddy's burial.

She only nodded stiffly, surrendering no points.

With a glance of apology toward Florence, I told Maxine about our cemetery lots at Pleasant Hill. "I'm sure Daddy meant for them eventually to be buried up there, side by side. He could not have anticipated the—the changes that were in store in the meantime."

I wished I had slanted my statement in a more conciliatory way. "*...the fact that Daddy would one day fall in love and remarry.*" But now that I had met Maxine, I felt even less inclined to believe Daddy could have been in love with someone as stand-offish and hard as she was.

Maxine seemed to weigh my words regardless, and I felt hope rising. Then she asked, "Well, dear, if Danny had wanted to be buried in East Texas, don't you think he would have told me he owned a cemetery plot there?"

I could not answer that. Of course, he may very well have so advised her, and she found it convenient to keep it to herself.

Maxine began, "I'll tell you something you may not know. Your father had been after your mother for years, to move away from East Texas. But she wouldn't listen."

Again, I was speechless. The fact that Daddy had told this to Maxine was deeply disturbing. Did he tell her also that it was his natural inclination—at least, in those days—to pick up and move, try out a new oil field, from time to time, no matter where we were living? And we often did that. When we didn't, it was because he and Mama had worked things out somehow. "Daddy built us a house up there," I argued, distressed that my voice was quavering. "It was the first home Mama and Daddy had ever owned. He—he had a high-paying job as a driller—he was excellent at what he did; everyone respected him—and there was no end of work in the East Texas field. Besides, Mama and I—we loved the New London school. And our happiness meant everything to him."

"Yes, it was for the sake of your happiness that he waited so long, despite the fact that he was miserable," she said.

"He was *not* miserable. He—"

Her eyes flickered. "Oh yes he was. On the night before your mother was killed, the two of them had a major falling out. I hate to say this, but from what he said, their marriage was in serious jeopardy."

Out the corner of my eye, I saw Florence's mouth drop open. I was livid. "How dare you say that!" I cried.

Maxine's eyes filled. "So, now you're accusing me of lying?"

"My parents were crazy about each other," I said hotly. "Even if they did have a fight, they would have never split up," I swore. Then I remembered Daddy's regret that he failed to tell Mama he loved her on the morning before she died. I started to tell Maxine, but again I had an aversion to trotting out details of my parents' life. I had already said too much. I was disgusted that I had managed to lower myself to her level. And now, all at once, I had a hollow feeling at the pit of my stomach. Had I only imagined Daddy telling me that, after all?

"Now, everyone, calm down," said Florence, her voice strained, the palms of her hands pushed forward as if in defense, fingers splayed. "We are under a strain right now. Making more out of things than we should." She paused, with a pointed glance at Maxine. "Wouldn't it be great if we all lived in the same town, with one cemetery, and we wouldn't have to be having this discussion! But we don't. So we are going to have to work it out like the grown-ups we are."

Even though I did not agree with Florence, I could not help admiring the way she had taken command. I felt comforted by her strength and clear head, and had a sense that somehow everything would work out.

"I'm telling you, the solution is to bury Dan in Fort Wayne," she insisted. "It isn't that far from here for Maxine and Daniel, a few hours on the train. And I have offered to have Delys stay with my family whenever she wants to, so that she can visit her father's grave. It's the most central location of all, for heaven's sake.

"And apart from that, it will be so helpful for Pop," she added, a note of pleading having crept into her voice that made me begin to appreciate what she may be up against, back home. I felt bad that I had never thought of this before. All I had thought of was myself. Her eyes filled. "He's very confused about my brother's death," she said thinly. "He doesn't understand. It was all so sudden. It isn't natural for the son to die before the father."

Maxine looked from one of us to the other with a withering stare. "Nor is it natural for a four-year-old boy to lose the father he idolized." She looked at me. "You had Danny all your life until now, and you didn't appreciate him. My Daniel has been cheated. His father won't be with him, or be able to provide for him, as he did for you. The least my son should be able to do is visit his father's grave whenever he wants." She glanced at Florence. "And not have to travel to another state, to do it.

"I owe him this. Danny owes him this. And, by God, over my dead body will he be buried anywhere else but right here!" Her hand slammed down on the table, giving both Florence and me a start, and upsetting the pencil and sending it tumbling to the floor.

She sat back, heaving her breath, her face florid.

There was only one thing for me to do, and my body knew before my mind had registered it. I was rising from my chair. "I can't stay here any longer," I said.

Florence looked at me wide-eyed, the color drained from her face. I remember her chair scraping loudly across the floor as she backed away from the table. "I've got my car. I'll drive you to the hotel where I've booked some rooms for my family. It's near the station."

To a hotel was not where I intended to go, but I didn't argue. I would sooner ride with my aunt than call a taxi then have to wait around for it to come, feeling completely ill-at-ease as the moments ticked by. I went to remove my hat and coat from the hat tree. I put them both on, then picked up my suitcase from the spot where I had put it down when I walked in.

Chapter 25

When we were seated in the car, Florence handed me my copy of Daddy's Will, hastily rolled up like a newspaper. "You will want to take this with you."

I thanked her and opened my handbag to slip it inside. "Please, will you take me to the station? I'm going home."

"But, the funeral—" Florence said, bewildered.

"It's all a travesty as far as I'm concerned. I want nothing to do with it."

She made no response, but drove down to the end of the block, then turned in the opposite direction from the way I thought we should go. Of course, maybe she knew another way to the station, or maybe I was disoriented.

At length she said, "Don't let Maxine get under your skin like that. She just wants to have her way."

I did not say anything. Florence had no idea of the persistent doubts about my parents' relationship that I managed to dismiss most of the time. Maxine could have easily twisted the meaning of something Daddy said, but nonetheless she had managed to raise the specter of doubt all over again. Oh why, of all the times to have a quarrel, had Mama and Daddy picked the night before Mama was killed?

As we drove on, Florence said, "I have to talk to you, and there is nothing I hate worse than trying to have a conversation while I'm driving down the street."

I had forgotten that she wanted to talk to me earlier. "Alright," I said. I felt calm now, more so than I had felt since I arrived here this morning. Or maybe I was just too fatigued to be upset or nervous anymore.

After a few blocks, Florence spotted a small park. "Ah, good!" she said. She pulled over to the curb and we came to a stop. The park was empty, its wood plank swings hanging limp from their chains, see-saws left with one end angled upward, and one down. The scene looked sad somehow. I found myself wondering if Daddy had ever brought his son here to play. Again I felt a pang of sympathy for the child. Poor little fellow....

I remember noticing Florence's hands, resting on the steering wheel. They were long and slender, like Daddy's. But the network of veins protruding from beneath the skin, and the smattering of mushroom-colored liver spots, reminded me of the difference in their ages. She exhaled a breath. "I'm glad we finally got some time to ourselves; and anyway, I didn't feel right talking about Maxine while I was under her roof," she said, turning to look at me.

"You've seen for yourself now. Maxine is not our kind. She has no class."

I nodded. Florence had put into concise language what amounted to my own general impression. The word *common* came to mind, a word Mama used to apply to certain people who did not behave according to her standards. "I've often wondered how Daddy got to know her, and especially now. She is nothing like Mama. It's hard to imagine him falling for—well, being attracted to her."

"They met in a bar, where she played the piano," Florence explained, then frowned. "Not a honky-tonk. Some sort of lounge connected to a restaurant, I gather. Dan told us about her when he came to visit Pop one weekend. They had learned Maxine was pregnant, and were planning to get married. Needless to say, the news came as a shock." She paused, took in a breath. "Dan was lonely, I think. Your mother had been gone for such a long time."

My eyes filled. "But he knew I was moving up here, within just a few weeks. I know you're speaking of a different kind of loneliness. Still, he should have thought before he got her pregnant and ruined everything."

Florence shook her head. "That's what I need to tell you. Maxine had lied to him and said they were safe, that she couldn't have any more children. Then, bingo! Too late, he realized she was just looking for a good man to support her, and finish raising her other children.

"Still, he felt—" she shrugged. "—Well, it takes two after all, and it was his responsibility to marry her and make the best of it. I remember him saying to me, 'Maxine isn't all bad; she has a lot of good qualities. And she seems to be a good mother, best I can tell.'"

So Daddy had been duped? I did not like to think my father was that naive. Of course, who was I to judge, when I wasn't around to see it happen? *"I thought I could count on you, Daddy,"* I lashed out when he called with the news. If he had leveled with me, at least I would have known he was trying to behave responsibly when she snared him. I would never have begrudged him a relationship that included sex, as long as it didn't interfere with our plans. "Why didn't he tell me the truth?" I queried, frustrated.

"I begged him to. I was afraid if he didn't, you would feel betrayed.

But he was afraid if you knew the truth, you would resent Maxine, and it would be impossible for all of you to live under the same roof.

"Maybe this way, you would still move up here someday, he said." She sighed. "It was a long time before he gave up on that."

I saw him climbing up the rungs of a ladder, with hammer and nails, his hopes as high as the rooftop....

"Why don't you let me drive you to the hotel?" Florence urged. "Take some time to think about all this, and get some rest tonight. Maybe by morning, you will feel differently, and stay for the funeral. Think how much it would mean to Dan."

But she was wrong. Daddy would hate the funeral Maxine was cooking up for him, and wouldn't blame me for skipping it. I shook my head stubbornly.

Florence exhaled a long breath as though in resignation. But then she said firmly, "Well then, you need at least to stop by the funeral home, see your father one last time."

At the words I felt panicked, as if I were a sick child who had been tricked into getting into the car only to learn I was headed to the doctor's office. Looking down at Daddy, dead, was what I had been so determined to spare myself. Besides, doing so would not bring him back. "I don't want to see my father. He's dead, and he has on a suit," I blurted out.

"Child, after coming all this way!" Florence cried. Her vehemence shocked me, and made me realize that my fractured relationship with Daddy must have brought her a good deal of pain; and this could only mean that it had grieved Daddy far more than I ever knew.

I imagined Daddy looking down on me from the heavens, frightened that I would abandon him without so much as saying goodbye. Still, I went on struggling. Surely Daddy would not want me to remember him lying dead, I told myself—

Then all at once, I knew what to do. I turned to Florence. Tears of defeat were running down her cheeks. Her finger rested on the starter button, as if she could not bear to depress it. "I'll go to the funeral home," I said. "But I'm not going to—to *view* Daddy's corpse," I added with distaste.

For a moment Florence hesitated, a puzzled frown on her brow. Then her expression cleared. She nodded slowly. "I'll fix it so you can just go in and sit with him for a little while. It'll be fine." She reached over and patted my thigh.

I remember her pressing the accelerator and making a wide u-turn in the street. Abruptly, another car appeared seemingly from out of nowhere.

I heard my voice cry out, "Watch it!" I was shrinking away from the door as the auto very nearly broadsided us. The driver swerved out of the way just in time. Florence hit the brake, the tires squealing. She waved apologetically through the window as the other driver sped by, a horrified look on his face. She said not a word, but released her breath and drove on. I felt partly to blame for what we had narrowly escaped.

A few minutes later we were shown into the room where Daddy lay. Just by the door was a pedestal holding a guest register and fountain pen. I ignored this. A lamp on a tall brass pole stood at the head of the closed casket, with a pinkish, opaque shade of swirled glass. The window blinds were drawn, which to me made the room seem like a tomb from which all signs of life were to be sealed off. How Daddy would loathe being shut up in here and gawked at. A small chair with a tufted back and arms waited beside the casket. The casket seemed larger than I would have expected for a man who was rather slight in build, really; it seemed to dwarf the little chair. It had bronze handles and trim, and was covered with some sort of fabric, deep brown in color.

There were no flowers. I felt bad about this, as I had felt at the absence of flowers on Mama's grave that first time I visited. I should have asked Florence to stop off somewhere so I could buy some to bring. Now I recalled Allie's request that I let her know the arrangements so she and Uncle Logan could send flowers. How long ago that seemed....

I sat down uneasily in the little chair. I would not stay long. I heard Florence say quietly from off to the side, "Take your time, dear. I'll wait in the parlor." She put an arm around my shoulders from behind, clutching me tightly, touching her cheek to mine. I could feel the wetness on her cheek. In that moment I felt a rush of warmth and longing for Florence, and I realized suddenly that never had I felt as physically drawn to any other woman, except for my mother. I found myself grabbing her hand with both of mine and squeezing.

I sat there alone for a long time before I could fully assimilate the fact that my daddy was right there, just inches away. Then, once I did, I wanted more than anything to be touching him. Imagined myself slipping down beside him on the cold concrete porch, edging up as close as I could get. I should have let them— But no, it would not be the same, and from this day I would always have to think of how Daddy looked right now, when I wanted to remember him alive and vibrant and sitting with me on that porch. Being Daddy.

Eventually I reached out and very tentatively touched the side of the casket, then withdrew my hand. The casket surface felt warm to my fingers, like flannel. Now I was possessed of an overwhelming desire to rescue Daddy and take him away with me because he did not belong here; it was a visceral sense of what I had reasoned out when I fleetingly thought I could bring his body back to Texas.

I don't know how long I sat there before I lost my self-consciousness and felt inclined to talk to Daddy in my head. I gradually became aware that it was the natural thing to do, to tell him what was in my heart as I used to do in the days when we sat out under the stars together. Haltingly I reached back and laid my hand on the casket again, this time the warmth reminding me of how his smooth khaki-clad thigh used to feel against mine as we sat together. First I railed at Daddy for not telling me the truth about Maxine, anger rising as I did, that if he had only done so at least I would not have misjudged him. He was right that I could not have tolerated living with Maxine, under the circumstances; but I didn't wind up living with him anyway, and at least he and I would not have been estranged for the last four years of his life.

When my anger was spent, my shoulders collapsed in regret and I was apologizing to him for not realizing that he would have never tossed our plans overboard in a moment of lust. This reminded me to say how much I appreciated his never-failing generosity to me. Finally, I found myself commending him for the fine job he did of building a room for me upstairs in his house.

This brought to mind the house he built for us in East Texas, and I began to reminisce about the life we lived there, as I often did while kneeling at Mama's grave. I told him that I often visited Mama, and that I knew his spirit now resided there with her, even though I could not manage to bring their bodies together as I wanted to. I described the special service I had dreamed of holding for him outdoors, and said I hoped he would have liked it. I somehow felt he might be conveying to me, "Why Dee, that sounds real nice, it sure does; but it's alright. You know what they say, it's the thought that counts."

After that I sat some more and let the tears drain down. And gradually I began thinking of these past few hours, how unreal they seemed, how little to do with anything that was important between Daddy and me. The words I had spoken to Florence echoed in my mind, and all at once a poem was flowing out, as naturally as the first poem I had written, in Mrs. Hathaway's English class:

I don't want to see my father.

He's dead and he has on a suit.
Which he never wore when I knew him,
would rise up in protest if he could
to the stranger who forced him into it,
to the second wife who hired the stranger,
to the men who took his first wife—
my mother—
who knew better,
would have had a fresh set of khakis,
starched and creased,
the kind he wore that day he clawed her body out,
bloodying his hands and forearms.

It was time to go. I promised Daddy I would come to visit him as often as I could, and said that I was thankful to have discovered my Aunt Florence. *She's so like you, Daddy! I love her already.*

I was searching for a way to tell Daddy goodbye, when I remembered Florence gesturing to the picture of me in my Brigade uniform this morning: *"Dan was so proud of you."*

I was proud of you too, Daddy. I will always be proud of you.

I leaned near and kissed Daddy's casket, pressing it gently with both my hands.

I knew then that Florence had been right. I needed to come here. I knew, too, as I turned and left the room, that I would write down the new poem when I was on the train. I knew I had to go back to writing the poems of New London that I had abandoned. I knew I was ready, that even if it meant I'd stumble and fall a few times, the poems were all there within me if I kept on writing.

As I sit here all these years later, I do not know even yet if my choice to avoid Daddy's funeral was right or wrong; and sometimes I wonder. I will say that I treasure that quiet visit with him at the funeral home. I will always believe that, on some deep level, Daddy and I did hear each other, and understand. I fear that if not for the blow-up that sent me fleeing Maxine's house, I would have gone to the funeral as duty prescribed then come home relieved it was over, perhaps never having had an intimate moment with Daddy, and no one else around.

Still.... I remember a visit to the sprawling American Cemetery in Normandy one summer. It was on one of those chilly, misty afternoons so common in that region of France, and I was shivering in my all-weather coat and lace-up shoes and rain hat. While walking among the neat rows of graves marked by crosses, or stars of David, the weight of collective loss was almost heavier than I could bear; it was so like being in the Pleasant Hill Cemetery that first time I went back. But what struck me with unexpected force was that the loved ones of those many heroes buried thousands of miles from home, in a foreign country, would have been ever so grateful for the opportunity that I had passed up.

Chapter 26

On the train I read Daddy's new Will in full, and in the last paragraph I discovered that Daddy had bequeathed to me Mama's engagement diamond. He had left the diamond in the custody of Aunt Allie, to be given to me at a "time of her choosing."

I was not aware that Mama's diamond had survived her. I had always assumed it was lost in the rubble of the explosion. Noting there was no mention in the Will of the ring in which the diamond was mounted, I could only assume that it had been damaged beyond saving. I could barely remember how the mounting looked, only that it was platinum and there was some sort of filigree curling around either side of the stone. The ring matched Mama's wrist watch nicely, I recalled, and looked pretty on her dainty hand.

Why had Allie never given me Mama's diamond? What was she waiting for? I wondered. For that matter, when had Daddy given Allie custody of it in the first place? And why? It seemed he should have been the one to pass on to me an article that was so deeply precious to my mother.

My train pulled into Houston at just after seven o'clock on Tuesday morning, and I took a taxi home. When I turned the key and walked through my front door, I felt I had been gone for a year. Exhausted, I pulled down the window shades in my bedroom, undressed down to my underwear, and burrowed beneath the bed covers, thinking a good nap on my own bed would refresh me, then I would call my aunt.

When I awoke the afternoon sun was quickly fading. The hands on the clock beside my bed pointed at four twenty-five. I rose and wrapped my house robe around me. I could hardly believe how long I had slept, but I still felt dopey with fatigue. My neck and shoulders ached from all the hours sitting on the train, plus, no doubt, the tension of the last few days. I did not feel like talking to Aunt Allie, or anyone else for that matter. I went into the kitchen to put on the kettle and brew a cup of tea, noticing a distinct and disagreeable odor of rotting pumpkin coming from the garbage. Naturally the pumpkin pulp and seeds I had quickly discarded on Sunday had bled through the garbage sack, soaking it good, and coating the enameled can that held it. Grimacing, I hastened to wrap up the sack of pumpkin in my half-read Sunday *Chronicle*, then hurried out to put it in the big can beside the Taylors' garage. I hoped my landlords would not discover me. I did not feel like encountering them, let alone explaining why I had come home sooner than expected and was attired in my house robe at four-thirty in the afternoon. It occurred to me that, as much as I liked the Taylors as neighbors, if I bought this duplex one day, I may not rent out the small side where I now lived as I had earlier envisioned, because that would mean neighbors around all the time. Maybe I would fix it up as a guest apartment instead; and if I did, I could remove the fence dissecting the two sides of the yard and create one large, nicely shaded space. Maybe my Aunt Florence would come to visit sometime, and we could sit outside and talk. How kind she had been. Though I could hardly wait to get out of Cleveland yesterday, I had hated to let her go. After pulling up to the station, we sat in the car for a while, getting to know each other better. She filled me in on details of her family, whom she was eager for me to meet. When she asked me to tell her about my life, I found myself talking about Bruce. I told her of my betrayal of him— which I had never before confessed to anyone— and explained how deeply I regretted it. I admitted that, for all my resolve to accept that I was never going to hear from Bruce again, I could not help hoping that he would forgive me one day, and return. "That is, if he made it home safely from the war," I said. I would have gone on to tell her something else I had never told anyone before: that I had once strongly considered writing a letter to the U.S. Navy, to try and find out if Bruce had survived, and the reasons why I had not done so after all.

But Florence was already asking cautiously, "Would he know how to find you?" I knew by the question that she had been closely following what I said. A good listener, like Daddy. Like Bruce. If I married Bruce, it would be like marrying Daddy, I reflected. I sensed from the look of concern on my aunt's face that she joined in my hope that Bruce would eventually return to me. Why had I not been sent to live with Florence, instead of Allie? I wondered, frustrated. Then I felt guilty. "Only if he contacted Aunt Allie, and she told him where I was," I told her. Which suddenly made me wonder if Allie would cooperate. Surely after all this time, she had given up trying to run my love life. She had never commented favorably or otherwise on the boys I dated at Rice while still living under her roof. Of course there were not that many of them, thanks to the war. Nonetheless, I sensed she was determined not to interfere lest I rebel on principle. So maybe Allie would cooperate if Bruce were to call or write me one day. Oh, why waste time thinking about it? He wasn't going to try to contact me. He had probably long since tossed out my address and phone number at Allie's.

Having escaped discovery by the Taylors, I returned to the kitchen to scour the stinky garbage can interior, and brew the tea. Minutes later I was taking my first sip of tea. Ah, that was better. It warmed me deliciously all the way down. Home. How glad I was to be here! I took my teacup to sit outside in the chair under my fig tree, and enjoy the brisk autumn air and the last few tranquil minutes of daylight. Then I knew I had to call my aunt.

Sitting there, sipping my tea and thinking of what I would say to Aunt Allie, I suddenly realized I would have to explain why I was home a lot sooner than expected. I dreaded this. No doubt she would find it very odd that I had chosen not to attend Daddy's funeral. I tried to think of a convincing excuse. It was none of her business what had taken place around Maxine's card table. If I told her of our disagreement, she would only reason that Daddy was foolish for marrying such a woman in the first place, her estimation of him lowered yet again. I did not want that. Just thinking of how defenseless Daddy was made tears return to my eyes. I certainly would not tell her what I had learned from Aunt Florence about how Maxine had tricked Daddy into marrying her.

I thought and thought. At length I decided to wait until tomorrow to call Allie. What day was this, anyway? Let's see—I had to think—Tuesday. Daddy had died on Saturday. Let Allie assume the funeral was held on Tuesday morning, and that I attended the ceremony then boarded a train shortly after, arriving home in the wee hours of Wednesday morning. Yes, that is what I would do. I felt better now, or at least more resolute. I still did not feel like being around anyone else, and was glad I had arranged to take the whole week off from school. My fellow teachers at Austin—many of whom had once taught me—were unfailingly kind. Likewise, the administrative staff. Sometimes I felt almost as if I were still a student there. I knew that their words of sympathy about Daddy would defy all my efforts to remain composed. It had been hard enough to hold myself together when I notified Mrs. Sessions.

On Wednesday around ten o'clock, I picked up my mail from the Taylors' and lingered for the obligatory chat. I was somewhat relieved that Mrs. Taylor was gone from home. Mr. Taylor did not arouse my emotions as she did.

Afterward I went home and dialed Allie's number, only to be met with a busy signal. I waited a few minutes, flipping through my mail, then tried again. The line was still busy. Again, fifteen minutes later, the same result.

As far as I knew, Allie did not go in for long telephone conversations. Maybe there was something wrong with the telephone. I decided to wait a few minutes then try once more. If I still did not get through, I would ask the telephone company to check the line.

Just before eleven I called again. This time, to my chagrin, there was no answer. Allie must have hung up the telephone and dashed out the door.

It was nearly two o'clock when I finally reached her. Her voice sounded weary when she said hello. "It's Delys. Is anything the matter?" I asked.

"Oh, Delys! Oh no," she said, distractedly. "Just aging parents, that's all." There was a pause as she realized she had made a blunder. "Sorry, hon. I didn't mean to—"

"It's alright. I know." My grandfather Roy had retired at the first of this year, and according to Allie, he had no interests in life to take the place of the work he had for so long enjoyed. He sat around, bored, and his health was suffering. It occurred to me now how unfair things had turned out. If Daddy had lived to be as old as Roy, he would have found no end of activities to occupy his time.

I had not seen my grandparents in a while. My grandmother was increasingly bitter over the loss of Mama. Sarah had reached the point where she could not encounter me without making some snide remark about Daddy. "It's her age," Allie had apologized. "She doesn't think before she opens her mouth."

Now Allie explained that the Maddens' hot water heater had gone out overnight, and she had spent the morning trying to locate a reputable plumber who could replace it today. Then she went over to meet the plumber and be sure everything was working properly before he left. "I stayed and put together some lunch for my parents. So now I'm behind on what I needed to get done for myself."

I could not help feeling sorry for Allie. I ought to volunteer to help her out; but how, when I had a full-time teaching job? And besides, I did not want to be around Sarah. "Let me know if there is anything I can do," I said vaguely. Who would care for an aging Allie and Logan one day? I wondered suddenly. Swiftly I realized that probably I would. Thank goodness, it was a long time before I had to worry about that.

"How was the funeral?" Allie asked now. "You didn't let me know about the flowers."

"I—I'm sorry. Everything was so busy and hectic," I apologized. I was not really sorry. I knew Allie only wanted to send flowers because she felt it was the right thing to do. They would have been just one more artificial gesture. Maxine probably would not even have recognized Allie and Logan's name on the card.

"Anyway, how did it go?" she asked gently.

Tears threatened. I paused, swallowing down the lump in my throat. "Eh— it was fine," I told her. "It's good to be home," I added, to close the subject. "Logan was right about Daddy having drawn up a new Will. It's why I called. He left me Mama's engagement diamond. Said it was in your keeping."

After some hesitation, Allie said, "Of course, I should have thought. Can you stop by in the morning? Say—oh—around ten o'clock?"

The weather was chilly and gray when I drove up and parked at Aunt Allie's curb; a wet norther was expected to blow in sometime today, the kind that usually came around Halloween. Tomorrow was the big night, I noted. I needed to stock up on "trick or treat" candy. There were a lot of small children in Eastwood.

I hugged my sweater around me and hurried up to the door. "Come in," said Allie with feeling, and closed her arms around me. "Good to see you," she said.

"You, too," I said, squeezing her back. I was still feeling guilty about how quickly I had developed a level of affection for my Aunt Florence that I had never felt for Allie. She released me and studied my face. "Well, you look rested anyway," she said kindly. "Come, sit down. I've got coffee brewing."

My aunt made excellent coffee. Soon it was steaming up from china cups on the gate-legged table between the two wing chairs where we sat in her living room. She handed me a small packet. "I had not thought of this for a long time," she said quietly. "It was tucked away in my jewelry box."

I did not want to injure her feelings, so I said, amicably, "I wonder why Daddy left the diamond with you. I mean, he could have given it to me at some point, and saved you the bother of keeping it."

"It was no bother," she said. "Dan was afraid the diamond would get lost, or stolen, as he traveled around," she said.

Admittedly, this did seem reasonable. The question remained, however: why had Allie held onto it for so long? Certainly there had been appropriate occasions for presenting it to me before now—my college graduation, for instance, or my 21st birthday. I removed the paper wrapping, and there appeared Mama's diamond, blinking up from a cushion of cotton. I don't know what I had expected to feel upon seeing it, but without the mounting it seemed... well...anonymous. I did not feel anything. Careful not to let it slip from my fingers, I lifted it up toward the front window, watching as the light through the Venetian window blinds caught the many facets of the stone. Perhaps someday I would have it mounted in a pendant to wear around my neck. I nestled it back down in its cotton.

When I looked up to ask my next question, I noticed Allie was staring at the diamond, tears in her eyes. I felt awful for not having realized this transfer would probably return painful memories to her. I imagined Daddy reaching out, handing the diamond to her. *"Keep this safe for my daughter, will you?"* "Mama was proud of her ring," I said gently. "I never saw her without it on her finger."

Allie sighed. "It is a pity the mounting was—was lost," she said weakly, then sniffed. She sat back.

"Was there some special event you were waiting on, to turn it over to me?" I asked now.

She did not answer right away. "I had imagined that one day when you became engaged to be married to some bright, promising young fellow, I would present the diamond to your fiancé, and he would have it mounted for your finger," she said finally. "Guess I'm just a romantic, huh," she added with a slow smile.

I thought then how pretty and youthful Allie was, now in her early fifties. She still had a slender figure, and she wore her hair in a less severe style than she used to—a little longer with ends loosely curled, and a little more fullness around her face.

How well I remembered Allie's attempts to prepare me for that day when I would become engaged to a young man who met with her approval, forcing me to go out with boys I did not wish to be with, in hopes I would forget about the only boy I ever really cared for. I could not resist saying, "As long as the bright, promising young fellow wasn't Bruce."

A leaden look came into Allie's eyes, and I regretted my words. "Bruce was neither bright nor promising. Surely you could see that when all was said and done," she pointed out. In one of my mutinous moments, I had told Allie that I drove to Overton after visiting Mama's grave for the first time, so that I could inquire about Bruce.

Once again I had an unsettling feeling that if Bruce tried to contact me one day, she might not inform me of it. "There was a lot more to Bruce than you realized," I told her, hoping she would take my point. Then, on the other hand, fearing I may have sounded like a defiant school girl, I allowed, "But I can certainly understand your reasoning back then. After all, we were so young." Only then did I think of the most obvious way to put Bruce in a positive light, should the need ever arise. "I'm sure that fighting in the war brought out the best in Bruce, as it seemed to have done for so many young men," I said. I started to remind her of the many stories of heroism in the papers, and in *Life* magazine, but decided that would be rather overdoing it. "I hope he made it safely home."

Aunt Allie sat back a bit. "Of course," she said quietly. Then she stared at me for a long moment before admitting, "I just wanted things to turn out right for you when you married. I still do. There's nothing worse than to wind up disillusioned."

As you did. I wanted to say, but did not dare.

Since writing down the poem that came to mind as I sat with Daddy, and determining that I was ready to return to work building an anthology, I had felt frustrated that I knew so little about the tragedy that inspired the poem's final lines. Daddy had shared some details of the rescue effort during his visits at my hospital bedside, but I was in no shape to retain much information then. Over the years we had scarcely raised the subject when we were together. And of course, early on, Bruce stopped talking. Only on rare occasions had Allie dropped a crumb from what she had observed. Usually her reminisces were complaints about the services held for Mama, and usually not to me: *"I could hardly make out what the preacher was saying about Vinia for all the other burials taking place nearby at the same time,"* she had remarked once to a friend on the telephone, after having attended a more traditional grave side service for someone at her church.

Not until one of our heart-to-heart conversations near the end of Allie's life would I learn what was really behind her occasional sarcasms: Daddy had refused to have Mama's funeral in her native city, which Allie and her parents regarded as fitting. Just one more reason to dislike Daddy....

As we sat talking over coffee that day, I knew I would be foolish to ask my biased aunt for help in developing background for writing poems, and my uncle knew little except for the legal aspects of the tragedy. But the newspaper articles in the file I had discovered in Logan's office promised to be a valuable source, and while I had avoided reading these initially because doing so was too painful, I knew that if ever I hoped to accomplish my aim, I would have to put my feelings aside and read them now.

Leaving Aunt Allie's house, I drove straight to my uncle's office a few blocks away.

The wind was blowing so hard that the wooden sign—E. LOGAN FLETCHER - ATTORNEY AT LAW—swung back and forth, screeching on its hinges. The sign appeared to be freshly painted. The small grass lawn, which had been closely cropped at the end of the summer, was turning yellow now. As I approached, Logan's dark blue sedan came slowly backing down the driveway. The car was spotlessly clean and the chrome was polished. The white sidewalls were gleaming loops on the tires.

I waved hello. Logan pressed the brake and rolled down his window. He wore his proverbial crisp white shirt, and tie. His suit jacket hung on a hook behind him. How perfectly in order Uncle Logan's life always appeared, down to the last detail. It wasn't that hard to imagine his horror when my aunt was in danger of bleeding on his car seat during a miscarriage.

Pleasantly he asked, "What brings you here this morning? Allie told me you were to drop by the house."

When I told him I was hoping to have another look at the file about the school explosion, he knitted his brow and leaned a little nearer, the better to hear. No doubt he hoped for some explanation. But I could not imagine him appreciating my fledgling efforts to write poems. "Daddy's death made me curious about some things," I told him.

He frowned. "I was sorry about your father. He was too young to go."

A lump forming in my throat, I nodded and smiled, "Yes, he was."

"Well. Help yourself to the file. In fact, you can take it home with you— ask Mrs. Jolly to delete it from the index. At this point, I doubt anything will turn up that we could use to build a case against the school board. It's been—what? How many years?"

"It will be ten years in March."

He shook his head slowly in wonder, then nodded farewell as he rolled up the car window, and continued backing down the driveway.

After stopping by Telephone Laundry to pick up my dry cleaning and buy a few groceries including three bags of Tootsie Rolls, to prepare for trick or treaters, I went home and spent the rest of that day with the New London folder contents spread out over my kitchen table, oblivious of time passing and only vaguely aware of the wind whistling and tossing the fig tree branches outside the windows. When the room grew so dark that I was having difficulty reading the small newsprint, I paused long enough to turn on the ceiling light. I realized with a start that my fingers were freezing. The wind had died down. Cold weather had settled in. I turned on the small gas heater in the corner, the irony of which never escaped my notice, even now.

As I had expected, interspersed among the stories of the rescue effort that was well under way even before the dust had settled, I found horrific tales of mutilation that I could not bear to read even after all this time, even when I did not recognize the victim's name. In spite of my serious purpose, I felt I was being voyeuristic somehow, poring over the gory details of someone else's tragedy that were none of my business. Of all people, should I not be privy to this, when it shattered my life as well? And yet, in a way, I was excluded from these poor innocent children and teachers: I had survived.

I often read three or four sentences into a piece, then fled as if I had wandered into a blind alley, my hand pressing against my chest. I wondered as never before how Doc Buckstrum and other medical professionals had managed to get through that experience, and Bruce, too, a grisly job forced on him by circumstances that most grown-ups would shrink from. I found myself wondering if I had set myself a task that I could never be objective enough to complete. I had wanted to tell the truth of New London that I was prevented from telling in my essay of long ago. Well, here was what the truth looked like.

I was surprised to find a long piece from *The New York Times*. Why would a major newspaper from up east take such a big interest? Then again, I had already run across a message of sympathy issued by President Franklin Delano Roosevelt and his family, from the White House. And people of all ages, from all over the country, and from other nations as well, had sent donations and letters of condolence. Jarringly, a message of sympathy had come via telegraph from Adolph Hitler.

I read through a few paragraphs in the *Times* story. The piece was certainly well written. I made a mental note to read it in full someday. But right now I needed the broad range of material found in the odd assortment of clippings.

One report of the rescue stated that the acetylene torches, which would be used to help cut through the steel girders, did not arrive immediately. In the meantime, desperate men— the majority of them oil field workers; many of them fathers of children who were among the victims— dug through the rubble with their bare hands. "Rescuers' hands were bloody as they clawed through brick and jagged framework," it said. The hair rising on the back of my neck, I looked up from the page. My poem.

Would the word, prescient, apply? I wasn't sure. The poem was more universal than I realized, as I had thought only of Daddy as I wrote it. This seemed an encouraging sign. I went on reading....

It took two thousand rescuers, working in shifts of around a thousand at a time, a little less than twenty-four hours to dig away rubble that was twenty feet deep. "Like a quarry," someone stated. At night they worked with the aid of flood lights from the football field nearby. Twenty heavy oil field wenches pulled concrete pillars and debris from the building.

I sat back and tried to appreciate the sheer scope of the effort, carried on as thousands of cars arrived at the scene, from far and near, and hundreds of people from around the community dropped what they were doing and hurried to the site on foot.

I found the article detailing my mother's heroic efforts to save her students. Thank God, there was no picture. The facts were pretty much as I remembered being told. The most chilling of all was that only one boy attending Mama's sixth period History class that day was missing from the room when the explosion occurred: Peter "Bucky" Buckstrum.

Bucky had been a few steps short of making it to the band room.

The randomness. It made my skin crawl. It made me angry all over again, not so much at the school board this time, but at life, at the injustice of life.

With trembling fingers I folded all the papers carefully and returned them to the file folder. I had positioned an open notebook and pen nearby, having expected to jot down ideas for poems as I went. Alas, a blank page stared back at me. Disappointed, I put everything away on the top shelf of the closet in the tiny hallway. I would have to think about all this, and try and digest it. I could envision this project taking many months, maybe even years, to complete. And how would I know when it was complete?

That night I awoke from a deep sleep, flew to my desk and wrote:

"Word Spread"

Women sprang from kitchens,
apron-clad,
supper kettles simmering on stoves.
Men scrambled from under leaky trucks
and wiped their greasy hands;
All around, drilling rigs shut down.
And they came.
Crossing miles in rushing steps,

Eyes wide and locked ahead,
Arms outstretched in readiness
for their children
who—God grant—
would be running to them.

I returned to bed wide awake and giddy with joy.

The next day I spread all three poems out on the table and read through them. I asked myself the hard question: What if Mrs. Hathaway was the only person who would ever take my poetry seriously? I realized I could not keep going, writing into a vacuum, spurred by my own wish to keep believing in my ability to do this.

I spent most of Saturday at the Houston Public Library, perusing the shelves of periodicals that published poetry. I wanted something a little more highbrow than *Readers' Digest* or some women's magazine. I was not so rosy as to aim for a magazine that was out of my league, like *The Atlantic Monthly or Harper's*. *Collier's* perhaps? *The Saturday Evening Post ?* On the other hand, maybe some regional publication that would have a mostly southern audience. I found two that seemed promising, both of them university presses that published a variety of essays, short stories, and poems. Appropriately, one was entitled *The Lantern*, and the other, *The Beacon*. I copied down the address and the name of the Poetry Editor for each. Imagine having a Poetry Editor, I thought with a small thrill. Someone who could guide you into refining your verse until it was all it might be. I thought of Emily Dickinson's mentor Thomas Wentworth Higginson. The years they corresponded together, and the fruits of all their labors.

I had acquired a typewriter while at Rice so that I would no longer need to rely on the one I had used at Logan's office. I lugged it into the kitchen that night— I was beginning to feel as if I lived in the kitchen—and sat down and wrote a query letter to the Poetry Editor at each magazine. I wanted to have two ready, though of course I would not dare to mail both envelopes at once. I went in alphabetical order by magazine title, and omitted the date from the second query, to insert later. In my letter I explained my experience of the New London tragedy that inspired the poems, and that my larger aim was to develop a poetry anthology about the pivotal event and its meaning. I wrote that I had graduated from the Rice Institute, and was now a high school English teacher.

Realizing I had no title for the poem about Daddy, I gave the matter considerable thought. I finally settled on "A Closed Casket." Then I typed fresh copies of all three poems, prepared two self-addressed, stamped return envelopes to tuck inside, then placed everything in two larger brown envelopes and addressed them, sealing the first. As I licked the distasteful glue and made a face, I congratulated myself on having the second one so near ready to send that I could not talk myself out of it, if the first were rejected.

On Monday I stopped at the post office on the way home from school. All day I had felt fluttery inside, at times believing fiercely in the poems, at other times convinced they were no good, that I was fooling myself. Imagining a rejection letter sailing back in my carefully self-addressed, stamped envelope. Then, after a second brave attempt, another. I would soon be dreading to reach inside the mailbox. Maybe I should not be doing this after all. Instead, keep writing and keep believing. Yet—

As I walked inside the lobby, I suddenly realized that in my zeal to get this effort under way, I had failed to go back to the first poem and explore other possibilities to replace the word *gaping*. I froze in my steps, clutching the envelope to my breast. True, the word had not leapt out at me when I typed up the poem on Saturday night. Yet.... Could my chances of being published rise and fall on one word? Perhaps so. One word in a short poem was probably the equivalent of a whole chapter in a novel. For a few moments I struggled, other postal customers zigzagging around me from behind. Should I take the envelope back home for now? Finally I braced myself. Mrs. Hathaway had not questioned the word. *Gaping* might be as good a word as any. I walked up to the counter.

When I handed the envelope to the clerk to have it weighed and buy the required postage, I felt I was sending off my message by way of a carrier pigeon. The poems seemed so very fragile and helpless against the vicissitudes of publishing weather. Nonetheless, when I walked away, I knew I had taken the first small step— risk might be the better word—in doing something that could matter one day.

That night after going to bed I lay awake for a long time, feeling overwhelmed with all I had lost, almost as if the weight of it were pressing my chest and shoulders down against the bedclothes. Why the sum total of loss struck me so hard then I do not know, except perhaps, since Daddy's death until then I had been continuously distracted by some obstacle to be overcome, or some goal to be achieved; yet now all I could do was wait, the unknown yawning open in the darkness all about me. Everyone I had loved most in the world was gone. Mama was gone. Daddy was gone. Wherever Bruce might be— alive and well, I hoped— there was no longer any reason to believe he might one day come back to me. As I lay there I saw that, starting with the tragedy in New London, I had been following a certain path in which all major turn posts were foregone. All I had become as a person, and all I might yet be, were a result of that one misbegotten moment in time.

I could see the future stretching out before me and knew I was always going to be alone. I don't believe I had any real sense then of why this seemed so inevitable, and I remember being seized by a wave of dizziness, a queasiness in my stomach, soon curbed by a sense of denial that at length allowed me to relax and fall asleep. But I have come to realize that in the wake of all those losses had come an indelible loss of part of myself: my ability to let go and love again.

Part Four

Chapter 27

Who am I to say anything about life? A retired high school English teacher and aspiring poet who received a letter on this day that something beloved to her heart is coming to a close.

But here I am, pushing age fifty-five (I don't feel that old; my face in the mirror always surprises me, how my features have softened and faded, as if I'm on my way to becoming indistinguishable from the paint on the wall), and I feel I should say that the loss heralded in the letter to which I refer and the loss that occurred on March 18th, 1937, have something of significance in common. Which is that change is change and cannot be helped, whether for better or worse, whether little by little, like inexorable drips from a leaky faucet—the letter from the Scottish Brigade only sets in typeface what had been happening for years—or in a flash, as in the case of the London School explosion. Though permit me to say that when I think about it, there was nothing instant about that calamity either. There were all those years of peaceful weekday mornings when the school bus crested the hill then trundled down, presenting to riders like Bruce and me a panoramic view of the red tile roof on the handsome school that we thought would always be there. Years when serious accidents were often reported from the oil field where danger is inherent, but rarely in the surrounding community. And thus were people lulled into complacency (and some into self-importance) so that they forgot that in the right circumstances, their greatest blessing could become their biggest curse. Loss of healthy respect over time was what it was.

So regardless of the reasons behind change and the wrenching pain it inflicts, there's only the going on, the trying to make something of what's left behind, and move forward. That is, I think, the reason for the farewell reunion of the Scottish Brigade which, according to the letter, is to be held on March 25th. To mark the place between epochs. I must say I find myself reflecting on Beatrice Lytle in light of this letter. If I were to make a conservative estimate, the number of young women whose lives she influenced directly through their membership in the Scottish Brigade, over the years, would be in the thousands. I can only guess at the range of emotions she will feel as she takes her seat of honor. Not that she is likely to let her guard down and disclose them to anyone.

Beatrice Lytle retired only a few years ago, at age seventy—after stepping down as Brigade Sponsor, she had stayed on as Senior Counselor for a whole decade—and though I never reflected on it until now, the gradual demise of the Scottish Brigade began shortly after she cleared out her office, turned in her key and drove away. It seems almost as if her continued presence on the campus, in her tailored shirt and sensible shoes, and the authority that radiated from her, had held back time and kept the organization from starting to unravel. And perhaps, in her heart of hearts, that is why she waited so long before taking her leave.

But who knows what good might come, when a bunch of women with a deep sense of community get together and start talking among themselves? Singing some of the old songs, maybe. Remembering. All the while thinking, teary-eyed as I am right at this very moment, how much it all meant and wondering if there isn't some remnant that could be salvaged and used to band the group together once again in a common purpose, to start something new that is wonderful and valuable in itself. I don't know what. I just feel suddenly, in my very bones, that these conversations will take place on March 25th, and they will gradually bubble up and converge—a change beginning right then and there—and something new and good will come: a form of redemption for what is lost and can never be brought back again.

Chapter 28

It seems doubtful that I will ever learn what became of Bruce.

It was shortly after the war that I considered trying to find out through the United States Navy if Bruce had survived—I was still living with the Fletchers then, looking for a place of my own. But I found myself reluctant to make inquiries. First of all, I could not overlook that letter I had written to Bruce just before he went away, and that he must have received, yet never responded to even after more than enough time had passed for him to forgive me for what I had done if ever he were going to. I envisioned him aboard his Navy ship, facing the wind, thinking of me, his jaw set stubbornly.

Otherwise, I had to carefully consider how much I really wanted to learn. How I would love to know that Bruce had survived. But on the other hand, what if he had not? I could not bear to know he was killed when his ship was destroyed by an enemy bomb, or that he was lost at sea. Such a fate would be morbidly similar to that of the hundreds killed in the New London tragedy, a fate Bruce had barely escaped. Once, long before I knew Bruce had joined the Navy, I saw a photograph of a young man in the newspaper. He was a handsome young sailor, with a slim waist and muscular shoulders, his white hat tilted at a jaunty angle and a bright, confident smile on his face. Underneath was a caption stating his name, then: "MIA. Presumed dead." Following this, a date that stared back at me as unequivocally as March 18th, 1937 engraved on a cemetery tablet. I gazed at that photo for a long time, wondering, how could someone who loved him bear to live with all the meaning contained in that brief caption?

The photo haunted me as I considered inquiring about Bruce after the war. And at length I decided, no; I have had enough grieving to last a lifetime. Let me believe that he made it back safely and fell in love with someone else, while I remain for him a bittersweet memory of what might have been.

It is a Friday afternoon in early autumn, a year after Daddy's death. A few moments before the three o'clock bell, I swing my classroom door wide open and set the doorstop with the toe of my shoe. The fresh air wafting toward me from the hallway always feels welcome after I've been cooped up inside, and I take a nice deep breath. I think about sitting under my fig tree in a little while, and watching the sun go down as though it were melting into the housetops of East End. There is not a more tranquil place in all creation, I believe.

I become aware of a tall male figure standing before the long line of steel lockers across from my room. From the waist up he is in shadows, but I see his dark pleated trousers on a slender frame, and his two long feet planted several inches apart on the granite floor. I assume the gentleman is a parent waiting to have a word with Mrs. Theroux, the Latin teacher, whose room is across the hall from mine. The bell rings—a sound that always makes my heart catch as I recall the day, in another place and time, when the sound of the final bell would not come. My sixth period class spills out in chaotic Friday fashion, everyone talking at once. I wish them a good weekend as they pass me by, and remind them to drive safely. Weekends are when teenagers borrow the family car, and most of my students are too inexperienced to know how fragile life and limb can be.

When everyone is out I head back inside to erase the blackboard and load up my satchel with a full weekend's worth of papers to grade. I have forgotten about the man.

"Delys."

My heartbeat stumbles. After all these years, how do I know it is Bruce? But the sound of his voice is as familiar to me as if I had heard him call my name only yesterday. *"Delys,"* he would say wonderingly, as if it were a miracle that I had slid in beside him in the car and closed the door. *"Delys...."* The second syllable drawn out long and low, his eyes tender and adoring. And we'd speed away to the cemetery.

I pivot around and look. Bruce has emerged from the shadows now and is coming toward me. He wears a white shirt with the collar open and the sleeves rolled up above the wrists. His hair is neatly parted up the side and cropped close; his face is shaved, and his straight dark eyebrows are knitted together above his brown eyes. His figure is more filled out and sturdy-looking than when I saw him last, and his complexion bears the healthy bronze of a person who spends a lot of time in the open air. A sailor home from the sea. Other than this, he has hardly changed at all since our last Sunday together, long ago in the Forest Park Cemetery.

My grip is so tight around the door knob, it is as though I am trying to hold the door upright.

"Bruce?" The name comes out in a breathless query as I regret more sharply than ever that I once abandoned him. I feel as though I had only just done it, and realized my error in shame.

Then he is less than a foot from me, smiling down, his eyes searching mine. "You didn't get my letter."

His voice is a little lower than I remember, I now realize, and has grown husky, mannish. "No," I tell him, my mind so scrambled with surprise that I can't begin to construct all that might lie behind his presumption.

"I thought not, at least I hoped that was the reason when I got to the bank and Mr. Wilson didn't have a letter waiting."

"Mr. Wilson—?" I ask, bewildered.

"At the bank in Overton. I told you in my letter that I'd be on the road, but to please reply in care of Mr. Wilson at the bank."

I am still having trouble reconstructing Bruce's movements. "You went back to Overton?"

He nods yes. "Doc set up a Trust at the bank before he died. But then I went away."

"Yes. To the Navy."

His eyes widen a little. "So it was—" he begins, but I cut him off.

"I was so afraid you didn't make it back," I tell him, and I wish I could put my hands on his face right now, to be sure it is really him and not my imagination playing tricks. Kids are whizzing past us on both sides. "How did you know where to find— You wrote to me?" I ask, finally beginning to catch up with what he has been saying. And then the culprit's identity becomes clear. Aunt Allie.

"In care of your aunt. It was the only address I knew, though I was going from memory—"

I hasten to interrupt again, reciting the address for him, 6707 Park Lane Street. I want to think Bruce remembered it wrong, maybe transposing the numbers somehow, and Aunt Allie never got the letter in the first place. Too, if you didn't put both the words "Lane" and "Street" at the end, sometimes your mail wound up going to Park Street in the Broadmoor neighborhood. Maybe—

"I think 6707 is what I put."

"And you put the word Street at the end, you are sure?"

"Yeah," he says, nodding. "I remembered that quirky part." Then he shrugs. "Maybe she didn't get it, though. I didn't put a return address on it. I didn't have one. Guess I could have put the bank, but it never occurred to me. It's alright."

But it isn't. Even though Bruce did find me in the end, the small hope

I once entertained, that Allie had finally realized she had no right to interfere in my life, is hardening into a knot in my chest. Then I wonder again how Bruce knew where to find me, and I ask him.

"I decided to drive down here and try the school. By then I remembered how much you thought of the woman in charge of the Scottish Brigade. I didn't remember her name, but I figured they would know in the office. I hoped that you had stayed in touch with her.

"It was a long shot, I'll admit. I didn't even know if she was still around, or if the drill team existed any longer. So many things have changed since the war."

"And Miss Lytle sent you up here."

Bruce presses a hand against his breast pocket and winks. "Gave me a hall pass." He smiles. "I couldn't believe my luck."

I cannot suppress a grin at the thought of Miss Lytle playing matchmaker. I may as well get this behind me right now. "I have always been sorry for what I did to you, Bruce. I still feel terrible about it."

His eyes flicker for a moment, then he shrugs. And I think: *No, you can't shrug it off.* He continues, "Anyway, after I got through at the bank, I stopped by to see Doctor Malone. He told me a young woman had come by a while back, inquiring about me. I asked him where she was from and he said Houston, he thought. He couldn't remember for sure. I asked him if she was tall and slim and had long auburn hair, kind of wavy, and was just about the prettiest young woman he'd ever seen. He said he could not remember the exact color of her hair, but that he was sure it was not blond. He was partial to blonds. 'I do remember she was right pretty, though,' he said."

I am suddenly conscious of my hair, the two sides swept up and clasped at the top because I overslept this morning and had to rush; and besides, I am way overdue for a trip to the beauty salon. "He told me about your father dying. I was very sorry to hear that. It must have been hard. That's how I found out you had joined the Navy."

Bruce is nodding. He has already put all this together in his mind. Now there is a barely discernable shift behind the look he is giving me. As if he has removed himself into some other dimension of thought; as if he wishes to shut out a very painful memory. Or maybe he wishes to shut me out because I was absent when he needed me most. I am fearful of this retreat, what it portends. But then abruptly he is present again, and I tell myself I was exaggerating. "So I decided that if you had gone out of your way to try and find me, then nothing would stop me from finding you." I find myself smiling, loving that nothing would stand in Bruce's way of getting to where I am.

He frowns. "You're not married, are you?"

Feeling shy as a school girl all at once, I giggle and drop my eyes. "Noooo," I say, lengthening the vowel.

When I look up he is grinning. "Say, can we go somewhere?"

Anywhere. To the cemetery.

Mrs. Theroux comes through her door and into the corridor, which I suddenly realize has emptied out as Bruce and I have stood talking. She is wearing her hat and carrying her tote bag. She waves goodbye to me, a look of mild curiosity on her face. And I love that I am standing here with Bruce. *"He came back for me,"* I want to boast. I wave to her, then turn to Bruce. "I'll just go in and get my things, then stop by the office and sign out. You can follow me home. I don't live far. We'll figure it out from there. Oh Bruce, I'm so glad you found me!"

It is a very short distance from Houston to Galveston, made all the more so when I am eager to be there yet somewhat trepidatious at the same time because I know what will happen once we arrive, have known since I was standing just inside my front door, being kissed in a way that took me right off my feet and left me breathless, my mind speeding back to a time when such kisses were only exchanged in an auto strategically parked under the low-hung branches of moss-laden trees. Ironically, there is no chance of my entertaining a visitor of the opposite sex for much longer than that kiss required, given the number of Austin students who live on Rusk and the surrounding streets, and the way people talk. And so discreetly I've packed a small bag, as naturally as if I had done this every day of my life. And even though there is nothing resolved and much to be talked about in the hours ahead, there is one thing, by golly, that won't wait any longer and that is making love with Bruce. We are fully grown, consenting adults now, owing no explanation to anyone.

Driving south on Highway 75, we make small talk somewhat self-consciously and answer each other's questions, how long have I been teaching, and how long since he got out of the Navy. Long enough to study and get his GED, he says. I find this encouraging. Except for telling him that Daddy died of a heart attack around a year ago, I don't venture into details of the past, and neither does Bruce. Maybe we are each waiting for the other to start. Reaching back to compare notes on the past can be scary, especially for me. I have explaining to do. And Bruce? Maybe he just wants to savor this long-awaited moment. Fine with me. I keep wanting to pinch myself, to prove this moment is real.

The Galvez Hotel is showing a little wear around the edges since the war, the furniture and rugs looking a bit dowdy; but we do not care. Twilight is closing in as we hasten up to a room on the third floor, and a low, barely audible rumbling can be heard, following us up the stairwell from afar. It is going to rain and it doesn't matter. Even in Galveston. My heart is thundering in my chest. Should I tell Bruce I have not done this before? That the farthest I ever went with any boy was when he and I came oh-so-close while burrowed down in the Buckstrum sedan, in Forest Park Cemetery? Does he guess? I have a perverse feeling that I am like a student showing up in class without having done my homework. But I do not like bringing up the subject of my inexperience now, as if to call his attention to the fact that he will need to treat me with special deference; and anyway, isn't the likelihood that I am a virgin all too obvious? *"You're not married, are you?" "Noooo."*

Moments after closing the door behind us we are kissing again, long, eager, searching caresses of the kind that never could go as far as we wanted in the cemetery before being abruptly halted. And then—well, there is none of that slow, teasing, slip strap sliding off the shoulder, business you read of in love stories, for us. We are both stripping off our clothes as if they had caught on fire. Bruce's arms go around my waist. As I am being lifted by the hips and put down gently on the bed, I think I have never experienced arousal that comes even close to that I feel from those two hands cradling my buttocks. Oh my. I want to remember this forever.

In the face of such longing, such readiness, I don't believe the rest of this could possibly be painful, but I am soon proved wrong when Bruce enters through the portal of my body. Or tries. His eyes widen slightly at the failed attempt, as though something has just registered in his mind; and there is a discernible pause. *Oh God, don't stop now.* My teeth clenched together, all I can manage to force out is, "Come!" His gaze at me is suffused with a look that is as close to adoration as any I have ever seen. *See? I waited for you.* What follows is an exasperatingly slow, labored forward thrusting, my hands firm on his bare hips now, my eyes shut tight, sweat popping out on my brow. *What if, in my body, there is nowhere to go, what if—?* Suddenly I feel a raw, snagging inside that makes me gasp and suck in my lips. Then warm liquid spreading out in there, and finally Bruce's breath blowing out on the side of my neck.

Afterward there is a prolonged moment in which neither of us seems to take a breath. We are as still as if the earth has ceased to turn. When Bruce removes himself, he sucks in his cheeks from pain and his straight brows hitch together, his eyes watering. I never even entertained the idea this might be as painful for him as it was for me, and now I know I should have warned him. Why is it I am never as thoughtful of Bruce as he is of me? His cheek collapses against my breast and we both heave a sigh. Bruce flips over on his back then pulls me into his arms and asks as worriedly as if he had just wrecked the car with me in the passenger seat, "Are you alright?"

"I am," I say, smiling, all but giddy with a sense of accomplishment. "You?"

"I'll live. You should have told me, though."

"I know it. I am sorry. Stupid not to realize it would hurt you, too."

"I'll be back," he says, then rises and goes into the bathroom. I hear the water running. Immediately I am mortified to imagine that my shattered maidenhead will be presumed by the hotel maid, and I glance down at the sheet, searching for evidence. There is none. Only what Bruce is washing away from his body and two bright red smudges on the inside of my thighs. I had always thought there would be more blood than this. When Bruce has finished in the bathroom, I go in and quickly wash the red stickiness off myself, thinking how awkward are all these maneuvers, for heaven's sake. Pain radiates between my legs. But it has to be gotten through. I have this idiotic sense of relief that I won't be found out by the maid and have the Galvez domestic staff tittering about me tomorrow.

When I return to bed, Bruce wraps me in his arms again and peers into my face. "I love you," he says softly, a smile spreading over his face that strikes me—paradoxically—as a wistful kind of goodbye smile, when we have only just begun to say hello. His eyes are sad, that's what it is; sad above the smile. I almost think he's going to cry, I really do. And why should loving me make him so sad, unless—. He kisses my forehead lightly.

"I love you, too. Always," I tell him earnestly. "I cannot believe this is happening." I kiss the hollow of his hand, which smells of hotel soap. I remember the time when I read Bruce's hands like a map, how I would open the palm of one and trace the lines with my index finger, then press my lips in that hollow, just as I am doing now. I remember it was softer there then.

"Me, either. I used to believe it just wasn't in the cards."

We are like honeymooners. There is no place to go and nothing to do but make love. It is more drawn out and easier on both of us the second time, and the third is downright slow and pleasurable. After that time we realize it has grown fully dark outside and rain is flooding down as though we had boarded Noah's Ark and set out to sea. I feel peaceful now, glad to be closed up in a safe cocoon.

We are famished, but unwilling to break the spell by going out to dine. So we order from room service. When the bellhop knocks upon the door to deliver our dinner, I slip discreetly inside the bathroom. I turn on the light and find myself staring straight into the mirror. My cheeks are scarlet; my eyes, luminous. The question that must have preoccupied legions of unmarried women at this juncture in their lives looms near: What happens now? But happily I already know the answer. Bruce is going to ask me to marry him, and go back to New London to make a new life. I'll teach at the new high school, of course, which looks much like the old one, I discovered while in the neighborhood, except it is built close to the road where the ground is level: a rectifying of one more mistake of the past. And Bruce will—what? I don't know. Take his Trust money and open a small business in Overton, maybe? *Oh my, who would have thought we would ever go back?* But suddenly it seems as right and natural as anything could ever be. And it occurs to me that being immersed once again in the community could very well make the poems I want to write come more readily. *"Dear Miss Lithingate, Your letter to Addison Vanzandt has been referred to me. I find the poems and subject matter most intriguing. As Mr. Vanzandt is on sabbatical this year, however, no submissions can be considered until he returns next fall. I hope you will forgive the delay in receiving a more meaningful response to your query. Thank you for considering The Lantern as a possible home for your poems. Yours sincerely, Floyd Canatollas, Editor."* The phrase, "most intriguing," is enough to send my spirits into the clouds every time I think about it, and has sent me chasing back to reread the letter so many times that I've memorized it. Every day that I do not find my self-addressed, stamped envelope in the mailbox I tell myself that Mr. Vanzandt has returned at last, and is working his way through a very tall stack of mail. Any day now— I must be sure to send him my married name and forwarding address. Mrs. Bruce Buckstrum, County Road ___, Overton....

I can already see myself packing up the duplex, Bruce hauling boxes out the door. Only a small voice inside my head asks: Can it really be that easy? And I think that surely I will pay a price for the way I let him down. But I won't think of that now.

When I've brushed through my hair, wrapped up in my robe and gone out again, I find Bruce dressed in trousers and ribbed undershirt. He has the firm chest, rounded muscles and taut waist of a man in sound physical condition. Smiling, he motions for me to come and seats me at a candlelit table spread with a white linen cloth, brushing my cheek with a kiss. Bruce pours two glasses of wine and we plunge into outsized seafood platters—stuffed crab, shrimp, scallops and oysters—with golden fried potatoes heaped high, and sizzling hush puppies. Outside is drowning in rain. The windows are cracked at the bottom. The room with its high walls smells wet and briny, and slightly musty. I want to remember the way it smells forever.

In between bites Bruce tells me about his experience on the aircraft carrier, USS Sommers, noting that he served as a signalman during the war. At once, this provokes an image of him perched high atop the mast of an ancient sailing ship, in a striped jersey and shoes with outsized buckles, looking out over the ocean for signs of land. But as he explains the various forms of light and sound and flag signals they used to locate other U.S. warships, or to warn of the danger of approaching enemy vessels, I like knowing that Bruce's job was to warn of looming disaster, saving lives without ever picking up a weapon. I tell him so.

He shrugs. "I was lucky that's where they had places to fill when I went in."

About this time we have eaten our fill. Bruce tops off our wine, emptying the bottle, and we lean back in our chairs, sipping. I tuck my feet up under me, content as a kitten after lapping a bowl of warm milk. I can easily look out and see a future of our sharing many such romantic, candlelit dinners. I think how in the past I fooled myself into believing that I would be happy the rest of my life, living alone. I feel now that I never want to be alone again; or rather, never want to be without Bruce, which seems to be one in the same. But there is so much I need to explain. At the least Bruce needs to know I did try and reach him when I sensed he needed me. I lean forward. "Did you come looking for me at a football game that October, before Doc died?"

He looks surprised at the question. "I tried to get your attention. But it seemed you didn't hear me."

"I knew it was you!" I exclaim, slumping back in my chair.

"Why did you ignore me, then?" he asks, his face stricken.

"Regulations," I hasten to say. "We were about to go out on the field."

At this information he hesitates momentarily. "When the game was over, I saw you were with a guy, so I left," he says then. And though he shrugs indifferently once again, I do not miss the telltale hint of jealousy in the steely set of his jaw. I am thrilled. I cannot help it.

"It was just a date; he didn't matter to me," I hasten to say.

He appears to let this pass. Yet I feel that unsettling distance stretching between us again. "Doc had gone into Mother Frances the night before, for tests. I'd seen the notice of your game in *The Chronicle*— I still kept up with that. I just wanted to talk, and I knew there wouldn't be another chance. We already had our hotel room. I was lucky how things came together, or so I thought."

"I had a premonition something bad had happened," I tell him. Now I explain how I was shaken to the core when he called out to me, and how I talked myself in and out of the possibility that I was only imagining what I heard. "And after the game, the parking lot was a zoo. I couldn't spot you," I tell him, though I do not say that I might have looked harder had I not been with someone else. I tell him how I called the Rice Hotel that weekend and even sneaked off on Sunday morning and waited for him at the back of the park in hopes he would come.

And now I recall something else. "I wrote to you about it shortly after, saying I was worried. That I would call you as soon as I had an opportunity, to be sure you were alright. Did you get my letter?"

His face hardens, bringing a clutch just below my sternum. "I got it," he says flatly, then shrugs. "It wasn't—it didn't change anything."

I remember how carefully I worded the letter, to avoid raising false hopes. Poor Bruce. I go on explaining, "I telephoned you at Thanksgiving— twice— but no one answered."

"I was probably at the hospital—"

"Daddy had asked me to move away and live with him up in Ohio—"

"I thought he was in California," Bruce says, looking confused.

"He moved to Ohio, to work in a refinery. It's a long story. As it happened, things didn't work out for me to join him after all. But at that point I assumed they would, and I hoped—very much—that you and I could get back together. I knew Daddy wouldn't stand in our way. Like Allie did. And is still doing, or trying to. I called you again, on the day Pearl Harbor was bombed, but—"

"That was the day Doc died."

I nod. "Doctor Malone told me. Anyway, I called another couple of times, and eventually I wrote to you again. Let's see...around the first of the year."

"I was long gone by then."

"Yes, I realize that now. I didn't try again until I was out of Brigade, free and clear of my responsibility. By then the number had been disconnected. I figured if you had really come to the game, you must have been trying to tell me you were moving away. Naturally you couldn't write to me—Oh, damn Aunt Allie! What a mess things have become. And it's all her fault."

Bruce doesn't say anything at first. He looks at me for a long moment. Finally he says, "When it comes right down to it, I guess it wouldn't have changed anything in the end. I'd still have gone into the Navy. Or the Army, something. I really didn't have a choice about that."

I lean forward again. "But at least we would not have lost each other for all these years," I tell him. And suddenly a question arises that has been dancing around the edges of my mind since we started this conversation. "What did you do with Rusty, when you went off to the Navy?"

Bruce hesitates. Then he says carefully, "You know, Rusty took that bullet not long after you moved away. I carried him to Doc."

I am nodding yes. "And Doc saved his life. I've always been so grateful to you both," I tell him, wanting this to be all that needs to be said about that bullet, and afraid it isn't.

"Yes, well he seemed to be getting better. But then the wound got infected."

I catch my breath. "But you didn't tell me—"

Bruce shakes his head, winces. "I told Doc afterward that I didn't think I could tell you that your dog was dead. And he said, 'No, after all that's happened, I don't think you should.'

"We buried Rusty at our place. I cried and cried." He reaches across and takes my hand. "I'm sorry, Delys. I guess I figured I would tell you someday, but I never could seem to do it."

I can hardly believe what I am hearing. I see my sweet pal with his red coat and lopsided ears trotting dutifully back to the house from Bruce's, day after day, waiting at the fence for me to come, confused as to where I've gone. And why I left him behind. And then, one day—suddenly, yet as inevitable as the disaster that blew our lives apart—a bullet rips through the air.

I feel angry and helpless as I have not felt since the day I found out that the London school board had betrayed us all. I bring my hands to my mouth and start to cry. Frightened, Bruce rushes over to my chair and takes my elbows. "Here. Come." We lay down on the bed and I bury my head in his chest, sobbing. It is as if the life I loved so much has been robbed from me all over again.

Chapter 29

In the wee hours of the morning I wake up and look around, orienting myself. Last night's white-draped, roll away dining table, with candle stumps and crumpled napkins and empty wine glasses, comes into view. My head aches and my eyes feel too large for their sockets. I am wrapped in my robe, lying on my back next to Bruce, his hand draped casually across my abdomen. I think of the placement of his hand as his one last way of saying, *"I love you and I will always be here,"* before drifting off to sleep. When I think of Bruce's tear-strewn face as he dug a grave for Rusty, I feel a tenderness that nearly brings me to tears all over again. I tell myself that surely Rusty was conscious of being coaxed out of his safe place under the house and carried off in Bruce's loving arms, and of Doc trying to help him. I find that comforting, especially when I had half-suspected that Bruce eventually walked away from Rusty as I had walked away from him. How could I have ever thought Bruce capable of such cruelty? I turn toward his sleeping figure, my heart so swollen with love for him that I can barely contain it. I riffle the hair on his chest until his eyes open. "I need you," I say with longing.

After making love we feel lazy. The rain clouds have grown lazy too, dissolving into a thin veil of pale gray that expends only a steady drip-drip on the window ledge. In all my life I have never felt so far removed from the rest of the world. We order coffee and orange juice, and prepare to lie about on the pillows all morning, talking. So much needs to be said, we hardly know where to begin. But I feel hopeful more than ever that everything will turn out right, and we'll leave here together and never part again.

Bruce makes a start, asking me to tell him about Daddy's death. I tell him the whole story of going up to Ohio, including my decision not to attend the funeral and how I wound up sitting beside Daddy's casket at the funeral home, talking to him as if we were sitting out on the porch together. Which reminds me of the poem that came to me there. I am too shy to recite the poem for Bruce, but I tell him about it, and about my efforts to build an anthology of New London poems.

"What's an anthology?" he asks.

Feeling uncertain all at once about having waded into this subject, I tell him it is a collection. Then I remind him that his own words, about the first day back at school after the explosion, inspired my very first poem. "I only have three written so far, but maybe you can help me with a few more."

His face closes up. "So many years have passed now. And a war," he says doubtfully.

I recognize the same wall going up as before. I would have thought the years passing and, yes, experiencing the war, would have distanced him from the explosion, made it possible for him to talk about it. But then, perhaps he is only afraid his memories of the event are no longer reliable. I venture, "You would be amazed at how much there can be in one tiny image that crosses your mind unexpectedly. I've come to realize that poems are the best way for me to tell the truth about what happened in New London."

"Maybe so, but I don't think anyone in New London wants to be reminded," he says.

His reaction gives me pause, as I realize he fails to appreciate the extent of my ambitions. I suspect he has in mind the kind of cloying poems that appear on the pages of the *Book of Memories.* I start to say that there are universal truths and themes to be derived from the tragedy. But then I'm afraid that will make me sound like a show-off to someone who didn't know the meaning of the word anthology until I told him. Bruce has not had all that much exposure to poetry, obviously— how could he?—and he doesn't know that when capably written, it can speak the truth to a great many people, on many levels. It can make a difference. I search for a different way to explain. "But that's not the audience I want to reach, Bruce," I begin, then immediately fear I've fumbled my opportunity by using the word *audience.* Oh well.

Now I notice Bruce is looking at me wonderingly, as though I've already achieved literary fame. So, he did understand what I meant. Still, I quickly add, "That is, if the poems are ever published." I am more than ready to move away from what has proven a tricky subject. Besides, there will be years and years ahead for me to acquaint Bruce with my poetry. And he will understand what I write on a very deep level; I know he will.

I lift Bruce's hand from the sheet and kiss his fingers. Then I raise up on an elbow and peer down at his face. I choose my words carefully. "Tell me about your dad at the end. Doctor Malone said it was liver failure. It made me sad. Doc was such a good man. And he had been through so much."

Bruce hooks an arm behind his head and stares up at the ceiling. I glimpse a bird's nest of brown hair in his under arm, and for some reason it stirs me. The body below the waist has a mind of its own, apparently. I'm just beginning to learn. "Too much," he says. "It happened so fast, though. There isn't a lot to tell. One day he seemed fine, and the next day he was jaundiced and feeling sick. He knew what it was when he went into the hospital, and he never came out. I went up to Tyler every day to be with him."

Poor Doc. Poor Bruce. "That time together must have meant the world to both of you. I wish I'd had time like that with Daddy," I interject with feeling.

"I'd already pretty much given up on school. My grades had sunk so low by then, and I was so behind, I knew I wouldn't graduate on schedule. Teachers breathing down my neck every damn day," he says, and I feel the slow turning of a knife inside me. *"Maybe you can find someone up there to help you...."*

"So I figured, the hell with it. I'd rather be with him."

I nod in sympathy. Yet, considering the years when Doc forced Bruce to sit with him as he drowned his sorrows in whisky—which had a grave effect on Bruce's studies—I marvel that he felt drawn to be present at his father's sickbed. After all, those weeks of pain and misery at the end of Doc's life were the consequence of his abuse.

"I came in one day and Mr. Wilson was sitting by the bed, taking notes. Typical teenager, it hadn't even occurred to me how much business had to be tended to when someone is about to die. Doc lived long enough to get things set up for me, the money and all. And what he couldn't do ahead of time, he instructed me how to handle.

"Then on a Sunday morning when I walked into his room, I found a doctor and nurse standing on either side of his bed. I knew immediately what was going on. The doctor had his stethoscope on Doc's chest. Doc's breathing was real shallow, and he seemed to be drifting in and out of consciousness.

"Another couple of hours, and he was gone." Bruce pauses, takes in a breath. "It nearly killed me, losing him. I stayed there beside his bed for a long time," he says. Then he turns his face toward mine. His eyes are glassy. He sniffs. "When I walked out of his room, the whole floor had turned into mass confusion. News of the attack on Pearl Harbor had arrived.

"I knew already that I was going to join the service. But I didn't know until then it was going to be the Navy."

I nod my head sadly, imagining Bruce boarding a train all by himself, going far away, with no one there to say goodbye and wish him well. I stroke his hand gently. "I'd give anything if I could have been there to see you off when you left."

Bruce looks closely at me but doesn't say anything. I get that unsettling feeling again that he is either retreating from me, or—more frightening—pushing me away. I wonder what I can say to him to make up for that night at the edge of the football field when I didn't turn and respond to his call. I don't know how you explain to anyone how a certain set of disciplines can be as deeply ingrained as were those in Brigade. Let alone why they were necessary to accomplishing the desired result. But surely in the armed services there is a similar—

"Being in the Navy gave me a lot of time to reflect on life," Bruce is saying now, staring up at the ceiling again. "That was the first time I felt secure; felt I could depend on things. I guess that sounds strange, given that we were fighting a war."

Again I think of that long period when Doc was drinking. "You mean, the first time you felt secure since our lives were yanked out from under us."

He considers this. "No, I think it was the first time, ever. When I was little, my dad was away and my mother might as well have been, for all she cared about her kids. Then she went out partying one night and got killed in a car wreck, and Doc moved us to Overton. It was better then, of course, but Doc worked long hours and he never did remarry. I don't know why, and I've often puzzled over it. Most fathers would, with kids to raise.

"It was pretty well left up to Edna, to be the mother of the family," he says. "I guess she did the best she could," he adds, and shrugs.

"Well, it wasn't fair to her. She was just a young girl, in school," I point out.

"I'm not denying that. It's funny, but I often remember that night Edna and I were invited to supper at your house."

"Valentine's Day; I remember it, too," I say fondly, and squeeze his hand.

"Your house was fixed up so nice inside, with pretty things everywhere," he recalls, and glances at me. "What are those ruffly things that go on the tables?"

I smile. "Doilies. Mama used to starch and iron them regularly."

"Yeah. And the food was a real meal, too, planned out ahead of time."

"Fried chicken and all the trimmings. I remember. It was Daddy's favorite. And apple pie."

"With red hearts in it. Just because it was Valentine's Day," Bruce reminds me, his mouth turned up at the edges. I am surprised, and touched, that he would remember such a small detail after all this time. "Later I went home thinking: Why couldn't it ever be like that at our house? And I wished I could turn around, and go back and live with you."

I chuckle. "It would have been fine with me."

Even as I utter the remark, I am hoping it will provide an opening. Yet, Bruce lets it pass. He says, "But that wasn't the only thing I liked about the Navy. It was the first time in my life I didn't feel I was being compared every day with my sister and brother, and coming up short."

I can literally feel the weight of injury in his words. "You never came up short for me," I assure him.

Again, he lets my remark pass. "Even that night at your house. I knew what your mother thought of me. I could tell by the way she talked to Edna, and made over her. She barely spoke to me."

Exactly what I remember thinking as we sat around Mama's table. It seems to me, if intuition counts, then Bruce is one of the most astute individuals who ever drew a breath. And isn't intuition important? Not that Bruce is less than intelligent otherwise, regardless of what he thinks of himself. While I resist seeing my mother in an unfavorable light, ever, I cannot deny Bruce his due now. "All the same, you were doing fine before our lives collapsed around us," I remind him. "So what, if Edna and Bucky breezed through school? I admired you for the way you kept at it, even when it was hard. That says a lot about a person." This is not strictly true, at least, back then it was not. I was worried that Bruce wouldn't pass, and if he was kept back, then we wouldn't be in the same grade anymore. And he might decide he liked someone else.

Bruce seems thoughtful for a minute. Then slowly he turns his face toward mine. To my chagrin, his brows are drawn together in a thunder cloud. In a flash I think how many times since yesterday he has looked as if he could turn and walk away from me, or maybe on some level already has. Darkly, he says, "But when you got to be s*omebody* in high school, you didn't want to associate with me anymore."

"What?" I ask, amazed that he could have had such a distorted impression of what happened. "You know why I broke off with you. It was my Aunt—"

"Don't bring her into it. She wasn't even in the picture when you called me up and said you couldn't see me anymore."

I feel the heat coming up in my face. I could argue that my aunt was still very much in the picture. But I take his point, just the same. "Look, Bruce, I had a responsibility to fulfill. People looked up to me—well, more so, to the office I held. For which I had *worked my heart out.* You knew this. I could not go on sneaking around with you. What if I got caught? And besides, what we were doing was very, very dangerous. You knew that as well as I did." I let out a breath. "I thought you understood all that," I tell him defensively. If he is expecting me to apologize, he can forget it.

"You're still not leveling with me, Delys," he persists. "The truth is, you thought someone better might come along, now that you were somebody important. Be honest. You won't hurt my feelings any more than you already have."

Helplessly I cry, "I don't know what you are talking about; I never wanted anyone but you." I am exasperated that he could fail to see this. I am now sitting up in bed, trembling, glowering down at Bruce. I cannot believe this conversation has devolved into an argument over something so completely unfounded. I find myself grabbing the edge of the sheet to cover my breasts, self-conscious for the first time since we walked into this room, as if Bruce had suddenly become a stranger.

He lifts one skeptical eyebrow. "Then, why didn't you ask me to wait? It was only a few months. And you knew that I would, that I all but worshiped you."

With a sting of regret, I remember the night I stood before my bedroom mirror in all my spanking new regalia, the epaulets and braids and whistle; how I suddenly felt that I didn't love Bruce anymore. How thick of me not to imagine someone as intuitive as Bruce would guess as much. Yet, I recall now, Bruce did not ask if he might wait for me. I can always point that out.

Or, can I? The fact remains that for all practical purposes I abandoned him, as he says. It would be cheap and cowardly to call on him to share the blame now. I slip back against the pillows, let out a sigh. "It was complicated," I say uneasily.

"I'm listening," he says, which sounds like a warning. He must have been thinking on this for a very long time. Again I envision him aboard his Navy ship, looking out over the churning waves, condemning me in his thoughts.

I take a few moments to organize what I will say. Finally I begin, "There was a moment when—I guess, I was so full of myself—I thought I didn't love you anymore." I glance into Bruce's face. It is as still as death.

"That you could do a lot better," he persists, his voice low.

"No. That never even crossed my mind," I argue. "I honestly believe I would have felt the same even if you were the smartest guy in the school," I tell him. Oh, why did I have to use a word with smart at the root? I wonder. But I'm at a loss to explain what had amounted to a feeling of rare singularity, fleeting though it was. By the time summer drill began I was tortured by what I had done to Bruce. "And— and anyway," I stammer, "it wasn't long before I wasn't so sure about that anymore."

"You mean, about not loving me?"

"Yes. But I still knew I had to break off with you. Calling you up—collect, of all things, though of course I had no choice–was so hard for me, Bruce. You have no idea."

He utters a short laugh. "You ought to have been on the other end of the line."

"I know, I know!" I cry, wagging my head back and forth. I face him again. "Look, you don't have to believe me if you don't want to, but only later did I realize I could have asked you to wait."

He thinks about this. "Well then, why didn't you–"

I cut him off. "I almost did. As the summer wore on, I felt more and more sure I had been wrong. I wanted to call you. But I was afraid your dad might answer—oh God, I felt so awful, because I was sure he would know what I had done to you. For Christ's sake, he had given my dog a home! And he had never questioned all those times I called you up and left him to pay the bill. Maybe he would slam the phone down on me.

"But when August came and I knew you would be bringing Doc to Houston, I decided to call you while you were there, and hope for the best," I tell him, feeling vindicated. Yet now I pause abruptly, remembering something else, something I am loath to admit. I waiver for a few breaths, considering. I could keep this part to myself, and say I lost courage in the end. But no. I realize I don't even want to. I want the whole truth out, once and for all. I take in a steadying breath. "But then—then, after I dialed the Rice Hotel number, I started to wonder if I would be able to go on respecting you, if you did take me back. For those few moments it took to be connected to your room, I wondered. And I realized I was afraid to test it out. I remember Doc answering the phone. I hung up.

"And that's the truth, Bruce," I tell him, my voice strained. "The whole truth. At least, the best I can remember. And I'm sorry, I really am."

Bruce's chest is heaving. His dark eyes are focused on me intently, with— what? Anger? Disillusionment? I cannot tell; maybe both.

I add, "But my hesitation had nothing to do with wanting someone else, or feeling you didn't measure up to me, somehow. No one ever believed in you more than I did. And still do."

Bruce blinks, then narrows his eyes at me as though he is trying to divine something behind my words. Yet I have never felt more transparent. His face relaxes, and I sense he believes me, and maybe appreciates my courage in being so frank. It seems his expression might soften now, and he might reach for me and hold me close, forgiving me. Is what I have done so terrible? Truly, my actions do not seem beyond forgiveness. But he goes on lying there, thoughtfully.

Finally I ask him sharply, "Why did you come all the way here, the way you feel?"

Bruce raises up, turns to me with a melancholy look. His voice tight, he says, "I came back because I love you, Delys—"

"I love you too, Bruce," I hasten to interject, my heart, and all my exasperation, melting like a wax candle under the heat of the flame. Bruce loves me. It is going to be alright.

"And I always felt like what we had between us was interrupted. But not finished."

"Yes, *interrupted* is the right word," I agree, though I'm not quite sure what he means by the word, *finished.* I smile up at him hopefully.

He lets out a breath. "At least I think I'm beginning to understand better what happened," he says in a conciliatory voice. He reaches for my hand, squeezes it.

My eyes water. "Forgive me?"

"Yeah," he says, and looks at me tenderly.

I wait. But he doesn't ask the question I am expecting. Is he fishing for me to turn the tables, and propose? Maybe so, since I'm the one who interrupted us. I can't quite bring myself to do this, so I dance around with words a bit, hoping he will take the cue. "I was intrigued when you said you were moving back to Overton," I tell him. Then I explain that I have returned to visit Mama's grave a number of times, though I have avoided driving into town since that first time, when I met Doctor Malone. "Too many ghosts. If you were there, I would feel differently, though," I add. Well, that's pretty direct, after all. Yet Bruce says nothing so I press on, "What did you have in mind to do in Overton, when you go back?"

He shakes his head. "I'm not going back to Overton, Delys. I see where you got that impression, but I only stopped there, to sign some papers, that's all," he says. Then for a long moment he studies my face. "I've decided to reenlist in the Navy," he says now. "And I was wondering what you would think about that."

It is the last thing I expected to hear. A wall of resistance rises in me. I want roots, I want to belong somewhere. I want my house and my fig tree. Or at least the equivalent of that, in Overton, or somewhere.

"You look as though you don't like the idea very much," he says quietly, as though he half expected this.

"I'm not sure I understand why you want to do that, Bruce, or how I figure into it. Why, if we got married— if—if that's what you have in mind—and settled down, I could give you back all you missed, growing up. A home that you could be proud of. A hot meal waiting for you, when you come home at night."

"But that's not the half of it," he barks, impatient. "Come home at night, from what?"

I hesitate, wishing I had something to suggest that would make his eyes light up. But I don't. "I take it you have a little money at your disposal. What about a business of some kind?"

"There's no future in Overton; have you seen it lately?" he replies dismissively.

"Well then, elsewhere. But even better: have you ever thought of going on to college? They've got the GI Bill now, you know. It was so smart of you to get your GED! And I could support us while you go to school," I suggest. "There was a time when you planned to become a doctor. You still could—"

Bruce is frowning, shaking his head. "Phooey, I could never have been a doctor. That was me trying to make up to Doc for losing Bucky. I think even Doc knew it was wishful thinking, but he didn't want to say so," he says, then adds stubbornly, "No. I'm not going to try anything ever again unless there is at least an even chance that I can succeed and make a real contribution.

"It's why I'm going back to the Navy. Maybe not forever, but at least until I feel I have some other compelling direction to take."

I am beginning to appreciate, only now, how deeply wounded Bruce's childhood left him. The cumulative effect of those times he was compared with an older brother and sister who were smarter. The slighting remarks in hushed tones that did not go unnoticed; the woeful shaking of teachers' heads. The bruising effect, finally, of my turning away at a time when he needed more than ever to have someone he loved believe in him.

Pensively he says, "You remember when you were telling me about that moment when you felt you didn't love me anymore? Hearing that, I realized something. You had looked at yourself and discovered you were on the way to becoming the person you are right now. But in that same moment, I stopped. Becoming anything. And I didn't get a foothold again until sometime after I joined the Navy."

He screws up his eyes. "I would love more than anything for us to be married, Delys. But what I've offered you is all I have," he says. "It's for you to decide if it's enough."

Suddenly I know exactly how Mama felt when Daddy informed her he had decided to work in the oil fields. Mama loved Daddy so much that she decided to tag along with his dream. She must have known one day she would have grounds to insist they settle down as she wanted to. Once they did, she refused to budge again. Whether or not that refusal would have busted up their marriage will always remain unknown, unfortunately. The problem is, I am already where Mama was, when she retired her suitcase for good. "Bruce, I can't do what you want now. I have a job that I love, and a good prospect of someday owning the house where I rent my duplex," I say, and I can see him retreating from me again. No, I cannot bear this. We have come so close. I have a sudden, desperate inspiration. "But I'll wait. Until you see what you want to do after...after a while in the Navy." I smile, feeling better. Of course. This is how it will be, and it is fine. We can do this. "There's no hurry. I am good at waiting," I tell him with a smile. "Send me your address as soon as you have one, and I'll write immediately, I promise. We'll never lose each other again, Bruce.

"Oh please, don't let's lose each other again!"

Bruce looks at me sadly. He doesn't have to put into words that he won't be sending his address.

At length, he kisses my forehead lightly. When he draws away, his face looks relaxed, peaceful, for the first time since he approached me in the hall yesterday. Maybe for the first time since I've ever known him, in fact. Was it really so hard, trying to feel worthy of my love? Gradually I realize that he is relieved, that he never hoped or believed it would turn out any other way. Could it be, he loved me enough to at least give me a chance to redeem myself, and—if I were able to—to take a risk and marry me, if I thought we could be happy?

I believe this is so; and I am struck, as often I have been, by Bruce's generosity of spirit.

He takes me in his arms and we lay back on the pillows facing each other. Tears are now running down my cheeks. It seems to me the grooves of our bodies fit into each other as though we were made to be a pair. I could never get enough of the soft, comforting warmth of lying with him this way. And I wonder if I'm crazy to let him go, if I should go with him, and hope for the best. One word, and—*Bruce*—

Lovingly Bruce kisses the wet spots on my cheeks. He begins, "You know, when I came here, I hoped that at the least I'd find there was something left of those two kids who fell in love riding the school bus, and thought they would go on growing up together, and there was no reason in the world for anything or anyone to ever come between them...." As he goes on talking, about how our letters to each other once sustained us, then the unexpected gift of those Sunday mornings in the shadows of Forest Park Cemetery, I close my eyes and enter into the picture he is painting of us. His voice becomes lower, and lower still, until it is little more than a whisper, a warm breath on my face. "Now I reckon there is something left, don't you? It's a sweet thing to hold onto, isn't it. Out of all we lost. And no one can ever destroy that, or take it away from us," he says finally.

"Yes, oh yes," I tell him, opening my eyes.

Bruce is not there.

How often I used to imagine Bruce's return. Yet I never did so until shortly after my aunt's claim from her sickbed—vaguely asserted, then later almost cruelly withdrawn—that a letter from Bruce had come to her house after the war. I was forty years old as Allie lay dying, and perhaps feeling especially vulnerable with my own youth beginning to fade as surely as a summer tan. Was there a letter, or not? I will never know for sure, but I choose to believe not, because if Bruce had written to me and received no answer, I know he would never have given up searching until he found me. Bruce was all too familiar with the views of my Aunt Allie.

For a long time the fantasy of Bruce's return sustained me. After all, the outcome was as good as any I had reason to hope for, and—I frequently told myself—if Bruce ever really came back to me, I would be prepared. But mostly it satisfied, if temporarily, an obsessive need to confess what I had done that was wrong, or at least beneath the standards I'd always hoped to live up to; and to be forgiven.

At the end of the fantasy I would despair to find myself in my own bed, alone. Or, standing outside my classroom, my hand still on the doorknob after everyone had gone, the fresh air wafting toward me from the hallway like a warm breath.

Then on one occasion I awoke in the middle of the night after having gone to sleep imagining the story, opened my eyes, and had a fright. If

I could so vividly imagine Bruce's return, I reasoned, then what if I had imagined much more? What if his visit to my room as I recovered after the explosion was only a figment of the imagination of someone who had suffered a head injury? Likewise, his coming to get Rusty? Maybe in reality I bent to Daddy's will, and let him find a new home for my dog. No one ever saw Bruce and me together after I left East Texas, so how could I prove that we were? And there were no letters from him boxed up and sitting upon the top shelf of my closet right now, to prove we had remained in touch.

What if Bruce had been killed along with Mama, and Bucky and Edna and Lanelle, and all the rest?

Panicked, my heart racing, I remembered the *Book of Memories*. Of course! Bruce sent it through the mail. Or, did he? Maybe, instead, someone at the school—. But then it didn't matter who sent it.

I leapt from the bed, threw on the light, and hastened to retrieve the volume from the closet shelf. I opened it to search among the leaves laced with flowers and sentimental poetry, to see if Bruce's picture appeared there along with the others. I stared so hard and for so long at one picture after another of sixth graders, going back again and again to the same faces, the same names underneath, checking to be sure, that eventually I felt my eyes had burned right through the pages and I could no longer focus them.

Bruce's picture was not there. I was all but breathless with relief and gratitude, for I knew that what we once had together did not end with that last day on the bus, cresting the little hill and seeing our handsome school building swing into view; that at least we had those stolen hours in Forest Park Cemetery, when we were old enough to tease at the edges of the grown-up world of pleasures that might have awaited us.

After that night of panic I stopped telling myself the story of Bruce's return; and since then I have resolved to be grateful for all I have left of him that is real.

Now you might say that I am a foolish old maid, for all my ruminations, that memories are not enough to pass for a decent life; and maybe you would be right. But I would argue that memories are all we have that can neither be destroyed nor taken away from us. And whichever ones I choose to call up of an evening, when I am sitting out here on my porch under the stars, mine are always within me, bearing witness to the truth about what happened.

Selections from
A NEW LONDON ANTHOLOGY

by
Delys Lithingate

School Pictures

Smiling for the camera
in the *Book of Memories*,
several hundred children can be found.

Young girls with taffeta hair bows,
young boys with hair slicked down;
Seniors wearing cap and gown.

The young ones had not lived
to see the next grade.

The Seniors had not lived
to cross the stage—
diplomas clutched in hand.

All they might have been
is captured here instead:
frozen in time.

Thirteen Minutes Before the Bell

What I am thinking of is
    the eerie silence
    that hung in the air after
    the earth heaved and
    the school erupted

those brief moments when
    the squirrel ceased nibbling
    at its nut
    and the deer raised
    its horned head
    from the brook

and they looked

    into nothing
    into nowhere

for it wasn't in the natural order
    of things.

Those brief moments when
    what happened was not to be
    conceived of, when
    the planet skipped
    its breathing

those brief moments just before
    the rise of panicked voices,
    squeal of sirens,
    rumble of tires
    rolling up

the rural road leading to New London.

Those brief moments of minds registering:

    The children are in there.

Ascension

They were gone long before
their funerals were held,

hasty rituals forming a gateway to grief,
sealing up loss in a context

comprehensible to the living

but having nothing really
to do with those souls

who were too occupied with
rising to look down,

who escaped from the
ravaged bodies they no longer

had any use for

through the opening
formed when the roof flew off

on a propulsion of gas;

were gone even before it
slammed down again

landing like a cocked hat
on the proud school's skeleton

and people on the ground
having the gift of second sight

might have seen all those
shimmering vaporous figures

and mistaken them for a bank of clouds
forced up by the sudden surge of air.

But sometimes I've dreamed that I saw
Mama unclasp her hand from the others'

and wave goodbye to me down there
as I landed unconscious on the campus

before I was taken away
to Mother Frances

where I awoke several days later
and learned from Daddy

that she had perished and her remains
had already been buried.

Blackboard Wisdom
found intact among the rubble

Oil and gas are East Texas' greatest mineral blessings.
Without them, this school would not be here and
none of us would be here learning our lessons.

I remember

we could not imagine
anything bad
ever happening to us

in our tiny hamlet
safely tucked away
on a patchwork of land,
stitched in on all sides
by two-lane rural byways

our allegiance
spelled out
with chalk in a
pupil's cursive hand.

Outsiders would never
find us unless
they were looking

and then
would have to
ask the way
when nearing
our small enclave,

often becoming
lost again as
they headed away.

In the end,
our blessings
would become
our undoing

I remember
how our bus of
indigo blue would
crest the hill each
weekday morning

our handsome school,
red roof sun-bedazzled,
sweeping into view

I remember
our pride's wellspring
retiring into shade
as we trundled
home at the
end of the day

and all the while
the force of our
destruction
building
stealthily within

as every day
brought us
one day
closer,
one day
closer still,
until

the hour when
our innocence was
rent in two

and laid bare
to the world.

The blackboard scribe
was presumed to be
among those who
did not survive.

Or so I remember
though it was long ago
and time wears away
the burred edges

that catch and
draw us in
to revisit our
worst memories.

Time is our
benediction.

A Young Teacher, After

No one knows
who she is.

She was new
that year,
they say;
she did not
appear in the
previous annual.

Wearing her figured smock
with Peter Pan collar
and lace-up shoes
she put on fresh
that morning,
dust-laden now—

dust whitens
the landscape
in the photo;
it was taken just after—

she sits atop some
fugitive object,
amid swells of
disgorged papers

scattered looking
as if she had been
flung there
along with them.

Strands of hair
shoot out
in wild disarray
about her head.

Her eyes,
underscored with
dark bruises,
blaze in accusation

above a mouth
turned down
at the corners,
set hard
in her jaw

her hands driven
deep in
her pockets
as if to stop
their quaking—

you imagine
two tight fists.

She might be
sitting
on her suitcase
at the railroad station
waiting
for the next
train out

no matter where
it's going; anywhere
but here.

It was her
first job, likely;
she taught
Art, by the smock.

And what else do we know?
Nothing.

For right after
the shutter
clicked she vanished
like so many
others—

spooked, they
hastened their dead away
in the backs of
wagons

as the Dallas
coffin maker
worked around the clock
to turn out
small ones.

No one has
seen or heard
from her since

and of her
there is
only left this
image
with blazing eyes, this
image right
after,
this
speechless fury.

A Note to the Committee

I'm not saying what you did was wrong.

In that situation, no one could
have known what was right,
how to right such a terrible wrong.

I'm just saying, while the
cenotaph is noble
rising from the esplanade;

and it's moving to see
all those names
engraved in stone

—you couldn't get a better sense
of the enormity by
walking through the cemetery—

I'm just saying,
there could have been a
memorial hospital—

such generosity!
We broke the whole world's
heart that day—

and I know two people
who might have been saved:

Doctor Peter Buckstrum,
who needed hope, to go on living,
after Edna and Peter, Jr.,
And too many others to name.

Imagine—
for every sheet he lifted,

forced to put down again
and walk away

there might have been
a life saved
on some future day.

And then, the youngest, Bruce,
who rose to gruesome duty,
identifying sister and brother.

Which—I've always thought—
revealed a valor
that would have served him well
had he pursued his father's vocation

as he longed to do until
Doc Buckstrum succumbed
to the ravages of heartache

and dragged the dreams of
his caring son
down with him.

Can You See?

This deed was not of God,
but heresy.

Can you see
all the little churches
redolent of homegrown flowers
spilling out with coffins
on a Sunday afternoon?

Children come to Jesus
as late as Wednesday night
borne down the steps
in caravans,
solemn, one by one,

Farewell Gospel
hymns borne
on heavy-laden air
as each passes by,
innocent still.

Can you see
all the little children
borne to sleep
on Pleasant Hill,
redolent of
fresh-cut pine,
wet with grave-diggers' tears:

Friends, brothers,
sisters, cousins
together in life,
and now in death,
borne from
ruin's ignoble dust
to lie in the Glory of
hallowed earth.

The Father frowned,
the Son wept; the
Holy Spirit drew in
a shuddering breath

as they peered—
Trinity of
despair— at

All the little children
borne away,
borne away.

The School Superintendent

That he was relieved
of his post afterward
is well known.

That he was
complicit in the
tragedy remains
a matter of
some doubt.

That he felt he was
seems all but certain.

That his tall,
lanky figure
used to be seen
wandering the
campus like a ghost,
searching in anguish
for his
missing children

—those who were,
and who were not,
his own blood kin—

is rumored to be true.

How well he was
loved
by faculty and
students
is remembered
by those, still alive,
who knew.

That his legendary
forgetfulness
was once cited
with affection

in the *Londana*
may not be known
anymore.

Those were the days
of automobile
running boards.

By now, many
who posed for
pictures on them,
grinning above
saddle oxfords,
are gone.

The *Londanas*
of that era—

those happy chronicles
of school life
before the deprivations
of war,

before the great loss of
New London was
compounded by
great losses, more—

are gathering dust
in a back room
of the small
museum

maintained to the end

that what happened
there
could never be
forgotten.

Fame

Not a one of us
dreamed of
being thrust into

the klieg lights
of celebrity

on most maps
we were not
even a dot.

Tyler and Longview—
for sure
and even Henderson—
maybe.

But New London—
where's that? People
would say
then one day
the manual arts teacher
flipped a switch—

this was
just before
the dismissal bell—

and suddenly
everyone knew
who we were

or who we had been
for most people
we were an After
before we had
been a Before.

All over the world
school children
writing letters
on ruled tablets

teachers
gathering them
to mail to a place
unheard of heretofore

facing Southwest
in Chicago as
they stood
to observe
a minute of silence

youth donating
pennies, nickels,
dimes and quarters

President and
Mrs. Roosevelt
writing they were
deeply grieved

heads of state
around the globe
expressing solidarity

our small
Western Union
pulsing as
never before

reporters sharing
typewriters,
filing stories
on us

no one could
say enough.

It wasn't how we
would have chosen
to bring attention
to ourselves

had we wanted any
in the first place
and by and by
we withdrew again

pledging never to
talk about the
incident

not among ourselves
for that would keep
the pain fresh,
the wounds bared

not with outsiders
for that would
suggest our disrespect.

Elsewhere life
went on
inexorably
hearts joined
in sympathy
missed not a beat
in the march to war

though even Hitler
paused to
wire condolences,

which goes to show

how much history
had yet
to be written

as we built
a new school and

used the pennies,
nickels, dimes
and quarters to

erect a monument
to our dead.

The Organization

Old high school Yearbooks
gathering dust on the shelf

picture me in plaid kilt and scarf,
black shoes and white spats,
glengarry hat

a bracing look,
a look of knowing
it is all up to me

and whatever comes of it—
success or failure—I own.

Don't tell anyone
you're from New London
says Aunt Allie.

Imagine me, suddenly, a girl
with a reputation

but here I turn the page
to something I can be proud of

calling for an intensity
that suits my nature

the rural spelling champ,
the honor student

Here, now, nothing
matters more than

being the best
you can be

so naturally
I fit right in, knowing

one day I will see
how my efforts have fared:

the weight of my whole heart when
the scales are balanced.

It would be better, Dan, if
Delys came to live with me now

and Daddy off to the
California oil fields,

Bruce still up there
giving Rusty a home

and writing letters to me until

It would be better if
you stopped writing Bruce

Christ! What more could she
force me to give up

than the sum total of
the remains of my life?

I'm kneeling before the toilet
vomiting

Please, let me help, she begs,
from outside the bathroom door.

Of course, Aunt Allie always meant well.

Phoned all her friends to say
I'd been accepted

and cheered me on
as I rose through the ranks

in something I valued that
would not be snatched away.

All I wanted.

As I look back on my
picture in uniform

I suppose it meant something
different for every girl, but

if I had to put into words
what it meant to me

I would say,
Everything.

Rusty's Aftermath

I have a pair of
bed pillow shams,
faded and familiar, and

most times in the
morning when I plump
them into place,

the corner of one flops down.

As I straighten it up,
my mind returns to
my dog, Rusty, how
one ear stood straight up,

while the other
flopped down;
how, every day for weeks

he ran off from his new home and

stood guard over our
empty house
believing with all his might

we would return

until one day a bullet took him
and he became
one more casualty

of our common tragedy.

Juxtapositions

Ads appearing alongside news columns,
Henderson Daily News, March 19th, 1937

Going back and rereading
the old newspaper,

I found the juxtaposition of
the tragic to the mundane
a little unsettling:

how Red Cross officials
asked that no more help
be sent to the scene, for

the throngs of people
were hindering the
rescue effort;

and at the same time
Double Dip Ice Cream
advertised a variety of sandwiches
for ten cents each,

the Salvation Army
gave out over fifty thousand,
free, to rescue
workers

from the oil field
as they used
electric cranes
to move huge blocks of
masonry
from the broken bodies
of children.

The governor

declared martial law
because people
kept coming

as if the place were a
magnet, or a movie
at the Strand, where

Banjo on my Knee, with
Joel McCrea and Barbara Stanwyck,
was listed on the playbill
next to where

the Death List from page one
continued on page six

and the Mayor of Overton
continued drawing up lists
at the city hall

while parents filed by
long lines of the dead
in morgues set up
in various places like

fellowship halls,
garage sheds, and
the Overton Skating Rink;

and outside,
witnesses said,
some parent busted
a leering photographer's
press camera.

The telephone company
board was covered
with emergency
calls, so that

death messages just had to
wait their turn

while radio companies
broadcast an appeal
for people with no
business there

not to approach the scene
or they would be
turned away,
for they just
kept coming.

All the while, shipments
of new Oldsmobiles
made their way to
Texas Motor Sales so

drivers could join the ranks of
thousands who were buying
America's most sought-after
fine car

and the traffic load
on the highways was
300 percent over
peak loads of
any previous calamity.

All ambulances in East Texas
were rushing to the scene and
when they ran out,
laundry trucks and
fire trucks were deployed.

You could DANCE
nightly except Sunday
at Mattie's Ball Room on the

Longview-Kilgore Highway

from which
you might see
convoys of
National Guard troops
rumbling by, on their
way to keep order

because people just
kept coming.

For Bruce, from Delys

Over you is the place I can
never make my way to,
too far away
to ever arrive I

imagine all the ports
you might have sailed to,
till one ended

in safe harbor:

in being what
you wanted to be

all I kept you from
by being me

imagine gentle fingers
once cradling my face
now binding up wounds

in a faraway place,

every stitch a closing of
the wound
I left in you.

This is my hell:

you sail through my dreams
on your ghost ship

always going away.

When I call out,
your name

sends echoes

over the wide
and deep

their answer
mocking me.

Knowing you have
heard me
is my hell. Still,

better this
than hear
you lost your life

at sea—

new fathoms
for the grief
I feel—

or know
your grave's

at Pleasant Hill.

A Fringe of Black Lace

Black satin slip
trimmed in dainty
black lace
on cream net

the kind my mother
wore to school
that last day

of her life
Is my slip showing?
She asked as I left
for the bus

and I said no
which was a lie
but Bruce was
waiting

and now
as I turn the same age
Mama was then

Aunt Allie
gives me a
black satin slip
with dainty
black lace trim

and says, more and more
as you get older
you remind me of
your mother

especially now,
with your short hair—

those pretty waves,
that kicked up so becomingly;
how jealous I used to be
growing up.

I still can't believe
she is gone, she says.

The words hover
between us, conspicuous

as the fringe of
black lace showing
below Mama's dress hem

on her very last day
she would have been
mortified

so my aunt's eyes are
misty, remembering
Mama,

and my face is
hot with guilt,
remembering Mama

at home, I write
a thank you note.

Six years later my aunt dies,
never knowing the black satin slip
with black lace hem

lies folded inside
the box it came in.

Aunt Allie

A lacy sleeve slides down
the woman's thin arm
as she clutches a pill
from a tray
then drinks it down

as she clutches what is
left of her life

in a house built high on
a terraced lawn sloping
down to a quiet street
sloping down to the banks
of the bayou

deep and
slow-moving
between us

saving me from her clutching
for a few stolen hours

on a few stolen days
for a few stolen months
many years ago

under moss-hung trees
over serpentine lanes
winding between the
monuments

high above the banks
on the other side

where only the dead stay
and others linger

and love
for a while, then,
like ghosts,
drift away.

Survivors' Reunion

We probably wouldn't even
recognize one another

after all these years— those
who left, and those who stayed—

I think, when I see the
circular posted at the drive-in
grocery

not far from the cemetery
where I usually stop for a soda

before the long drive home.

Besides, what would we have
to talk about

except what happened to us
that we'd all rather forget?

And anyway, someone might see
my name tag—

assuming we wear name tags—

and remember Bruce and Delys
riding the bus together
or walking down the hall

how we hardly knew
anyone else was around,

and might say they had heard
Bruce joined the Navy during the war

though they aren't for sure
Do I ever hear from him?

Or if it's a teacher—
oh, especially if it's a teacher

Bruce had, say for math or
chemistry—

she might remark how sad
it was that Edna and Bucky
were lost,

the smartest kids
in the school, whereas
poor Bruce...

...but she hopes he
did alright for himself.

And I will say *Yes ma'am*
obediently,
as if I were still in sixth grade

and think how tenderly
Bruce held onto Rusty

as we drove away,
and gave him a home,

and how he made
patients feel at ease

when helping out
in Doc's examining room

and how I know in my heart
Bruce was so much more

than most people
gave him credit for.

All the same—

Mama would want
me to be there,

so I make a mental note
to see if it falls on a weekend.

Yet as I slide behind the wheel
and turn the motor on

I realize that something
long since put to rest in me

has begun to stir
troublingly again.

It isn't so much what
others said of him, but

my greater sin:

Bruce went away to war
believing
I was just like them.

Idylwood

Woman past middle age,
wearing sensible shoes,
walk the sloping streets

of Idylwood, greeting neighbors,
in the cool
of the mornings when

the sun warms
a slow-moving bayou and
old trees cast
silkscreen shadows upon
park grounds.

Trace the steps
of late Aunt Allie;
reflect on her life's work in
the art of dividing.

Move to an empty house
on a terraced lawn
above the bayou

and remember
the four-door sedan
in park shadows,
idling;

remember the boy,
one hand on the wheel

the other, tender around
the hand of the girl;

remember the thrill,
the speeding away,

the eyes
peering through glare

for prying neighbors
who might see
and tell.

Live beneath
a late aunt's roof,
not subject
to her will;

wave hello
to an aunt's neighbors,
now silver-haired;

and know one
sacred secret
kept, even still.

Longing

This is a poem about sex
This is a poem about love

about how the imagination
can expand to the far
reaches of the mind

conjure two bodies entwined
on a Galveston night
when rain slides down
a hotel window

This is a poem about how
that did not happen
because you never came back

This is a poem about
how I wish you would so
it could

This is a poem about
longing.

Forwarding Address

Bury me where I
left my heart;
bury me
in Forest Park.

Practical matters
to tend to
when one has achieved
a certain age:

the drawing up of the
Last Will & Testament.

The lawyer behind
a broad wooden desk
with a leather top;

a lamp at the edge
with a green glass shade;

his legal pad; his fountain pen;
every tittle and jot.

A fitting end for
the last one left:

the small estate sale;
proceeds to favored charities;
what little I possess

scattered
in all directions,
as we were.

Half a page of
lines filled in,

the lawyer's voice,
quietened:

Eh, Miss Lithingate,
where are you to be buried?

In East Texas, with
my mother? Or Ohio,
with my father?

My life has been
a problem of
long division.

How can I be buried
at Pleasant Hill,
where Mama's surrounded
by her pupils?

And Daddy's beside
the woman who schemed
to take my mother's place.
(She would not welcome me.)

Move Mama to
another space,
and ask that she
wait for me there?

Over these long years past,
I have featured her teaching
class after class,

writing History
in morning's mist
upon the gravestones.

No, I could not
disturb commingling grass,

wrest her from such long tenure.

In Forest Park, I answer.

In a grave near
the duck pond,
under the trees;

in the shadow of
chapel arches, where
we would walk
sometimes, after

and tell each other
the only way for
time to end
would be with us together.

Lay me down where I
left my heart;
lay me down
in Forest Park

where you might
one day trace
our steps and find that,

to my dying breath,
despite my sin,
I loved you best.

A NOTE FROM THE AUTHOR

The tragedy that struck the New London community on March 18th, 1937, has haunted me for years, since my first visit to Pleasant Hill Cemetery, where I noted that fateful date marking the end of life for so many innocent victims.

It seemed inevitable that I would one day weave a story around the event that would have lasting ramifications, not only for that small hamlet in rural East Texas, but far beyond. As I began my research, I wondered: What would it be like for a survivor who is hastened away from the community she knew and loved, and where schoolmates, teachers and friends could share in their grief and support one another, as the days went by and they inevitably found a path for moving on from the tragedy? Would this forced separation lessen the unbearable pain of loss? Or, rather, would she be denied her only chance to overcome her loss, and be healed?

The answer to the question lies in the pages of AFTERMATH.

The novel does not attempt to recreate the many details—both terrible and heroic, moment by moment—of the tragedy. For such a recounting I would point interested readers to several works of nonfiction available, and urge them to visit the London Museum and Tea Room for one of the most compelling historical collections and narratives that I have seen.

Suzanne Morris

ABOUT THE AUTHOR

Suzanne Morris (www.suzannepagemorris.com) is the author of seven previous novels, including the bestselling *Galveston*, *Wives and Mistresses*, and *The Clearharbour Trilogy*. She and her husband have lived in Cherokee County for eight years.

CPSIA information can be obtained
at www.ICGtesting.com
Printed in the USA
LVHW091725220519
618749LV00005B/797/P

9 781622 88116